# FLATTENED

CHASE WALKER

authorHOUSE®

*AuthorHouse™*
*1663 Liberty Drive*
*Bloomington, IN 47403*
*www.authorhouse.com*
*Phone: 1 (800) 839-8640*



*Published by AuthorHouse 12/02/2019*

*ISBN: 978-1-7283-3422-6 (sc)*
*ISBN: 978-1-7283-3420-2 (hc)*
*ISBN: 978-1-7283-3421-9 (e)*

*Library of Congress Control Number: 2019917546*

*Print information available on the last page.*

# CONTENTS

# CHAPTER 1

## We Met by Accident

"Mister, are you okay?" A faint voice of a little girl came to Jonathan's ears. As he slowly opened his eyes, a blurred, upside down vision of a little girl with short, black hair came into sight.

Again the voice said "Mister, are you okay?" Jonathan couldn't answer because he's not sure if he was ok or not. Slowly he began to move his head side to side.

"He's alive!" said another little voice. Jonathan's face was squished against the passenger side window. Vertical, wide, brown lines comes into focus. More children that also came into focus. A second after that, he is able to speak.

"I think so." Jonathan finally replied. His numbing arms and legs feel like they are weighted down as he tries to move them. He noticed a large spinning object that he made out to be a tire. The tire was attached to maze of pipes and rails. When the yellowish blur came into focus, panic and rush of adrenalin began to set in.

It all started to come to him, The yellowish blur, The tire, The children's voices, and now the sounds of screaming, crying children. He was in an accident with a school bus. Jonathan suddenly was in a hurry to climb out of his truck; but he literally didn't know which way was up.

He tried to figure out how long he was unconscious. Some of the children were out of the bus and walking around. He felt he was out a long time, but the spinning tire that is now stopped, makes it seem like he wasn't out that long.

The pickup truck he was lying in was on its side. Jonathan had difficulty climbing out, but he managed to do so.

"What happened? Are you okay?" Jonathan asked the little girl with the short black hair. She was the first person he saw when he had starting waking up.

"Yes I'm okay, but I think some of the other kids are badly injured" She replied.

Jonathan was somewhat still dizzy from the accident. He sat down for a moment and tried to stare at the crash site. Looking at the way the bus and his truck where settled. He just couldn't figure it out. He had no idea how it all happened. Jonathan tried to remember the time before the accident. Nothing. He couldn't remember hours or even the start of the day.

It took him a short time to regain energy physically and mentally to head toward the bus; which had clouds of smoke bellowing from its front end. There was the smell of burning oil and antifreeze in the air.

Once he was able to walk without the feeling of passing out, he approached the bus. The rear emergency door was already opened. He could hear the screaming, crying children. Jonathan was aw-struck at what he was seeing. At first he couldn't see all the kids, because they are hidden between the high-back seats. Some kids seemed to almost hanging in mid-air, still strapped in by their seatbelts. Not to mention the bus is littered with thrown about luggage.

Walking through the bus gave Jonathan an unsettling feeling. Aside from seeing the children that were crying with cuts, bloody noses, and possibly broken bones; the bus is on its side. He was almost walking on the ceiling. What would normally be the center isle is now to his side. And he is walking on the windows. The only thing giving Jonathan a good feeling was that all the children seemed to be alive.

Jonathan began to aid the children by carefully unbuckling the kids that are still strapped in their seats. They also seemed to be the least injured. While he was looking for some kind of first-aid kit, He noticed the bus driver was unconscious. As he approached her, he noticed her eyes were still opened, with blood running out of her nose and left ear. The left half of her face was a dark purple, and a chunk of her scalp was torn off. He didn't see where she might have hit her head, but he wasn't looking very hard for it. This made him want to vomit. The thought came to him how horrified the children would be if they saw the bus driver in that condition, but on the other hand they may have already. There's nothing he could do about it now.

He finally found the first-aid kit. Unfortunately, it wasn't going to be much help, but it was better than nothing. There was about fifteen children. The only good thing is most of them had minor cuts and burses. It didn't take long before the First-Aid kit was all used up. He was forced to use some of the clothes from the scattered luggage as bandages.

It appeared the worst injured were two kids that had broken bones. One of them was a little boy about the age of six or seven. He was screaming and crying so hard he started choking when he gasped for air. When Jonathan reached him, he saw his leg was bent sideways and thought it must be broken. He tried to talk to the boy to calm him down.

"Hey what's your name?" Jonathan asked. The boy couldn't give a reply; he was in far too much pain. Jonathan didn't know what to do. His first thought was to pick the boy up, but he knew that would hurt him even more. He decides to leave the child there for now, and help the less injured. Jonathan hoped the boy will calm down by then.

He discovered the second of the worst injured children. She is a little girl who was crying just as hard as the little boy. She was trying to hold her wrist, but every time she touched it, she cried out in pain. There was blood dripping from her wrist, through the fingers of the hand she was holding her wrist with. Jonathan had a horrible image of what her wrist will look like when moves her hand away.

"Hey, it's going to be ok. I'm going to help you. Let me take a look at your wrist." Jonathan said. Much to his surprise, she was able to hold up her wrist and almost stop crying. Suddenly he pulled her arm back as soon as Jonathan went to reach for it. Once he was able to gain her trust, He slowly uncurled her fingers. reveling bone that has popped through the skin in two places. The girl noticed the cringed look on his face and began to cry again.

Jonathan found a shirt from the luggage that was thrown about. He ripped it into pieces to use as a bandage. He managed to tie a loose bandage around her wrist and reassure her that she will be alright. He knows sooner or later he would have to retie the bandage in some kind of splint, but this will have to do. He heard that voice again, but this time it wasn't so faint and distant. The familiar voice was right next to him.

"Mister!" He looked up and saw a girl with slender build and short black hair. She seemed to be older than the rest of the children. She was about fifteen years old.

"Hey!" Jonathan says in a confused panic. He was both, surprised and thankful she was not crying.

"Who are you, and why did you hit our bus?" The girl asked.

"I'm Jonathan. I don't know what happened. I just wake up and saw"..... It was the same girl that he saw when he regained consciousness, while lying in his truck. This time she was right-side-up, instead of up-side-down.

"Saw what"? She inquired.

"Saw you, you're the first thing I remember seeing you when I was waking up in my truck. Who are you?" Jonathan asked

"I'm Stephanie. Are we going to be alright?"

"Yes we're going to be alright. Some of the kids are badly injured. I may need your help tending to them."

"Yeah, I figured that. What do you need me to do?" She asked with a shaky tremble in her voice.

"Can you go to my truck and see if you can find some kind of first aid kit? And I may need pieces of straight wood, I think I have to make a splint or two. I'm afraid that boy may have a broken leg, and I know the little girl has a broken wrist."

"Okay, I'll see what I can find, by the way his name is Chaz" She says with slight sarcasm.

"Chaz?" Jonathan asked.

"... As in Charle.." She said with a puzzled look on her face as if to say, *You didn't know that*?

"Oh right." Jonathan replied, *how should I know that?* He thought.

Random voices of children wanting to volunteer to help aid the injured filled the bus. Jonathan explained to the older kids what he was doing, and asked them to make sure the rest of the younger kids where ok. He went over to Chaz to see how bad his leg was. Just as Jonathan feared, it looked like it was broken. It was bent outward at the knee. He once again tried to calm the boy down.

"Hey Chaz, my name is Jonathan" The little boy just looked at him with disbelief and tears.

"How did you know my name?" Chaz shuddered between sniffles.

"That girl Steph told me. Can you move at all? Or try to sit up? I know it hurts." Jonathan attempted to straighten the leg. Chaz screamed out in pain. Jonathan was getting frustrated, but he had to keep his cool.

"Okay, OKAY I didn't mean to hurt you buddy. You have to try to move for me. I know it hurts". It's been about fifteen minutes since Stephanie went to the truck. Maybe she was caught up trying to find the wood. Jonathan thought to himself. He decided he is going to pick the child up. First he gave Chaz fair warning.

"Chaz I'm going to pick you up. I want to move you out of the bus and away from the broken glass and the smoke." Jonathan wasn't sure how to pick the child up. He wanted to support the leg some way. Any movement would hurt Chaz. Luckily for Jonathan the boy was small and skinny kid. He probably weighted only 40 lbs. Just then Jonathan figured out how he was going to move Chaz.

"Chaz, I want you to lean back against on my arm, rest your head on my shoulder, now put your arms around my neck. I'm going to support your leg with my other arm so it doesn't move. Ready?"

"I, I'm afraid.... It, It's going to hurt."

"It'll be fine we'll move slow.. okay? Here we go buddy" Jonathan slowly to lifted Chaz up. The child was light just as Jonathan suspected. Surprisingly Chaz didn't scream; he just winced and grabbed on to Jonathan's neck tighter. While Jonathan was carrying the boy to a safe location, he took a quick scan to find out where Steph and the other children are at. He put Chaz down in a pile of leaves. Knowing the boy is in a lot of pain, Jonathan tried to make it seem like it is all ok.

"That didn't hurt so bad, did it?" Jonathan asked.

"A, a little." Chaz replied holding back tears.

"I have to check on the others real quick. You'll be ok here for now." Jonathan made his way to the bus to aid the little girl's broken wrist, when he noticed Stephanie was wondering around with a puzzled look on her face. Almost as if she was supposed to meet someone in a crowded theater.

"Hey!" he called out to her. "What did you find?"

"I found a few heavy branches; there're the straightest ones I could find. There was nothing in the truck to use." She said.

Jonathan though for a second how odd it was that there was nothing in the truck. He'll look in the truck later, but first he wanted to get started setting the splints. He knew this was not going to be easy. He was surprised and thankful Stephanie found such straight, clean branches.

"Good job on finding these splints, they're perfect. I may need your help setting them. Can you do that?"

"Sure, I know a little first-aid."

They started with the little girl with the broken wrist. Jonathan carefully took her wrist and slowly unwrapped the bandage. She pulled her wrist away and started to cry.

"I know it hurts, but you have to let us set the splint. It'll take a second and we're all done. Can you tell me your name?" He asked as he began again to slowly unwrap the bandage.

"M, my n, name is, is K Kasey." She stuttered. He managed to get her wrist unwrapped, but a piece of cloth got caught on the edge of the bone that was poking out through the skin but, Jared lose when she twitched and screamed out in pain. Even Steph flinched, but regained composure remembering she had to be brave for Kasey. Jonathan had a split second to decide how to take Kasey's attention away from her wrist. He was also wondering If Stephanie was thinking the same or was she just as panicked as Kasey is.

Before anyone could even say the words "broken wrist", Stephanie grabbed a Pieces of rag she found from some of the clothing that was thrown about from the accident. She tied it around Kasey's arm slightly above the elbow and used a piece of wood she found to make a tunicate. Then she turned it tight to slow down blood flow to the wrist. Stephanie knew that would make Kasey's wrist numb in a minute or two. Just then Jonathan took two pieces of wood and set the splint tied in place.

"Done!" Stephanie said proudly.

It all happened so fast; even Kasey didn't know what was going on. She even stopped crying. A look of relief came to Jonathan's face. He looked a into Kasey's eyes with a soft smile, cradling her chin in both hands.

"See, that wasn't so bad. It's all done. You did great." She almost smiled back or at least almost stopped crying.

"Let's get her to safety and check on Chaz. This bus is filling up with smoke." Stephanie suggested.

With that, Kasey managed stand up and walk over to Chaz, holding her wrist like it was going to fall off any second.

"I'll tell Chaz you'll be right there to fix him" Kasey said without looking back.

They didn't notice how much the bus filled with smoke. The thick, heavy smoke made it difficult to see if any children are still on the bus.

"I'm going to make sure everyone is off the bus then I'll meet you where chaz is?" Jonathan asked Steph.

"Okay, I'll meet you there." She agreed.

Jonathan made his way the front of the bus making sure everyone was off. The only person he wasn't worried about was the bus driver. It has been too late for her.

On his way out, he tripped over something. It sounds like glass clinking. He looked down and picked up an empty Whisky bottle. Maybe this accident wasn't his fault, he thought to himself.

"THE BUS IS ON FIRE!" Jonathan heard a voice cry out. By this time he almost couldn't see the exit door because the smoke was so thick. Suddenly, a hand broke through the thick smoke and grabbed Jonathan by the wrist.

"The bus is on fire! Get out of here!" It was Jett, one of the older boys about ten years old. He grabbed Jonathan by the wrist and led him out of the bus. Once he is out of the bus, he noticed that Stephanie has a splint on Chaz's leg. Jonathan was impressed by this and thought to himself, *wow! she's good.*

"Wow! You're good." He says.

"Thanks." Stephanie replied.

"I have to try to put this fire out before this thing explodes. I need you to get all the kids away from this thing incase that happens."

Jonathan tried to tell Stephanie without letting the other children know what was going on.

"OKAY. I'll get them over to your truck. That should be far enough. Be careful. If I don't see you in three minutes, I'm going in after you." Stephanie said.

Jonathan didn't want to waste time arguing with her, so he just answered OK and ran toward the bus to look for some kind of fire extinguisher. He made it into the bus that was filled with thick black smoke. He proceeded to the front of the bus, flailed his arms to act as a human fan trying to wave the smoke so he can see where he's going. He reached the front of the bus. Still doing the "Human helicopter". He finally found the fire extinguisher being blocked by the corps of the dead bus driver. It appeared a reddish blur through the thick smoke. He reached down and unlatched it. The fire extinguisher is small, much too small, but it was the only thing he had. Jonathan thought he found the source of the fire. He gave a few short blasts. He didn't want to use the entire extinguisher in one shot. *This better work.* he thought to himself. He didn't see any more frames, just a lot of smoke. If nothing ells, all this smoke should make a great signal for help.

# CHAPTER 2

## Movin On

"Is the fire out?" Stephanie called out in a frantic panic.

"I think I got it out." Jonathan said.

With the bus engulfed in smoke, chards of broken glass, and one dead bus driver; the bus wasn't going to make good shelter. Jett noticed Jonathan mumbling to himself and nodding his head in rhythm. Jett finally realizes Jonathan is counting, and answers the question bouncing around in Jonathan's head.

"Fifteen. There are fifteen of us." Jett said. When Jonathan looked over; there stood a boy about ten years old, too shy to look Jonathan in the eyes.

"Oh. Okay. What's your name?" Jonathan asked. Jonathan has a feeling that's the boy who grabbed his hand and led him out of the bus.

"My name is Jett. I grabbed your hand and dragged you out of the bus. We were on our way to a camp for the gifted and talented. Why did you hit our bus?"

At first Jonathan couldn't give an answer because he couldn't remember the accident. He couldn't even remember waking up that morning. But he does remember the empty whisky bottle he found on the bus next to the bus driver, which makes him feel confident that he didn't cause the accident.

"You saw the accident?" Jonathan asked with anticipation that there is a witness, but at the same time doubtful because the witness was only ten years old with an active imagination.

"Yes." Jett answered without hesitation. "You where coming around the curve head-on and then you tried to swerve out of the way, but it was too late. The bus driver blew the horn to try to get your attention, but you didn't react in time. She turned the wheel to avoid hitting you, and we collided. The next thing I knew I felt the bus turning over. It was the loudest crash I ever heard." Jonathan just stood there. Shock, fear, and sorrow overwhelmed him. He really didn't know how to respond.

"I'm sorry. I didn't mean to… I just can't remember what happened." Jonathan said.

"Are you some kind of doctor? I saw you trying to put a splint on some of the children. How are we going to get out of here?" Jett asked being both shy and out spoken at the same time.

"No I'm not a doctor. I just want to help you kids. I'll get us out of here somehow. Don't worry someone will come along and see us. All that smoke from the bus will act like a smoke signal." Jonathan said trying to reassure Jett and all the other children.

"That is unless the trees block the smoke. We are off the road in a deep valley, and the breeze is blowing our signal away." Stephanie had said with a disappointed, worry tone to her voice.

Jonathan took a second and realized that she was half right. The trees gave him an idea. "Steph, can you climb trees?"

"Yeah! I'm the best climber here" She said with great anticipation.

"Do you think you can climb that tree almost to the top and see what is around here? Maybe there is a nearby house." Jonathan suggested.

"I know! I can climb all the way to the top and see what is around." That request seemed to lift her spirits a little. Before anybody knew it, Stephanie was half way up the tree.

"Be careful!" Jonathan yelled from below. Stephanie just looked down at him as if to say "Dah" A few other voices called out volunteering to climb trees. Jonathan didn't want that. Being worrying about one falling child was enough. And there were already two broken limbs. Fortunately, the volunteering children where to short to reach the bottom branches.

"I'm going to make my way back up to the road to see if I can flag down someone." Jonathan said to some of the older children. He reached the top where the road had the skid marks from the accident. He took notice of the broken glass and the tire marks. He still couldn't Piece together what happened. If and when someone drives by, they may stop to see that people need help. You can definitely tell there was an accident, and the direction the vehicles skidded off the road from the scuffed ground.

"Hey! I see something!" Steph's voice rang out.

"What is it?" Jonathan shouted back still feeling the warm pulsating throb of his head.

"It looks like a small village. It's hard to tell." Jonathan braces himself for the next pain throb.

"How far away does it look?" Jonathan winced.

"I don't know… a mile or so." Stephanie said.

"Do you see anybody?"

"No." Stephanie said.

"Okay. I'll meet you at the bottom." he said. Jonathan was thankful he could stop shouting.

Once Stephanie was at the base of the tree, and the children were accounted for, it was decided that they are all going to hike toward the small village. *There has to be some kind of help there.* Jonathan though. Plus it was going to be dark soon. One of the main concerns was getting Chaz there. Clearly, he could barely walk. He may even have to be carried. Jonathan took a deep breath, giving himself a silent pep-talk for what he was about to say.

"Okay kids." Jonathan announced, as he was about to explain how they were going to pull off the imposable. "We're going to have to work together if we're going to make it to safety. I think we should start hiking. There is a small town that maybe able to help us out." This was not going to be easy with fifteen kids. One of which has to be carried.

They took one last round up of things they might need for their hike to the place Stephanie had spotted. If they played there cards right, they should reach the village by dark. Jonathan was hoping this hike wasn't going to be as difficult as it sounded.

The children seemed to be smarter than Jonathan was ready for. They managed to make some kind of stretcher using four heavy branches and thick rooted vine for chaz if needed. They did this without Jonathan's help. Chaz started out using a heavy branch for a crutch. Good thing Chaz was a small kid.

They have been hiking for about an hour or so, and some of the kids started complaining, as expected.

"Hey mister, this hike is a long way. Are we almost there?" Said a tiny voice.

"Yeah you're right, it's taking a little longer than I thought it would. But it's not so bad." Jonathan said stopping to take a look around. He couldn't see the accident site or the road anymore. It appeared they where hiking through some kind of valley. After the second hour of hiking everyone agreed to stop for a rest.

"Hey Steph, Do you think you can find an easy tree to climb to see how close we are?" Jonathan asked.

"Not a problem" she replied.

It almost seemed like she was waiting to be asked. You could tell she loved to show off her athletic, climbing skills. Within a minute or two, she was twenty feet in the air with ease, as if she were walking on the ground.

"I see somebody! And I think they see me!" Stephanie yelled down.

"Who do you see?" Jonathan asked.

"I see a little girl. She is pointing at me and she's waving others to look as well."

Stephanie described a little girl with reddish hair about six years old; who was franticly waving other people over to see that Stephanie was in the tree. It almost seemed like the little red headed girl never saw another human before. She finally climbed down to tell the others what she saw.

"How far do you think we are?" Jonathan asked.

"It looks like we're getting close, about half mile away. It's just that we can't see the village from the ground. The forest is so thick you'd never see where it is, unless you where high up."

"As long as we're getting close, let's just get there. We'll get help and hopefully get out of here." Jonathan suggested.

The younger kids were starting to show signs of giving up, they getting too tired to move on.

"Come on kids, we're almost there. We'll rest when we get there."

Jonathan was trying to have a positive attitude and keep everyone's spirits up. The forest was getting thicker as they hiked on.

"What the heck!" Jett shouted.

"What?" answered Steph, as if Jett where her annoying little brother.

"These woods are too thick, we'll never make it." Jett protested.

"Yes we will. Just keep going, besides I think I finally see a clearing." Stephanie said in an attempt to reassure the kids everything will be ok.

# CHAPTER 3

# Civilization

Hiking though the thick woods is taking its toll on everyone, even Jonathan is getting tired. Finally, they broke to a clearing. A wide open, plush, green field stood before them. A few hundred yards away or at least the lengths of two football fields stood a rundown looking structure. The structure resembled some kind of boarding house of some sort. It had at least two floors, two chimney stacks, and a long porch that wrapped around the house. The house was surrounded by a few smaller houses. Some of the kids were getting excited.

"Where saved!" shouted one boy,

"Yay!" the voice of a little girl rang out. Jonathan was leery about what kind of people they were about to encounter. Even though the children are very excited, they where to tired to run across the field.

"Hang on everyone." Jonathan commanded. "Let me do the talking. We don't know what kind of people they are".

"What do you mean, Kind of people?" Stephanie asked sarcastically.

Jett and some of the other children expressed the same thought, as they looked at Jonathan with a doubtful looks on their faces.

"You never know. They could be nice, but they could also be not so nice. We just have to be careful." Jonathan said.

Also in the distance emerging from the structure, a small group of people started gathering. First three, then six, then quickly to about twenty or more. They seemed to be all ages; ranging from totter to almost elderly. One gentleman stood out from the rest. He was tall, over six feet. He had long white hair and a beard to match. He had a stocky build, but not heavy set. His face seemed to have been chiseled, showing a perfect well rounded looked. He boldly stepped ahead of the rest of the group. Soon enough the two groups where marching across the field toward each other, like two small roman armies coming across the battle field to meet in the middle. This was far from any war. This was more like a peace treaty, a cry for help. Finally the two groups met up just about half way.

Jonathan stuck his hand out to his side, about waste high with his palm turned facing behind him. As if to resemble a backward stop signal. His small army of injured children slowly came to a stop. The two small groups of people stood there checking each other out, sizing each other up. Jonathan kept walking a few feet to meet the muscular burly man. Jonathan wasted no time jumping into a begging introduction.

"We need your help. We were in a bus accident about three-four miles away. The bus overturned and most of the children have miner cuts and burses, but two of the kids need medical attention to broken bones." Jonathan pleaded.

"I'll see what we can do. You're far from any hospital or doctor. You're far from anyone else for that matter." replied the burly man.

"One of the boys may have a broken leg, and one of the girls has a broken wrist." Jonathan said.

The burly man had an expression on his face as if to doubt the group of intruders. They were trespassing and they were not welcome. He sees the two injured children Jonathan is talking about. The man turned his head around, looking back at his small army. His eyes pointed to a middle aged couple. He flicked his head sideways in the direction of the children. The couple quickly ran over to the children. The woman noticed Kasey's wrist, and saw the make shift splint. She held Kasey's good hand and led her back toward the main house. The man of the couple saw Chaz's leg and he just picked him up and carried him following the woman back to the main house. It's amazing how much can be said with such little body language. This guy must be the leader Jonathan thought.

"Come on back to the main house. You and the other kids get cleaned up." said the burly man.

"Thanks we need it." Jonathan replied. "We also need to call for help." The burly man and the rest of his people he was with just looked at Jonathan funny. After a short awkward pause, the burly man looked at Jonathan.

"Sure, Let's get you cleaned up first." On the way back to the main house, Stephanie tugs on Jonathan's shirt to slow him down so they could talk quietly.

"Did you see the look they gave us when you mentioned calling for help?" Stephanie asked with a mixture half panic and half concern in her voice. "It's sounded like he was being sarcastic, the he said, *sure*"

"That's what I meant when I said, *kind of people.* We probably stumbled on some kind of commune or cult. The burly man appears to be the leader." Jonathan said.

"What kind of cult do you think they are?" Stephanie asked.

"I'm not sure. I could be wrong. Let's keep this to ourselves. No need to mention it to the others and cause a panic."

"Gotcha." Stephanie said.

When they got back to the main house the burly man rounded up the rest of his group. It looked like about twenty people. He makes a brief announcement that there are new arrivals. *New arrivals*? Jonathan thought to himself.

In the main house, Jonathan notices this cult like family seems to do everything in groups. He is wondering if this may be true for even bathrooms and showers. He is also planning the fastest way out of there. His first concern is getting himself and the kids cleaned up, rested, and hopefully fed.

"You and the kids can get a shower and get cleaned up. You'll have to share towels, I'm sure that won't be a problem." Jimmy said.

"Thanks, that's very nice of you. I'll make sure we get cleaned up as fast as possible. We don't want to inconvenience you any more then we already are." Jonathan replies.

"Take your time, no hurry." With that the burly man orders a young woman from the group to get some fresh towels. Jonathan decides to finally to introduce himself.

"By the way my name is Jonathan."

"The names Jimmy" replies the burly man. "I'm going to check on your two injured kids to see how they're doing."

"Thank you Jim." Jonathan motions for Stephanie to come over. He suspects that he and the kids were rescued by a commune or some kind of holy-rolling religious cult. He also can't find a telephone anywhere.

"What's up?" She asks.

"I'm afraid we're going to have to shower as groups" Her eyes just got really wide.

"What! w, w," Her nervous stuttering is cut off by the young woman returning with fresh towels. It's not enough for each kid to have their own, but they were already warned about that. It's better than nothing.

"Here are some towels for you. By the way my name is Star."

"Thank you my name is Jonathan and this is Stephanie."

"Hello Stephanie "Star said. It's almost like Star is trying to break out of a shy personality. It also seems like this is the first time these people have seem other people in a long time.

"Well, I have to get going, I can't keep Jimmy waiting. He doesn't like that." Star hurried off leaving behind a fading annoying swishing sound corduroy pants make when the legs rub together.

"Now what do you mean we're going to shower in groups?" Stephanie asked with an almost angry tone.

"Relax; we're going to shower in two groups, Boys and girls. I don't know if you noticed what's going on in this place." Jonathan said.

Stephanie looks at Jonathan with the expression on her face that asked, *what do you mean*?

"I think this place is a commune." Jonathan said.

"A what!"

"A commune, It's when a group of people live in solitude, cut off from the rest of the world. They are usually religious, claiming they know god and the bible and all that stuff. The burly man, his name is Jimmy. He must be the leader."

"Are you sure? They seemed to be friendly and caring." Stephanie said second guessing Jonathan's logic.

"I'm not a hundred percent sure, but I have a good idea. Take a look around. Did see any telephone? Any technology? TV, And the clothes they are wherein?, Who wares Corduroys?" As he is expressing his thoughts, Stephanie starts to look around in search of his claims. "Who names there kid Star? For now, I just want to get us cleaned up. Like I said, we'll be in two groups, boys and girls. Besides, it would take too long for each of us to shower one by one. Trust me. You take the girls and go first, than I'll take the boys." After a short while Jonathan and the other kids got cleaned up, even Chaz and Kasey. They even got proper splints for their broken limbs.

By this time it was getting dark. Jonathan was thinking about putting off calling for help till the morning. Everything was so up in the air about how they would contact for help, or if they even could. So far he still doesn't see any kind of phone, cell phone, or even a TV. He dose notice a lot of candles and lanterns. That tells him this place has little to no electricity. He would soon find out what the deal was. It wasn't night fall yet.

"Come on, It's time for dinner" Jimmy commands. "We have extra for you and your group. After dinner, you can help us clean up. Everyone dose there part to help out around here". Jonathan really didn't like being ordered around like that, but he figured he would let this one slide.

Dinner was not as strange as Jonathan thought it would be. They had grilled chicken and vegetables. Jonathan told the story about the accident. It also gave him a chance to try to remember how it all happened. He still couldn't piece it together. He also was relying on what the children's revision of the story was, which puts Jonathan at fault. Now would be a good time to mention the empty whisky bottle he thinks.

After dinner they all helped clean up. Everyone was working together; people washing dishes, people drying, and putting away. Once dinner was cleaned up, Jimmy showed the new arrivals where their sleeping quarters would be for the night, and possibly for some time after.

By this time it was well into the night hours. As the rest of the kids where getting settled, Jonathan pulled Stephanie aside, and once again explained where he thought they ended up. He also tried explained why the people where acting so funny.

"Don't worry. I'm doing my best to get us out of here ASAP." Jonathan told her.

"Yea, I get it" she said with a doubtful look on her face. That gave him the feeling of failure, which he didn't like or accept. That put the fire in him to make a promise to him to be gone from this place by tomorrow night.

It wasn't long before they all got settled in, and they were just hanging out. Some of the new comer children are already trying to let their shyness fade and are making friends with the commune children.

Some of the younger new comers, ages five-eight, are getting drowsy. First, they asked for bedtime favorites to help fall asleep, a favorite blankly, teddy bear, dolly. Soon they were asking for mommy or daddy; sometimes both parents. Jonathan and Stephanie knew they had to try to calm the children down. Some of the children started crying.

Jonathan and Stephanie reassured the kids that they would be home soon and we're just having a sleep over. Luckily they were so tired, it wasn't long before they fell asleep. What a relief, they though to themselves. It was like Jonathan and Stephanie are reading each other's minds.

"I'll be right back. I'm just going to the bathroom." Jonathan told Stephanie.

"Should I wake the others; we'll make it a group effort perhaps." She jokes. You're such a wise guy Jonathan thought to himself as he looked back at her with a *shut-up* look in his eyes.

"Ha, ha wise guy." he said. There wasn't much privacy in this place.

Jonathan was on his way back from the bathroom when he notices there's a campfire burning. That brought a peaceful calmness to him. Jonathan sees Jimmy, that young lady he will soon know as Star. He also few of the older people sitting around the campfire.

When he returns to the sleeping quarters, he tells Stephanie what he saw.

"Let's go check out what they're up to." She says. From that remark, Jonathan could tell Stephanie was board out of her mind.

"I guess, we have to be careful. I don't know if they're having some kind of cult meeting or just casually talking." Jonathan warned.

"Careful, Smareful, we're already in. They fed us, let us use their showers, and gave us shelter. We're probably the only people they've seen in years."

"Ok, but let me do the talking." Jonathan said.

"Yes sir!"

They headed toward the campfire that was giving off a bright

Orange-Yellowish glow. Jonathan positions him and Stephanie so they can be seen and not startle anyone. Jimmy stops talking in mid sentence thrusting his chin upward slightly, and poking his eyes at Jonathan and Stephanie as if to say *can I help you?* This kind of bothers Jonathan, but wanted to find out what kind of people lived here and no better place than around a campfire.

The roaring campfire gave off the right temp, and right glow. It seemed to be throwing off shadows that showed the contours of the faces around the campfire, which was very soothing. Jonathan and Stephanie slowly walk up to the group. They realize they're stirring up their energy circle like when you throw a new log on a fire. Starks fly.

"Hey, mind if we join you?" Jonathan asks.

"Not at all; come on over, have a seat." Jimmy says with a warm inviting voice. "How are Chaz and Kasey doing? Are they settling in? I know it must be hard for them to try to get any rest." Jimmy adds.

"They are doing much better. They are so tired with all that's going on they may actually fall asleep, thanks to you guys." Stephanie said, jumping into the conversation. Perhaps to help break the ice, or just to be heard and let the group know she wasn't shy.

"I'm glad to hear that. So Jonathan, how are you holding up? I know it a challenge guiding fifteen injured children on a three-four mile hike after being in a overturned bus. You must have a strong feeling for children." Jimmy asked.

"Yeah, I guess." Jonathan said.

Just then the thought of his sister's kidnapping triggered in his head and made him realize that's why he is trying to help these children to safety. After all these years, he still hasn't forgiven himself and still takes the blame.

"When I was about 17 years old, my little sister Sylvia, went missing. She was about 6 years old. One minute she was there, playing in the yard; and the next she was gone. I was in the driveway changing my oil on an old ford F150. Somewhere in between me fighting with the drain plug and me getting out from underneath the truck, she vanished. I think she was calling my name; I couldn't tell. Her voice sounded muffled and distant. I was too busy fighting with a rusty drain plug.

After running around in a panic for about twenty minutes, I started asking neighbors if they saw anything. They claim to have seen a strange car driving around at an unusually slow speed. They say it was an older Chevy, green, 4door sedan. I guess I never got over it; even fifteen years later. I hate to say this, but sometimes I almost wish someone would find her body. At least that way, I would know where she was and will always be. Having my little sister missing, not knowing if she is alive, hungry, scarred, in pain and always fearing the worst twenty, four-seven takes its toll on you. Especially Knowing she was just a few feet from me one minute, and gone the next. That's a guilt I'm willing to hold on to and never let go."

Everyone remained silent...... There was a soft high pitch whimper, then a sniffle. Jonathan looked over to where the sound was coming from. It was Stephanie. There was a tear running down her cheek and her eyes where squinted as if she were looking into the sun. Jonathan puts his arm around her and gives her a hug.

"Wow man, I'm sorry to hear that." Jimmy said, probably just to break the quiet tension in the air. "Well, that explains the energy to guild fifteen kids to safety. All this time the police never had a single lead? What did she look like? I know it's been a long time." Jimmy asked with a soft tone in his voice.

"No, not a single lead. She looked like any other little girl; blond hair in ponytails, skinny, about four feet tall." Jonathan's voice now has that shaky, nervous tone. After brief pause He finally collects himself. "Well that's all I have and that's how we got here." Just then Star gets up and hands Jonathan a glass with a reddish liquid in it.

"I'm sorry Jonathan, I won't say sorry for your loss; because that's what you say when someone dies. She may still be alive. Why don't you have some of this, it may settle you a bit." Star suggests.

He unwraps Stephanie from his arms and takes the glass Star is handing him. It smells like real homemade wine.

"Come on; drink up, just a little." Jimmy says in a reassuring voice as if to tell Jonathan *it will be alright*.

"Thank you." Jonathan replies. He can taste and smell the wine is in fact homemade. He is grateful and manages to slug down a few glasses.

# CHAPTER 4

Jonathan's eyes popped opened. He sprang up, only to wrack his head on an invisible hangover that hovered over him, then he quickly went back down again. Once again, there was that blurred vision of a girl looking down at him. This time it was different. The girl had a name.

"Jonathan, are you ok?" Stephanie asked with sarcasm in her voice knowing he was hung over. He just moaned softly and tried to regain his vision.

"Coffee" he said in a winy whimper. "Water, aspirin, something. I at least need coffee." He was hoping there was some coffee close by. He could smell some kind of food in the distance. He gave it another try at sitting up. It isn't going to be easy, but he did it.

As he looked around the room, he noticed some kids are still asleep. He was trying to guess what time it was by using his biological clock. He really had no idea what time it was. He was guessing it was around 9:30am or so.

"Steph what time is it?" Before she could answer, Jimmy walked into the room where the new comers are.

"Morning everybody, there's breakfast down the hall. You know the rules. You eat, you help clean up. That's how we do it here." Jimmy commanded in a nice way.

"What time is it?" Jonathan asked.

"It's 7 o'clock." Jimmy replied with a sharp tone.

"I just need some coffee for now" Jonathan replied.

During breakfast Jonathan checked on Chaz and Kasey. Chaz couldn't walk without the use of a crutch. He still had some difficulty, but the reset splint helped out a lot. Kasey was starting to feel a lot better with her new splint.

Jonathan reassures the children they will be going home soon. Some of the younger kids had that *"I'm about to cry* look on their faces. The truth is that Jonathan had no idea when or how they were going home. He still didn't find any way of communicating with the outside world.

Meaning he still hadn't seen a phone or anyone using a cell phone. He also doesn't see any wiring going to or from the building. That makes Jonathan wonder how they are getting electric if any; unless everything is running underground.

After breakfast, Jonathan's hangover has dwindled down to a headache. He decided to start looking for help once again. He still has an unsettling feeling about where they are, and the people around them. It was nice of the cult-like group to take Jonathan and the children in and care for the injured as if they belong, but it is getting time to try to contact help.

Jonathan actually set off to look for Jimmy, the self-proclaimed cult leader. At that moment, Jett and Stephanie come running up to him in a somewhat of a calm panic. They try to explain the conversation they just had. It was hard to get a solid story between the gasps of air. And the alternating voices; since the two kids were taking turn speaking.

"Jonathan! These people… These people aren't going to help us… contact anyone for help… or get out here!" Stephanie starts out try to catch her breath.

Jett continues, "They claim they don't have any contact with the outside word…. That's why we don't see any phones or power lines."

"These people haven't had any communication with other people in at least fifteen years and that's they want it to stay." Stephanie finishes.

Jonathan suspected the information the two vast sources just told him didn't come from other children, but one of the adults. That would probably mean Jett and Stephanie where sent as messengers. Well, that explains a few things, Jonathan thought to himself.

"Who told you all this?" Jonathan asked, now with the same panic in his voice.

"Jimmy!" answers Stephanie.

Surprisingly a wave of relief washes over Jonathan. His wondering can finally be put to rest now that he knows where he stands about if these people are going to help them out. Best of all, it came from strait from the horse's mouth. He now knows they are on their own If they are going to be saved.

"Jimmy? First off, you'd think they would do anything to help us leave. We invaded there space or whatever this place is. What did he say to you? And more importantly, what did you say to him?" Jonathan inquired.

"I just asked where the phone was so we could call for help. That's when he said they didn't have a phone or any means of contact with the outside world and it's going to stay that way. He also said everything they need is all right here. There was no need for anything ells." Jett's description of what had been said was all Jonathan needed to hear.

"Oh-ya, Jimmy said he'd talk to you, and explain everything." Stephanie added. Jonathan couldn't help but to feel almost threatened. Stephanie leaned in close to Jonathan.

"We are getting out of here?...right? I mean they're not going hold us hostage."

"No! There're not. I think you're forgetting one thing, There are going to be many sets of parents looking for you kids when you didn't reach your destination." Just then a light bulb went on over Stephanie's head, so much her eyes brightened.

"Oh ya, that's.. right." She answered with a sense of hope in her voice.

"I may need you to do that tree climbing thing again. In the mean time Let me talk to Jimmy and find out what exactly what he's talking about. Where was he at?" Jonathan asks.

"He was in the main house." Jett replied.

"Keep your cool you two. I don't the other kids hearing any rumors. And don't say anything to anyone ells." Jonathan said. The three of them started heading toward the main house.

"I get the feeling I should do that tree climbing thing soon.... Like now soon." Stephanie says out loud; not really addressing anyone specific. After a second or two Jonathan agrees. He knew he had no choice; she would have done it anyway.

"Ok, try not to be seen. I don't want you drawing attention to yourself." Jonathan said.

"I'm going with you Stephanie." Jett expresses in a over excited burst of adrenaline.

After a short hike in the nearby woods, Stephanie found what looked to be the tallest tree. The only problem was that she's too short to reach the first branch. She needs to be two or three feet taller. *Dam!* She thought. She hesitated for a second, than she had an idea.

"Jett, I need you. You have to help me get to the first branch. I can get the rest of the way from there."

"How am I going to help you do that?" Jett asked.

"It's easy. Get down on your hands and knees, and I'll use you as a step stool. I won't hurt you, I promise." Stephanie explained. Jett got down as she instructed, but she is still about six inches too short.

"How's it going up there?" Jett asked.

"I'm still too short. Can you raise me up any? I just need six inches."

"Not really. I can barely hold you. Can you jump?"

"No, that would hurt you. But that gives me an idea, I'm getting down, but I want you to stay there for a sec." Stephanie gets down and takes a few steps back, as if to get ready for a running start.

"What are you doing" Jett said.

"Just stay down. I'm going to run and jump up to the first branch, but I still need you as a stepping stool so I can keep the momentum going."

"You mean like inertia?" Jett asked.

"Correct."

"Hang on. If that's the case, I'll crouch down facing you, once I feel you leap off my shoulders, I'll see if I can stand and boost you to the first branch. With you already going in the up direction, you shouldn't weigh that much. At that point, I'll be guiding, your weight not lifting." Jett explained. Stephanie pauses to think for a second then nods her head in agreement.

"Ok, sounds good. You ready?" Stephanie asked.

"Go!" Jett shouted.

Like a starter pistol telling the runners to start running. Stephanie jogs toward him. Jett can tell she is going to use her left foot, because she has an off-beat step pattern. Sure enough she puts her left foot on his right shoulder. There was a slight tug on his shoulder, than the tugging sensation went away. Her body weight lightened. Jett thrusts himself upward, then moves quicker once he relies how light she has become.

“Got it! I’m up!” she shouted.

Star runs up to Jimmy with stern concern. “The new comers are asking about telephones and ways to contact the outside world.” She said with a panic tone in her voice.

“I know, I was talking with two of the kids a moment ago. I believe their names where Stephanie and Jett. I informed them that we have no communication with the outside world, and we like it that way. I told them I would talk to Jonathan later.” Jimmy said.

“So we’re not going to help them?”

“We helped them plenty. We cleaned them up and fed them. If they want to try to seek rescue, they’re on their own.” Jimmy said.

“What if they decide to stay?” Star inquired.

“They won’t” Jimmy said with a promising tone in his voice.

Star’s expression went blank, but her eyes widen when she saw Jonathan approaching. Jimmy turned around, sees Jonathan and turns back at Star.

“You better get going.” Jimmy instructed.

Jimmy confronted Jonathan and had no problem explaining that they are isolated and cut off from the outside world for a reason. They lived that way for 20 years and they are staying that way. Jonathan doesn’t understand the reason why, but he doesn’t really care.

“So there are no phones here? And you haven’t had any communication with other people in 20 years?” Jonathan asked.

“All we need is each other. We know how to live off the land and rely on Mother Nature. It’s true what they say, *you teach a man to fish, and he eats for a lifetime.*” After a short speech how to live off the land, Jonathan is surprised Jimmy didn’t mention God at all.

“What do you see?” Jett yelled up to Stephanie, who didn’t respond right away. “Well!” He yells again. A minute later he finally gets an answer.

“I don’t see anything.” She yelled down. Her voice was full of sorrow and disappointment. When she reached the base of the tree, Jett asked her again as if to hope the answer will change.

“What!? you see anything?.. At all?” Jett asked in desperation.

“No. there was nothing around, just forest. We’re in the middle of no ware In case you haven't made that connection." Stephanie said, trying uplift Jett's broken spirit.

"H-how are we going get home? I-I want to see-see my mom and dad! W-we're never getting out of here!" Jett's voice is a quivering stutter, holding back tears.

"Calm down Jett. Jonathan will know what to do. I'll tell Jonathan and he'll find a way to get us home." Later that afternoon Stephanie told Jonathan what she didn't see.

"There was nothing out there. All I could see was forest. I couldn't even see the bus, No bus, no road, nothing." She is getting more and more panicked every time she explains it.

"Are you sure you where high enough? Try the tree across the field. Maybe it will give you a different angel." Jonathan tries to encourage her and Jett not to give up and stay positive.

"I guess I could try that." She replies in a not so agreeing tone of voice.

"Look, first of all don't forget, there's going to be people looking for us, or at least for you kids."

"How do you know that?" Stephanie asks crossing her arms.

"As I tried to explain to you once before; you never made it to your destination. There are people waiting for you, not to mention all your parents. Fifteen missing kids, assuming each kid has a mom and a dad, that's 30 people. Don't forget about camp counselors and staff. I bet people started looking already, once they see your bus didn't arrive." Their faces suddenly gain a hopeful look. It was true; he wasn't just making it up just to try to make them feel better.

"Yeah, I guess, I never thought about it that way. I'm going across the field to find higher tree. You are coming Jett?"

"You bet! Let's go." Jett replies. Stephanie and Jonathan both looked at each other knowing that was the happiest Jett has been in a long time.

"Make sure your back by dinner time. I'm going to check on the other children. We can't stop looking. God only knows when help will arrive." Jonathan says heading into the main house.

Jonathan enters the main house and the first thing he did was check on Kasey and Chaz. Kasey seemed to ok for the most part. She almost doesn't notice the splint anymore. Chaz can manage a lot easier now that he got use to the crutch. The other children seemed to be doing just fine, helping out with chores, such as farming, hanging wash, preparing for dinner. Best of all doing the chores seemed to occupy their minds. Jonathan decided to ask chaz if he feels like coming with him, only because he is the second oldest and most mature.

"Hey Chaz, I'm going sightseeing. Do you want to come with me?" Jonathan asked.

"Yeah! What are we looking for?" Chaz asked with excitement.

"Nothing really, I just want to look around. Do you remember how Stephanie climbed the tree to find this place? I'm kind of doing the same thing." Jonathan explained.

"Aren't these people calling for help for us?" Chaz questions with a shaky stuttering tone of voice. Jonathan is hesitated to give him an honest answer.

"Not really, it seems they have no form of communication with the outside world here."

"What?, why?, How do they…?" Chaz has temporarily lost the ability to form complete sentences. This didn't concern Jonathan; he knows Chaz will return to normal in a few seconds.

"Come on, I'll explain on the way. I'm not sure what's going on here, but I'm going to try to find out." Jonathan says.

The main house had two smaller houses and what looked to be a barn. Close by is a nice size garden, about at least an acre. People and some the *bus* children are working in the garden. Some are hanging laundry; some are carrying jugs water from here to there. Someone was milking a cow. It really looks like they have everything they need. Why go anywhere for anything? How did these people wind up here Jonathan is wondering. Maybe they only started off as only 10 people and then… a mini population growth perhaps?

# CHAPTER 5

## Exploring the Commune

Jonathan and Chaz decided to see what's inside the barn first. The door swung open without a sound, not a creek or even a squeaky wine. And it was a smooth swing. The door was perfectly even with the dirt floor, so the dirt floor didn't have any rub marks on it. That was somewhat odd, Jonathan thought. He thought a barn door would make some kind of noise or at least have sagginess to it. Inside the barn was just what should be in a barn, cows, chickens, hey, ect. The structure was long and narrow, with a loft.

"Eew, It stinks in here" Chaz complained.

"What did you think a barn would smell like?" Jonathan asked rolling his eyes. "Just as I thought, there's not much to see here. Let's check out the house next door." Jonathan said.

As they shut the barn door, it had a heavy smooth swing. And a solid *thunk* when it slammed against the other door.

The house next to the barn is a small two story white house with green painted trim around its windows and door frames. The paint was faded and chipped. The windows have a dirty haze to them, so hazy and dirty it is hard to see through them. Surprisingly, none of them are broken.

The front and back doors are locked, and the windows are too high to reach. In the back of the house there is a pair of wooden doors almost level with the ground. *These doors must lead to the basement.* Jonathan thinks to himself. The doors are unlocked.

"It's open!" Chaz belts out. The hinges were rusty and stiff, so stiff they only let the doors open half way. They give off a stuttering low pitch moan. There is a set of crumbling, concrete steps that lead down and disappear in a pool of darkness.

"We'll have to make our way in the dark to the find the stairs that lead to the first floor. Try not to trip over anything" Jonathan said as he looked back at Chaz.

"Let me go first. I can see in the dark. My dad says I have infer-red vision. I'll find the stairs faster than you will, I promise." Chaz claimed.

Jonathan moved aside and lets Chaz lead. In seconds Chaz disappeared into the darkness, followed by the fading *thud* of his crutch. *Thud, thud, thud, thud, thud. Clank, reeeeee.* From all that racket Jonathan is guessing Chaz made it up the stairs to the first floor.

"I guess you're up stairs? What does it look like?" Jonathan yelled down. Jonathan made his way to the bottom of the concrete steps. Chaz began to tell Jonathan directions so he can navigate through the dark and find the stairs.

"Go straight forward about 20ft. The stairs will be on your right. Be careful of the…" Before Chaz can warn Jonathan; there's muffled *BONG!*

"Son of a….!"

"Pole, right in front of you. Are you ok? What happened?"

"I wacked my head." Jonathan moaned as he pulled himself up the stairs, holding on both sides of the railing that aligned the staircase.

Upstairs was well lit from the sunlight beaming in through the windows. There was a rank stainless in the air. It's almost a suffocating musty odor. The house seemed to be in good shape. It looked like it was barely lived in. At the top of the basement stairs was the kitchen.

"This is a big house. It looked much smaller from the outside. I wonder why nobody lives here, or it seems like nobody lives here." Chaz remarkd. Jonathan went to the sink to try the faucet. The water ran, both hot and cold work.

"How does the hot and cold water work if there is no electric on?" Chaz asked.

"I'm not sure." Jonathan replied. "Maybe it's tied in from the main house." They continued exploring the house looking for some kind of way to call for help. While searching through the house, they come across one of the rooms that were locked.

"Should we try to get in?" Chaz was suggesting with high level of excitement in his voice.

"Absolutely, I think I can find a way to get us in." Jonathan said.

*This field is taking forever to cross.* Stephanie thought to herself, as she and Jett were high stepping through the tall grass and a beaming sun. She was also afraid Jett is going to start whining.

"How are you holding up little buddy?" Stephanie asked. She thought she'd give Jett up-lifting nickname to keep his spirits up, in case he was running low.

"Great! Are we almost there? It looks like we're getting close." Jett said.

"Yeah. The highest tree is just ahead. Do you see it? It's not far. We'll be there in about ten minute's tops." Stephanie said.

"yes, I see it. Are you going to the very top? I bet you could see everything from up there. Can I come with you this time?"

"No, I need you to stay on the ground. I have a very special job for you. And only you can do it.

"What's that?" Jett was so excited. He admired Stephanie as if she were a super hero.

"You'll see when we get there." She said as she was trying to think of a special job he could do. They finally reached the edge of the field. From this point on, it was thick brush, rocky terrain, and a log or two to climb over. Finally, they reached the base of the tree.

This tree's first branch was a lot higher than the last tree she climbed. There's no way she is going to jump high enough to reach it.

"Ok, Steph I'm ready" Jett said. Before Stephanie could say anything Jett was in a crouch position just like last time.

"Hold on, do you see how high the first branch is? I'll never be able to jump that high. That's at least ten feet up." Stephanie aid.

"How are you going to get up there? You have to get up there to see what's around us and look for help and…." Stephanie cuts him off in mid sentence.

"Slow down you." She firmly demands. "Give me a minute. I'll think of something. I didn't hike all this way only to have to turn back and tell Jonathan and the others I faulted. We just have to stop and think."

The two wondered around for a minute aimlessly looking around. Jett sat down on a log to rest, they both did. Then Stephanie sprang up.

"I got it Jett! Help me lift this log. We'll lean it against the tree like a ramp and I'll just walk up to the first branch."

"Great idea!" Jett says "But you'll only be half way up. How are you going to reach the rest of the way?"

"Don't worry about that for now. Just help me with this log, I'll show you later." Stephanie said. The log is about twelve inches in diameter; about eleven ft long, and weighs about thirty-forty lbs. They both struggled, but got the log leaning where they need it. Stephanie walked up as planned.

"Dam! I'm still too short." Stephanie said. "Alright, I got another idea." She yelled down to Jett. "We have to reposition the log so it will be straighter, up and down. I just need the end of the log to be two ft higher. You follow?"

"Yeah, the log needs to rest at a sharper angle." Jett said.

"Correct! Good job little buddy." Stephanie said.

The nickname thing seems to work out well. Stephanie ran down the log and she and Jett struggled once again to reposition the log higher on the tree.

"That looks perfect!" Steph says proudly as she pats Jett on the shoulder. "Well here it goes."

Stephanie gets a small running start. She climbs back up the ramp. She pushed off with her left foot when she reaches the end of the log, jumps up and just enough to reach the first branch.

"Got it! We did it! The rest of the climb is easy. It's just like a ladder from here."

"Yes!" Jett cheers from the ground.

Chaz and Jonathan stood in front of the metal door as if they were just asked a brain teaser. The riddle being how to unlock the door and see what's inside. The door was standard size, and had a lock in the knob and a dead bolt.

"Do you think you can get us in?" Chaz asked as Jonathan swung his foot up, and kicked the door so hard he broke the wooden framing. It made a loud *Crack*! It startled Chaz so much he almost fell backwards tripping over his crutch.

The room was like a storage room, with random stuff everywhere. They just stood there for a minute in wonder at everything they see. Chaz hobbled over to the far wall and picked it up by its curved frame as if he's held one before. The wood has a faded clear coat that must of looked great when bran-new. The string was tight. Jonathan was watching Chaz test how tight the string is, but he didn't have enough strength to pull back all the way.

"You know how to use that thing?" Jonathan asked.

"Yea, my dad taught me how. This one is made for a right handed person. I'm left handed, but I could still us it." Jonathan was Surprised a kid that age knew about that type of stuff. Chaz handed it over to Jonathan because he has the strength to pull the bow back to its fullest range.

Jonathan took it, resting the handle between his index finger and thumb. He drew the string back to its full range, then released pressure, never letting go of the string. Rule number one, never dry fire a bow.

"60lbs pull" he claims, handing it back to Chaz.

"Is it? I'm used a 30lbs. My dad uses an 80lbs bow." Chaz said.

For a moment, they got lost in the craftsmanship of the bow and the love of the sport. As fast as their minds wondered, they quickly snapped back into reality. Chaz hung the bow back where he found it. Both took a mental note on where they could find it again.

Among the rest of the clutter, there was a wooden desk. It has a narrow drawer in the center and three drawers going down its right side. The desk is piled high with random junk. The top of the desk wasn't even visible. Paper, books, magazines, boxes of what looked to be electrical outlets and zip ties, a small tool box with random tools inside, were piled high on this desk. They overlooked probably the only thing they desperately needed, if they had any chance of getting help and leaving that place.

Kasey walked to the main house. There was sadness in her eyes; almost all of the newcomer children had the same look. They miss their homes, mommy and daddy, probably a pet or two, maybe even a sister or brother. She just got finished helping Star hang wash on the line. All she did was hand Star the clothes from the basket so Star didn't have to bend over. They seemed to have a bonding moment. She was Star's "Little helper." Helping out and being needed made Kasey feel better.

"How are you feeling Kasey?" asked a deep, burly voice from the side of her.

She turned to look, It's Jimmy. She was startled at first, and then she becomes shy. He was walking over toward her; he knows she is shy and frightened of him.

"How are you feeling? Does your wrist still hurt?" he asked in a soft gentle tone. At first she looked down at the ground, than finally looked up at him. In a shy almost whisper she answers

"It's feeling better."

Jimmy is over six feet tall, Stocky build, White hair pulled back in a pony tail, And a white beard. To Kasey he is ten feet tall and three feet wide. He kneels down on one knee, still looking down at her.

"Are you sure you're not in pain? We can fix it, if you are." He calmly says.

"I'm sure, it's ok." Seeing Jimmy kneeling on one knee, Made Kasey feel a little more at ease.

"Mr. Jimmy?" she asked with a heavy shyness.

"Yes Kasey" he answers with a look that says ask me anything and I'll tell you honestly. She reads this look and asks,

"Are you going to keep us hostage here?"

"Oh, no sweetie. What makes you ask that?" She looks down at the ground again, too shy to answer. "Did you hear that I wasn't going to help Jonathan call for help?"

She looked up at him as if she's saying *yes*. He looked into her eyes and realized she was too shy to say it, but she is thinking it. He sat down next to her. She looked into his light blue eyes and thought to herself, that he is tough but gentle at the same time. He looked at her and starts explain why he said that.

"Kasey, did your parents ever tell you they wish they could take all the bad out of the world, and make it so that nothing bad could happen to you?" She looked up at him shyly and replied.

"Yes"

"Well, I can do that here. And it took me a long time to make it like that. I'm not keeping anybody hostage. Anyone can leave anytime they want. Nobody dose because we're happy here. You see Kasey, This place..." As he explains further, her eyes widen with surprise and maybe some joy. "And with any luck, Star will learn how to hang shirts on the line the correct way." Jimmy ends. A smile came to Kasey's face followed by a small giggle.

"I know" Kasey giggles, "I tried telling her by hanging the shirt the way she does; It makes people look like a football player or Frankenstein."

As they both laugh about it, he puts a burly, warm, muscular arm around her and gives her a kiss on the forehead. They kind of look like a Grandfather and Granddaughter.

*CRACK!!* Followed by the sound of a high pitch screaming girl's voice shatters the silence,

"UMFF!"

"STEPHANIE!!" screamed Jett. "Steph!" he repeated.

He heard the crack of the branch, her screaming, he even saw the branches shake in the area of the tree she landed in. But now he couldn't see or hear her. He starts franticly circling the tree, repeatedly calling her name. By this time he is almost crying. He finally decided to use the log ramps she did, even though she is almost twenty feet up. He has to at least try. He reached the top of the log, but he is to short, much too short. He began to cry, and cried her name out loud almost as if screaming for help.

There was a good chance no one will hear them, they're almost a mile away from the main house. Between his gasps for air and his cries, he finally heard a slight moan. Hearing that seemed to shut him up fast; and made him come to his senses.

"Stephanie?" Jett said again.

"uuuhhhh" Stephanie moaned.

"Steph?" he called out look straight up the tree. He wasn't too far from her, so he didn't hear where the moan came from. He remained on the log. He couldn't circle around the tree, but at least he was higher up closer to her.

"Uuuuuhhhh" She moaned again. This time he was waiting to hear for it. He looked in the direction from where the sound came from.

His breathing was heavy and loud. He even stopped breathing for a second, thinking that will increase his hearing power, than continues breathing. He waited a few seconds more to see if she moans again.

"Steph?" he said once again.

"Uuuuuhhhh"

There she is. She is high, very high above him, maybe ten ft high and over to his left. He still couldn't see her. *Wow, she must be really high up*. He thought to himself. He suddenly heard leaves rustling; he looked in the direction of the rustling and saw a pair of legs hanging on one side of a heavy branch. Her torso is hanging over the other side. She was perfectly balanced. A helpless feeling washed over him. He couldn't get to her to help her; she had to help herself and make it to him.

"Steph, I see you. I can't make it to you. Can you breathe?" He called out. She can only push out a death-like moan that sounded like his name.

"jjjeeeet" she managed to say.

He could hear in her voice. She could barley breath. She knew she had to get up somehow, but there is nothing for her to braes herself on. She's just hanging perfectly balanced on a thick branch, as if she is in mid-air. He called to her again, hoping she'll respond.

"Steph, Steph, say something!" Jett pleaded.

"Something!... is …stabbing…..me." She moved her head slightly, then her legs. It's not much, but it made Jett feel better.

"Can you tell what is stabbing you?" Jett asked.

"No, I'm too weak to left myself up. It hurts every time I try to move." She said.

Jett doesn't know what to do. The main house was too far away, and he had no idea where Jonathan was. Jett had to do something to save Steph, she couldn't do it by herself. Standing on top of the log, he is still four ft from the first branch. Steph was at least a foot taller than he was, that's why she could reach it easily.

If he takes off his pants, he may be able to use them to lasso the first branch and climb up. That would mean he would be in his underwear, but he didn't care; he's going to try it. *Well, here it goes.* He thought.

"Hang on Steph, I have an idea" he shouts up.

Stephanie is trying to free herself in the mean time; she doesn't even answer back. Jett throws his pants up holding on to one pant leg. Almost, still to short by at least six inches. He then gets another idea. He takes off his shirt so now he's just in socks, shoes and underwear. He ties his shirt on the end of one plant leg, and tries again this time holding on to the shirt. The end of the pant leg wraps around the first branch and snags on the rough bark of the tree.

"Got it!" he shouted excitedly.

He gave a tug to make sure it caught, than he tugged harder. He applied steady pressure, places one foot on the trunk of the tree and slowly pulled himself up. Once he realizes the pants will hold, he pulled himself up to the first branch.

"Made it Steph!" She looks down with amassment and thankfulness in her eyes.

"What is this?" Chaz questioned holding up what looked like a large metal lollypop. Jonathan looked at Chaz as if he's holding the winning ticket.

"Where did you find that?" Jonathan asked.

"On this desk, it looks like it's wired to this radio" Chaz replied.

"Radio?"

Jonathan hurried over to the desk where Chaz was. Chaz was surprised why the radio is interesting to Jonathan, that he took a step back.

"What?" Chaz asked as he looked at Jonathan with anticipation.

"Don't you know what this is?" Jonathan asked, as he uncluttered the desk by pushing almost everything on the floor.

"A… microphone?" Chaz answered in a question tone.

"Yes, it's a microphone wired to this CB radio. Do you know what a CB radio is?" Jonathan could tell by the look on Chazs face the answer was no. "A CB radio is a radio used to talk to random people." Jonathan said not waiting for an answer.

"Oh, what does the C B stand for?" Chaz asks.

"Citizens Band; You know like 10-4. We can use it to call for help" Jonathan finally says.

"We can?" Chaz finally understood.

"Yes! Now you get it." Jonathan said excited that Chaz finally realized.

"Ok then how do we do that? Does it work?" Chaz inquired.

"I hope so. We have to find out if this place has power. It's plugged in but it's not turning on. There may not be electric to this house." Jonathan said.

"Let's try another plug maybe?" Chaz suggested.

"Yea we could." Jonathan began to plug the radio to random plugs in the house, but nothing, no power to any of the plugs.

"Anything?" Chaz asked.

"No, nothing. Well if nothing ells we at least know that there is a radio here in case we do find some power." There wasn't much to the rest of the house. The exploring pretty much stopped in that room. There was enough stuff in there to keep busy for a while.

*I can do this* she said to herself. If Jett can manage to climb to the first branch, I can do this.

"Steph, I'm coming for you. Or try to at least. You're right, after the first branch the rest is like climbing a latter." Jett said.

His voice is just a muffled distant noise to her ears. She knew it was his voice; she just couldn't make out the words. She hoisted herself up and holds herself there for a few seconds; the effort is made her dizzy, and disorientated. Her hearing was fuzzy and her sight was blurred.

She was wondering if this was how Jonathan felt when she first found him in his truck after the accident. She let herself back down to rest for a few seconds. Just then she felt the branch slightly vibrating. *Oh no not again, don't snap,* she thought. It was Jett, or at least his hands, they made it to the branch she was balanced on. That meant the next lower branch wasn't far down. That also meant he could reach her legs which were hanging in front of him.

"Steph, I'm going to hold on to your legs and guide you down to the branch I'm standing on. Can you handle that?"

"yeah." She replied running out of breath, with that she hoisted herself up and said

"Ok let's do it."

Jett grabbed her legs and lifted up slightly to help support her body weight. She pushed back and let gravity, and Jett's guidance, do the rest.

She managed to still hold on to the branch on her way down. *Easy, relax,* she told herself. This is just like the uneven bars in gymnastics. It's only four feet to the next branch down to Jett, but it feels a lot further way when you're dizzy, and you have a slight stab going across your stomach.

"Gotcha!" Jett said, still holding on to her legs. He only lets go when he felt her standing on her own.

The first thing she does when she lands is check to see how bad the cut is on her stomach. A small stub of a branch ripped through her shirt and gave her a nasty cut across her stomach. She lost a good amount of blood, that's half the reason for her dizziness.

The bleeding can be stopped, it's not gushing. Once they find out she is somewhat ok, she leaned forward and gave Jett a hug, trying not to get blood on him; but he didn't care, he's so happy she is standing there and not dead or passed out, he gently pulled her closer and gave her a more firm hug. He also didn't want to hurt her.

"I was trying not to get blood in you" she explained.

"S, so what" he stuttered out of joy and happiness. "Looks like you're still bleeding" he said. He took off his shirt again and carefully wrapped it around her waist as a make-shift bandage to help stop the bleeding.

"We should probably start heading back hom…" Stephanie stops herself from saying the word *Home.* She is stunned for a second not knowing why that word would pop into her head. "Start heading back to the main house and find Jonathan and the others" she said.

"Good idea" Jett agreed.

They slowly made their way down the log-ramp, holding hands for balance purpose, now finally on the ground again.

"What did you see up there? Anything?" he askd with excitement.

"Yes!" she said.

# CHAPTER 6

The *new comer* children were gathered around Jimmy. He was explaining to the rest of the kids what he told Kasey. The children are hanging on every word he says. It's like they are hypnotized by the sound of his voice. He explained that where they are. There isn't anything that can hurt you. There are no bus/car accidents, no robberies, murders, or violence; and that's why he and his followers will not contact the outside world. He also explains that he's not keeping them hostage and they are free to leave anytime they want. All the while explaining; he gets theatrical with lots of body movement and hand gestures. That seemed to keep the children interested, and helped them relax about being stranded there.

"...And there you have it my young friends." Jimmy ended with a warm smile. "Now, who wants to help out making this evenings dinner?" he asked in a warm burly voice as only Jimmy can. Almost everyone raised their hand. That's a great example of leadership skills; being able to get ten kids aged six-twelve years old to willingly help set up and make dinner.

The young couple that tended to Kasey's wrist; were in the in the garden picking fresh veggies for that evening's dinner feast, the man's name is Travis, and her name is Terry. They're a cute couple, soul mates. Bonded together not by marriage, but common law and a glue stronger than any wedding ring could ever be, their five year old son, Hazelton. They named him that because the day was hazy with overcast when he was conceived. What better thing for a young couple to do on a hazy day.

"Travis do you think this is going to be enough for our new friends?" Terry asked as she picks the last few cucumbers that barley fit in the basket. She not looking at him, however she is waiting for a reply just the same. "Travis?..... Travis, I'm trying to..." She stops in mid sentence when she noticed he is in a hypnotized stair. She looked in the direction he was looking; now she too found herself in the same hypnotized stair.

Two child figures were walking toward them, one half naked not wearing a shirt, and the taller one with hair a mess, a dirt streak across her face and blood stained shirt wrapped around her waist. Her slight limp made them look like walking zombies. As they got closer, Travis and Terry notice its Jett and Stephanie. They walked over to the kids in a fast pace, both in a puzzling concern. Terry gently rested her hand on Stephanie's shoulder. "Honey?.. What happened to you?" The kids were still a little shaken up.

"We were out goofing around and Stephanie fell a hundred feet out of a tree." Jett nervously belted out. Stephanie shot him a sarcastic look that says *shut up*.

"No I didn't. True I was climbing a tree. The branch I was on broke and I fell four feet to the next tree limb below flat on my waist, which game me this gash and lower rib on this side hurts" she explained cradling her right side.

"Let me take a look at you" Terry said reaching to lift the bloody shirt. Steph and Jett didn't think the cut was that bad till they saw Travis and Terry's recoiling facial reaction.

"Eeww, we better get you inside so we can dress that cut." Travis said.

"Yea we have to get that cleaned up before it gets infected" Terry agreed. "And Jett you need to get a shirt on. I'll have to get this one soaking to try to soften the blood." The four of them walked inside when Travis remembered the basket of veggies they left in the garden.

"Terry, we left the basket of veggies in the garden, I'm going to bring them in the kitchen, you got this?"

"Yeah, when I am done here I'll catch up with you" Terry said.

"Ok, but take your time." Travis said. The young man continued to finish gathering the food for dinner. He's not really worried; he knows Stephanie is in good hands.

"This is going to sting, a lot, you may want to hold your breath" Terry warranted.

The look of horror washed over Stephanie's face.

"I'm kidding, you should see the look on your face" Terry said as she bursts out in uncontrollable laughter.

Jett thought it funny too. Stephanie however did not find it funny, but it made her feel better to know the cut was miner enough to be a joking matter.

When the cut was all cleaned and bandaged up, Terry was trying to figure out why Stephanie's ribs hurt. She figures if Stephanie's rib had broken, she would be in a lot more pain.

"I think you just bruised it real bad. Take it easy for a while, no more rough play, got it!" Terry said as she tassels Jett's hair. That seemed put a smile on Jett's face.

Terry went to join Travis and the others in the kitchen preparing for dinner.

"Don't forget what I said about not telling anyone what I saw in the tree, I'll tell Jonathan when the time is right." Steph whispered in Jett's ear.

"Ok, I won't say anything" Jett promised.

They both headed out to get cleaned up for dinner. After a short while Jett and Stephanie met up with some of the other new comers. They told Jett and Stephanie everything Jimmy had explained to them.

"When did he say this?" Jett asked.

"Earlier this afternoon, where were you two? And have you guys seen Jonathan? Jimmy was asking about him earlier." One of the girls said.

"We haven't seen Jonathan since this morning." Stephanie replied. "I hope he shows up soon, it's going to be dinner time soon."

"If he isn't here to help set up, he'll be sticking around to help clean up, Jimmy will make sure of that. We all know how we all have to do our part." Said another little boy.

Jett and Stephanie just look at each other in confusion. *Who brainwashed you guys*? Stephanie and possibly Jett thought.

"Yeah, we get it." Stephanie said just to end the conversation. "Come on Jett, let's go and find Jonathan. We'll see you guys at dinner."

Just as they were about to head outside, they saw Jonathan and Chaz heading toward the house. All four walked toward each other, meeting up just outside the main house. Stephanie realized she must of forgotten about the streak of dirt smeared across her face, judging by the look Jonathan and Chaz were giving her. It had only been a few hours since they last saw each other; however to Stephanie it seemed more like a few days.

"What happened to you?" Jonathan asked, indicating that there was a smear across her face.

Stephanie explained to Jonathan and Chaz everything she saw for the brief moment she was in the tree, before the branch snapped. She also explained the injuries she acquired on their journey.

"....And my rib is badly bruised, possibly fractured. It hurts when I take deep breaths." It also hurt when she laughs really hard, as she'll find out later. "Where did you guys go off to?"

"We found this really cool abandon house, it was so cool, we went inside it." Chaz say's excitedly almost as if trying to compare adventures.

"What? Where?" Jett asked,

"And we found a way to call for help! We can get out of here and go home!" Chaz continued.

Jonathan had to put a hand up in a *slow down* motion, indicating he is going to explain the exactly what they saw.

"Slow down kid. We got in the house over across the field. It has running water, but no electric. We broke into one of the room that *was* locked. There was an old CB radio on the desk, but since there was no electric, we couldn't turn it on to see if it worked." Jonathan explained.

That news seemed to give Stephanie and Jett a glimmer of hope. Stephanie goes on to fill Jonathan in on the conversation Jimmy had with the newcomer children and how the children seemed brain washed.

"That dose sound strange, but I think they are tired and happy to be alive." Jonathan said.

"Oh! That's another interesting thing Jimmy told the kids. He claimed everything they needed was right here." Jonathan stood there and thought for a second.

"I can understand that." Jonathan said.

Stephanie, Chaz, and Jett all look at him with questionable doubt in their eyes. He saw this and explained further.

"Look around, do you notice the gardens, the live stock, meaning the cows and chickens. It must rain here often; don't you see all the Rain barrels?"

"What's a rain barrel?" Jett interrupts.

"It catches rain water to be used whenever someone needs it." Stephanie explains.

Jonathan shot her a look that said *now you're getting it.* An *ah-ha* moment just washed into her eyes. Her face and body expression soon follow.

"That's why there are candles everywhere, for light. Only a few things have power." Jonathan continued.

"Like the stove for cooking?" Chaz asked.

"Yeah, the big stuff, but things such as light, they use candles for. And the food here, it's always farm fresh, because that's all that's here. At dinner time, take note of what you are drinking, it's almost always water. If there is any juice it's pure" Jonathan said.

"You mean with bits of fruit floating in it?" Jett's face pinched.

"That's called *pulp*, Lab partner" Stephanie said rolling her eyes at Jett, who just melted in them.

As they continued talking, they were slowly realizing these people weren't so strange, it was just how they lived.

# CHAPTER 7

He leaned against the building with his arms crossed and a satisfied look on his face. *They seem to understand how life is going to be here,* he thought to himself. Over hearing conversations was his forte. He didn't want anything altering his place of peacefulness and tranquility.

"Jimmy!" Jimmy turned his head, without moving his torso and shoulders. The starting of the sunset exposed his facial features, casting a shadow; making him look like a statue that was chiseled in his honor. "Jimmy, sorry to bother you, someone broke into the room in the guest house." Said one of Jimmie's *next in command;* she goes by the name of Flo, short for Flower, not Florence.

Jimmy's eyes squinted for a second; but at the same time he wasn't surprised. He had a few people in mind who could have done it. The question was which one of them.

"Oh yeah? Was anything stolen or broken?"

"No, but they tried to get the CB radio to work. Most of the stuff that was on the desk is on the floor now. And they left behind a sneaker print on the door." Flo explains.

"I see." Jimmy said calmly. "I'm sure we'll find out who did it at dinner time. These no power to the guest house anyway, and even if there was, the radio has been disabled for years, no chance of it ever working."

"What should we do?" Flo asked.

"Nothing." She looked at him with surprise.

As they walked over to the kitchen help prepare for dinner, he explained to Flo what he just overheard and assures Flo that the new comers are starting realize what life will be like here. She was clearly not happy about this and wanted the new comers to leave.

"They're going to rune everything we established here. Maybe we should help them contact the outside world and get home." She lowered her tone of voice when she saw two of the new comer children go running past them.

"Hi Mr. Jimmy, hi Mr. Jimmy." The voices said as they ran past.

Jimmy just gave a heartfelt smile, with no time to reply, but at the last second, before they get out of earshot he turns in their direction and called to them in that burly voice as only he can.

"Get washed up for dinner kids."

"Ohhkayyy" a pair of fainted high pitched voices shouted back.

Jimmy put his hand on Flo's shoulder, just like as if a father would tassel his son's hair. A parental sing language that says; *everything will be ok; I even cleared it with mom.*

"Look, Flo I know you're concerned. Believe me, I thought of all the risk it was taking in these new comers. I admit, when I saw the injured children, I let my guard down. There was no way I would turn them away. Don't forget, even they are god's creation and are in need of help, and he is the higher power." She just looked at him mentally saying; *I guess.*

"However", he adds "There is one key facture that I may not know what to do until the time comes."

"What?" Flo asked.

"At some point, there will be some kind of search party perhaps, a large search party; looking for the new comers. I don't want them here anymore then you do." Jimmy explained.

"Oh great! You see? This is what I'm afraid of; I want to help these people just as much as god wants me to, but if they're going to break in places they don't belong and attracting other outsiders, what am I to think?" Flo stated.

Again, Jimmy put a hand on her shoulder.

"Relax; right now I need you to calm down. I can't think straight with you frazzling me. We have time to think of something. Tonight after dinner we'll invite Jonathan and that Stephanie girl and maybe some of the older kids to join us around the fire. That way we can get some answers on what their plans are. And I'll tell Jonathan to stop kicking doors. But for now, don't say anything at dinner. I would like it to be peaceful." Just as they are about to walk in the house she shoots him a look that say, *I hope you're right.* And he shoots her a look replying, *I am, don't worry.*

Travis stood in the doorway of the main house. He was bellowing out that *dinner's ready*, as he also rang the dinner triangle. All the adults are already there from helping in the kitchen. Kids come running from out of everywhere it seemed like. Everyone was hungry, it was a long day. Tonight's dinner was chicken and veggies. They all shared stories of what they did that day. Mostly people did chores, some of the new comer children learned new skills, and seemed happy about doing so. Kasey bragged about how she helped Star hang laundry.

"I can tell Star hung your shirt." Kasey said pointing at Flo. "It makes you look like a football player." she added with a giggle.

Jimmy, Star, and some of the others laughed. Flo hesitated for a second, then turned to look at one of her shoulders, rolled her eyes, looked at Kasey.

"I was thinking more like camel." She said winking at Kasey.

That made Kasey giggle harder and cover her mouth; so that she didn't spit out half chewed food. Some of the people, even the new comers could tell it was a long time since Flo said anything funny like that. Jimmy gave Flo a satisfied look that says *well played*. She saw this and replied, *I know*. Dinner lasted longer than usual, because of better moods and sharing stories. After dinner everyone helped out cleaning. It seemed to go by faster than normal.

"Hey Jonathan join us again by the fire later. Maybe bring some of the other kids this time. It was a good time last night." Jimmy said.

"Sure, ok. Thanks" he replies.

Jimmy caught up to Flo. She smugly looked at him; with a quick up and down, head to toe glands and landing her gaze dead in his eyes that said. *What can I do for you now? I made nice-nice with the little brat.*

"Thanks" Jimmy replied as he read the look.

Jonathan ran up to Stephanie to ask how she is feeling, thinking a bruised rib would hurt while eating not forgetting about the cut on her stomach.

"Hey, how does your rib feel?" Jonathan asked.

"Well, it only hurts when I walk, breath, lie down, laugh, and now eat." She answered with a very sarcastic tone and a smile to go with it. He is speechless. He takes a step back and stares at her for a second.

"Oh"... is all he can say at that time. "Hey! We have been invited to the fire later tonight."

"I guess. There's nothing better to do." She sighs,

"Jimmy said to invite some of the other kids too." She just shrugged, as if to say *I guess so.*

A good number of the new comer children, even some of the younger ones sat around the campfire. The fire was a three foot wide ring. It gave everybody a reddish-orangey glow. There were about twenty people sitting around, being hypnotized by the fireball that roared and occasionally popped in front of them. The others can tell that the new comer children don't see campfire very often, by the way they are gazing into it. As if they are watching a movie.

"How did you kids like your first day of hard labor?" Jimmy asked with a smile in his face.

There was no need to address who he was asking. It's obvious the new comer children had sheltered lives. Jimmy didn't ask them that question to be mean. He knew they grew up in a very different life style then the children that lived in the commune.

"I don't ever want to milk a cow again" said one of the younger boys.

"Why not? That's the freshest milk you'll ever have." Terry added.

"Grouse!" The little boy said.

"Oh you'll get use to it. Then you'll be doing it without even thinking about it." Terry said.

"I guess so". The little boy replied. Stephanie and Jonathan look at each other, *Get used to it?* They thought to themselves. *Are we going to be here that long?*

"There are no cows at the Wilkinson's Camp for the gifted." Stephanie quickly jumped in.

"Where?" Terry asked. The facial expression on everyone's face was also asking the same question. Even Jonathan, who surprising enough didn't know.

"The Wilkinson's Camp for the Gifted. That's where we were all headed before the accident. All of us kids where pick from different schools to attend camp for the summer. As you can see we never made it." She said giving Jonathan *the stare.* He looks over at her and does a double take.

"What the hell you looking me for?" he half whispers. She just looks at him and says nothing.

"Oh, so all you kids are gifted?" Travis inquires.

"Yes. Our IQ's tested superior to our piers. Some of us specialize in one thing, and some of us know a lot about everything. I'm sure they're sending search party by now to look for us. We were scheduled to arrive yesterday afternoon." Stephanie explains.

"I imagine they would, I can't see why not." Travis says lifting an eye brow. Jimmy got up and through another log on the fire.

"Who wants a little wine?" he announces breaking an awkward silence. Cheers for booze sounded off from around the campfire.

Jimmy returned with an unmarked one gallon jug filled with what looked like the homemade wine. Jonathan offered Stephanie some wine. She was very mature for her age and he knew she could handle herself. She took a small sip, pinched her face and handed it back to Jonathan, looking at him like he was crazy for drinking the stuff.

The circle of friends gradually got smaller and smaller as the night went on. They actually talked, until the early morning. This time Jonathan was sure not to overindulge like last night. As they all got ready for bed, Jonathan thought to himself *one more day gone. Is help coming? Too soon to try to find us maybe.*

"Jonathan, can we talk?" Stephanie asked with a nervous tone.

"Sure, what's up?"

"I didn't get a chance to tell you what I saw when I was in the tree just before the limb snapped. Or it was more like what I didn't see." She said.

"What do you mean? What you didn't see?" He looks at her like she has three heads.

"I mean.. I was up in that tree and I was looking around and I saw the skid marks from the accident, but the bus and your truck where gone."

Jonathan is still looking at her funny.

"Are you sure? I can't imagine hiding a bus. Are you sure you where looking in the right direction?" He asked.

"Yes, I was up higher then I was before, I know exactly where we started. The skid marks where still there, but the vehicles were gone. Don't you find that strange?" Stephanie asked.

"Yeah, that is strange. Why would anyone go through all that trouble to move and possibly hide a bus?"

"Do you think they're trying to hide us? And prevent us from being rescued? Why would they do that? What if...." Jonathan cuts her rambling off.

"Look! Nobody's trying to hide us. I can't explain how the vehicles went missing, provided you even looking in the right direction. Like I said before, People will be looking for you kids soon. And I think these people would be happy to see us leave. It's only been a day and a half so far and..." Now she interrupts him.

"Soon two days will be three, then four, then a week then..."

"Ok, I get it" Jonathan said. "You're getting all worked up for no reason. I don't know what to tell you. Look, I'm tired and you need to get some rest to. You're going to have a hard enough time sleeping with that bruised rib and that stinging cut. We'll discuss this in the morning, ok."

"Fine, Goodnight" She says, knowing she's not going to rest easy. They go separate ways to their beds and wait for the next day to come.

# CHAPTER 8

## 48HRS LATER

The next morning was gray, rainy and a little chilly. Everyone seemed to be trapped in their beds; under a warm blanket of cozy. The sound of the tapping rain against the windows felt so soothing, that it even lulled the early risers back to sleep.

Jonathan just lied there with his eyes open, wondering what the other kids were thinking. He was wondering if they are still shaken and scared from the bus accident. They all were hopeful about help coming, but at the same time they seemed to be handling it better than he thought. Not to mention accepting how the way of life is here.

Jonathan also started wondering about his sister. He never forgot about her, but explaining to Jimmy and the other people about what happened the day she disappeared; made it feel like she just went missing yesterday. He keeps replaying that day over and over in his head as he was lying somewhere between falling asleep and a daydream, listening to the rain tap against the windows. He heard a soft voice echo in his head.

"Jonathan.... Jonathan" Said the soft echo.

He leans up on his elbows and looks around and doesn't see anything.

"Jonathan!"

It's the voice is of a little girl. *Sylvia*? He thought to himself. Suddenly he saw a shadowy image, which turned into the faded little girl, coming into focus more and more. After a second the image reached out her hand, and then he heard the voice call to him again.

"Jonathan, why did you ignore me that day? Was the car more important? I was screaming at you help over and over and you just ignored me." She said with a fainted voice.

"Sylvia" Jonathan moans in a slight whisper at first.

"Jonathan they pulled me in the car and drove away. They covered my eyes so I couldn't see."

"Sylvia" He says a little louder. This time Stephanie heard him.

"Jonathan, I thought you loved me. Who were those people that took me away? Did you know them? What did I do wrong?" This time he felt the emotional stabbing pain in his heart. *Is that what my little sister is thinking? That I didn't love her.* Hearing this made him scream himself awake.

"SYLVIA!" he shouted, springing sitting up; and breaking the silence of the room. He was covered in a cold sweat. Some of the children in the room are startled awake. Stephanie was one of them.

"Jonathan! What the hell was that? What happened?" Stephanie asked. Just then Star and Jimmy come running in the room.

"Is everything ok in here?" Jimmy asked.

"Jonathan you're covered in sweat." Star said as she pats the sweat off his head with her sleeve. He answers in a out of breath panic.

"I'm ok… I just had a bad dream, that's all." Jonathan claimed.

"That's a hell of a dream you had, care to tell us about it?" Star said with concern in her voice.

"I don't want to talk about it now." Jonathan replies. Just then Jimmy chimes in.

"Jonathan after you wake up I need to talk to you for a bit, but first get some coffee and pull yourself together."

Jonathan started to answer, but Jimmy was gone. He walked away as if he has better things to do.

"What's his problem?" Stephanie asked.

"Someone broke into one of the rooms in the house next door and Jimmy is not happy about it. So what the hell kind of dream did you have?" Star inquired.

"It was like she was right in front of me. I could have sworn I was talking to her." Still dazed from just waking up, he continues telling about his life-like dream.

"Are you sure it was your sister?" Star asked.

"Yeah! I can still see her. Oh god, she thinks I was ignoring her. She doesn't know how much I miss her. She.." Star cut him off and gave him a hug before he totally lost it.

"Let's get you some coffee." Star suggested. He calms down after a few seconds.

"Good idea, I need coffee." He agreed, looking at her still dazed and tired. Star tells him to stay there and get dressed; she would get him some coffee. He thanks her and she hurries off.

Stephanie has a look on her face that Jonathan can read. He just turned to her and gets in detail about the dream and what his sister looked like when he last saw her fifteen years ago. He tells her because she asked about it without physically speaking. Stephanie didn't know what to think. She was saddened, shocked, and angry, all at the same time. Saddened because the guilt he is feeling about his sister, shocked because she never knew anyone who had a loved one kidnapped, and angry because she wants to help him, but she can't. Star finally returned with a large mug of steaming hot coffee.

"Here, it's a little strong, but it'll wake you up and make you come around." Star said.

"Thanks, I need it. I better get motivated; I know how Jimmy doesn't like to kept waiting." Jonathan says rolling his eyes.

"Relax, finish your coffee first. He'll wait. He gets inpatient, but he knows you had a rough morning. I'll go with you." Star said as she leaned against his shoulder, tilting her head over to touch his. She was giving him one of those arm-less hugs. They both go off to meet up with Jimmy.

"Feeling better?" Jimmy asks

"Yeah, thanks. Sorry about this morning I didn't mean to startle everyone." Jonathan goes into brief story about the dream he had, knowing Jimmy wasn't really interested.

"Good. Glad to have you back." Jimmy said placing a hand on Jonathan's shoulder. "I need your help doing some carpentry work. We need to fix a door frame. It appears someone got into our storage house and broke into one of the locked rooms." Jimmy said holding a dead stare in Jonathan's eyes, as if to say *I know you did it. But why?* Jonathan just looks back at him with a blank stare.

"Sure, I've done some carpentry work. A door frame shouldn't be a problem." Jonathan said.

"Yeah we just have to fix one side where the door lock is. Someone kicked it in. Any ideas who would do that?" Jimmy asked.

Jonathan is stuck between a rock and a hard place. Should he tell the truth? Or just play stupid and hope it passes? Either way he's going to look bad.

"I did. I'm sorry Jimmy. It was the day after the accident; me and Chaz were looking for some way to call for help. We found our way in the house and came to this locked room and I just kicked it in. I'm sorry that I damaged your property. "Jonathan said.

"I see." Jimmy replied with a look that expressed, *I knew it.* "So what ells did you break?"

"Nothing ells. The only thing I tried to do was get the CB radio to work." Surprisingly Jimmy wasn't as angry as Jonathan though he would be. He actually felt better telling the truth. Jonathan felt Jimmy had a new found respect for him.

They continued to fix the door frame and Jonathan explained to Jimmy that some of the kids seemed to actually like the farm lifestyle, except the fact they miss home and want to be with their families.

"So what are you trying to tell me Jonathan? You all decided to stay?" Jimmy asked.

"No, I'm just saying the kids seemed to have adapted to life here. It's almost like this is the camp they never made it to." Jimmy's eyes squint slightly. A crossed look between mad and surprise washes over Jimmy's face. Jonathan is not sure how to read this look. "We're still looking to get out of here. So don't worry."

"Oh I'm not worried, you are all welcome to stay as long as you like. Just stop breaking stuff. Oh, as for the CB radio it will never work, I made sure of it." Jimmy said with a knife piercing stare that sliced though Jonathan.

After a few hours the door and some other things managed to get fixed. Despite the minor disagreement, the two worked well together. They managed to fix a leaking pipe, rewire a switch and tighten three loose steps on the staircase. All for a house nobody stays in.

"Thanks for your help." Jimmy said with a warm smile. Jonathan was taken by this odd turn of attitude, but he just played along with it.

"Glad to help. Sorry again about the door. It won't happen again."

"It's ok Jonathan. I know you and the other kids are under a lot of worry and stress, being in a strange place and away from home." Jimmy said.

"Oh Jim, why is this room kept lock anyway? There doesn't seem to anything crazy in here?" Jonathan asked.

"I keep this room lock because I have that bow on the wall. I don't want any of the kids getting a hold of it."

"Oh, ok." Jonathan shrugged off.

As they were leaving the storage house, they met up with Flo. She knew what they where up to; she didn't even ask. She looked at Jimmy purposely ignoring Jonathan. Jonathan noticed this and decided to have fun with her smugness. He gave her tight lipped smirk.

"Hello Flo how are you today?" Jonathan asked still holding that tight lipped smile she hates so much. She rolled her eyes at him and returned the same smile.

"I'm doing fine, thanks. How was your melt down this morning? Everyone is so concerned about you." She emphasis the word *everyone*. Foolishly, Jonathan should have saw that one coming. He was so caught off guard, he almost stutters his next few words.

"I'm much better now, thanks for your concern." Jimmy loves the mental and verbal sarcasm between these two, but he has a lot to do and he could use Jonathan's help.

"Alright you two, send me the wedding invitation. Jonathan I need your help with a few things in the barn now that I know you have good carpentry skills" Jimmy said.

"Yes, Jonathan seems to be good at screwing things up." Flo interjects; holding the same tight lipped smile. Jonathan gave Flo a wink and turns to Jimmy.

"What's next?"

# CHAPTER 9

Kasey was walking around and met up with Terry.

"Hello Kasey."

"Hi Mrs. Terry." she said looking down at the ground at first, then finally at her.

"How's your wrist feeling sweetie?" Terry asked.

"It's ok. When do you think I can take the cast off?"

"Oh dear, It's only been two days. I'm afraid a broken bone takes longer than that to heel. Why? Is it bothering that much?"

"Not really, I just want it off." Kasey said sadly looking at the ground.

"Aww sweetie, I understand. It gets in the way." Kasey gave her a sad look as she replied.

"Yeah..." Terry explained that she had some laundry to hang up; and asked Kasey to help.

"Do you hang shirts to make people look like football players the same way Star dose?" Kasey asked with a smile.

"Only if you want me to." Terry said giving her a gentle hug, and then they headed out to the clothes line. Terry put the basket of clothes on the ground and held out a hand for Kasey to hand her an article of clothing. Kasey picked up a shirt and hands it to Terry to see how she hangs it up. Terry held the shirt upside down and clipped it on the line.

"Is this how Star puts clothes on the line?" Terry asked.

"No, She hangs them by the shoulder."

"I See." Terry answered giving a long drawn out nod. "So Kasey, can you tell me more about this camp you and the other kids where headed to before the accident?"

"You mean the Wilkinson's camp for the gifted?"

"It's a special camp for very smart children? That sounds so nice." Terry comments.

"Yeah, I guess." Kasey said in a doubtful voice. Terry understood Kasey's sadness, and tried to give her some encouraging thoughts.

"Is it possible you can think of this place as the Wilkinson camp?

I'm sure you're learning something. Right?" Terry asked with a hopeful smile. "You learned the right way to hang shirts on a clothes line." Kasey looked up at her and handed her a pair of jeans as if to say *not really.*

Chaz, Jett, and Stephanie walked across compound and took notice of some of the commune children, who are living there farm life, doing farm chores; Such as milking cows, collecting eggs, and picking veggies in the garden. Chaz turned to Stephanie and Jett, and explained he's going see if he can help out around the farm.

"You guy's, I'm going to see if I can help out around here. I just need something to do. I'm going crazy." Chaz said.

"I guess, we're going to see if we can find Jonathan. He went with Jimmy this morning." Jett said.

"Sounds good, catch-ya later." Chaz said.

Chaz hobbles over to a boy who is about twelve years old, the same age as he is. The boy had long blond hair pulled back into a ponytail. The boy gave off a long tired sigh as Chaz approached.

"Hey you need a hand with that?" Chaz asked. The boy seemed surprised at first. "I can help you with that. If you just show me what to do. My name is Chaz. I'm from..."

"I know who you are." The boy interrupts. "You're one of those kids from that bus accident." The boy said without breaking stride from milking the cow, as he gave Chaz a sarcastic look.

"Hey, sorry to bother you." Chaz said as he starts to limp away.

"It's not all fun and games here, ya know." the boy said. Chaz stopped, not believing what he thinks he just heard. Did he imply that I'm having fun? as if this is the time of my life.

"What?" Chaz turned around looking down at his leg and crutch, and then looked at the boy. "You're right kid, I'd much rather be back on that over turned fire ball of a bus. I also rather be hiking and carried three miles through heavy woods with a broken leg."

The boy just looked at Chaz and realized going through all that probably wasn't fun. As he turned to limp away, the boy called out,

"Hey, my name is Arbin. Want to learn how to do this?" he asks. Chaz wasn't all that enthused about milking a cow. He mainly wanted to sit down.

"Sure I guess." Chaz said.

Jett and Steph hear Jonathan and Jimmy causing a ruckus inside the barn. Apparently they're fixing one of the barn stalls.

"Hey kids." Jimmy said with a burly grin.

"Hey, wha-cha fixin?" Jett asked.

"What does it look like they're fixing lab partner?" Stephanie replied, even though nobody asked her. This made Jett have a bigger crush on her more so then usual. Jimmy just looked at Stephanie with a facial expression that said*, that's not nice to say.*

"What? He likes when I talk to him like that. Tell-em Jett." She said giving him a love tap on the shoulder.

"Yeah, that's true, I like it." He said with a nervous, choppy tone.

Jonathan leaned in closer to Jett to give him some big brotherly advice about women.

"Get use to it kiddo, they'll be doing that to you from here on in." His advice is followed up by a slight head nod and a wink.

"Hold that a little higher please." Jimmy requested. Jonathan is held a plank for Jimmy scratch a line.

"Ok got it." Jimmy said.

They repeat the same step for two more planks. After the planks are nailed up, Jimmy tells Jonathan there is some pluming to be fixed in the main house.

"What are you kids up to for the day?" Jimmy asked.

"We're just wondering around. Chaz was with us, but split off to see if he could help some of the other kids." Stephanie answered.

"Oh good. Do you two want to help us with some pluming?" Jimmy asked.

Jett looked at Stephanie before answering. When she didn't give any facial expression, he agreed to help out with some pluming.

"Sure". Once again Jonathan leaned into Jett and said,

"Good job. You're getting the hang of it." The four of them headed over toward the main house the sky was finally starting clearing up and the sun was breaking through the clouds.

"I'm guessing you have some pluming skills? It's ok if you don't, I can show you." Jimmy said to Jonathan

"Yeah, I have some pluming skills." Jonathan said. Jimmy was impressed at what Jonathan knows about pluming. He was even more impressed that the two kids where actually interested how minor repairs got fixed.

A few days, soon turned into a week. Some of the kids who were crying for mommy and daddy; where still doing so, but not as much. Jonathan started to get worried, but he didn't want to mention it to any of the other kids or even Stephanie. He figured they would just start to freak out. The curiosity was killing him. Was help sent out; and they can't find us? Did any of the parents contact the Wilkinson's camp about the missing kids?

Jonathan wanted to ask Stephanie to do that tree climbing thing again. She still had a bruised rib from the last time she fell. He was really starting to think they were never going home. For some reason, the feeling of worry and doubt washed over him so bad, it becomes visible on his face.

"What the hell is wrong with you?" he heard a familiar, but unpleasant voice said from behind him.

"Flo, always nice to see you. How is your day going?" Jonathan inquired, holding a fake smile.

"What the hell is wrong with you?" She repeated.

"What are you talking about? There's nothing wrong with me. What's your problem?" Jonathan protests. Now he was really wondering how obvious the worried look on his face was.

"I'm not the one with the problem. You're the one in a trance. Are you doing drugs? Why are your eyes blood shoot?" She knew there's something bothering him, and she was loving it.

"Look, I'm not on drugs. I'm tired; in case you haven't noticed. I know you don't like us here and we get it. Believe me; I'm trying to get us out of here. Don't you have anything better to do?" He finally asked in a peeved tone. She just tilted her head to the side, looked up, and gave a sarcastic answer.

"Mmm, no. I have the rest of the day. Why? aren't you enjoying our conversation?" She asked again with that famous smile, he now hates so much. He can see she is just enjoying his misery.

"Oh good, your voice playing a symphony in my head right now. Why don't you please stay and help me hang some laundry." He said sarcastically.

"Uh, no! I'll just stand here and watch you. This is fun for me." She replied.

"Glad to entertain you. So tell me Flo, is Flo short for Florence, or Florida, flour of my eye?" This conversation with Flo actually made Jonathan snap back to reality. Surprisingly, he started to feel better.

"Neither." She said, staring at him dead in the eyes. She must have noticed that he was feeling better, because she turned and walked away.

"Hey, where ya going baby? I thought we were having fun." Jonathan said.

She spun around so fast, Jonathan flinched. Then took two steps toward him so their noses were two inches away from each other and said,

"You call me baby again and I'll make so you can never reproduce. Got it! Jonathan!"

*Yes I'll marry you.* He thought to himself. Man, he fell for her. He loved her wavy blond hair, the shape of her body, and her greenish eyes that were piercing through him, like a knife, she wants to plunge in his chest.

"Gotcha!" was all he could say. He suddenly had a new found respect for her; at the same time he couldn't figure out why.

"Jonathan!" said pleasant, familiar voice of a little girl. He turned around.

"Hi Kasey, Wha-cha doing?" Jonathan asked, yet again snapping back into reality.

"Nothing, are you going to make people look like football players?"

"what?"

"You know, if you hang shirts the way Star does, by the shoulders, it makes people look like football players."

"Oh, I didn't realize that. That's interesting. So how's your wrist? Is it feeling any better?" Jonathan asked

"Yes a lot better." He was waiting for her to mention something about going home, or when help will be coming; thankfully she didn't.

"What were you and that Flo lady talking about? She seemed mad at you when she was leaving."

"Oh nothing, just stuff that had to be done around the place. She's a little high strung." He said with a smile. He tried to make Flo seem like a friendly person.

"She's a little something alright." Kasey said with a giggle. "Do you need help with the rest of this?"

"Yeah, that would be nice, thanks Kasey." Jonathan said.

"You're welcome." She said picking up the last few articles of clothing. "Are you ok Jonathan?" Kasey asked. He wasn't expecting that.

"Yeah, I'm fine why? Do I look bad?"

"You look a little pail, like you're going to through up" *Wow,* he thinks to himself. Even a small child can see I'm not all there.

"I'm ok; I just have a lot on my mind." He said trying to cut the conversation short.

"Oookkaayyy" she stretches out.

At that point Jonathan decided to try to go off and be by himself till he feels somewhat normal. He suddenly found himself taking a walk across the field that Jett and Stephanie walked across to get to the tallest tree she fell out of. He reached the base of the tree and looked up. He was somewhat impressed that she climbed that high, even more impressed she fell. What a brave kid he thought. He wanted to talk to Stephanie and tell what he's been thinking. If she was brave enough to climb that high and almost fall to her death, she can handle what he had to say.

Taking that walk and making the decision to tell Stephanie made him feel a lot better. He hurried back to the main house to find Stephanie. It seemed like the longest walk ever. Before he could reach the main house to get to Stephanie, Jimmy caught him.

"Hey Jonathan!"

Jonathan looked over and saw Jimmy running toward him.

"Hey you got a second?"

"Yea, what's up?"

"I just wanted to say thanks for your help the last few days. It helped me out a lot." Jimmy said.

"Sure, Thanks for helping us out ya know, taking us in and everything."

"Sorry things aren't going the way you planned. I'm afraid it may be a while for you and your people to get out of here. I hope you can accept that." Jimmy said.

"Yea, I get it, but it's been only a week and a half. Help should be coming soon." Jonathan said with a hopeful thought.

"I wouldn't count on it." Jimmy said.

Jonathan just looked at him with a blank stare. Jimmy just nodded his head as if to say *think about it,* and walked away.

That conversation made Jonathan more driven to find Stephanie. For some reason, he knew she would understand, remain calm, and not freak out. He reached the main house and saw Jett. He assumed Stephanie was somewhere close by.

"Hey Jett, have you seen Stephanie?" Jonathan asked.

"I haven't seen her in hours. What's up? Is everything ok?" Jett asked.

"Everything is fine. I just had to talk to Stephanie about a few things, so if you see her please tell her I am looking for her."

"Gotcha." Jett replied.

Jonathan gave him a warm smile and tasseled his hair, in hopes to reassure him things are going to be ok. Jonathan is continuing his quest to find Stephanie, when Travis called him over.

"Jonathan, I need your help in the barn. One of our cows broke through one of the stalls. I hear you're an expert in stall repair." They both burst out in laughter, so loud other people stop and look. The two walked toward the barn like they were best friends their whole lives.

"I heard you had a small tiff with Flo earlier, what was that about? if you don't mind me asking." Travis asked.

"Oh, I got a little defensive and called her *baby* out of slang, and she got all pissed for some reason. I know she doesn't like me; and she shows it." Jonathan explained.

"Women." Travis shrugs off.

# CHAPTER 10

Travis and Jonathan got so wrapped up in *man talk*, before they knew it the dinner bell was ringing. They looked at each other in surprise, thinking the same thing; *Dinner time already?*

"Wow what time it?" Jonathan asked.

"Dinner time apparently." Travis said. By this time Jonathan knew the routine. If you didn't help prepare dinner or help get dinner ready, you better help clean up. That was completely fine with Jonathan. Finally, he'll meet up with Stephanie, like he' been trying to do all day.

Dinner was a feast of meat and veggies, which was a change from the usual chicken. Stephanie noticed Jonathan was looking at her funny. She could tell he wanted to talk to her, and it is going to be important.

During dinner, Jonathan was getting the feeling other people could feel the tension between him and Flo. He made sure to keep his eye contact with Flo to a minimum. The few times they did make eye contact, her green eyes seemed to slice through him like knife through an apple.

"What was that?" Stephanie asked while she was brining in dirty dishes from the table to the kitchen.

"I'll explain when I'm done. I need to talk to you." Jonathan said. She reads the look on his face and was getting the idea this was going to be a different kind of talk. She guessed some kind of news about being rescued or the lack there of.

After dinner was cleaned up, Jonathan finally caught up with Stephanie. She was chumming it up with some of her new friends. He didn't want to pull her away from the fun she was having. He figures, he'll just walk by and be seem, maybe she'll pull herself away. As he walked by pretending to be casual, he heard her voice making the announcement that she has to get going and find Jonathan.

"OK! Let's talk! Out with it!" she demands. He really has so much to say, he doesn't know where to start.

"Hey, I don't need you to freak out, but I don't think help is on the way. They should have found us by now. I wasn't going to tell you, but

I couldn't think straight holding it in. I knew I could confide in you." Jonathan said.

"What makes think help is not coming?" Stephanie asked.

"Because, I was thinking about it, somebody must have known the rout the bus was taking, and knowing you're arrival is a week overdue; I was sure they would have sent a search party by now." She could see and hear the panic in his voice. She's also tempted to ask him if he is afraid, as silly as it sounds.

"Jonathan? Are you scared?"

"Yes." For the first time, since they were stranded together, she could see doubt in his eyes. There wasn't even a glimmer of hope to be found, a look that said *we're on our own*. At that moment, a warm feeling of panic started to set in. From the top of her head, then trickled to her ears, then her cheeks, down the sides of her face. The panic feeling, left her head feeling numb. That warm fear continues down her neck, shoulders, arms and finger. Soon she was wading in the same invisible pool of panic and doubt Jonathan was in. All she could do at that time was stand frozen in place. She didn't even notice the tears running down her face until Jonathan reached over and wiped them away.

He expected and was ready for her reaction. He took a step toward her and put his hands on her shoulders and looked into her eyes. She was teary-eyed, but not crying, yet.

"Look we'll all be reunited with our families, it's just taking more time than I thought. Besides, help could be on the way. I could be wrong… It's happened before." He added that last bit to try to make her at least smile and ease the tension. She dose and it did. "Just do me a favor, and don't tell anyone we had this conversation. I don't want people to know I'm doubtful. Flo is already feeding off it, and she is killing me."

"Oh-ya, what's with you two? I saw the way she looking at you during dinner. I thought she was going to throw her knife at you." Stephanie asked.

"I don't know. Sometimes people can tell they won't like each other at first sight. It's just a vibe people get. And to piss her off; I called her *baby*. I guess it worked; I just didn't think calling her that would have a lasting impression." Jonathan explained.

"I would say it did; you keep it up; I'm going to have to rescue you from her." That almost made them almost laugh; they at least gave a big smile to each other. Jonathan was feeling much better getting that off his chest. He felt even better knowing Stephanie didn't totally lose it.

The night became cloudy and humid. It was starting to lightly rain. This was going to affect the nightly campfire. Maybe it would be canceled; or maybe it would be held in a different place, but where?

Jimmy catches up with Flo and wanted to know what was with the death stare.

"Hey Flo, Flo." Jimmy called out. She turned around in a surprised reaction, like she is honored that he was looking her.

"What's up?" she asks bright eyed. She actually had that butterfly feeling in her stomach, as she gets lost in his eyes.

"Hey is everything ok with you and Jonathan? I noticed the death stare you where giving him." He leaned back against the wall, with one leg bent and his foot flat against the wall. From a distance they look like couple of teenagers making plans for the weekend.

"He peeved me off by calling me *baby*." For reasons nobody really understood; Flo hated being called *baby*. Jimmy tried not to laugh; only because Jonathan hit the only nerve Flo had. "It's not funny." She wined, giving him a light slap on the shoulder.

"I wasn't laughing." Jimmy countered

"You wanted to. I know when you're holding back laughter." Flo claimed.

"Sorry, It's not funny, well maybe a little." Now she starts to give him that wicked stare. "Ok, it's not funny. You want me to say something to him?"

"No, not a big deal, it just peeved me. We having campfire tonight? It looks kind of rainy." Flo inquires.

"I don't know, probably not. We'll see if the rain stops." Jimmy said.

The rain got heavier as the night went on. This seemed to make everyone tired and worn out. Some of the adults found themselves at the kitchen table suddenly having an unplanned poker match. This was a nice surprise. Pretty soon the table was full, so full that they needed another deck of cards and they had to split off in two groups. Some of the kids even joined in teaming up with the grownups. Jonathan paired up with Chaz, as did Travis and his wife Terry. Stephanie wasn't interested; and Jett was interested in whatever Stephanie told him. Flo and Jimmy soon joined in.

Outside became both; a place of *do not enter* and a place of total interest. The rain was pounding sideways and the wind kicked up in a circular motion from time to time. Judging by the way the kids where gather around the windows watching the trees sway side to side; you could tell it didn't rain that hard often. The sky started to flash; a quick flash, like a camera, then a full on eye blinding brightness lighting up the whole sky.

The thunder got louder as well. Stephanie, Jett and some of the other kids were counting from the lightning, to the sound of thunder. You know, to tell how far away the storm was. If you counted two seconds between the lightning and the thunder, the storm should be two miles away. There was a loud crack of lightning that hit the ground in the center of the field. This terrified some of the smaller kids; who started screaming and crying. The sound of the kids screaming, made some of the adults run out to see what was wrong.

"What happen? Everything alright?" Jimmy asked.

"Yeah, a bolt of lightning crashed down in the center of the field. It was blinding and made the loudest crack. Didn't you guys hear it?" Arbin said.

"Yes we heard it. You kids stay away from the windows." Jimmy ordered.

Jimmy and the rest of the adults returned to the card game, it wasn't long before the lights flickered and then cut out completely. Everyone bellowed out "aww" at the same time. It sounded like it was practiced over and over just to get it right for that moment. The kids soon started chattering down the hall about what just happened. The card game was temporarily broken. Travis and Terry went to check on the children, Jimmy went to go find some candles and Star and Jonathan went to look for some candles AS WELL.

"I got some candles." Star called out. She hands Jonathan three big, wide candles, each with three wicks on the top of them.

"That should help" Jonathan said. They made their way back to the table, where they met up with Jimmy. Once all the candles were lit, the card game resumed.

"I'm going to run to the bathroom." Jonathan announces. Star hands him a lantern to help light his way.

"Here, you'll need this." She said.

"Thanks" he replied as he headed off. The bathroom is down the hall a little bit, it was almost kind of isolated. When he approached the door Flo came out, she didn't know it was Jonathan until he got closer with the lantern. At first she had a casual look on her face. Then she realized it was him and instantly her face transformed. When he saw this he took two steps back. She just stopped and blocked the door, knowing he wanted to go in. For a second there's an awkward silence. Jonathan decided to break it otherwise they could be there all night.

"May I get in there?" He asked as if he was defusing a bomb. She just stood there with her arms crossed and leaned against the door frame still blocking the way. "Look I don't know what your problem is with me, but whatever I did I'm sorry." Again, no response; Just a stare. "Yea know what? Have it your way. I'll use another bathroom." As he turned to walk away, she grabbed him by the shoulder and spun him around so they're face to face.

Thirty minutes passed by, and the game was back in full swing. Flo and Jonathan came walking back from the direction of the bathroom. Flo had that look on her face that said *see, I told you I could do it.* He had a look on his face that said *she's right*. Jimmy looks at them and did a double take.

"I see you two made up." He said. The two sat down and seemed to blend into the game as if they never left. Everyone was getting tired, and retreated off to bed. Jonathan just laid there and thought about Flo. *Shake it off.* He keeps telling himself; and soon faded off to sleep.

# CHAPTER 11

"How's that feel? Put a little pressure on it, but not too much." Travis told Chaz. The cast was off. Chaz put a little pressure on, then a little more. "Ok, take the pressure off. Can you bend it?" Chaz manages to bend his leg slowly.

"I can bend it. It still hurts a little. I can put a little pressure on it." Chaz said. Travis stood in front of him and put his hands on Chaz's sides to support him.

"alright, good. Try taking a step toward me. I'll help you." Chaz just gave Travis a doubtful look. "It's ok, I got you. Slowly put a little wait on it, I'll hold you up." Chaz slowly lifted his good leg and put all his weight his bad one. It didn't hurt as much as he thought. He hesitates for second, then slowly moved his foot forward and placed it down; taking a step. Then he lifted his injured leg and slowly bent the knee and swings it forward. He gently placed down. He looked at Travis with a surprised wide eyed look.

"I did it!" Chaz cheered.

"Good! Try it again, slowly." Travis said. With Travis still holding Chaz by his sides; Chaz took another step. "How does it feel? Can you do another?" This time Travis is a good distance away from Chaz. Travis slowly let go of Chaz's sides, but his hands still in place ready to catch Chaz if he has to. "Come-on, you can do it. Try two more." With great confidence, Chaz slowly took two more steps.

"I can do it!" Chaz said proudly. Travis can tell Chaz is holding back pain.

"Good. I would say at least keep using the crutch, you may not need the cast anymore. Just take it easy on it. You're still healing." Chaz felt like a new person as he limped away without the cast. Jonathan looked up and saw Chaz limping toward him without a cast on, and almost not using the crutch. Jonathan gave him a wide smile.

"Hey pal, I see you're doing better. Can almost walk on it huh?" Jonathan said.

"Yea! Travis just took the cast off! It hurts a little." Chaz explained. "What cha doing?"

"We're chopping up some of the trees that fell down from the storm last night. Want to help?" Chaz just looked at him puzzled. "Just kidding." Jonathan said as he continued chopping away at the fallen tree. Chaz decided to keep trying his new leg, showing off that he doesn't need a cast anymore.

Arbin is inside the barn cleaning up from the animals. The storm made some of the animals go crazy.

"Hey, can you give me a hand with this?" Arbin asked as he tried to piece the stall door that got knocked off its hinges.

"Sure, what do you need me to do?" Chaz asked. He was feeling pretty good about being able to help out. He felt so good he almost forgets his leg is still injured. He actually was reminded by Arbin, who commented that he didn't have a cast on.

"No cast?" Arbin commented.

"Travis looked at it off this morning and said the cast could come off. I just have to take it easy for a while." Chaz explained.

"Oh, here hold this straight while I try to reset these screws" Ardin said. Chaz braced himself on his good leg and grabbed the door at both ends. He lifted it to high at first, then levels down so Arbin can reset the door in the right place.

"Thanks." Arbin said

"What ells need to get done?" Chaz asks with enthusiasm.

"If you want to help me in here, that would be great. I have to just have to make sure everything is in order, make sure nothing ells I broken, collect eggs, I'll even let you milk the cow if she has it to give."

"Ok." Chaz replied. The two boys started doing whatever they needed to do to get things back to normal. *Thunk*, Chaz hits something with crutch. *Thunk, thunk*, "What's this?" Chaz asked tapping his crutch on the floor of the barn.

"What's what?" Arbin asked. He walked over to where Chaz is.

"This." Chaz said as he tapped the floor again *thunk*.

"I don't know. It looks like a door of some kind." Arbin said. In the floor of the barn, there was a wooden door, about four feet long and four feet wide. The door was level with the dirt floor of the barn and it was painted to match the dirt floor in the barn so it couldn't be seen.

"Have you ever seen it before?" Chaz asked.

"No, I never noticed it before." The two proceeded to look for some way to open it, but they couldn't find any handles or hinges for that matter. There was however several screws bolting it to the floor.

"Nobody ever mentioned any kind of trapdoor in the barn?" Chaz asked with surprise in his voice.

"No, nobody, like I said this is the first time I'm seeing it. Maybe it's some kind of storage space." Arbin suggested.

"Or maybe it's a secret underground room." Chaz added for effect. "What kind of screws does it have?"

"It's not a star or a flat head. It looks like you need a square head of some type. We better finish up here first. I'll ask someone about it later." Arbin explained. Chaz shrugged in agreement.

Later that afternoon, Jett met up with Chaz. Jett was actually without Stephanie. Chaz found this to be strange. He didn't question where she was, because he was so excited about finding the trapdoor in the barn. He asked Jett where Jonathan went off to.

"I don't know, why? What's up?" Jett inquired. Chaz explain to Jett how he and that Arbin boy were in the barn and they found the trap door that was bolted down with these odd screws. Arbin claimed not to know anything about it, nor did he ever see it before.

"Wow! What do you think is down there? You think these people are trying to hide something?" Jett asked.

"I don't know. It almost seems like it. I figured maybe Jonathan could find a tool and take the screws out. Where's Steph? I'm surprised you're not with her." Chaz said.

"I haven't seen her all day. She's probably with Jonathan." Jett said. Jett and Chaz went off to see if they could find Jonathan or Stephanie.

The evening was starting to set in. There was a lot of clean up of fallen trees that got done. Although, there was plenty of firewood. Jonathan and Stephanie where in the mess hall helping get dinner ready. Chaz and Jett came walking in, before they could say anything; Stephanie handed Jett a pile of plates and a warm smile. He understood what needed to be done, it happened every night. It was either help set up or cleanup. Chaz stepped close to Jonathan.

"Hey," he pauses for a second and waits for Jonathan to make eye contact. "I found a trapdoor in the barn!" Chaz said in a whisper.

"What? What did you find in the barn?" Jonathan asked.

"A trapdoor, it's bolted to the ground with six square indented screws. Did you ever see it before?" Chaz asked.

"I never saw it. Where is it?" Jonathan asked.

"It's in the back corner of the barn. I was in the barn with that Arbin boy. We were fixing some things that the animals stirred up during the storm."

"Dose Arbin know you know about it?" Jonathan asked.

"Yes, we found it together. He claimed he never saw it before. He also said he would ask someone about it. Do you think we could get the trapdoor open?" Jonathan was remembering the last time they broke into some place they weren't supposed to.

"Do you remember the last time we broke into a lock area?" Jonathan reminded Chaz.

"Yeah, but this has screws, we'd be undoing, not breaking in." Jonathan looked off into space for a second as he gave the idea some thought.

"We'll check it out after dinner and see what we need." Jonathan said. They were in such deep conversation they didn't notice Jett and Stephanie listening in. As Stephanie asked what time they were going, Jonathan and Chaz both jumped out of their skin.

"Nobody say anything to anybody. Chaz and I won't even mention it to Arbin again. They may be trying to hide something." Jonathan said.

Dinner was a feast as usual. The four were unusually quiet at dinner time. Hell, Dinner time was unusually quiet. At times the only sounds going around the dinner table were the clinking and clanking of silverware and plates. When those times of quietness reared its head, there was usually slight tension in the air. Jett, Chaz, and Stephanie kept shooting looks at each other. Some other people noticed and would look at them funny. Jonathan tried to cover this up by giving the people that noticed an eye shot that said *kids.*

"Clean up, clean up, everybody clean up." Kasey started to sing when dinner was over. That actually broke any leftover of tension. Cleaning up couldn't go fast enough; As far as Jett, Stephanie, Chaz, and Jonathan were concerned.

The four made their way to the barn and they found the trap door Chaz was talking about. Jonathan looked at the door and saw the screws Chaz was talking about. The door was four ft by four ft. There were six square headed bolts holding it to the floor. For a second they all just stood there and stared at it.

"Do you think we can get it open?" Chaz asked.

"It shouldn't that hard. It looks like all you need is an adjustable wrench. I know where I can get one. I don't know how Jimmy and the others would react if knew we were trying to open this up, assuming these's even something down there." Jonathan said.

"Why don't we just meet back here later tonight? Maybe during the campfire." Chaz said.

"I don't think that's good time, everyone will be outside." Jonathan replied.

"Why don't we just open it now? The campfire doesn't start for a few hours. I bet we can get this open in ten minutes." Stephanie said with high tension in her voice. She was also circling around the door like a vulture circling its prey.

"Alright" Jonathan said after a minute of dead silence. "I'll be back in five minutes."

After a short time, Jonathan returned with an adjustable wrench and some matches. The bolts came off easier than they thought. While they're doing this, Jonathan was keeping watch at the barn entrance ready to stop should somebody come by. The trapdoor was heavy, but they managed to get it open. There was a set cement stairs leading to what looked like a tunnel. They all just stood there for a minute hypnotized by what they were looking at.

"I'm going to check it out real fast" Jonathan said.

"I'm going with." Stephanie commanded.

"Me too." Jett said. It was obvious that everybody wanted to down and check out the new found territory. They decided to all go take the journey into the unknown.

# CHAPTER 12

## Exploring the Tunnel

All four of them headed down the cement stairs. Jonathan led the way using the pack of matches. The stairs were narrow and they had to walk down single file.

"We're only going to be down here long enough to take a fast look. These matches aren't going to last long." Jonathan said. Everyone agreed.

At the bottom of the steps, a tunnel trailed off in two directions, right or left. Since they only had matches lighting their way, they couldn't see very far ahead. They decided go right because, above ground, that direction would bring them to the abandoned house that Chaz and Jonathan where in. The air in the tunnel was cool, but not cold. The air was also dry. The tunnel was about ten feet tall and about 8 feet wide, pretty big for a group of people to walk in. They walked about one hundred yards then came to another set of stairs leading upward to another trapdoor and that's when their last match went out. Now they were surrounded by total darkness.

"Jonathan?" a panicked voice asked. Jonathan could tell it was Chaz talking. Jonathan made an announcement that they had to turn back and head back to the barn.

"Common, you guys, we have to head back. Everyone hold hands so we don't lose anyone." Jonathan said. They all headed back in a human chain. There was a small amount of light illuminating from the barn trap door they all focused on.

"We'll have to come back down when we have a flashlight or something. We have to check this place out." Stephanie suggested. Even though nobody said anything, she could tell everyone agreed.

Suddenly they heard a thud, and then footsteps coming toward them. This freaked them out. Now the human chain was running. They finally made it to the stairway leading to the trap door in the barn. One by one they all hurried up the stairs. Once they all reached in the barn, they slam the door back in its place, and bolted it down.

# *Chapter 12 1/3 At Wilkinson's camp for the gifted.*

*There sits a woman in tan cargo shorts, and matching tan button down short sleeve shirt. She is dressed as if she is going on a safari. The desk she is sitting at is covered with stacks papers and files. Her name plate is at the front of the desk that reads "Mrs. Schmerginhertz" There are other desk like trinkets, such as the mini sand trap with that mini rake that is in it. There are also a few stress reliving toys such as, a stress ball and some kind of slime oozing hour glass. You know; the one when you flip it upside down you can watch the slime slowly drip threw the openings of the divider that is placed in the center of the tube. Nobody would ever know that there was a telephone on the desk until it rang.*

*"Good afternoon Mrs. Schmerginherts, how you doing this fine day?" The woman looks up and gives a big smile.*

*"Please Tom, call me Linda." Said the five foot, 120lbs, nicely figured woman.*

*"Ok Linda. I'll be on the docks if anyone is looking for me" Tom said trying to navigate his way out of her light brown eyes and wavy blond hair. Tom grabbed the two way radio and headed for the docks. When Tom reached the dock, he stopped dead in his tracks, whispered a curse word to himself and hurried back to the office. The door flew open and this sent Linda back from mini vacation of word searches.*

*"What's wrong Tom?" she asked in stunned, concern.*

*"The guard boat is half sunk. Looks like we're down a boat again. Can you get Rich on the phone and tell him what happened. He has to come and fix this A.S.A.P."*

*"Really? We just got that thing back two days ago. You got it Tom." Linda says.*

*"Thanks Lin.." Tom says as he leaves the office. Lind returns to her cluttered desk and without looking she finds the tiny torn corner of the paper that had the number of the shop scribbled on it. And she even knew which stack of papers it was buried under. Not the neatest filing system, but it worked.*

*Before she could make the call, the phone rings.*

*"Hello, this is Linda Scherginherts at the Wilkinson's camp for the*

*gifted. How may I help you?" There is a woman at the other end of the line who is speaking in a frantic panic. "Mam, I need you to calm down. I don't understand what you're saying."*

*"I'm trying to find my son! He should have been there! I haven't heard from him in 2 and a half weeks!" yelled a frantic woman on the other end.*

## Flattened

### Tunnel vision:

Chaz, Stephanie, Jett and Jonathan Made it up the staircase and slam the trapdoor down and bolt it back in place. They Just stood there for a second; waiting to see if they hear anything. At the same time they all leaned closer to the door. It sounded pretty quiet down there. THUD! All four jumped out of their skin. Stephanie gave a starting of a scream until she managed to cover her mouth.

"What, what was that?" Jett managed to blurb out in a frantic panic. They all just looked at him with the same thought. *I don't know.*

"Maybe it was one of the kids? What if we just locked them in? What if..?" Chaz is suddenly cut off.

"Chaz! Calm down. We didn't lock anybody in. we had to unbolt it to get in, remember. I think we should cover the door with some of the dirt, so it doesn't look obvious someone opened it." Jonathan explained.

"I bet the tunnels lead to the other houses." Jett suggested.

"What if zombies live down there and they eat anyone who goes down there?" Chaz fantasized.

"There's no such things as zombies you knucklehead." Stephanie said as she rolled her eyes. That seemed to stark a slight discussion about which monsters could be real or fake. Jonathan wanted to break up this conversation before he himself got caught up in it.

"We need to get one of the lanterns." Stephanie said as they headed back to the main house and making a plan to return to the tunnels.

Stephanie started to gather what was going to be needed. As people where setting up for the campfire; Stephanie managed grab one of the lanterns and a good size candle. She set them off to the side by her mattress, when she was caught off guard by Hazleton, Travis and Terry's five year old son.

"Hey wha-cha got?" For a second she doesn't know what to say. *Tell him you keep candles and lantern there in case you have to go to the bathroom.* She thought.

"Oh, I need it in case I have to get up in the middle of the night. Isn't close to your bed time Hazey?" she asked. He looked up at her and gave a puzzled look. "Come on I'll take you there and tuck you in." She said holding her hand out for him to take.

Once the darkness set in and the crickets where chirping, It was almost time. It was almost time for the campfire to light up. It was time for Stephanie, Jett Chaz, and Jonathan to plan their journey into the unknown.

"I have two candles just in case." Stephanie said looking at him with fear and worry in her eyes. Jonathan looked in his pockets and makes sure he had the matches. Jonathan got the feeling that there is something ells worrying her; something she's wanted to tell, but isn't.

"What wrong?" Jonathan finally asked. "Look, I get it if you're scared. I'm a little nervous too." She continues to stair to the side of him. The truth was that she was scared, but didn't want to admit it.

"Arbin keeps looking this way" Stephanie said. Jonathan casually looked in the direction she was looking. He saw Arbin staring at them. After a second, Arbin looks away and leaves the room.

"Do you think he knows something?" she asked.

"He might, he has lived here long then any of us. Try not to let it worry you. We don't have to do this tonight." She looked at him sternly.

"No! I want to do this tonight and find out what is going on around here and where those tunnel lead." Jonathan could tell she really meant it, and was probably going with or without him. He really didn't want to do this tonight. Jonathan figured, if she was going to go in the tunnels he could at least be there to protect her.

"Okay, as long as you're sure you want to do this tonight." Jonathan said.

"Yes. I'm sure. Should we find Chaz and Jett?" She notices the eye roll he gives.

"I almost want to leave them out of this. It'll be bad enough worrying about the two of us. I really don't want to have to worry about those two. Unless you think they'll be fine down there." Jonathan was questioning. Her hesitation to answer; is an answer in its self. She was trying to say *no.*

Without Stephanie saying anything; Jonathan answered the question she didn't ask.

"I'll see if they want to stay up here and not go with us; I doubt they will." Jonathan said. She just nods in agreement.

There is brightness illuminating from the court yard. Jonathan and Stephanie Stop to take a look and see Jimmy getting the campfire going.

"Hey guys joining us tonight?" Jimmy asked.

"Yea we might. Chaz and Arbin had repaired some planks in the barn; I just wanted to make sure they did it right and the boards didn't come loose." Jonathan said.

"Yeah, good idea. Thanks we don't need anything falling apart." Jimmy agreed. Stephanie and Jonathan make their way to the barn.

"I didn't know we had to fix anything in the barn." Stephanie inquired

"We don't, but now we don't have to worry if people see us in there. And best of all, the head honcho thinks it's a good idea that we're in there. Understood?"

"I guess." She shrugged. As they entered the barn, they notice the trapdoor is missing the bolts that hold it down. They just looked at each other for a second. They both know that Jonathan bolted the door on with all the bolts. Stephanie helped bolt it on.

"Ok now what? Do you think Chaz and Jett are in there without us? Do you think they would be brave enough to go down by themselves?" she asked.

"I doubt it. More importantly, where are the bolts? I got an idea. I'll go in and you stand here and make sure no one bolts the door down. Are you good with that?" Jonathan asked.

"No way! I want to see what's in there, and besides, I went and got the lantern and candles." She protested. Jonathan kind of figured she would react that way.

"Ok, so you want to go down there by yourself? You're going to be fine with that?" Jonathan questions.

"Sure, I'll be ok." He hesitated for a few seconds. Trying not to think of what can go wrong.

"Ok, listen, this is the plan. Once you go in, I'll put the door on crooked so it isn't sitting flat. I'll ether be in here or at the campfire. I'll be keeping my eye on the barn and watch to see if any one comes in or out. The only thing is, how are we going to communicate with each other? I guess I could just check the door every so often." Jonathan said.

"I'll try to come back up in half an hour. I should have an idea what's going on down there. I'll try to see if Chaz and Jett made their way down there too." Stephanie said.

"Ok, go to the right. If the houses are connected by the tunnel that is the direction of the abandoned house me and Chaz where in." Jonathan said.

"Ok, gotcha." She replied. He put his hands on her shoulders in a consoling concern.

"Sure you're going to be ok?" Jonathan asks one last time.

"I'll be fine. Stop worrying." She says as if she talking to one of her parents. He watches her descend down the narrow stairway, turn to the right as they planned, and faded out of sight. He put the door in place crooked. He stood there for a while just listening, listening for anything; footsteps, voices, screaming, or something. After a while he makes his way to join the others at the campfire.

On his way back to the campfire, he decided to look for Chaz and Jett. When he approached the group of people sitting around the fire, he looked to see if the two kids were sitting with them. They aren't, so he headed toward the main house to look inside for Chaz and Jett. Before he made it inside, Star called out to him.

"Hey Jonathan, saved you a seat." She said with a smile.

"Thanks, be there in a few. I just have to go to the bathroom." Jonathan said. He really doesn't; he just wanted to take a quick look for the two boys. After looking for them for about 10 minutes, he headed back to join the others at the campfire. On his way back he met up with Kasey.

"Hi Jonathan." She said waving her wrist that had a cast on, but now is a heavy bandage.

"Hey it looks like your cast is off. Is your wrist feeling better?" Jonathan asked.

"Yeah!" she said excitedly. "Mr. Travis looked at it and said it was healing great. He replaced the cast with this bandage." Kasey explained.

"Oh good. Do you want to join me at the campfire?" Jonathan asked.

"Sure, ok." She said. He gently takes her tiny hand and leads them to the fire of *all knowing*.

Jonathan took a seat so he could keep an eye on the barn. Kasey sat next him. This also put him next to his favorite person, Flo. He didn't realize he was going to be sitting next to her. He probably would have sat next to her even if he didn't have to watch the barn; just to annoy her. Jonathan was concerned with keeping an eye on the barn and worrying about Stephanie.

He looked over at Flo and gave her a tight lipped smile and a slight nod. She returns the greeting with a half lip curled sneer. The few people that notice this greeting exchange held back from laughing.

"So, Jonathan how did the kids do making the repairs in the barn?" Jimmy asked to break the tension.

"Oh they did pretty good; I just have to go back in there and finish little odds and ends. Otherwise they did a really good job. I'll run back in there in a few minutes. I don't want to forget." Jonathan replied.

"That's a great idea, the sooner the better." Flo suggested, raising then quickly lowering her eye brows. He thought he would return the compliment.

"Good idea; I agree." Jonathan said slapping a hand on her thigh. If looks could kill, Jonathan would have been dead where he was sitting, talk about a death stair. He just gloated in her eyes. Travis got up and threw another log on the fire. While he was up, he asked if anyone would join him to have some wine. Everyone seemed to agree. Jonathan decided that is a good time to break away and return to the barn, and check on Stephanie.

# CHAPTER 13

## No Rest for the Wicked

She looked up as Jonathan put the trapdoor in place. Now it was just her and the glow of the lantern that splashed a dull brightness. She just stood there in place for a second, more like a minute or two. She moved the lantern around to see how far the dull brightness would light her way. Soon her eyes would adjust to the darkness that swallowed her.

She turned to the right as her and Jonathan planned. The air that surrounded her was dead. She couldn't hear anything. It was so dead quiet; she can only hear her heartbeat racing. She could only see a few feet in front of her. As she made her way down the darkened tunnel, she waited for something or someone to jump out at her. The tunnel was wide, which made her walk in almost a zigzag pattern. She did this because she didn't want to miss any hidden passage ways.

Her fear tried to consume her. She fights it off the best she could. *Just pretend you're walking across the compound to meet up with Jett* she told herself. Who was she kidding? That trick didn't even come close to working. She felt as if she was in a horror movie that was coming to life and no one was going to save her. The walls of the dark corridor were crumbling cement in many places. She estimated the distance she walked so far, was a lot further then the first time they went down there.

She tried to imagine where she would be, if she were above ground. It's been a straight path without any other direction to go. The smell was faint, but it was there. The smell wanted to choke her, but it was too faint. Finally, it clicked in, burning. It was a smoky smell. It smelled like something was burning and the odor still lingered.

That stench was actually subsided her fear. Now she's picking up her pace. Her footsteps got wider as she walked faster. She didn't walk faster out of fear, but mixed emotions. Curiosity and adrenalin were pulsating through her body. The burning, smoky smell has made a new friend. It's accompanied by a smell that is almost familiar to Stephanie; but she just can't describe it. All of a sudden the words *cheep and leather* popped into her head. She kept asking herself why those two words. As she kept walking down the tunnel, the smell kept getting stronger.

There was a break in the wall; another passageway. This one was on her right. She turned and went down the narrow passageway. After she walked the distance of about a football field, she came to an opening; an opening where the smell was pungent. She felt the air expanding all around her; this made her think she walked into a much larger space; a room perhaps.

From what little light the lantern casted out, she saw many shadows. One of those shadows made her stand frozen in her footsteps for a second. The tag-teamed feelings of fear and confusion had a wrestling match inside her head, and no referee to call cheap shots. It did however explain where the stench was coming from. Along the wall to her right was a row of seats. They are either two or three seaters. That's pretty much all she could make out from the shadow until she got closer. She took a few steps forward and it all came together; the two familiar smells are cheap leather and smoke.

She reached down and touched and ran her fingers along the back edge of the seat to make sure she's not dreaming. This was not a dream she was really touching the ugly green seats to the bus. *Wait! How did they?.. Who got?.. Where did?* She couldn't finish a thought. She slowly walked down the row of seats. *Maybe they're from a different bus*; she tried to convince herself. Then she saw something that confirmed her fear. On one of the seats, scribbled in pen, it said; C h a z w a s h e r e.

Jonathan sat by the trapdoor using a pile of hay as a pillow to sit on. It felt good to get away from everyone for a while; because he was getting overwhelmed sitting by the fire listening to everyone talk about the day they had. He leaned his head back against the wooden stall and just wanted to close his eyes for just a few minutes while he waited for Stephanie to pop her head through the trap door.

His eye snapped opened. He sprang up and one of the first things he realized is that he slept through the night. Even sitting on a dirt floor and leaning against a wooden stall; somehow, he slept all night. He could feel that it was the next morning. He looked at the trapdoor, and was terrified to see the door was still in the same position that he left it the night before. He was terrified because he didn't know if Stephanie managed to come up and put the door in place as he left it, or did something happen to her while she was down there and never made it out.

It was easier for him to look for her in the main house and see if she made it inside; rather than troll in the tunnel looking for her. He also was wondering what happened to Chaz and Jett. He ran out of the barn. The early morning daylight rinsed off the night before and he feels cleansed with a new day that he tried to catch up with.

Jonathan ran toward the main house past people wishing him a good morning to which he replied by shouting back of the same greeting he was greeted with. People could tell something was up by his actions. It wasn't in his demeanor to be so vague. He didn't care at the time he was prepared to explain later. He almost reached the room the new comers were sleeping in, when Flo met up with him. This caught him off guard.

"Where's the fire Jonny boy?" she bellowed out.

"Nowhere." he replied and keeps going. He noticed Flo gave him a strange look to his answer. He really had no time to play games with her now, but he'll make up for it later. They had a mutual feeling of, *We'll talk later*, in their eye contact.

When Jonathan reached the sleeping quarters where the new comers were sleeping, he looked for Stephanie, Chaz, and Jett. He only found Jett sleeping peacefully.

"Hey!" Jonathan whispered crouching down next to Jett. "Jett." He whispered again, this time he gently shook him. Jett eyes popped open, then slowly retreated to a normal groggy facial expression once he realized it was only Jonathan.

"What's up?" Jett asked, still half asleep.

"Have you seen Stephanie last night or this morning? I think she's missing."

"I haven't seen her. What do you mean she's missing?" Jett asked.

"Last night I went looking for you and Chaz. I couldn't find either one of you. Stephanie went down in the tunnels to look around, when I went back to the barn to wait for her to come up; I fell asleep and didn't get up till this morning. The trapdoor was still in the same place where I left it. I don't know where she is. I didn't know if she made it back here to bed or; is she maybe still in the tunnels. In any case I have to find her." This made Jett more wide awake and his eyes widened.

"Where ells have you looked?" Jett asked getting up and changing into clothes to wear that day.

"This was the first place I started. I have to go in the tunnels and look for her, but I don't want anyone knowing I'm in there." Jonathan explained in a panic.

"How are you going to do that? Everybody will be roaming all over. Someone is sure to see you" Jett said. On their way over to the barn; Jonathan was explaining how the trapdoor was offset and he and Stephanie were betting that the tunnels connected the houses on the compound.

# CHAPTER 14

## Missing

Once they reached the barn the first thing they noticed was the trapdoor is now bolted back in place. Seeing that only made Jett more confused; but it ran a chill down Jonathan's spine that gave him goose bumps. They just stood there for a second not knowing what to do. Just then Jonathan got an idea.

"I have this idea." Jonathan said. "We have to find Chaz. If these buildings are connected by the tunnels; we need to go into the abandoned house. Chaz and I were in there once before. We need to back in there and see if we can find a trapdoor like the one in the barn." Jonathan explained.

"Why don't we just ask someone about the tunnels? And explain that Stephanie may be trapped in there." Jett asked. Jonathan really didn't have an answer. He knew there was probably no reason not to just ask. There wasn't any harm in asking.

"I suppose you're right. I'll ask Jimmy the next time I see him. I thought Chaz asked Arbin about it when they discovered it the other day. I don't think Chaz got an answer." Jonathan suggested. They decided to split up. He instructed Jett to find either Arbin or Chaz. And he was going to see if he could talk to Jimmy about the tunnels the kids found. Jett agreed.

Jonathan was franticly making his way toward the abandoned house. He was actually hoping to run into Jimmy for a change. The compound was unusually quiet for some reason. There was always a lot of hustle and bustle going on, with people doing various chores. This morning was not like that.

On his way to find Chaz or Arbin, Jett ran into Kasey and Star. They were hanging clothes on the line. It seemed to be Kasey's new favorite thing to because she liked the way Star hung shirts to make people look like football players.

"Hey Jett, wha-cha up too?" Star asked.

"Nothing, I'm just trying to find Chaz or Stephanie. Have either one you seem them by any chance?" Jett inquired. Star looked at him puzzled for a second and shook her head.

"I haven't seen them. Have you Kasey?" Star asked looking down and giving Kasey a love bump with her hip. Kasey liked that. She looked up at Star with a grin from ear to ear and gave her an answer caught inside a giggle.

"N, noo." Kasey said. Star asked Jett why he was looking for those two. Jett claimed there was no reason and he was just wondering where they were.

Jett made his way over to that abandoned house he heard so much about, in hopes to meet up with Jonathan. Making his way to the abandon house was going to be a little harder then he thought. On his way over he ran into Travis who, asked him to help stack a pile of firewood. Jett was glad to do so, but he was in a hurry after all. Twenty minutes later, wood stacked.

"Thanks pal." Travis said as he gently slapped a hand on Jett's shoulder.

"Anytime." replied Jett with a smile. Jett's journey continued. It wasn't far to the abandon house, but he seemed like he was running through an obstacle course of chores. He heard a loud thud, followed by a snort, and then whoosh; like something waving in the air. It was Arbin, he was struggling to milk one of the cows. *Let's see,* Jett thought to himself. Ask Arbin if he needs help and waist more time, or Ask Arbin if he needs help and get some answer about the tunnels. Now Jett understood why Jonathan is so hesitant to ask just anyone about the tunnels.

"Hey, Arbin, you need a hand with that?" Arbin looked up in surprise. Jett has made a decision that he is going to ask Arbin about the tunnels. "You need a hand with that?" Jett asks again. Arbin didn't know what to say. Milking a cow is really a one person show. Arbin decided to let Jett have a try, since he's so willing to help out.

"Ok, have a seat." Arbin instructed Jett on milking a cow. Jett had somewhat of an idea, but to actually do it, is a little different. Arbin was surprised to see Jett was doing a good job at it. Jett was just trying to warm up to Arbin before he bombards him with questions about the tunnels.

"Hey, how am I doing at this?" Jett asked. Jett really didn't care at all how he was doing. He just needed an ice breaker.

"Not bad." Arbin replied. *Now that the stage is set,* Jett thought to himself. Let the questioning begin.

"Hey Arbin!" Jett said looking up at him, but not breaking stride of the milking action he acquired. For a second there's a quiet moment except for the tinning sound the streams of milk that were pelting the sides of the bucket. Arbin just looked at him blankly. "What's with the tunnels? And where do they lead to?" Arbin hesitated for a second or two. They both lock eyes; Jett still not breaking stride of milking.

"I don't know." Arbin claimed. "There are rumors about the tunnels. We were always told never to go in the tunnels. And nobody really talks about them."

"If you know something about them; I need to know. Stephanie may be trapped in there. After you and Chaz found the trapdoor, Stephanie went down there last night and she was supposed to meet Jonathan back in the barn in thirty minutes; but Jonathan fell asleep till this morning and now we can't find her. Not to mention that the trapdoor is now bolted back in place."

"What do you mean she went down in the tunnels? So there's a chance she may still be in there?" Arbin asked with a nervous shake in his voice. "We have to find her! Now!"

"Is she really in that much danger, that we have to leave now, this second?" Jett asked.

"Well, we should; and you're spilling the milk. We need that." Jett was so worried about Stephanie, for a moment, he forgot he was milking cow. He looked down at the bucket snapping back into reality.

The two boys set off bring the milk back to the main house. Each of them has two buckets full of fresh milk. On the way they discussed a plan to find Stephanie. Arbin explained to Jett the layout of the compound. Jett had no choice but to listen to Arbin.

"There's more than one of those trapdoors. There's one in the barn as you know, one in the abandon house in the basement, and one in the main house in the basement." Arbin said.

"Where should we start looking?" Jett asked.

"I would guess the barn, but there are too many people around. We can sneak to off to the abandon house and enter in the outside doors leading in the basement." Arbin explained.

Lunch time was rearing its head; and still no sign of Stephanie and the day will be getting late soon. Jonathan was in the main house searching for a lantern and a candle. He decided he was going back to the abandon house and look for a trapdoor to the tunnel. He didn't see one when he was down there, but he also never looked for one. The one thing he was going to remember was the pole in the middle of the basement; and make sure he wasn't going to run into it again.

Once Jonathan had everything he needed; he wanted to see if he could find Chaz. He didn't want to waste too much time looking for him. While he was looking for Chaz, Star called out to him. Star has to call his name twice before Jonathan responds.

"Jonathan.......Hey Jonathan!" he finally looked up and saw her looking at him with concern.

"Oh hey Star. What's up?" He answered trying to give a warm smile but is not doing a good job at it. She noticed the bad attempt at a fake smile and could tell something was wrong.

"Are you ok? What's wrong? You seem distant." Star said. With that being said, he started getting concerned about himself. *Am I that worried that people can see it on me?* He thought to himself. *I must be.* He has decided he was going to finally ask someone about the tunnels and Star will be the one. He trusted her. He dropped the fake smile.

"Hey, I need your help Star; but first what did you need from me?"

"I can use your help in the basement moving some furniture. You seem like the strong type." She said with a finger gently running down his bicep. She did this to try to break him out of his distant trance and make him forget what has been bothering him. For a minute it was working. His eyes softened and that smile returned; but this time it had a warm feeling powering it.

"If you are not too busy. And you can tell me what you need my help with." Star said.

"Ok you first. Lead the way." *Perfect!* He thinks to himself. *The basement, just the place need to go.* He was truly happy about going down there. He was betting there would be a trapdoor down there.

The stairs heading down to the basement were made of wood and a little steeper than the average staircase. The basement was cool. It was also petty large and spacious. The floor was not dirt, but concrete. They walked almost all the way across the basement. There was boxes of food stored down there; mainly veggies. There were also jars of what he guessed to be homemade tomato sauce and ageing booze; also assumed to be homemade.

He was trying to find a trapdoor while he was down there, but it was dark and difficult to see. She led him to the far wall where a couch sat. Behind the couch there was some lawn chairs.

"Jimmy asked me to see if there were any extra chairs down here. Do you mind helping me bring them up?" She asked.

"Sure" Jonathan replied. "Let me get these for you." He gathered all the chairs to be brought upstairs.

"Ok, now you, what did you need my help with?" Star asked. Jonathan's face and tone of voice suddenly get serious. He leaned in closer to her, as if there is other person around and he has to tell her a secret; even though they both know they are alone.

"Star, what do you know about the tunnels that run under ground here? I know one way you can enter them is through a trapdoor in the barn. That girl Stephanie may be trapped in one. I need you to tell me anything you know about them. Is there more than one way in them?" Jonathan asked. The first thing she did before answering is takes a step back. *That's not a good sign.* He thought as he reads her body language. Next was her silence.

"What? What's wrong?" He asked out of desperation. Star just looks at him and shakes it off before answering.

"N, Nothing. It, It's just that we were always told never to go down there." Star said.

"Why? What's down there?" This time he grabs her shoulders in hopes she'll realize how serious he is and not hold back information that could help Stephanie.

"I know that it can be dangerous because it's dark and a lot of passage ways. If you don't know where you're going you'll get lost down there, and good luck finding your way out. When did Stephanie go in there?"

Jonathan explained how he fell asleep waiting for Stephanie to come out last night. And when he woke up the trapdoor she entered from was still in the same place as the night before, and now the trapdoor is bolted back down.

"There is a trapdoor in this basement." Star said. "Help me move this couch forward." When they moved the couch there was a trapdoor; just like the one in the barn. It too was bolted down. Jonathan looked at it and figured out he can get a tool to get the bolts out.

"Ok, that helps me out. I know what I need to get. Let's get these chairs upstairs first so you don't keep Jimmy waiting." Star agreed. Jonathan finished helping Star get the chairs up, and then he set off to get what he needs to go find Stephanie.

"Jonathan?, you're not going down there, are you?" Star feared.

# CHAPTER 15

## Jett and Arbin in the Tunnel

"Ok Jett, You got the matches?" Arbin asked putting the candle in the lantern. Jett handed Arbin a half used book of matches. He lit the candle and they started descending down the steps leading into the basement of the abandon house. They closed the outside doors they just entered from. When they reached the bottom of the staircase, they noticed the pole in the center of the basement. They walked past the pole toward the back of the basement.

"There it is." Arbin said holding the lantern over the trapdoor. They both just stood there for a second and stared at it; watching their shadows sway back and forth made by the swing of the lantern.

The door was bolted down with six bolts, two on each side. Arbin had the wrench to unfasten them. This door was also about four feet long and four feet wide. They are both nervous and scared. Slowly Arbin knelt down with the lantern in one hand and the wrench in the other. Jett can see the hesitation in Arbin's body language. He put the lantern down and began to unscrew the bolts. They seemed to come out easier than they looked. The bolts were half rusted and some have started to lose their shape, and become rounded.

They managed to remove all six bolts. Now they just needed something to pry the door up.

"Here, try this." Jett said, handing Arbin a flat screwdriver looking piece of metal. Arbin took it and wedged it between the floor and the trapdoor. He pried the door up enough for Jett to slip his fingers under it. Arbin dropped the piece of metal and slipped his fingers under the door. The two boys lifted the door up. This one had hinges on it. As the trapdoor opened; it exhaled a soft cool breeze at them; as if it tried to blow out a candle.

The boys just sat there at first. Arbin moved the lantern over the trapdoor opening. A narrow concrete staircase was daring them to walk down to the bottom. The boys looked at each other as to ask who is going first.

"Who's going first?" asked Jett. Arbin just looked at Jet as if to say *you go first.* "Ok, I'll go first" Jett volunteered. "Give me the lantern." Arbin gladly handed Jett the lantern.

The staircase that seemed to be leading into the depths of hell, the staircase is steep and falling apart as they climbed down. The air was cool and dry. They walked so close together, they were almost stepping on each other. The lantern was only shining a few feet in front of them. They finally reached the bottom. The staleness of the air made it hard to breath. As they walked forward they were swallowed into the darkness.

As he approached the house, Jonathan noticed the cellar doors had been closed from the inside because the outside lock was unlocked. He reached in his pocket, grabbed the matches and lit the candle. He handed Star the lantern and told her to go first so he can close the door behind them. She called his name in sudden surprise.

"Jonathan! someone's here!" He hurried down the steps; and saw what she was talking about. They both walked slowly toward the open trapdoor. Jonathan reached down and took the bolts that were on the floor. "Who do you think is here?" Star asked.

"I don't know. Maybe Jett, but I don't think he's ever been here before. The only person that was here with me was Chaz. Maybe Jett told someone who knew of the tunnels and that's who's here. I'm taking the bolts with us; I don't want to get us locked in here." Star nodded her head in agreement.

They both just looked at the narrow staircase that is daring them as it did the two boys. Jonathan went first. He told Star to stay close to him. Before he could finish his sentence, she has a hand grabbing his shirt. Soon they too are swallowed into the darkness, like the rest.

"How far do these tunnels go?" asked Jett.

"I don't know I've never been down here." quivered Arbin. The tunnel was wide enough that they walk side by side. Their pace gradually picked up. They adapted to the tunnels dark passageways.

"Ok, we started at the end of the tunnel. I'm going to try to keep a mental map in my head as we go." Jett suggested.

"Yeah, good idea. So far we have only been going straight." Arbin said.

"I wonder what the purposes of these tunnels are." Jett said out loud not expecting an answer, more or less just making a statement. "Do you have any idea how long we've been down here?" Jett asked.

"I'm not sure." Arbin said. They both stop to collect their thoughts.

"Do you think going this way will lead back to the main house?" Jett asked to reassure his sense of direction was good.

"I'm pretty sure. If I remember the stairs headed toward the main house and we went straight, we didn't turn right or left." Arbin explained. The boys continued to make their way down the tunnel. After a while they come to opening in the wall. It seemed to be another connecting passageway. Arbin shined the lantern in opening. They walked in a few feet just enough to know it's not a room, but they wanted to confirm it is another passageway.

"It looks like another passageway, should we take it?" Jett asked.

"I think we should make a mental note of it and keep going straight." Arbin replied. Jett agreed. After a while they noticed a burning smell that was faint.

"You smell something burning?" Jett asked. They both stop to smell the air.

"Yea, a little. What is it?" Arbin asked.

"I don't know" Jett answered. "I don't see any smoke, do you?"

"No." Arbin replied. They both decide to shrug it off. As they walked further, the smell gently and slowly consumed their nostrils. It didn't seem to be getting any stronger. They held the lantern higher to make sure they didn't see any smoke.

"Should we turn back?" Jett asked with a slight tremble in his voice.

"I don't see any smoke. It kind of smells like something was burning at one time." Arbin said.

"Yea I suppose you're right. We'll keep going." Jett said. Soon the burning smell was not along. It had partnered up with some other smell. The second smell would have been more familiar to Jett.

"The smell is getting worse. Arbin stated.

"I don't think it's worse, I think it smells like something ell is with it." Jett said.

"I guess, but what?" Arbin inquired.

"Not sure, but I do recognize it. I just can't place it." Jet said. The two smells intertwined and danced around them making one putrid odor. After a little while they came to another opening in the wall. The now strong smell was coming from the opening. At the same time, without questioning; they turned and walked through the opening. The air changed now. It's felt more stale and heavier. This was not a passageway, but a room of some kind.

Star had her arm looped around Jonathan's. Jonathan can't help but to look at Star in disbelief. The look on her face said that she has never been down here before. He finds that hard to believe. Soon they came to same opening that the two boys first saw.

"Look!" Star said grabbing Jonathan's arm even tighter. "It looks like another way to go." They walked in a few feet.

"Yea, it sure is, I'm thinking we should keep going straight for now so we keep track of where we are."

"Yeah, you're right." She agreed. They continued going straight.

"Are you sure you've never been down here before?" Jonathan asked with a doubtful tone. She just gave him a funny look.

"No. This is the first time I'm seeing this. I never had any reason to come down here." she protested. He just shrugged it off and they kept walking.

Arbin and Jett stood at the entrance of the room, only seeing what the lantern will allow, which was only a few feet ahead of them. Without realizing it, their fear was been washed away by curiosity. They walked through the room, as a surgeon would do micro surgery. The nauseating odor they have been swimming in is almost invisible to them by now.

There was something that had penetrated the air, a recent freshness of some kind. Jett noticed this and was wondering if Arbin did also.

"It feels like someone has just been here, maybe just a few hours ago." Jett questioned.

"What do you mean?" Arbin asked.

"It feels like someone has been here before, like there's a break in the staleness." Jett was hoping Arbin felt the same thing. If he does not, then that only means Jett is filling himself with fails hope. If Arbin does, then Jett's predictions are correct. Arbin stopped and took a second to absorb the air around him.

"Yeah, I guess. I almost feel it. Are you trying to say your friend Stephanie was just here?"

"Yes, that's what I'm hoping." Jett said. The two boys began taking a closer look around the room. The lantern being so dim made it difficult to see the lay out in the room. As they made their way across the room, the air seemed to lose that stale feeling. They noticed a bench like shadowy figure a little ways ahead of them. When they got closer Jett was confused.

"Is that a seat to a school bus?" Jett asked as he quickly starts to go over to get a closer look. Arbin soon followed. They soon discovered that is was the same row of two and three seaters Stephanie found. Looking closer at the row of seats, they saw scribbled in pen, the words C H A Z W A S H E R E. Jett just freezes. He soon realized these are the seats to the bus they were on when they were on their way to the camp. Numbness was slowly being washed over Jett. He was also nonresponsive when Arbin tries to talk to him.

"Jett.....Jett!" Arbin yelled to break him out of his trance. For a moment Jett was frozen in place like a mannequin. "Hey!" Arbin finally shouted. His voice echoed through the room and possibly also the tunnels. This seemed to break Jett out of his trance. Jett flinched back into reality.

"What! what!" Jett said still half in shock.

"Are you ok? What's wrong?" Before Jett could answer, they heard a voice in the distance call out.

# CHAPTER 16

## Still in the Tunnel

Star and Jonathan stopped in dead in their tracks. Star grabbed on to Jonathan so tight she knocks him off balance.

"Jonathan, who was that? Who ells is down here?" she asked with a heavy tremble in her voice.

"I don't know. It sounds like one of the kids. Hello!" he shouted. This only seemed to echo his voice back into their ears. Jett and Arbin both are now in a frozen trance starring at each other. The air all of a sudden seemed heavy and thick. Fear over came them. They tried to talk but can't. They find that they can only whisper. After about two seconds Jett broke their silence.

"Who was that?" he asked in whisper. W, what should we do?" this time his whisper was accompanied with a stuttering tremble.

"Hide!" Arbin said as he franticly looked for a place big enough for the both of them. After a few seconds of them running in circles, Arbin grabbed Jett and told him to crouch down in the corner and blow the lantern out. He explained the room is so dark whoever it is probably won't see them. Hearing the patter of footsteps getting closer, Jett had no choice but to agree. They went to the end of the row of bus seats, crouched down almost cuddling each other, blew the candle out and waited.

"The voice came down here; come on let's see." Jonathan said. Star wanted to turn back and didn't want to see who was yelling. Jonathan can tell this by the way she was grabbing on to his arm. "It'll be ok I promise, I'm right here." Their faces cringe as the pungent burning smell grabbed them in a strangle hold. The abandon air that was once a structure in the tunnels was slowly withering away. That was the feeling Jonathan was getting as he and Star quickly and carefully walked down the corridor.

As they were walking, Jonathan was looking for another opening, perhaps the room where the voice shouted *hey!* After a short distance they came to a break in the wall.

"I think here, the shout may have come from in here." Jonathan suggested. The pungent stench had swallowed them completely. They could actually taste it.

"EW! That stench is nauseating, I can taste it." Star said while possibly trying to hold back vomit. Jonathan agreed. Standing the doorway they looked around as far as the lantern allowed. She leaned close to him and whispered in his ear.

"I feel like we're being watched, and we're not alone."

"I know, so do I." He whispered back. The walls to the room made it feel dungeon like. They were a grayish cinderblock. The floor was half dirt, half crumbled cement. The room itself was too large for the lantern to light up. Jonathan and Star would have to walk the perimeter of the room so the lantern illumination would reach from the wall outward about five feet.

"Come on, let's check over here." Jonathan suggested pulling Star along. She was still clinging on to him like Velcro. They walked to the opposite side of the room of where the bus seats were. Along the darkened grayish cemented wall there was metal two Hospital beds possibly from the 1920's. The round, tubular, rusted metal bed were placed side by side. They both had old, worn mattress' there was two sets of handcuffs latched on the metal frame at the head on one of the beds. The other bed had thick cloth straps. There was three sets straps; One at the head, one in the middle, and the last at the foot of the bed. The straps looked fairly new with fairly new buckles at the ends or them; as well as the handcuffs on the other bed.

They both looked at each other with the same thought; *what's with the beds and the restraints?* Above the beds, hanging on the wall was what looks to be some kind of medieval device. It looked to be some kind of whip. It had a handle wrapped in leather. The whip end consisted of ten or so thin strips of leather tails about one foot long. It looked like it wasn't hanging there very long. Jonathan thought he'd try to be funny by taking it off the wall and lightly batting Star on the butt. She didn't find this very funny, but he did. She gave him a slap on his bicep and told him to serous and act his age.

"Ok, chill out would you." He said as he took a step back. They continued walking across the room and along the wall. That nauseating stench was now almost gone, only because they have gotten use to it. About twenty feet further, they came to a set of heavy gauge chains. They were about five feet from the ground, and about three and a half to four feet apart. The chains were only about one foot in length. At the end of the chains were adjustable leather straps. Directly below the chains; almost on the floor is another set of chains with leather straps. There was really no questioning what the chains were for.

Jonathan was thinking of joking around with Star and put himself in place where a person would be if they were in the chains. But he figured it would be a bad idea, since she didn't think his last joke was funny.

"What kind of room was this?" Star asked, with a wide eyed discussed look on her face.

"Judging by the looks of everything, I almost want to say what kind of room IS THIS?" Jonathan comments.

"What are you talking about?"

"Look at the straps and chains; the "cat-of-tails" hanging on the wall. Don't you notice everything is fairly new looking? The chains aren't rusted, the leather straps are worn, but they aren't even dry rotted." She took a second too looked at what he' talking about. Once she realized what he was talking about; she gasped an inward breath and placed a hand over her mouth.

"Oh my god!!" she mumbled through her trembling fingers. Jonathan saw the fear in her eyes and gave a comforting remark to snap her back into reality. He needed her to be focused and not have a meltdown.

"Hey relax. I highly doubt they used recently. Let's keep looking around and see who's been watching us." Jonathan wasn't sure if he should have said that or not. The only reason he did, was because she said it when they first entered the room. He was surprised, but thankful she didn't freak out over that comment.

Arbin and Jett were no longer scared for their lives. In fact their fear subsided as soon as they saw it was Jonathan and Star entering the room. They remained quiet because they wanted to see what Jonathan and Star were going to find. They were shocked at the whole other side of the room they completely missed. Even though the two boys weren't physically speaking to each other; they could almost read each other's mind. And that was, when should they blow their cover.

Jonathan and Star reached the end of the room where they found another opening or an exit maybe a new entrance. As they got closer to the newly found passageway, the lantern's illuminating brightness just about reached the two boys crouched in the corner. The glow of light was only about six inches from them; that's how dark it was down there. Both boys knew that all they would have to do is extend one leg into the glare of the lantern's brightness to be seen.

"I think there is another passageway." Jonathan said leading toward it. Star was reluctant to go enter the newly found passageway. She pulled Jonathan back toward her.

"Wait! What if… where is that leading to?" Before Jonathan could answer, Jett accidently knocked into the lantern he and Arbin were using; causing it to make a loud *clink*. Star grabbed Jonathan even tighter. They both spun around so fast the candle in the lantern flickered. This time Jonathan backed into Star wrapping one free arm behind him and around her. He held the lantern out and saw two pairs of sneakers. In them there were two sets of legs dressed in denim jeans. Star and Jonathan loosen their grip on each other. He took a step closer and couldn't believe what or more or less who he saw.

"How did you guys get down here?" Jonathan said. Jonathan and possibly Star were trapped between relief and bewilderment. "Who ells is here with you?" Jonathan asked.

"Just us." Jett said.

Jonathan started looking down the row of bus seats in disbelief. At first Jett could see doubt in Jonathan's eyes, until he sees the writing on the seat that reads C H A Z W A S H E R E. He does a double take just to make sure he's reading it right. He looked at Jett as if to ask him *have you seem this?* Jet looked back at him as if to answer *yes I have.*

"How did these get down here?" Jonathan inquired with a puzzled look on his face.

"What is it?" Star asked.

"These are the seats to the bus that I got into the accident with.

How did they make it all the way here? And where is the rest of the bus?" Jonathan asked in half a panic. Star gave him a doubtful look.

"Wait, these are the seats to the school bus you got into the accident with?" Star asked.

"Yes, look, there's Chaz's name scribbled in it." he pointed out to her. Star took a step closer to check out the scribbling for herself. Her mouth opened in surprise as she placed a hand over it.

"OH MY GOD! How'd they get here?"

"That's a good question. We were just thinking about that." Jonathan said with a load of sarcasm so heavy it even blew away the Tension. For the next few moments they just stood there in wonder of what to do. Should they keep exploring, or should they head back and come back later? Should they stick together, or spilt up again?

"Does anyone have any candles on them? This one's almost burnt out." Jonathan asked out loud in general to anyone who was willing to answer. The boys still had an extra candle, but it was the only one all four of them had; which meant they should stick together. They decided to go through the doorway at the end of the room and not turn back as previously suggested.

They walked down the corridor in a square formation. Jonathan and Star were in front holding one lantern with the full candle in it lighting the front, Jett and Arbin in the back holding the other lantern with one other candle that will burn out soon. The two lanterns made it a lot brighter and easier to walk. They could actually walk at a normal pace without fear of wondering what was around them. The putrid stench was soon faded and the air once again became that familiar staleness they got to know and love.

"Does anybody ells feel that?" Star asked slowing her pace down. They followed her lead and soon weren't walking at all. They tried to absorb what she's feeling.

"Feel what?" Arbin asked. There is a break in the staleness of the air; almost freshness she is having trouble describing.

"I don't know, the air seems clearer than before." Star attempted to explain. Jonathan held the lantern up toward the ceiling. He's thinking they may be under another trapdoor and not realize it. There wasn't a trapdoor above them, but the air diffidently was clearer in that area for some reason. There wasn't any break in the wall for the new air to be entering. So where was this fresh air penetrating from? What was it? And how did it find its way to them?

Soon the candle Jett and Arbin were using burned out; leaving them with only one lantern lighting their way. This made them walk in a tighter square formation. They finally reached a break in the wall; leaving them with two choices. They could either keep going straight ahead, or follow the narrow staircase leading to the wherever it lead.

"Wait here; I'm going take a look to see where that staircase leads to." Jonathan volunteered as he headed up the crumbling steps. No one second guessed his decision. They really had no choice in the matter; he just did it. In a few seconds the three where blinded by the darkness that swallowed them as soon as Jonathan trailed off with their only source of light.

# CHAPTER 17

## Failed First Try

It took awhile for Jonathan to reach the top of the staircase, which lead him to trapdoor that appeared to be bolted down from the inside.

"Well?" Jett yelled up. For a second there was no response from the top of the staircase but darkness and silence. A faint light was coming from the top of the stairs and was getting brighter; shortly after a voice.

"It's locked." Jonathan said appearing once again from the darkened staircase. "There is a trapdoor, but it's bolted down." He announced to the three waiting at the bottom. "Does anyone have a knife of some kind?" Jonathan asked.

"No why? What's up?" Arbin inquired.

"I'm going to mark the bottom of the trapdoor in case we ever find it again on other side; we know the place we were at."

"I bet we're somewhere under the barn." Jett said.

"I think we're past the barn" Arbin disagreed. After a short while realizing nobody had any kind of knife; Jonathan bent down and grabbed a jagged Piece of crumbling cement from the staircase. He climbed back up the narrow staircase. This time Jett went up with him.

"Here Jett, hold the lantern for me." Jonathan said. Jett held the lantern as close the trapdoor as he could without getting in Jonathan's way. Jonathan took the piece of jagged cement and lightly carved a small map of how far they traveled through the tunnel. He scratched the words *We are here.* And put an arrow on the spot where they made it to.

Jonathan and Jett descended back down the staircase and were reunited with Star and Arbin. Jonathan explained once again to them what he had carved into the bottom of the trapdoor and the reason he did it. Being that the trapdoor was locked they really had no choice but to keep going straight ahead.

The tunnel's air seemed to be getting cooler as they walked further.

"Do you guys think we should maybe turn back and head the way we came from?" Star asked.

"Nah, let's keep going a little further; If we don't find anything soon, then we'll turn back. There is still that passageway we passed to look in yet. That sound good to you guys?" Jonathan asked the two boys. Arbin and Jett looked at each other for a second as if to hold a wordless discussion and both nodded in agreement. It was settled, that was the plan. For a while there was a dead silence as they walked. Finally Star broke the silence only to announce that the candle was almost gone and they should turn back before they are left with no light at all.

"Hey, that candle is getting low. We should start heading back before we're stuck down here with no light at all." Jonathan looked at the candle just to make sure. She was right, she could have mentioned it sooner even.

"Yeah, you're right. Let's turn back. We can come back down soon as we get more candles. We need to find out if Stephanie ever made it back out of the tunnels last night." Jonathan said. The four turned around and started to head back the way they come from. Soon enough they came to the trapdoor Jonathan carved in.

"Hang on a sec." Jonathan said. He ran up the cement steps, leaving the others, wondering what he was up to.

"What's he up to?" Jett asked the other two.

"I don't know your guess is as good as ours." Arbin replied. Jonathan came back down a few moments later.

"What where you doing up there?" Star asked.

"I wanted to see if I could hear any noise coming from the other side of the door. I was trying to see if I could figure out where the door might lead." He explained.

"And did you hear anything?" Jett asked.

"No." Jonathan said. Once again they came to that corridor that none of them went down when they first discovered it.

"Should we go down, or should we keep heading back?" Jett asked.

"Ah, we don't really have the candle light to do it. We should get back for now. I want to know if anyone heard from Stephanie. We'll come back down A.S.A.P. That will happen tonight during campfire stories." Jonathan explained. Everyone agreed and planed on a place and time they would meet up. They continued walking straight and once again left the unexplored corridor lost, but not forgotten.

They reached the end of the tunnel and came to the crumbling narrow staircase leading up to the trapdoor that would bring them back to the basement of the abandon house. Jonathan led the way up the staircase and lifted the door open and climbed up on to the basement floor. The rest of the four followed out of the tunnel and into the basement. The air seemed cleaner and fresher. That reminded them just how they got use to the darkened, stale air in the tunnel. On their way back to the main house they split off to go separate ways.

"Star." Jimmy called out. His eyes are Pin pointed on her like a sniper pin points a target. At first she didn't respond. He called her name again this time with a little more loudness but a friendly tone. "Hey Star". She finally turned around. She had a feeling of why he's calling her and what he wants to know. She decided *act natural* as not to give herself away.

"What's up Jimmer?" she called him to add a friendly, casual *nothing wrong here* tone to her voice. He gave her a stern but easy look.

"Hey what were you, Jonathan and the two boys doing in the guesthouse? You know that no one is allowed in there." She is not caught off guard but at the same time she didn't know how to answer this question. Suddenly she finds what she hopes is the perfect answer.

"OH, I was looking for the chairs in the main house basement like you told me. I saw Jonathan nearby and asked him to help me look. I wasn't sure if I had the right place because there wasn't as many chairs as you said there should be, and I didn't want to disappoint you, so I asked him to come with me to the guesthouse and look in that basement. On the way we met up with Arbin and Jett. We figured we could use their help, so asked them to tag along. I just didn't want to disappoint you."

Jimmy stares up into space for a second as if he is trying to figure out a math problem and looked at Star as if he found the answer.

"I know someone entered the tunnels through the trapdoor in the barn. I had to reset the trapdoor. You do understand that nobody is to go down there; it is forbidden. Do you know who might have been down there?"

Jimmy's voice was stern. Star doesn't know what to say or how to react. She knows who might still be down there. The four of them where just looking for her. Star decided to play dumb for the time being or at least until she talks to Jonathan.

"I do understand the tunnels are forbidden territory. I haven't heard of anybody going into them. Should I ask around to see if anyone knows of anyone going in the tunnels?" Star asked.

"No, don't say anything to anyone. I don't want to cause a panic. You better help out getting dinner ready soon." Jimmy said. Star just nodded in agreement and hurried off.

Jimmy closed his eyes, took a deep breath, and slowly exhaled. He didn't want to think the worst, but he couldn't help it. He won't mention it to anyone if he doesn't have to. Jimmy realizes getting mad or frazzled isn't going to help.

The first thing he wanted to do is find out who may or may not be in the tunnels. As he walked across the compound he noticed Flo in the garden. He called out to her. When she didn't respond the first time, he doesn't call out again; he just walked up to her and lightly touched her on the shoulder. She was startled for a split second but quickly relaxed once she sees its Jimmy.

"Hey Jimmy what's up?" She could read his body language, a body language she hasn't seem in a while, a long while. She read; *there's big trouble brewing and I may need your help.* He made a promise to himself a second ago not to tell anyone. At the same time he knows he could trust Flo not to freak out or spread rumors.

Jimmy was going to ask Flo to go with him to a private place to talk. He suddenly changed his mind and decided where they are was just fine; they are the only people in the garden. He didn't want to look out of place sneaking around. He knelt down next to her and began to help her picking veggies for the evenings feast. He calmly started to explain the situation.

Star saw Jonathan in the main house down the hallway by the sleeping quarters. She ran up to him calling his name in that loud whisper voice people do when they want to be quiet and loud at the same time.

"Jonathan! Jonathan!" She ran up to him almost knocking him over. He was taken by surprise by her behavior and has to take a step back.

"What? What's wrong?" He asked. He himself is now in that jittery frame of mind.

"Jimmy was asking me if we went into the tunnels and why me, you, Arbin and Jett were in the guesthouse across the way. I told him that I asked you guys for help looking for chairs like the ones we got from the main house basement." She said in that loud whisper voice.

"Oh, ok. That was fast thinking. Good job. What did he say about the tunnels?" he asked.

"He wanted to make sure that I understood that the tunnels were forbidden territory. But he didn't explain why. I always knew that. Nobody ever talks about them; so nobody really knows why, or what's down there." The look on Jonathan's face was cross between frustration and confusion.

"That doesn't really help. I have to find out what happened to Stephanie. Not to mention I have to think of an alibi where Stephanie is, if she doesn't show up for dinner." Star was feeling guilty at this time and was thinking back to past years. She was thinking back, trying to remember anything about the tunnels she might have heard.

"I'm sorry Jonathan I can't tell you any more about the tunnels." She said with worry and doubt in her voice.

"That's ok. It's not your fault." Jonathan said giving her a reassuring hug. She pulled away and looked into his eyes.

"I have to get back and help out in the kitchen like Jimmy told me to." She said.

"OK. I'll see you at dinner." Jonathan replied as he gave her a soft gaze into her eye.

"What do you mean someone may have found their way in the tunnels and may still be down there? What makes you say that?" Flo asked in disbelief.

"I was in the barn this morning and I noticed the trapdoor in the barn was open and off set in its place. I had to bolt it back down. I was guessing it was one of the new comers." Jimmy suggested.

"That sound s about right. Our people know never to go down there for any reason. Do you have any idea who it might have been?" Flo asked.

"I'm not sure, but I would say Jonathan knows who it might be. I'm guessing it was that Stephanie girl. She seems to be the most outgoing of the new comers."

"Are you sure somebody actually went down there? Maybe they just lifted the lid to look down there; and they put the lid on wrong?" Flo said.

"To be honest I don't know. I'll have to ask Jonathan if he knows anything. If he does, he's the one going down there and looking for whoever it may be. I just wanted to let you know what I am up against. I know I can trust you not to say anything to anyone." Flo nodded in agreement. Jimmy grabbed the basket of vegetables and stood up. Flo did the same. "I'm going to bring these to the kitchen and look for Jonathan. I have to find out what's going on. Someone may be waking a sleeping beast." Jimmy stated firmly.

"Alright, let me know what I can do. I'll be done here in a few minutes, and then I'll be in the kitchen if you need me." There is a heavy concern in her tone of voice. Flo didn't get worried very easily or often. Jimmy read this as he walked away.

Star and Flo meet up in the kitchen. They didn't plan on meeting up on purpose; they happened to be there at the same time helping out. They seem to hold a conversation without talking. Flo with her aggressiveness and Star with her shy passiveness seemed to be all that was needed. The body language between the two ladies was so riveting, that's what made a wordless argument happen.

Flo started out with a squinting stare, *I know you know something. Why don't you just tell me?* Star replied by looking her up and down, *I don't know what you're talking about.* Flo replied back with the same stare adding a sheer to her gaze, *you're lying and I'm going to prove it.* To this Star came back with a wide eyed gaze, *I dare you.*

# CHAPTER 18

## She's Alive!

The room was cool, dry, and dark. She couldn't even tell if her eyes are open or closed. She can feel her eye lids do the movement but it looked the same; there's no change in vision. The mattress she is lying on was stiff and brittle. She could feel the worn, weakening stuffing and springs though the faded cloth. She tried to remain calm as she slowly moved. She noticed that she was not held down by any restraints. She can sit up and stand if she wanted. The only restraint she felt is no sight because of darkness.

She began her dark exploring by just lying there for a few minutes as she tried to collecting her thoughts. She had no idea how she got there or even why she is there. She didn't remember Jonathan placing the lid in place as she descended down the crumbling steps. She thought there was somebody waiting for her, but she was not sure. She decided to regain her senses listening, trying to hear anything. There was silence all around her. Once again, she blinked her eyes open and closed to try to gauge how dark it was; there's no change. She was caught between fear and confusion.

She began by slowly attempting sitting up. Leaning up on one elbow, she paused for a second. She did remember and feel the matches in her pocket. She lit one; the match threw off a bright glair when it first lit, then quickly dimed down as it settled to its normal light power. She held the match in front of her.

The flame was a steady, small, and tear drop shaped. The only good thing about the total darkness was that the small flame carved a window of brightness through it. The air was so still the match didn't even flicker. She only had a few matches maybe three or four. She had to find the lantern she was using. She held the match over the edge of the bed trying to see if there was anything in her way on the floor. The floor seemed clear. It was made of dirt and horror. She slowly swung her feet down off the bed to the floor. As she did this, she was using her feet to feel for the lantern she had. There was nothing.

She only had a few seconds; maybe ten at the most before the first match will burn out. Stephanie began to look around for something that she can use as a torch to light her way. She thought she saw a chair in the corner of the room. Soon the match went out. *I'm not going to waste another match* she thought to herself. She made her way over to the corner where the chair is.

The frame of the chair is wood. *Thank god* she thought to herself. The seat of the chair was made of wicker. She wanted to break one of the legs off the chair and wrap some of the wicker from the seat around the top of the leg and use it like a torch. She doesn't want to waste all that time and make a lot of noise if it's not going to work. Unfortunately there's only one way to find out.

In the total darkness, guided only by a strong will and a good sense of touch, she begins Go forth with her plan. The wood is brittle and broke easier then she thought. Then she started to unwind the wicker from its seated frame. The wicker is brittle too. It wanted to break as she was wrapping it around the broken chair leg. She managed to get ready for the moment of truth. *If this works, I'll have at least 3 other torches* Stephanie thought to herself. She finished the last wind for that chair leg; she also left a little extra unwound; almost like fuse to get the fire started. She counted the remaining matches she has left. She only has three. Retrieving the matches out of her pocket; she is almost too nervous to try. Feeling the box for the striking strip; she finds it and lights the match. Once again the half the room is slightly brightened by that steady, tear drop flame. She held the match to the tail she left hanging off the chair leg; slowly it started it ignite.

At first she has doubts of it working, than the flame gets bigger and bigger. She turned the leg so the flame was burning up the fuse. Now the flame got much bigger than the match. She was holding both at this point. The wicker that is wrapped around the chair leg slowly started to catch. Suddenly, Stephanie felts a sharp pain at her finger tips. It was the match burning her. She was so intensely watching the flame on the wicker wrapping; she forgot about the match she was holding. She dropped the match out of reflex. There was a slight smell of burning flesh in the air. This made her wince; all the while she was intensely watching the catch fire more and more.

There was a feeling of victory that wanted to wash over her; but she was holding it back on getting excited until she was convinced her dungeon made torch is going to stay lit. After a few moments the whole top of the chair leg was a full blaze. Stephanie was amazed it actually worked; now she was hoping that the rest of the leg doesn't catch also. Worried this may happen, she has to act fast. If the rest of the leg does catch fire and she can't hold it, she'll just lay it in the middle of the floor and let it burn itself out; but for now she has plenty of light to explore her way out of there.

The burning wicker gave off a pungent, putrid stench. There was also going to be the problem of smoke piling up. Her second thought is to first circle the perimeter of the room to see what is the corners. After she realized there is nothing in the room she can use; she headed for the doorway or what seemed like it wants to be a doorway. Still shaken up from waking in a strange place; she tried to keep calm. She had no idea which way to go, right or left. *I guess it doesn't matter at this point* she thought to herself.

She made a right out of the doorway. All the while she was trying to remember how she wound up in that room. She didn't think she would just decide to lie down and take a nap. She doubts someone put her there; surely she would remember that; or at least she wanted to think she would remember that. What seemed like walking forever; finally ended at yet another right or left decision. She was trying to keep a mental map of how to backtrack. That room wasn't the greatest place, but it was the only starting point she can remember. She turned right.

The onset of panic came and went. *I'll never get out of here. It'll be ok. I'll never get out of here. It'll be ok.* Those two thoughts were playing tug-of-war, or having a wrestling match inside her head. The corridor seemed never ending. At times she just stopped and looked around. To her disappointment, it's the same all around her. She has walked so far it may be pointless just to turn around. *I should have gone left. What if I had just went left? I'd be somewhere by now.* She silently yelled at herself.

She saw another passageway on her left. She turned left going down the passageway. There was something different about this passageway. It seemed smaller somehow; maybe narrower, not as high? She couldn't really place it. After a while she came to an opening in the wall on her right. It appeared to be another room.

Inside the room, hanging on the walls are backpacks; about ten of them. She took one off the wall and looked inside of it. She found clothes and school supplies; pens, pencils, tape, and stuff like that. Her eyes widen as an eerie thought came to mind. *Is this stuff from the bus?* She asked herself. She continued to look in the others to see if she could recognize if they belonged to any of the kids. She didn't find anything that would link the backpacks to any of the kids. She put everything back exactly the way she found it.

On the ground under the backpacks is an empty bottle of booze. She bent down to pick it up. She examined the bottle and its label; it's some type of Scotch from what she's read. She remembered that Jonathan had mentioned that there was a liquor bottle on the bus the day of the accident. She put the bottle back down right where she found it; even facing the same way.

On the other side of the room was a set of bunk beds. Each bed was made up of a heavy board. The first bed is two feet from the floor and the second bed I two feet above the first one. There is a small step latter beside the bottom bunk so someone was able to climb into the top bunk. There are no mattress or bed sheets to be found.

The rest of the room was a reminder of what horror and loneliness feels like. Looking around at the dirt floor and the stone walls; Stephanie was wondering who might have been sleeping in here.

She was imagining someone that it was held against their will. What was this place she found herself in? Why was it built and who built it? Stephanie knew she had to try to keep her cool if she wanted to get out of there. What was above ground didn't seem so bad after being in the tunnels.

She has to keep moving. She was worried about the smoke build up from her torch. There was really nothing ells to see in this room. She was getting the feeling of being watched; and the person watching her was just a few feet away. Whoever made it to the bus and bought this stuff down here must know she was down here and was probably watching her now. Her mind was starting to race with paranoia. Surprisingly the torch is held up better then she thought it would. She exited the room and made a left and continued straight. She forgot how much the passageway narrowed. By now she almost couldn't remember how to backtrack the way she came. Her fear was starting to turn into anger. The sound of her footsteps turned into slight pounding as they got faster. She is almost not afraid; after a while.

He was staring at her making sure not to enter the circle of glow that was being radiating from her torch. He was tall and his broad shoulders almost roadblock the narrow passageway of the tunnel. He stared at her with a hunger like gleam in his eyes. He stroked the hairs on his trimmed beard and slid his finger down his neck, to the finger bone that hung off the necklace of discipline, as he referred to it. The finger bone was just one of the few of the charms, and far from good luck charms, that hung from the necklace of discipline. He called it that because it's a reminder to all who have did wrong against him. He wears it proudly; unfortunately they are other people's battle scars; much like the finger bone that is representing the finger of thieves. One mustn't steal.

He didn't think she would wake up so soon. *I should have killed her when I had the chance* he thought. He didn't want to be seen by her. *I should kill her; I should do it right now* he continued to think to himself. But he doesn't. He just stood there and watched her as she exited the room.

# CHAPTER 19

## A Generator?

Star and Flo were still in the kitchen continuing their silent argument via body language; creating their own very private game of charades. The two girls were at a staring deadlock. They were waiting for the other to break the death stare they held on each other. Without warming their silence was broken by a dropped pot. The ear piercing clang sliced through the kitchen and ears of those closest to it. People flinched and some jumped out of their skin even. Flo and Star managed to physically stay deadlocked on each other. Their death stares soften as a soft little voice came from across the silent kitchen.

"Sorry," said a tiny, shy, soft voice. It was Kasey; the pot slipped out of her hand and clanged on the floor where it bounced around and finally came to a rest right side up. That ear piercing clang happened just in time; acting like a referee breaking up a fight between two athletes. Star quickly walked over to Kasey; squatted down and put a warm consoling arm around her shoulder.

"That's alright Kasey dear. It was an accident." Star said picking up the pot that had slipped out of Kasey's hand. She finished drying it off, gave Kasey a gentle pat on the head and put pot on the stove to be used again. Star turned back around to return to where she was stationed and was relieved to find Flo has gone away. The rest of the kitchen continued as they were only moments before.

Arbin didn't know what to make of what he just saw in the tunnels. For now, he just wanted to walk around to clear his head. He couldn't stop thinking about Stephanie and what kind of trouble she may be in; or where she went, what happened to her.

He wondered into the barn, not knowing Travis was in there tending to the animals. Arbin was both surprised and relieved. Surprised to see someone ells in the barn; relieved, because it'll help keep his mind off Stephanie and the tunnels.

Arbin was trying to mask a guilty look from Travis. He thought he was succeeding by looking down, having a fixed stare on the barn floor. He also thought doing the more unpleasant chores without being told; with an unusual ambition was a good cover. Arbin doesn't realize shoveling fresh poop shouldn't be a pleaser, no matter how great of a day you're having. Travis Knew something is going on from Arbin's behavior; but he didn't want Arbin to know. Travis decided to play along with Arbin and try to get some information.

"Hey buddy, doing a good job. When you're done there I have something important I need your help with." Travis said almost sure that Arbin would agree to anything, since he was in that *I'll do anything to shake this guilty feeling,* mind set.

"Sure, what is it?" Arbin asked.

"Finish up there first; I'm not quite ready for you yet" Travis said.

"Ok". Arbin said with a great feeling, as though he just pulled off the lie of the century. Arbin was trying like hell not to stare at the trap door that was hidden over by dirt and hay. Travis kept walking over it. *Does Travis know about the trapdoor?* Arbin thought to himself. *He must. He's been in here a million times. He must know about the trapdoors and the tunnels; but why weren't they ever mentioned? What other secrets are the adults keeping from us? What is down in the tunnels that have to be kept a secret?*

Flo met up with Jimmy Just outside the kitchen doors; he was making sure things were getting set up for dinner that night and the campfire afterwards. At first, Flo didn't want to seem to frazzled or just start rambling on aimlessly. She took a second to collect her thoughts. She was not going to let Star get her all frazzled; she took a deep breath, tilted her back straightening her spine. She slightly flings her head to one side whipping her hair out of her eyes and starts to firmly strut over toward Jimmy.

By now Jimmy has made his way outside of the main house. He heard the door slam shut. Without even looking in her direction; he could tell who it was and what she probably wants. He probably guessed what she's going to say next. He turned around with an expression on his face that says *what up Flo?* Before he can stop the motion of turning his head and following torso; his demeanor changed. In front of the closed door where Flo should have been standing was Jett. Jimmy stood straighter as if he is standing to attention and softens his gaze. Jett has a scared, puzzled face that seemed to be looking at Jimmy, but at the same time looking through him.

"Jett! What's wrong?" Jimmy asked. Jett appeared to be lost in thought, and not in a good way. His scared and puzzled look is causing his face to become flushed; soon he was almost ghost white. Jimmy ran over to him and caught him before Jett can plant face first in the ground.

"Man down!" Jimmy yelled out. That's one phrase that needs no explanation. It was almost never heard, but everyone knows what that means. Everyone that was part of the commune that is.

Travis and Arbin came running out of the barn randomly looking around to see where Jimmy's voice was coming from. A few seconds later Star and some of the others working in the kitchen came running out. Flo pushed her way though with a jug of cool water. By now a small crowd had gathered around. Jimmy poured some water on Jett's forehead. Jett started to come awake.

"Oh my god, What happened?" several people asked.

"I don't know. He just came out and then fainted. Help me get him inside." Jimmy ordered. Jimmy carried to the sleeping quarters where the new comers were staying, and rested Jett on one of the mattress. Now Jett was almost fully awake.

"Alright everyone Thanks for helping; but let's get back to prepping dinner. He'll be fine. I have it from here". Without hesitation, they all returned to their chores as if nothing just happened.

"Hey buddy, you'll be ok. I'm right here. Just relax. You just passed out from the heat and possibly some anxiety." Jimmy said in a calming soft voice; gently rubbed Jett's forehead. Jett was looking up at Jimmy's chiseled facial features. He also feels his warm burly hand on his forehead. Jimmy is slowly talking to Jett trying to get a story out of him about what just happened.

"How ya doing?" At first Jett remained quiet. Jimmy understood the boy's confusion and just continues to talk to him. "I know the last few weeks have been not so easy for you; the accident, being away from your family and everything. I will help you, but you have to tell me what's going on. I know you might have been down in the tunnels.

That's ok, No one's mad at you. I just need to know so I can protect you and whoever might have gone down there." After a few moments Jett finally broke his silence.

"Jonathan brought us down there." Jett whispered.

"Who did Jonathan bring down there and why did you all go down there?"

"Me, Arbin, Star, and Jonathan went down there to look for Stephanie. She went down there last night and never come out, so we went down there to look for her; but we didn't find her."

"Did you see anyone ells down there?"

"No."

"What did you see down there?" Jimmy asks.

"It was dark down there. The tunnels where dark. We saw what looked like the seats to school bus we were in. How did they get down there? Where is the rest of the bus?" Jett asks.

"How do you know it was the seats to the bus you guys were in?" Jimmy asked.

"Because we saw written on one of the seats *Chas was here.* I saw him write it myself. What ells is down there? And why are the tunnels there in the first place?" Jett asked.

"Nothing, it's just dark and unsafe for people to be down there. And you people need to stay out of the tunnels." Jimmy said with a stern, but kind voice. The remark was followed with a raised eyebrow, slight nod, and a slighter smile; as if to say; *I'll let this one slide kid.*

"But we have to find Stephanie." Jett protested.

"We will. Just try to get some rest. It's almost dinner time soon." Jimmy said with a final smile as he gave a gentle squeeze to Jett's shoulder. Jett gave Jimmy a smile as if to say *ok, will do.*

Jonathan emerged from the basement. He had no idea what just happened, despite hearing the commotion that was coming from the upstairs. The first person he saw was Star, who is giving him a wide eyed look as if to warn him of something. He also noticed that everyone around him had the same look on their faces. The look of wondering how what they just saw will turn out. Then he heard it; he heard what the look on Star's face was probably going to warn him about.

"Well look who decided to finally show up. Where have you been? Your little friend passed out. What did you do to him?" Jonathan recognized the voice and rolled his eyes. He turned to the direction from where the voice was coming from and gave a snarky reply.

"What and who are you talking about Flo? And what have I done to who?" Flo shot Jonathan a look that a little sister would give her brother, when the brother was about to be in big trouble, mister.

"Your little pal, Jett." Jonathan suddenly went from sarcastic, to worried when he heard Jett's name. That was one of his kids, that he wasn't watching. Jonathan was only in the basement for 30 minutes; but it all at once felt like 30 days.

"What about Jett? Where is he?" Flo cut him off before he could blurb out another aimless question.

"He's with Jimmy." She started out with a squinty eyed head tilt. "He's ok now, no thanks to you."

".....WELL?" She could see he was literally sweating as she watched a stream of sweat roll down his face.

"Alright, calm down. I was walking out of the kitchen about to go outside to talk to Jimmy, when Jett came running out in front of me and quickly went out the door. He almost ran into me. Little bugger! Didn't you hear Jimmy yelling *Man down?*

"Yeah. What was that about?" Jonathan asked.

"That means someone needs medical attention! Your little friend passed out probably from the heat or whatever you put him through earlier today. Jimmy caught him in time before he fell to the ground. I came out and gave him some cold water; who knows what would have happened to him if I didn't show up when I did."

Jonathan didn't know how to react. He felt relieved that Jett was ok, at this same time he was still very concerned and wanted to see him as soon as he could. There was a big part of Jonathan that wanted slap Flo for being so vain and self-loathing. He was about to pivot 180 degrease and head down the hall to where Jett was, but then he thought twice and didn't want to be rude, even to Flo. "Thanks Flo." Jonathan said. He wanted to say a few things more but he didn't have the time or know what to say.

"You're welcome!" She shouted at him snidely. He just held his right hand up as if he was waving to someone in front of him, but it was meant for Flo. He was proud of himself to keep all his fingers pointing upward and just the middle one like he wanted.

Jimmy was coming out of the sleeping quarters Jett was in, when he met up with Jonathan. Their eyes locked for a second. Jonathan could see a slight hint of anger in Jimmy's eyes.

"How is he doing?" Jonathan asked, not sure how Jimmy would react. To Jonathan's surprise, Jimmy seemed very understanding and didn't give him a hard time, at first. Jimmy did make it a point to let Jonathan know they would be having a serious talk after dinner.

"He's doing fine. He just needs some rest. It was probably the heat and everything ells that happened to him in the last few weeks. Go ahead and see him, he'll be glad to see you." Before Jonathan entered the room, Jimmy grabbed him firmly by the arm and looked him dead in the eyes. "We'll be talking after dinner; just you and me. I have some things to tell you." Jonathan didn't say anything; he didn't have to. They both understood what each other was thinking.

"Jett!" Jonathan cheered in a whisper. "Hey, how ya feeling? I heard you passed out." Jonathan asked.

"Yah… I guess so. I feel better now." Jett said he felt better; but Jonathan could tell there was still something heavy on his mind.

"What happened? Why did you faint? Was it the walk through the tunnels?" Jonathan was sitting on the floor so he can be closer to Jett. He could tell Jett told Jimmy about how they went in the tunnels. Jonathan could also tell Jett wasn't sure what to think. After a moment of silence Jonathan reassured Jett that whatever he said was ok, and he didn't say anything wrong. "It's ok if you told Jimmy about us going in the tunnels; it kinda needed to be mentioned sooner or later. We have to find Stephanie. Right now, we just want to make sure you are ok. Ok." Jonathan explained.

Jett looked up at him with a doubtful stare, wondering if this was one of those reveres mind games adults do to try to get kids to say what the adults want to hear; or was Jonathan really telling the truth and not mad at all.

"I was in here thinking about the tunnels when everything kind of got cloudy. The air became hard to breath, and my tummy hurt; it felt like I was going to throw-up. I got up and left the room to go outside for some fresh air. I ran to the front door, almost bumping into that Flo lady. I went outside; looked at Jimmy and the next thing I remember I was back in here again. It was then I told Jimmy that we went in the tunnels. He didn't seem mad, but he told me we were to stay out of the tunnels and never go in there again." Jett explained.

"Don't worry Jett; you're not in any trouble. I'll take the blame for going the tunnels. I had a feeling that no one was supposed to go down there."

"What's down there? Why is it a big secret? "Jett asked.

"I not sure yet, but I'm about to find out. Jimmy wants to talk to me after diner. I'll be getting some answers then. Don't worry about it. Just get some rest, ok?" Jonathan said giving Jett a pat on the forehead. Jett gave a faint smile, a slight head nod and closed his eyes to rest.

Jonathan didn't know what to make of that evening's dinner. It was nothing like how he expected it; he actually didn't know what to expect. Everyone seemed happy and cheerful, even Flo. She almost managed to laugh and carry on interesting conversation through of dinner. Jimmy seemed equally as cheerful as well, even though Jonathan knew He and Jimmy were going to have a little talk afterwards. There was almost no mention of what happened to Jett about an hour ago. This was totally fine with Jonathan.

Jonathan couldn't help but to keep looking at Jett all though dinner, reading his eye contact to make sure Jett was holding up ok.

"So Jonathan tell us, what you think is the best way to change motor oil." Flo asked. Jonathan wasn't expecting Flo to talk to him in any way, shape, or form. It was hard enough to believe she was even in a good mood. After a few seconds of a daydreaming, a nonresponsive Jonathan was still in a daze. Flo almost shouted his name.

"Jonathan!" Jonathan suddenly snapped out of his trance, shakes his head for a split second and returns back to earth.

"What? I'm sorry I had, I was, I just didn't hear you." Jonathan was thinking about Jett and how he was feeling. He was also thinking about Stephanie and she was doing. Flo was disgusted with him but just pretended like they where old friends, gave a slight chuckle and repeated the question.

"Motor oil! How do you think it should be changed? hot or cold?" At first Jonathan didn't know why she even asked such an off-beat question. These people haven't used a car in decades. Maybe she was asking out of spite, knowing his sister was kidnapped while he was changing his oil at the time of her disappearance. Whatever the case may be, he just answered with a slight smile. Even though the question ripped his heart out and he really wanted to answer *I would start out by making you drink whatever oil the car drained out.* But he kept his cool and answered.

"Hot! Definitely hot. That way it heats up all the dirt and sludge and drains it out also." Jonathan explained. *Motor oil?* He thought, *how did that become the topic of conversation? And why was Flo of all people involved?* Jonathan made it a point from here on in to pay attention to dinner topics for the rest of the night. He felt silly and left out of the loop.

"That's what I've been trying to tell you all. You should always change oil hot. Thank you Jonathan for clearing that up for them." gloated Jimmy.

"Sure, Not a problem." Jonathan replied, pretending as if he were in the conversation the whole time. When dinner was over, Jonathan was more than happy to help in the kitchen. Half of him wanted to prolong having his talk with Jimmy as much as he could; but the other half had to talk to Jimmy to find Stephanie.

"So Jonathan." Said a voice that was calm and easy; but at the same time was bold enough to be able to cut through all the kitchen noise. He didn't need to turn around to know it was Star talking to him. "Flow really set you up for a good one" she said looking at him as if to know how to get him out of trouble he didn't he was about to find himself in.

"What do you mean?" he inquired with doubt in his eyes.

"Motor oil?" Star said still looking at him knowing the secret he didn't. He just maintained his stare. "Oh, you probably didn't know we have a generator. It hasn't been used in years." After a slight pause Jonathan finally guesses.

"And the generator needs an oil change, and they want me to do it?"

"Close, they want you to help get the generator running. I'm not sure about any oil. I know the question was to see how much pride you have in your work. Now that Jimmy knows that, I'm sure he'll ask you to help get it running."

"Oh," Jonathan's eyes suddenly brightened. His farcical expression went from very worried to now curious, almost excited even. The thought of doing mechanical work really cheers a guy up, *men.* Star thought "What does the generator have to do with anything anyway?" Jonathan asked.

"I'm not sure but I think the generator has something to do with the tunnels. I overheard Travis and Jimmy talking about it just before dinner. Jimmy said you would need the generator to help find that girl Stephanie." Star said.

Jonathan started getting concerned about why he would need the generator to be running to help find Stephanie. "Maybe the generator would power light in the tunnels." Jonathan said.

"I guess." Star replied. Now Jonathan wanted to talk to Jimmy and find out what he had planned for him.

"Thanks Star, I need to find Jimmy and talk to him. I'll need your help soon, but I'm not sure how yet. I'll let you know?" Jonathan was asking more so then telling.

"Ok Jonathan I'm here for you." Star said as she put a hand on his shoulder and gave it a gentle squeeze. Jonathan gave her a soft smile and patted her hand that was still touching his shoulder.

"Hey." said a tiny, shy voice from behind. Jonathan turned around to see Kasey looking at him with a humble look in her eyes. "Is Jett going to be alright? I heard he fainted!" She asked emphasizing the word *fainted* in a louder whisper.

"Jett's going to be just fine Kasey. You saw him at dinner, he seemed ok? Right?" Jonathan asks.

"Yea, I guess so. I'm just worried about him. I'm worried about all of us. Are we ever going home? I miss my mommy and daddy." With that being said Kasey started to cry softly; as if she didn't want anyone to hear her. This pulled at Jonathan's heart. Hearing her cry made him want to cry himself. She reminded him of his sister that was kidnapped many years before.

Jonathan knelt down one knee and put consoling hands on her shoulders. "Oh Sweetheart, We're going soon. I know you miss your family, we all miss our families. I'm just trying to find a way to contact the outside world and let them know where we are." With that he pulled her close and gave her a big hug.

She finally stopped crying and gave him a look that said *ok that's fine*. He read this look and gave her a kiss on the forehead. "I'll see you at the campfire?"

"I don't know, maybe" She replied in soft voice that seemed more at ease. Jonathan gave her one last reassuring hug and hurried off.

When he walked out of the main house, he saw Travis and Flo talking. He also noticed they suddenly slowed down to a lower tone of voice and then eventually stopped talking once he reached them. *That's not a good sign* he thought to himself; but Jonathan wasn't going to worry about it right now. He has more important things to worry about. Despite their actions, Jonathan decided to pretend like everything is normal.

"Hey, have you guys seen Jimmy around?" Jonathan feels no need to explain why he is looking for Jimmy; they probably already know what is going on anyway.

"Yeah, I saw him; He's a medium height, well built guy, White hair in a ponytail and a beard to match. What ells do you need to know about him?" For a second Jonathan was speechless. Even Travis was caught by surprise. Actually, Jonathan had so much to say, he didn't know what to say. Right now he was going to let this opportunity pass and just give a sarcastic answer.

"Thanks Flo. You're a life saver I would really be in *it* if you weren't here." Travis couldn't hold back laughing. He knew Flo needed to be put in her place quite often.

"Oh you're in *it* alright" she replied with a wide eyed, tight lipped smile and a head nod that made her wavy blond hair bounce. Jonathan almost got lost in her blond wavy hair. She noticed this and gave him a look that said *really?* With that Jonathan ran off gave her a look that said, *huh, Woman*.

# CHAPTER 20

## Looking for Stephanie

Jimmy and Jonathan stepped out of the barn with the look of accomplishment on their faces; they were almost smiling. Like two high school class mates that haven't seen each other in decades. Travis and Flo had the look of shock on their faces as they walked up.

"Travis, take Jonathan over to the generator, he knows what to do from there. Got it!" Jimmy said with a sternness that was hidden behind a faint smile. Jimmy's request and sternness took Travis and Flo by surprise. He was only that stern with people for two reasons, when he *wanted* something to happen and when he *did not* want something to happen.

"Sure Jimmy, everything ok?" Travis asked with some doubt in his voice.

"Everything is fine. Just do what I ask please Jonathan has a child to rescue." Again, Travis and Flo just look at each other in disbelief. Before they could turn around to take Jonathan to the generator, Jimmy called Flo over to him.

"Flo I need you to stay here and give me a hand with a few things. Travis and Jonathan have a few things to discuss." Flo just gave Jimmy a *sure, why not* look.

"Ok, whatever you need." She replied. Travis and Jonathan headed off to the generator which was hidden near the abandon house. On the way over Jonathan explained to Travis what's going on; about Stephanie being missing and everything that Jimmy told him.

"I-I would love to help you out Jonathan, but I'm-I'm not going in those tunnels" Travis managed to stutter out with a quiver in his voice. He didn't care how afraid or unmanly he sounded. "I've heard about Groady and what goes on in those tunnels. I'm sorry to say; but I doubt your little friend is still alive." That fueled Jonathan's fire.

"I don't care what anybody says about anyone or anything down there! I'm going down in the tunnels and I'm finding Stephanie. And I don't need anyone's help!" Jonathan said almost stopping in his tracks, but he didn't want to break stride and waste time. He knew it wasn't going to be easy to get the old generator running. Travis didn't know what to say at first.

"The least I can do is help you get the generator running. What did Jimmy say about the generator?" Travis asked. Jonathan was too preoccupied worrying about Stephanie to remember what Jimmy said. He could only remember bits and pieces.

"I think he mentioned the generator powering some kind of lights that were down there. I'm not going to waste a lot of time trying to get this thing running. I have a lantern and plenty of candles and matches." Jonathan said.

Jonathan wanted to ask about who Groady was. He was ashamed to admit to himself that he was to afraid to find out. Besides Jimmy made it care enough, even if Jonathan didn't understand it the first time. The only thing he had to know was that Groady was a nonbeliever who got banished to the tunnels many years ago and he's pretty angry; and he may or may not have killed Stephanie by now.

The generator looked like a big solid rusty chunk of metal. There was spider webs spun in the corners and in between the pulley wheels. All the moving parts seemed to have been rusted together. You couldn't tell if a nut and bolt was once there or is the part supposed to be welded on. That's how old and rusted this thing was. The belts looked somewhat new for some reason. At first Jonathan didn't know what to make of it. He almost didn't even want to try to get it running. If Travis wasn't sent to watch him; Jonathan probably wouldn't have even bothered.

After staring at it for a minute or two, they both seemed to have the same idea that the lantern and candles may be good enough. On the other hand, they also promised Jimmy they would get the old rust bucket running.

"Well, I guess the first thing is to make sure it has gas." Travis nodded in agreement. There was half a tank.

"So far, so good." Jonathan said with amazement.

"Yeah! The rest should all be downhill from here." Travis joked. They both started laughing, mainly out of frustration that didn't even set in yet. on one side of the generator was a pull cord, just like you would see on a lawnmower. Next to the pull cord was a red button that was labeled *stop.* At this point Jonathan is really wishing Travis would say *I got it from here; I've done this a hundred times.* No such luck. Travis just looked at him at the same time tilting is head and pointing an eyebrow in the direction of the pull cord. Jonathan clearly understood that meant; *you're up. Let's see what you got.*

Jonathan grabbed the pull cord and at first gave a slight tug. Once he saw the starter box was pretty lose; he gave it another try. This time he put some *umph* into it. Much to their surprise it actually sounded like it wanted to start. Jonathan tried again; this time it started and ran for a second and then shut off.

"Dam this thing is loud. I'm almost thankful it died." Travis said. Jonathan was hesitant to try again. He knew once this thing was running the noise would carry though out the compound and everyone would know what was going on and Jonathan didn't like that.

"I don't think this is a good idea." Jonathan stated.

"Why not?"

"Because if the generator gets running and powers on the lights in the tunnel; that may wake the sleeping beast more than it is now. I think I should just go with my plan using the lantern. That way I can kinda stay hidden when I want to be."

"Yes but we promised Jimmy we would get the generator running." Travis said expressing great loyalty.

"That's true; we promised to get it running; however we didn't promise we were going to use it. Got it?" Travis thought for a second and then agreed. Under one compromise; they had to leave the generator running for more than second. Jonathan agreed. Besides he wanted to get down inside the tunnels and find Stephanie.

Jonathan pulled the cord and metal beast gave off a loud roar that had a clank to it; and snorted out a cloud of black smoke. After about five seconds the thing finally stopped rattling and knocking. Soon it came to a compromising pace; which was still loud and rough. After another five seconds Jonathan pressed the chipping, faded red stop button and the metal monstrosity slowly come to a stop. It left behind a shattered silence, a choking haze and a ringing in their ears.

"Well, mission completed." Jonathan said relieved finally being able to shut that thing off. Travis was just as glad to do the same. Jonathan lit the candle inside the lantern and they headed inside the house down into the basement steps at the back of the house. Once inside the only light was the lantern. They unbolted the trap door and swung the lid open. It opened with a slight creek and a small whine since it was opened just recently.

Travis was wondering if he should stay at the house while Jonathan was in the tunnels. He was even wondering if he should dare go down in the tunnels with Jonathan. At first he told Jonathan there was no way he would ever go down there, but something stared to change his mind. He couldn't quite place it.

"Hey do you think I should stay here and wait for you? Or… maybe not." Travis asked starting to doubt himself. Jonathan was actually surprised that he even thought of offering. *That would be super cool.* Jonathan thought to himself, but didn't want to say that and sound like one of the kids.

"Sure, but isn't Jimmy waiting for? If you can that would be great. I could use somebody up here."

"Jimmy's not waiting for me. I just figured you may need someone to check in with every so-often." Travis said.

"Ok great. But I'm not too sure what you could do. I mean, just wait here and see if I come up in a few hours. I know you said you would never go down with me."

"If I where to go down with you, how would I help you? It really sounds like a one man job."

"Just having somebody there with me in case I run into trouble and I think you know what I mean." Jonathan said. Travis just looked at him with a second thought in one eye and fear in the other. Jonathan started to think he blew his only chance at having help down there. After second of silence Jonathan headed down the trapdoor steps, but before he could make it to the second step, he felt a hand on his shoulder.

"You mean it would be two against one; right?" Jonathan was starting to think Travis wasn't so bad after all.

"Right." Jonathan replied almost smiling. "Take the bolts to the door with you so we don't get locked down here."

"Do you think someone would really do that knowing we're down here?" Travis asked.

"People know I'm down here and would probably want me to stay down here. But they don't know you decided to come down here with me, got it?" Travis really had to think for a second and then he realized what Jonathan was warning him about. Travis shoved the bolts in his pocket, and followed Jonathan down into what he always believed to be entrance to hell.

The campfire crackled, and popped throwing off a spark once in a while. That added a little extra light to the darkness. The fire's illuminating glow silhouetted almost everyone's facile features; by casting shadows around eye sockets, cheek bones and noses.

Some of the new comer children were there enjoying the campfire and the conversation, but at the same time they also noticed that Jonathan wasn't sitting with them. Not having Jonathan there was a big missing peace to *their* puzzle. Jimmy noticed Jett and Chaz looking for their fearless leader as they tried not to let it show who they were looking for. Judging from the looks being thrown around, people noticed Travis was missing also. It isn't mandatory to attend the campfire, it's optional. But if you went all the time, people noticed when you were not there.

"Star would you please get the jug from the kitchen?" Jimmy asked

"Sure Jimmy." She replied. With that she sprang up almost as if she was waiting for him to ask. Flo was looking at Jimmy funny as if to say, *I could have gotten it for you.* Jimmy reads this and jokingly comments to her.

"What? You look like you had a rough day Flo. Sneering has tired you out. Relax, take a load off girl." Jimmy said giving Flo a gentle pad on the thigh.

"I'm just saying you could have asked me to get it for you." She protested.

"No need Florence, we got cha covered." This made big laughs around the campfire, some people even threw in some sound effects like *eew* and *woow* knowing how much she hated being called Florence.

Nobody called her that. Star almost spilled the jug over she was laughing so hard as she returned. This made people laugh even harder. Flo's face was turning bright red

"Oh Lighten up Flo." Jimmy said poring her a cup of wine. Flo tried to shrug it off and pretend it didn't bother her. As the night went on the missing people didn't seem missing anymore, they just weren't there.

Jimmy knew he was using Flo as a scapegoat. He had to loosen the tension that may have started to build. Some people knew what Jonathan was up to, and knew Travis was with him. They didn't know if Travis actually may have gone down in the tunnels with Jonathan. It didn't sound like anything Travis would do.

# CHAPTER 21

## Search and Rescue

"This way." Jonathan said after looking at the map he carved in the underside of the trapdoor. Travis glanced up at the trapdoor to see what Jonathan was looking at. Travis was impressed and scared; impressed that he would think to make some identification as to where they are located, scared to think the tunnels are that big.

"First time down here?" Jonathan asked, as he noticed the worried look on Travis's face. Jonathan was also gloating because he felt he had one up on someone that lived here. He had been feeling left out ever since their arrival over one month ago.

"Y-yeah, N-Nobody even talks about down here." Travis quivered.

"Sure you're up for this? I really don't need you freaking out or passing out because of fear, or something like that. I won't be able to help you if that should happen. I need to find Stephanie." Travis took a short pause to think about it. *I'll take that as a "no"* Jonathan thought to himself.

"How far do the tunnels go down here?" Even with the doubt of Travis going, they still kept walking.

"Far, I'm guessing they span at least a quarter mile. And I don't plan on being down here all night." Jonathan stated.

"I don't plan on it either." Travis insisted. Jonathan had no idea where to start looking for Stephanie. They continued walking in the direction to where the bus seats were spotted.

"So, what direction are headed?" Travis inquired.

"For some reason the seats to the bus we were in made their way down here." Travis sudden cuts him off.

"Wait! The actual seats to the bus? Like the ones you sit in?" Travis asked in shock and disbelief.

"Yes." Jonathan just looked at him funny. "I hoping she made it back to those seats for some reason." Jonathan was leading the way since he had been down there before.

"It smells like something is burning down here." Travis stated.

"Yeah, last time we were down here we took to burning whatever we could find for a source of light. Don't be alarmed at whatever you see down here." Jonathan said.

"What do you mean?"

"I mean there are some strange things down here, like chains and shackles mounted on the walls. There are old metal beds with chains and shackles on them too. Makes you wonder what went on down here."

"Did they look like they were recently used?" Travis asked.

"I doubt it, at least I hope not." The air is stale and Jonathan smells that abandon smell again.

"The air down here...." Travis started but for some reason never finished. Jonathan knew what he meant. They made it to an opening in the wall, except Jonathan doesn't remember this one. Travis is feeling a little more at ease as he started to lead the way in the opening. Jonathan suddenly grabbed his arm. Travis stopped walking and let Jonathan shine the lantern in and led the way.

The lantern only shined a few feet around them. Jonathan went ahead carefully entering the blackened area. The room was bigger than they imagined.

Jonathan turned to the right and shuffled his feet as not to step or trip on anything. Six feet later he found shelf on the wall that was holding an empty booze bottle. As Jonathan looked at it closer, he noticed it was the bottle he found in the bus.

"What is it?" Travis asked.

"When the accident happened and I was searching the bus, I tripped on an empty booze bottle and this is the bottle."

"This is something from the bus and it found its way down here?" Travis questioned with a slight squeal in his tone.

"Yeah, this and the seats; I'm telling you someone was at the site and brought this stuff down here. That tells me two things. There is a way to the outside and the rumors about Groady being banished down here are true." Travis couldn't do anything but look at Jonathan with fear and shock.

"D-Do you think G-Groady is down here now? P-Probably watching us? Is that what you're telling me?" Travis asked with a stuttering, crackle in his voice.

"I'm afraid so, but I wouldn't bet on it." Jonathan replied. Twisted, morbid hallucinations about Groady started playing in Travis's mind. And all the rumors of all the evil Groady has done and the people he tortured that were unfortunate to find their way down in the tunnels, overwhelmed Travis. After a few moments Jonathan didn't hear any response. He looked over and saw Travis in a frozen, statue like trance. *Oh god, not now. Snap out of it.* Jonathan thought. For a moment Jonathan left Travis in his trance and went ahead a few feet. There was nothing after the shelf, just a solid wall. He shuffled across the floor to the other side of what he believed to be a room at first. Jonathan kept walking ahead still leaving Travis behind.

Guessing he walked about twenty feet or so, he found an area of the wall, that seemed to have random shaped stones wedged in place, as if the stones were meant to close off an opening. The stones were not lose, but not cemented in. He could almost break through if he had to. *We're going to see what's on the other side.* Jonathan thought to himself. Jonathan went back to see how Travis was doing.

Travis actually moved, he started making his way down the corridor toward Jonathan.

"Hey, how ya doing?" Jonathan asked holding the lantern up to Travis. Still in a world of confusion; Travis managed to nod his head. *I guess this means you're ok.* "I found something up ahead. There is a piece of the wall that look like in was once an entrance to somewhere. There is some kind of stones wedged, as if someone was trying to close it off." This woke Travis up a little bit.

"Do you think we should try to break through it?" Travis inquired. This made Jonathan have faith in Travis. *Now we're getting somewhere.* If Jonathan didn't know any better he would actually think Travis wanted to do so.

"Are you up to it? It's not going to be easy and it may make a lot of noise. I wanted to try to keep it quiet." Jonathan said.

"Yea! Let's give it a shot. I bet we can do it and not make a lot of noise. Do you think your friend Stephanie is held behind there?"

"I hope not. This place is a dungeon. I hate to think what it looks like behind that opening someone wedged over." Jonathan said.

"Is this the spot here?" Travis said with excitement. Even before he got the words out, or even got a reply from Jonathan, Travis was pressing on the wall seeing if he could budge the stone free. After a second or two, Jonathan joined him. Not long after the first try, pressing soon turned into kicking and now body slamming, Still not a budge. *This may take the work of a sledgehammer.* They both thought. All they could do now was look at each other.

"Wow! That stone is really set in; maybe it's cemented in from the other side." Travis suggested. Jonathan didn't even consider that.

"Maybe you're right" Jonathan agreed not wanting to waste time arguing.

"Are there any cracks between the stones? Maybe we can see the other side." Travis asked. With that Jonathan lifted the lantern up to the stone and gave a close look. At first all he could see was blackness. There are gaps between the stone, but to dark on the other side to see.

"I can't see if there is anything on the other side. It's too dark." Just as Jonathan said that, there was a white blur that shot across one of the cracks and back again. They both jumped and took a step back.

"D-Did you see that?" Travis almost yelled.

"Yeah!" "What the hell was it?" Jonathan put the light up to it again. This time he wasn't going to back off.

"I-I don't know!" Travis said. Jonathan held the lantern up to the biggest crack he could find. The white blur came back and stopped at the crack. The white blur was accompanied with a color. It seemed to be a brownish, blue. Whatever it was kept, bouncing around and making it hard to identify.

"It's an eyeball! Someone's looking back at us!" Travis yelled grabbing Jonathan's arm in a panic, making Jonathan have to shrug him off.

"Ouch!" Jonathan yelled in a whisper.

"Sorry man.. I didn't mean, I just," Travis just trailed off in apologetic rambling.

"I get it! Just relax." Jonathan commanded. The blur stopped long enough to blink. *My god it is someone looking back at us.* Jonathan whispered to himself, or so he thought.

"I-I told y-you." Travis stuttered out in a panic. Jonathan got close to Travis, and motioned for him to be quiet, and then turned back to the crack in the wall. This time Jonathan was looking close in the crack in the wall. He had the lantern right next to his head.

"Stephanie. Are you in there?" He doubted anyone could hear him through the wall. All he heard was silence, than he heard some kind of muffled noise coming from the other side. It almost sounded like someone was trying to talk, but they were muffled. Jonathan turned back to Travis for a second opinion.

"I can't make out what is going on. Could you make it out?" Travis was almost too scared to talk.

"I-I heard something, b-but I couldn't make out what it was." Jonathan took another look inside the wall. Travis crouched down to try to look inside the wall. Again, they saw that white blur and then that brown or blue ball. After a second or two it disappeared. Jonathan tried again to call though the wall.

"Stephanie? Who's in there?" There was no reply, just that muffled noise again, but louder. Jonathan tried to call to the other side. "Who's in there?" Still no reply. Travis and Jonathan kept looking the crack, but now all they saw was darkness.

All of a sudden they heard a loud thud! than a soft pop. Like someone's head smacked against the floor. This was all accompanied by a gagged *uummph!* This made Travis take a step back as he placed a hand over his mouth in disbelief. One thing Jonathan knew was that he had to reach the other side of that wall. And find out whose head went *thunk*.

"Travis we need to find the other side of this wall and find out who is maybe being held there. Maybe that generator thing may save us a lot of time." Jonathan finally suggested.

"Y-you think t-that's a good idea now? W-we should stay here for now. W-we're at least an hour in these tunnels." Travis said.

"I suppose you're right. We'll at least keep going till we run low on candles. We have to pick up the pace." Jonathan said. All Travis could do was nod in agreement.

They started to pick up the pace to a fast walk. Soon they came across what looked to be a trapdoor and possibly another staircase. They tried pushing it up, but it wouldn't move. After a while they decided leave it and keep moving. Before they left, Jonathan took a piece of stone and carved a map of where they were showing the way out. Jonathan and Travis stopped walking at the same time. They both stood frozen in that, *I hear something pose.* The air was dead silent, except for the faint echo of clinking chains. They seemed to be coming from all the way down the darkened corridor. The two just looked at each other almost as if in total fear.

"Come on" Jonathan commanded. Before Travis had time to protest, they were almost jogging; not really seeing where they were going or about to trip over. The lantern was only shining a few feet ahead of them. They both stopped for minute. The chains were getting louder.

"The chains seem to be getting louder." Jonathan pointed out. Even with the lantern it was still too dark to see where the chains were coming from.

"We better keep going before we lose whoever it is." Travis said, and then the two stared up again. They soon come to a corner; they had no choice they had to turn right. They kept going trying to hold a conversation and jog at the same time, which only proved how out of shape they both were.

"Da… ya…. Still…. Hear….. them?" Jonathan managed to puff out.

"N-no….. m-maybe we……. Should slow..... d-down……"

"O-oh…..ok" The clinking of the chains seemed to have stopped. The two stopped walking, mainly to catch their breath. Again the air was dead silent.

"I don't hear them." Travis said. After a pause, Jonathan agreed.

"I don't ether. We couldn't have passed them. We would notice someone with chains. And we didn't pass any doorways. We went in a straight line other than that right turn we had to make." Jonathan said.

"I don't get it. Maybe it'll start up again. Do you think it's possible we didn't go far enough?" Travis suggested.

"I guess, let's keep going." Jonathan said. Travis nodded. Without warning, Jonathan felt a sharp pain the side of his face, at the same time heard an inhuman grunt. As he went down, he looked at Travis who was wearing the look of horror on his face. And then Jonathan saw, felt, and heard nothing at all.

# CHAPTER 22

## Groady's Layer

"Anybody in for more wine?" Terry asked as she stood up announcing how much she had to *pee*. Cheers of *yes* came from random place around the campfire. "You my young friend are too young to be drinking," Terry said walking past one of the children, tapping them on the head with her index finger. Jimmy just smiled and pointed at the youngster as if to say *Nice try kido.* Terry was on her way back to the campfire grabbing a bottle of wine when she ran into Kasey.

"Is Jonathan at the campfire?" she asked in her shy little voice.

"No sweetie; I'm afraid not. Is there anything you need?" Terry asked crouching down. Kasey had a sad look to her.

"No, I thought he was going to be there. I wanted to join everyone ells."

"You can still come out there with us. Some of the other kids are joining us." Terry replied holding out her hand for Kasey to grab. Kasey wasn't really sure what she wanted to do. She wanted to go and join everyone, but she didn't want to go without Jonathan. "Why don't you come out for a bit and sit with us. You know my son Hazleton, he's there. You can sit with us. The campfire is roaring and pretty to look at, I think you'll really enjoy it. I'll sit with you and Hazleton." Terry suggested still holding her hand out.

"You will?" Kasey asked, lifting hand to Terrie's. Terry grabbed her hand with a big smile.

"You can sit right next to me." Terry stated in a promising voice. And the two walked out of the house hand and hand. Kasey sat right next to Terry just as promised. Terry handed the bottle of wine to Flo who took some, then passed it on.

The conversation around the campfire was both adult humor and kid friendly, which meant a lot of those *one liners.* The night was getting late. Some of the younger children were starting to yawn, which was making some of the older kids yawn also.

"I think it' somebody's bedtime." Terry said looking at Kasey and Hazleton then ending the comment with a smile and a friendly gaze.

The two children knew it was true but didn't want to admit it. Terry gave them a helping reassurance. "Come on kiddies, I'll tuck you both in." They didn't protest, they just gave a slight nod and took Terry up on her offer. This prompted a *campfire break*. Many people had to go the bathroom. Some of the other kids wanted to go to bed as well. Some people just wanted to stretch, and others wanted refill the beverage glass.

Terry walked Kasey and Hazleton to their beds, tucked them in and gave them both a kiss on the forehead. Kasey was so tired, she didn't even reply when Terry said *goodnight*. It seemed like some of the other kids were just as tired, they went right to sleep. Terry was doing her best to hide the fact that was worried about Travis. She was praying to god he didn't go with Jonathan down in the tunnels. She wanted to go and check on where he was. He should have been back by now.

People started gathering around the campfire once again. The amount of people got a lot smaller. Most of the children and some of the adults decided to turn in for the night. Terry wanted ask Jimmy if he had talked to Travis before he went off with Jonathan, and what was said. *Maybe I should just go there and see for myself.* She thought. The curiosity finally got the best of her. She grabbed some matches and one of the lanterns from the hallway. She quietly walked out of the side door and headed toward for the forbidden.

On her way to the house, she was trying to stay out of the moonlight so she wouldn't be seen. She looked back a few times to see if anyone was watching her. She wasn't scared at all about being alone however; she probably should have told someone where she was going, just in case. She honestly was planning returning before anyone knew she was gone. That was the plan anyway...

*I'm staying right here.* Jonathan thought. He knew he was lying down on some kind of table or bed. There was a sharp pain pulsating from the back of his eye to his forehead and then to the soft spot on the side of his head. It hurt just to take a breath. He wasn't even going to try to move. It was so dark where he was, he couldn't tell if his eyes where open or closed. He even thought his one eyes is swollen shut, it sure felt like it from the stabbing pain.

He tried slightly moving his arms and legs. He wasn't even sure if was tied down or not. His whole body was numb. Was he beaten that bad? Or was he numb from being tied down. Where was whoever attacked him? He suddenly remembered Travis was with him. What happened to Travis? Did he manage to get away or was he in the in the same distress as Jonathan? Travis could be right next to him. It was too dark to tell.

The pain in his head was starting to fade, or maybe he just got used to it. Jonathan tried to take an inventory on his injuries. He was having trouble with this because he kept flashing back the accident. He could see Stephanie standing in front of him. There was a background of trees, brush and smoke. "Stephanie?" he finally whispered. When he heard no answer, he called out again, still no answer. He slowly faded back into his reality and darkness swallowed him once again.

He was slowly able to move his head back and forth. It felt like his brain was rolling back and forth and bouncing off the inside of his skull. He can pick his head up about six inches, but that's all. His neck was killing him. The blow to the head must have pulled something in his neck. He then slowly moves his fingers. He managed to move each finger tapping them on the platform he was lying on. He can almost make fist. *Hands, check* he thought. By doing this he realized his arms are tied down. Now he tries to move his feet. From what he could feel they are not injured, but his legs are tied down also. He could slightly bend his knees, but he felt a sharp pain on his right thigh. *Waist down, check.* He decided to slowly take a deep breath to see what hurts when he does. As he breathes in slowly he feels pain in his right lower rib cage. He really was hoping he didn't have to cough, because that's going to hurt. He tried to move his arms, they are tied down. From what he could move, they seem ok. *Arms, check.*

Finally he tried to put it all together. His right thigh, lower fib cage, eye, head and neck hurt on the right side hurt all the same. His eye and head hurt the worst. And he was tied down at the feet, legs, waist, and chest. Now he can rest again.

He still couldn't see anything. He heard what he thought is a faint moan. Jonathan holds his breath as not to make a sound; after a moment, he breaths slowly. He decided call out. "Travis?" Jonathan didn't hear a reply for a minute or two, then he heard another moan. "Travis!" Jonathan whispered louder. "Travis, I'm tied to a table of some kind. My right side is hurt. I think my eye is swollen shut." Jonathan has to take a rest. He still wasn't getting any reply. "Travis…if that's you….Moan for only a split second."

"Uh" Jonathan was guessing that must be Travis. He was also trying listen for any movement Travis may be trying to make. Jonathan was trying to wiggle free, but the aches and pains make it difficult to do so. *Man, Travis must be hurting real bad. He can't even speak.* Jonathan was wondering. There was a sound off in the distance that was getting closer. As it gets closer, Jonathan realized that the sound was footsteps. Travis started to moan again. Jonathan told him to" *sshh*." Soon the footsteps end right next to Jonathan. He heard heavy breathing. And it's exhaling was the rankest breath he ever smelt. Whoever it was, was radiating body heat and a nauseous stench.

Jonathan was guessing it was Groady from what he was warned about. The mystery person lit a match, throwing off a flash of light that sent shooting pain into back of Jonathan's eyeball and felt like something was pushing the eyeball out of its socket. Once the flash died down; there only a steady illumination that remained. It must have been a lantern that was lit. At least Jonathan could see what was going on around him. It was than, he realized his eye was swollen half shut. He tried to turn his head to look around to see if he could find Travis, but it's too painful. He decided just to remain lying still.

A tall wide figure stepped in front of Jonathan. He has long, stringy dirty blond hair. A trimmed beard, a rough, hardened look on his face. He's wearing a necklace. The necklace is made of some kind of homemade rope. It looked like it was made from a heavy grass. Hanging from the necklace Jonathan noticed what looked like bones and other objects, but his vision was too blurred to make it out. *OH MY GOD! That's disgusting.* Jonathan is finally able to make out the objects on the necklace. Hanging from it appeared to be a human finger bone, a tongue, a big toe bone, and an eye ball. *Are they real? And what would make someone wear such a thing?* The devilish man took a closer look at

Jonathan. In return Jonathan got a closer look at him and the trophies he wore around his neck. His breath was rank and his body order was death.

Travis gave off a soft moan, which caused the Groady turn and give Travis a closer look. As he got closer to Travis, Travis just flinched and turned away. Even Jonathan could smell the fear. Believe it or not, Jonathan is actually getting board of being held captive.

"Where's the girl?" Jonathan managed to whisper out. Groady remained silent, as he slowly turned back to Jonathan with a snarl. "The girl, where is she?" Jonathan repeated again. Still no answer from Groady. After a few seconds Jonathan puts his head back down in the conclusion he isn't going to get an answer. With that Groady stormed out of the room without saying a word taking the lantern with him, leaving Travis and Jonathan to be once again eaten by the darkness.

As groady left the room, Jonathan was listening to his footsteps; Trying to follow them. Which direction they were going, how far they go. A minute went by and the footsteps just faded away into the unknown.

"Jonathan?" Travis whispers.

"Travis! You can talk thank god. How bad are you hurt?"

"I can't feel the left side of my face." Travis slurred. Jonathan could tell Travis's face was badly swollen, causing him to not have full use of his mouth. Travis sounded like he was practicing to be a ventriloquist. "The light hurts my head." Travis said.

"I know, I feel the same way. I'm tied down. I can't move. Can you move at all?" Jonathan asks.

"I think so. My body feels numb." After a minute he continues. "I feel some kind of restraints on my feet, legs and chest. It feels like heavy chains. My neck hurts when I move my head. What happened to us Jonathan?"

Before Jonathan could answer they hear the faint sound of rattling chains getting louder and closer. As the rattling chains get closer, they also hear the sound of a muffled girl's grunts. Soon the rattling chains and grunts are in the room along with the illumination of a lantern. Whoever was chained and muffled was now thrown in Jonathan's direction and landed on the floor. Jonathan could tell it was Stephanie. She got to her feet as quickly as she could and plopped the top half of her body on top of Jonathan. She was crying uncontrollably. Since Jonathan was tied down and Stephanie had her hands chained behind her back, they couldn't hug to console each other.

"It'll be alright. We'll get out of here." Jonathan protested. While Stephanie was lying on top of him, Jonathan grabbed the cloth gagging her mouth with his teeth and managed to chew it lose and pull it down to her chin so she could speak, but all she could do was cry even harder. As Stephanie and the illumination from the lantern danced around each other, Jonathan saw something that both horrified and filled him with rage. There was black and blue bruises around Stephanie's neck and went down under her shirt that she have managed to keep from falling off her. The bruise went up her cheek and covered the right half her upper and lower lips.

"Steph." Jonathan said in a whisper. She could tell Jonathan was both concerned and angry. He couldn't tell if her eyes were swollen from crying or did Groady beat her that badly. Before Stephanie could take a breath to answer, Groady grabbed her by the hair and shoulder. He pulled her backward, scooped her legs out from under her; and places her sitting on the floor. Then he finally put her hands in the shackles that are cemented in the wall. Jonathan went to yell, but a sharp pain stabbed threw he head. Groady then pick up the lantern and left the room, all without saying a word or even a grunt. Once again the three are swallowed in darkness.

After a minute or so, Jonathan started the reunion conversation. "Stephanie! My god! What happened to you? I'm sorry I didn't get to you sooner. Did that Groady touch you? Dose that guy even talk? I'm sorry I fell asleep that night. I'm just so glad to see you again." Stephanie tried to stop crying and pull it together enough to talk.

"Af-after I was in the tunnels for-for about t-two hours, I-I felt someone come from behind an-and hit me; I was knocked out. I-I woke up on a-a table or a b-bed of some kind. I-I haven't eaten or had anything to drink since then. He –he didn't touch me at all, yet. H-how do you know his-his name is Gr-Groady?"

"Jimmy warned me about him and told me who he is. Groady once lived above the tunnels with the rest of the commune, but he was an outcast and didn't want to follow the rules Jimmy made. He was banished, and locked down here. Looks like we met him and Jimmy was right, he's pretty angry. What do you mean he hasn't touched you yet?" Jonathan asked.

"I-I'm just surprised he hasn't tried anything. I-I mean a guy who probably hasn't seen a girl in-in god knows how long. And I don't think he talks. I don't remember hearing him. I only saw him a few times since he held me captive down here. Thank god you made it down here, but I believe Groady was going let me starve to death." Jonathan and Stephanie were talking so long, they almost forgot about Travis. They were reminded when Travis spoke up and made a comment.

"There is some kind of food somewhere, Groady sure isn't starving." Travis stated.

"Sorry Travis, we didn't mean to leave you out." Jonathan said.

"That's ok I understand. I needed time to recuperate. I'm starting to come around a little. I can at least move my head without it hurting."

"That's good to hear. Now all we have to do is figure out a way to get free, and do it in total darkness." Jonathan joked. Then Jonathan suddenly remembered, someone must have matches in their pocket. There are three of them down there. "Hey! One of us should have some matches handy. And I'm not joking this time." Jonathan said.

"Wait! I think I still have, unless Groady took them while I was out cold. I just can't reach my pockets to check." Stephanie replied.

"I'm pretty sure I still have some on me also. I can't reach my pockets either." Jonathan second. "Travis? Did you take any with you when we left?" Jonathan asked.

"I do feel matches, but the book is thin. It's just that my hands are tied and I can't reach in my pockets to get them." Travis said.

"That's fine at least we know we have some matches. Now we just have to figure out how to get free. Stephanie any chance you can slip one of your hands threw the chains?" Jonathan asked.

"Oh, I was always able to do that, I thought it would be more fun just to stay down here." Stephanie replied with a sarcastic tone. This made Travis snicker out the start of a tiny laugh, that suddenly turned into a moan once he realized it hurt to laugh.

"Ya-know, I'm at least trying to wiggle lose." Jonathan said as he was trying to wiggle lose, but all he could do was make the chains clank together. Jonathan finally gave up and took a rest.

The sound of Travis's struggling was making the chains clank echo in the room Then it fell silent. After about three-four minutes Travis's voice made a slight victory cheer, then there was a small flash of light slicing through the darkness and then died down to almost nothing.

The small amount of illuminating light was just enough for Jonathan to see the expression on Stephanie's face, which was of surprise and shock. He could also tell she was almost smiling. This made Jonathan so curious he almost forgot about the pain in his head.

"What, what is it?" Jonathan asked. For a second Stephanie was frozen in amazement, and then she pointed at Travis forgetting that Jonathan couldn't turn around to look. Again Jonathan calls out. "What is it? I can't see."

"It's Travis! He's halfway free!" Stephanie replied with in total excitement.

"Soon to be all the way free" Travis managed to blurt out between painful breaths. And with that chains hit the floor with a rattling, clanking thud. Travis just sat back for a moment in exhaustion.

"How did you do that?" Stephanie squeaked out.

"When that beast, Groady was tying me down I puffed out my chest and extended my belly as far as I could. I held my body like that, then when he was done I slowly sucked in my gut and chest; that made the chains just lose enough for me to wiggle out of."

# CHAPTER 23

## Terry to the Rescue

Terry pulled the outside wooden basement door open. It made a rickety creaking sound. She stopped for a second to look around to see if anyone may have followed her, when she convinced herself she was alone she carefully descended down the cellar steps. As she was going down, she pulled the door closed. She stopped at the bottom of the steps and looked around. She didn't remember if she had ever been in this basement since her time in the commune. It didn't look familiar. The floor was half dirt and half cement like the basement floor in the main house.

Once she felt brave enough and was sure there wasn't a boogie man; she slowly started walk around and look for that trapdoor. It didn't take her long to find the trapdoor that was only a few feet in front of her. It wasn't bolted down; in fact she was able to pry it up easily. Once she did, she held the lantern over the entrance to the tunnel and took a minute as she studied the unknown. This was the entrance to the forbidden, the passage to hell, and the place she was always warned never to go.

She took a deep breath and began down the staircase of the crumbling cement steps. As she descended down the staircase, she was putting the trapdoor lid in place; it was then she noticed what appeared to be some kind of map covered into the bottom of the lid. She looked at it for a few minutes, and when she though she knew what she was looking at, she started walking down the darkened corridor. She was trying to remember what the direction the carved map was showing. She really had no idea. Giving in to her better judgment, she chose her own way.

The feeling of curiosity washed away any fear she might have had, which gave her the courage to keep going and not turn back. Somewhere in the back of her mind, she knew wanting to find Travis all the fuel she needed. She hadn't been walking for very long. The burning smell filled her nostrils and she tried to mask it with her shirt pulled over her nose. That didn't last very long. She either got tired of holding it there or she just got used to the smell. She was surprised at how wide the tunnels were. She soon began to wonder what all the fuss was about; why they were never to come down here, and then she saw why.

She soon came to an opening in the cinder block wall. She looked inside and the first thing she saw was a metal bed with chains on the head of the frame and leather straps on the foot of the bed. Then she saw another bed set up the same way with chains and straps. There were chains and shackles cemented in the wall. Seeing this sudden made her heart start to pound rapidly. Now she was starting to realize all the warnings and the forbiddances about going down in the tunnels. She all of a sudden didn't want to be down there. *I have to find Travis.* She kept thinking to herself. It was the only way she would keep from just running out of there and returning to the others around the campfire.

The room was big, but mainly empty. Once she determined that there just wasn't much to see; she turned around and walked out. As she continued though the tunnel, her pace gradually got faster. She was getting more and more familiar with her surroundings; or so she thought. She noticed the tunnel getting narrower. She almost had to duck a few times to keep from hitting head. She isn't very tall, just a few inches over five feet.

The feeling of loneliness covered her; until she spotted small light down the corridor. This made her Stop and stare; trying to follow it to see where it was going. The next thing she saw almost made her scream out loud. She flinched as she placed her hand on top of her mouth to tell herself, *keep quiet.* The rumors about… *what's his name;* flashed in her head; followed by the warnings. *Nobody has ever seen again once they entered the tunnel. That's why the entrances bolted shut, and the tunnels are never talked about.* That thought ran such a chill down her spine; she actually turned around to make sure no one snuck up behind her. The flickering light was getting closer, but still pretty far away.

Terry wasn't sure what to do at first; brilliantly she decided to extinguish the candle in the lantern and allowed herself to be swallowed by the darkness. Now she was virtually invisible. All she had to do was remain totally silent. She kept waking using the wall as her guild, running her hand along it as she walked down the corridor. She made sure to pick her feet up as not to stumble on any lose flooring, make any noise.

She stood there listening to the faint sound of clunky footsteps that was walking with the flickering light. As the light and its footsteps got closer and closer; Terry stopped and began to retreat. She kept her widened eyes on the light. She started walking backwards feeling the wall trying to find the opening so if she had to, she could hide in the room. By this time she could make out a shadow and some facial features. It was a tall muscular built man. He seemed to have a beard, and wearing a necklace with about five or six trinkets hanging off it.

The light and bearded figure suddenly vanished right in front Terry. She was half relieved and half shouting *wait up!* to herself. She didn't want to lose sight of him, and behind him was the best place to be. She could still see the lanterns faded glow from where the wall sucked him in. She started walking faster and faster. She was trying to make it to turn before the glow completely disappeared.

At one point she forgot she was in total darkness and she tripped. On the way down she managed to hold on the lantern cradling it like a football making sure she it didn't hit the ground. She hit the ground so hard she slid on her knees and one hand leaving a deep scratch for a few inches. She quickly got up and attempted to continue her stride, but the pain in her knees made her struggle with a heavy limp for a few feet. Terry was in such a rush she managed to limp off the pain until she could continue her fast walking pace again.

Terry made it to the corner faster then she thought she would. She actually had to slow down. She didn't want to get too close to whoever it was. She followed the mystery person leaving a great distance between them, but not too far. The mystery person vanished into the wall again. This time Terry carefully stuck close behind, making sure not to trip and fall. There is a dim light splashing into the corridor from where the person vanished. As she got closer to what appeared to a room she stuck close to the wall. When she was about two or three feet from the entrance; she stood with her back plastered against the wall.

She was trying to listen to whatever sounds are coming from the room. She even held her breath trying to be as quiet as possible, she thought this would make her hear better. It was dead silent, until the cracking sound of wood and a bunch of grunts made her jump out of her skin. She put her hand to her mouth to hold back a scream. Voices shouted from the room.

"I got him!"

"Grab his legs!" The sound of chains rattled and clinked furiously. There was a loud *thud* and then a heavy grunting moan, then more shouts of commands rang out.

"Hold him with all your weight!"

"I'm trying!" another loud *thud* followed by the same heavy grunt. More chains rattled and clanked.

"I got him by the neck!"

Terry thought she could hear a girl's voice being bounced around in all that ruckuses. Along with the thuds and the grunts, a high pitch "oh!" or an "Oh my god!" She quickly started to recognize the other voices. *Travis?* She thought to herself. She looked in the room but it was too dark to see anything. She couldn't make out who was who. All she could see was a ball of dull shadows and silhouettes being casted from the dim lantern that was already in the room. She quickly lit the lantern she was holding. While she was trying to light the candle, she noticed Travis's face managed to poke through the illumination of the lantern.

She didn't know what to do. Half of her wanted to scream his name, but on the other hand she didn't want to distract him if he was fighting for his life. She couldn't just stand there and do nothing. She decided she wanted to jump in and help. It was still too dark to see what she was doing. She managed to get the candle lit and was able to see who was where. She saw Travis and Jonathan wrestling a tall muscularly built bearded man. It was then she noticed Stephanie was with them. *Is she chained to the wall?* Terry thought to herself. With Terry about to be added to the mix now it was going to be three against one. There was no way to lose this fight. They had to win.

At this point Terry was still unnoticed. Terry ran up and when she was in position, she swung foot up full force as hard as she could. Kicking tall, muscular bearded man right where it hurts. He belted out a loud drawn out moan that started as an "UMF!" For a split second

Jonathan and Travis looked in shock at Terry, not believing it was her. A second later all three came crashing down falling right on top of Terry knocking her over and sending the lantern clanking to the ground. Surprisingly the candle managed to stay lit. Terry couldn't move.

Travis and Jonathan managed to get tall bearded man hogtied with the chains they got themselves freed from. They also chained him to the shackles that where mounted into the wall next to Stephanie. The chained man was in so much pain he couldn't put up a fight. He was almost unconscious. Stephanie just sat there and looked at him and that hideous necklace. Travis, Jonathan and Terry sat on the ground in exhaustion. After about two minutes Stephanie spoke up.

"Can someone get me out of these things?" she protested waving her arms making the shackles rattle. Jonathan, Travis and Terry looked at Stephanie all thinking the same thing. *Shut up!*

# CHAPTER 24

## The Necklace of Discipline

Jett and Chaz were lying in their beds; which are placed next to each other thinking the same thing, but neither one wanted to say anything. Finally Chaz broke the silence and whispered to Jett.

"Did you see Jonathan? He's usually at the campfire. He wasn't there tonight."

"I haven't seen him since after dinner. I wonder if he went back in the tunnels looking for Stephanie. Me, Arbin, Jonathan and that girl Star where in the tunnels earlier. I bet that's where he is tonight" replied Jett.

"Yeah, I heard about you guys exploring the tunnels, Arbin told me. Are there really chains and shackles cemented into the walls? Chaz inquired.

"Yeah, it's creepy down there. And there's no light down there at all. The air is stale and hard to breath." Jett described.

"I get the feeling he's not coming back tonight, as much as I hate to say it. I'm surprised he didn't ask one of us to go with him." Chaz said.

"He probably wanted to go alone. I wonder why. We wouldn't have slowed him down." Jett stated.

"He probably knows there's a chance he may not come back." A third voice whispered out from the darkness. There was a long pause for about five seconds. The boys suspected it was Arbin talking.

"What makes you say that?" Jett inquired. Even though no one could see who Jett was addressing. Chaz and Jett heard movement, it sounded like someone shuffling their way through the darkness across the floor. It was getting closer to Chaz and Jett. The two boys lay still, then they realized it was Arbin. He is now sitting against the wall between Jett and Chaz. He didn't want to have to talk louder than a whisper; what he has to say was not for everyone to hear.

"Over the last few days I overheard Jimmy talking to Flo and some of the other adults. He mentioned this really bad guy, His name was Groady. He was sent down in the tunnels to live there as punishment." Arbin began.

"By who? And Why?" Jett interrupted.

"I'm getting to that." Arbin said. "I heard that Groady was this bad guy who lived in the commune and he didn't want to listen to Jimmy or follow any of the rules. I heard once…. he threatened to kill Jimmy and take over."

"Take over what" Chaz asked.

"You know, be the new leader." Arbin explained

"The new leader?" Chaz questioned.

"Anyway! The rest of the commune got together and helped Jimmy get rid of This Groady person. They banished him to the tunnels and bolted down all the trapdoors that lead down inside them. Once in a while you would hear Groady banging on the underside of the trapdoor trying to get out."

"Woow! D-did you ever hear him banging?" Jett asked in a stuttering panic, trying to hold back fear.

"I never did, but other people have. I heard rumors that's why nobody sleeps in the house across the field. Eventually no one went there at all. That's why it's abandoned." Arbin explained.

"And Jonathan and Stephanie are down there alone!" Jett said raising tone of voice.

"Shhhh!" Chaz reminded him. "Since you two have been down there, do you think we should try to find them?" Chaz asked. Arbin and Jett just sat there, turned their heads and looked at each other for a few seconds; even though it was pitch black in the room. "I mean I'll go with you of course, if you want. I just wouldn't put it on you guys." Chaz offered.

"I think we should at least wait till the morning or afternoon even. Who knows they may return by then. That will give us time to figure out what to do." Arbin suggested.

"I agree." seconded Jett. The three continued plotting out their rescue mission. With a few disagreements here and there, they finally pieced together a solid plan of action. This plan of action included an escape plan if need be. Arbin made his way back over to his bed, being careful not to disturb anyone. Chaz and Jett had difficulty trying to fall asleep. They wanted to exchange last minute thoughts, but didn't want to leave Arbin out.

Kasey woke up in her room to the sound of her mother calling the dog *Rex* to come inside. She sat up and looked around her room. It was just how she remembered it. It was white with pink trim on the window and wall moldings. The curtains were light purple; with stripes running vertically up and down them. The stripes were the same shade of pink as the molding. The furniture in the room was painted glossy white. There was a night stand to one side of the bed where Kasey put a glass of water in case she got thirsty during the night. The headboard to the bed was on the same side of the room as the windows. The foot of the bed was pointed toward the door; which by the way was painted light mint Green. The ceiling was bright white that supported a ceiling fan with yellow fan blades to resemble the sun. To Kasey no matter what the weather was outside, it was always warm and sunny in her room.

Just then she heard a sound that was both familiar and unfamiliar at the same time. It was unfamiliar to her in the dream; but familiar, because she was getting used to hearing it. She woke up and still remained laying in her bed just listening to the sound. It was one of the chickens outside. She suddenly realized she was not at home, but just dreaming. This made her start to softly cry. She didn't even realize she was alone. Everyone ells had woken up for breakfast. She eventually sat up and looked around. She didn't know if she wanted to cry more or just stop and see where everyone went off to.

"Kasey?" She heard a voice call out. "Kasey dear?" the voice called again. It was a woman's voice. She stopped crying and looked up, it was Star. She almost started to feel better. As Kasey's crying slowed down, the look on her face went from sad to a blank gaze.

"W-Where is ev-everyone? She managed to stutter out between gasps of breath. Star squatted down and rubbed a hand over her forehead.

"It's time for breakfast dear. What's wrong? Did you have a bad dream?" Star asked looking at her with a heavy concern in her eyes. Before Kasey could answer, Kasey thought of the dream she just had and started to cry again. Star leaned over and placed her chin between Kasey's shoulder and cheek so they were cheek to cheek. Then Star whispered in her ear. "It's ok sweetie. You can tell me. Did you dream you were home again?" Kasey was in such surprise she almost stopped crying.

"Y-Yeah… I-I dreamt I… was h-home again…… and I hear-heard….. my mommy call-calling…..Rex, my dog." Kasey continued crying once again.

"And then what happened honey?" Star asked while still stroking her forehead.

"An-and then-then…..I-I heard your voice….call…my n-name." After a few seconds Kasey finally softly shouted out. "I-I want to-to go home!…. I want to go h-home n-now!" And then she just cried out loud. louder than ever. Star didn't know what to do, so she just hugged her and promised she would be home soon.

"Kasey, why don't we join the others or breakfast? We're having pancakes and eggs. Come on sweetie. You can sit next to me." Star suggested.

"O-ok" Kasey finally agreed. As Kasey got up she commented about the boys going in the tunnels and she didn't think it was a good idea. For a second that comment made Star stop in her tracks.

"What do you mean honey? What boys?" Star asked with a slight head tilt and a concerned look.

"Jett, Chaz, and Arbin. I overheard them talking last night about going in the tunnels and looking for Jonathan and Stephanie."

"They were? When?" Star inquired.

"I think today." Star wanted to find out more, but didn't want to bother Kasey anymore about it. She figured Kasey had a bad enough morning and decided to let it go for now.

"Oh, ok. Let's grab a bite to eat before it's all gone. I'm starving, how about you?"

"I guess." Kasey answered, still feeling the effects from the dream she just had. Star held her hand out and Kasey reached up and grabbed it. The two walked hand and hand to the dining hall. Once they reached the dining hall, breakfast was almost done. They had just enough time to have what was left over and help clean up. After helping clean up; they decided to stay together and try to find out what the boys were up to.

The shackles still felt heavy on her wrists, even though she was free and no longer had them on. She kept staring at him as the flickering candle from the lantern distorted the contours of his face; casting odd shadows. She couldn't tell if the candle was making him look like some kind of monster, or was he really that ugly. It was the first time Jonathan and Stephanie got a close look at him.

For a short moment they all just stared at Groady. Groady, Terry and Travis stared at each other. Jonathan and Stephanie stared at those three and then looked at each other. Stephanie was getting the feeling Terry, Travis and Groady knew each other from another time. Terry and Travis just sat there for a moment not knowing what to say to Groady. They wanted to ask Groady how he got down there.

Still feeling the effects of Terry's attack and Jonathan's chain tightening strangle hold that was tightening every time the half beast tried to wriggle free; Groady seemed to be fighting off a state of confusion.

The unsteady silence that held all of them down was getting heavier. Everyone was wondering who would break it first. Travis and Terry wanted to ask Groady *Hey man how have things been since banishment in the tunnels?* And Groady may have wanted to ask, *How are thing s going in the commune without me?* Jonathan and Steph wanted to ask, *what's going on with you guys and how do we get out of here?* Everybody wanted to ask Groady, *What's with that hideous necklace you're wearing?*

Jonathan and Stephanie looked at each other with jittery frustration. Travis and Terry saw this eye contact and they now knew one of them was going to break the unsteady silence that seemed to hold them down.

Jonathan tried to ask Groady where they were and what kind of place this was, how long had he been down here and how did the seats to the bus get down here. But all Groady did was spit out grunts and grumbles; all the while shearing at Terry and Travis. He was also trying to wiggle free, but the tie-downs only seemed to be getting tighter.

"It's a slip noose lab partner." Jonathan addresses Groady with heavy sarcasm. "It only gets tighter the more you move." This comment almost made everyone chuckle. Everyone except Groady that is.

"Do you think he was down here for so long he forgot how to talk?" Stephanie asked leaning behind Jonathan; of course not caring if Groady could understand what she was saying.

"I'm not sure. It's possible I guess, but I would imagine he would catch on quickly." Jonathan replied not trying to be sarcastic. *I'm guessing you three have some catching up to do?* Jonathan thought to himself and very badly wanted to say aloud. It was pretty known that Groady couldn't free himself; this made Stephanie, Jonathan, Travis and Terry relax a bit more. Travis decided to chime in and fill in some missing pieces.

"Believe us, we're better off he's down here and doesn't speak." Terry nodded in agreement.

"Jimmy explained a few things, but I'm sure he probably didn't tell me everything." Jonathan stated. "I'd feel better hearing it from a different source; he might have altered some things or not. I just want a second opinion I guess."

"Yeah, well did Jimmy tell you how Groady wanted to takeover and be the new leader?" Travis said.

"I didn't know there was a job opening." Jonathan inquired

"There wasn't" Travis pleaded. "That's the thing. Did Jimmy tell how Groady forced himself on some of the women, and how he's the biological father of some of the children up there?" That thought ran a chill up Terry's spine and made her wince.

"You mean he....?" Stephanie started to question in half shock and suddenly couldn't get the rest of the words out.

"Afraid so. Or at least that was always the rumor." Travis reassured.

"Look, I don't care if he stays down here forever; we just want to know of a way to contact the outside word for help, and a few other things." Jonathan demanded.

"You're never getting out of here!" said a voice in a growly, grunting tone. All four sharply turned and looked in disbelief. Stephanie reached out and grabbed on to Jonathan and pulled him close to her using him as a human shield. Terry was so startled she spit out a screaming "OH!"

"Jonathan!" Stephanie cried out in a panic while still clinging on to him. "What does he mean? We're never getting out of here? We're going to be locked down here just he is? We have to get out of here! We're not getting locked down here; no way!" Jonathan put his hand out about waist high, palm facing down almost bouncing it in midair. He was giving the hand signal to *slow down*; at the same time turned around and gave her a look that said *calm down.* This made her finally stop rambling on.

"chiil-ax! Just calm down. We're getting out here." Jonathan reassured her. He was pretty sure they were going to leave the same way they entered. He went to take a step forward toward Groady, but Stephanie grabbed him tighter and held on to him. He didn't fight Stephanie's grip. He understood her fear. "What are talking about Groady? That we're never getting out of here? I think you my friend are the one who is never getting out of here." Jonathan suggested with a hint of sarcasm. Jonathan couldn't tell if Groady meant that comment for him and Stephanie, Travis and Terry since they were past acquaintances or did he mean that for everybody? Groady seemed to have his eyes and his sneer fixed on Travis and Terry; who just sat there not sure how to react, staring at Groady.

"None of you are getting out of here." There came that growling grunt once again; still having a gaze on Travis and Terry. Jonathan was getting tired of this guessing game. He wanted answers and wanted them now.

"What are you talking about? And how did you get the seats to the bus down here? That only proves there is a way out of here." Jonathan was losing his cool so much he finally breaks Stephanie's hold and takes a step toward Groady.

"Didn't you're friends tell you? How that looser Jimmy likes to keep control of everybody and what they do and how they act." Groady protested.

"Is that why you're locked down here? You didn't want to follow rules? That and forcing yourself on women you pig!" Jonathan said keeping a gaze on him. That comment put a queasy knot in Stephanie's stomach. She suddenly realized or more so remembered she was unconscious down there for some time. She held her midsection and slowly looked down at her clothes to see if there were any tears, or stains; but it was too hard to see in the darkness of the tunnels. She was almost too scared to want to know.

"I didn't do anything wrong. I did what that looser Jimmy wanted. He wanted a bigger family. People don't grow on trees." Nobody saw that comment coming. They all just looked at him twice and then looked at each other. Travis and Terry are glad Jonathan is doing all the talking. They had no idea what to say to Groady; and Jonathan was taking the awkwardness away.

"Jonathan, ask him how we get out of here and back to civilization." Stephanie commanded. Before Jonathan could respond, Groady jumped in and answered her request.

"I told you. You're never getting out of here. There's nobody around for at least fifteen miles. This is the middle of nowhere. Jimmy made it that way. He wanted to make sure to be as far away from people as possible." Groady said almost with pleasure. Stephanie didn't know what to say, think, or how to react. She just turned to Jonathan as if to ask; *is that true?* Jonathan read the look on her face and just rolled his eyes.

"He was just trying to scare you. Even if that was Jimmy's intention; it wasn't meant intended for us. We're not staying, sorry to tell you." Jonathan said that last part with full sarcasm. Stephanie leaned over and loudly whispers in Jonathan's ear.

"That necklace he has on scares me more than anything." Stephanie said.

"Necklace?" Jonathan questioned as he took a step forward to get a closer look. "Are those human bones? And is that an eyeball?" That made Stephanie's face crinkle as she took a step back. Terry's face is crinkled in the same nauseated pose. Travis mouths the words *"what the?"*.... leaving his jaw hanging open as he made no attempted to finish the sentence. Then they turned to look at each other, and then back at Groady and his, what looked to be a body part necklace. Travis and Terry read the look on each other's faces and realized they needed to get out of there. They saw and heard enough. Jonathan and Stephanie however needed to know a little more.

"Groady, what, the hell, is that necklace?" Jonathan asked putting exaggerated pauses between words.

"It's my newest collection, the necklace of discipline. It represents what happens to people when they cross me." Groady sneered.

"Care to explain what it means?" Jonathan almost hesitated asked. Everyone took an emotional step back; breaths were held and faces were in a half cringe. The story of how Groady pieced together such a badge of honor made up of specific body parts, was not going to be pretty.

"It's really self explanatory. The finger of thieves, the toes of trespassers, tongues of liars, eyes of people who looked at me wrong. Get it?! So if I were you, I would be careful around me." Groady warned.

"And how, or should I ask who donated to your collection?" Jonathan pressed on.

"The bus driver you left for dead." Stephanie gave a disapproving shout of *what!* as she remembered the bus driver and how she gave her advice that; "stupid boys only grow up to be stupid men."

"What?! you mean you?...." Stephanie paused for a moment as she thought of that monster cutting up the bus driver's body for his trophy piece. "What did she ever do to you, that she deserved that?" Stephanie commanded. Groady looked at her with a slight smug smile.

"Well, for one thing she's probably the reason why you're stuck here in the first place." Groady protested.

"You're a liar. What are you talking about, she's the reason we're stuck here? What do you know anyway?" Stephanie countered.

"Did she always drive drunk?" Groady smiled.

"What do you mean? What proof do you have?" Stephanie asked

"I guess you didn't see the empty whisky bottle she had?" Groady inquired. Stephanie began to counter argue, but Jonathan cut her off.

"He's right." Jonathan said sharply. Stephanie just looks at Jonathan in disbelief. As if to ask *whose side are you on?* She just remained looking at him crossly. "He's right! When I was looking in the bus I kicked an empty whisky bottle. I saw the same bottle in one of the rooms down here." This made Stephanie finally realize maybe Jonathan didn't cause the accident after all.

Now that the mystery of the necklace and even its donor was explained, there still one last question to be answered. What happened to the rest of the bus driver's body? That was the question nobody wanted to ask in fear of what the answer would be; nobody except for Jonathan that is.

"So what did you do with the rest of the bus driver's body?" Jonathan asked with enthusiasm. Much to everyone's surprise, Groady gave a very noble answer.

"I gave her a proper burial. That's more then what I can say for you people; you just left her there to rot." He said with a sneer. To this Jonathan and Stephanie just looked at each other possibly feeling same guilt; not wanting to believe he was right.

# CHAPTER 25

## Leaving the Tunnels Forever!

Jett, Arbin and Chaz found themselves in the abandon house up the stairs at the locked room. As far as Arbin could remember; this is where the two guns and a bow where held at one time, hence the locked door.

"Explain to us again why we're here." Jett and Chaz inquired with Arbin.

"This is the room where Jimmy keeps whatever weapons we have. I know there is a bow and arrow and I think two guns." Arbin stated.

"Yeah I know" Chaz agreed. "I was in here with Jonathan once before. We kicked the door in to look around and we found the bow; but I don't think we saw any guns. Do you have the key? I don't want to kick the door in again. The last time me, Jonathan and Jimmy had to fix it. And why do we need weapons anyway? Are we in danger?" Chaz asked almost stuttering.

"No, we're not in any danger, yet! I doubt those guys are going to make it out of the tunnel. I heard some pretty nasty stories about that Groady person. I heard once he kidnapped someone, killed them and ate pieces of their body." Jett and Chaz just looked at each other in half confusion and half horror. Looking for the weapons seemed like good idea all of a sudden. Arbin reached in his pocket and pulled out a key, put in the key in the lock and turned it. It turned half way around followed by a faint *click*. Then he grabbed the door knob and pushed the door open.

The room was just as Chaz remembered it; there was a stale and stillness to the air. That feeling of an abandon house swallowed Chaz once again. Jett and Arbin Just looked around in wonder. All the random stuff was just so overwhelming. There it was, hanging on the wall just as Chaz left it a few weeks ago. A recurve bow, 60lbs Chaz remembered. This time Chaz could walk over to it, instead of limping like last time. He grabbed it off the wall and held it in his hand. The last time he held the bow, couldn't quite pull back on the bow all the way. He just wasn't strong enough; it was 60lbs pull after all.

"Don't dry fire that!" Arbin commanded.

"I know how to use a bow; my dad taught me how." Chaz said. He held the bow as he did only a few weeks ago. This time he was almost able pull the bow back to its full draw. He surprised himself, he must have gained some strength; maybe all that farm living. Chaz hung the bow back on the wall and continued looked around. He never thought he would be back in the same room again. He honestly though he would be home by now he thought to himself, looking at the ground feeling sorry for himself.

"What exactly are we looking for?" Jett asked. Arbin started rattling off a short list.

"We should try to find the arrows to that bow, the two guns and the ammo. And whatever ells we think we can use in the tunnels." While the boys were on their miniature scavenger hunt; Chaz noticed what he didn't find. The radio that he and Jonathan intended on using to reach out for help. The CB radio and that funny shaped microphone simply vanished. A clear area on the desk where it had been sitting remained in its place. For some reason made Chaz's heart sank even deeper in his chest. He remembered the excitement he felt when he and Jonathan almost got it to work.

"Hey, what's this?" Jett asked aloud making Chaz *snap out of it* and look up. In Jett was holding what looked to be a miniature spear carved out of wood. There seemed to resemble arrows, home-made arrows. They where the right length of an arrow; one end was pointed. And the other end had a groove carved in it. They had no feathers at the grooved end like arrows did.

"Do you think these are arrows for that bow?" Jett asked. For a few seconds the three remained silent in deep thought.

"I don't know." Chaz said. Arbin grabbed one of the arrows and rolled it on the floor to see how straight it was. It rolled smooth, and steady about three feet in a straight line; revealing that the arrow itself was perfectly straight and smooth.

"Well there's only one way to know for sure how they will work" Arbin decided. He picked up the arrow off the floor and walked over to the wall and grabbed to bow. He looked across the room then walked out in the hall. Jett and Chaz suspected what Arbin was up to. Arbin stood in the hallway for a moment then Chaz and Jett joined him. Without a word being spoken; they all knew what was about to happen. Arbin put the bow string in the slot of the arrow, managed to pull back to the bows full draw and released. The arrow took off with a *whizzing swoosh;* the bow made a *snapping slap* sound. A split second later they heard a distant, faded *knocking thud* sound. The three stood there in bewildered confusion as to where the arrow went. They stood in place scanning the floor, then the walls, then the wall about twenty feet at the end of the hall.

"There it is!" Jett called out. Arbin and Chaz looked at the direction Jett was pointing. They all slowly walked toward to the end of the hallway, as if walking on eggshells. Once at the end of the hall they all stared at the arrow in satisfied amazement of the outcome they all just witnessed. The arrow was imbedded at least two inches into the drywall and perfectly straight.

"I guess that solves that one." Arbin stated. "They work." Chaz and Jett could only agree.

"Nice shot!" Chaz said, and Jett nodded.

"Thanks, looks like we found our weapon of choice." Arbin declared.

With lanterns, candles, bow, arrows and now a new found bravery; the boys made their way down the stairs to the basement. The random bouncing of the candle light made the trap door appear to be something out of a horror movie. It also put them inside an invisible bubble like force field that was fighting off the darkness that was trying to swallow them. Deep breaths were taken as if they was going to be the last ones.

"Well, let's do it." Arbin suggested as he reached down and pulled up the trap door. They took notice that the door wasn't bolted down as they usually are. After a very brief discussion about it; they all agreed it was better that way as not to get locked down there. Arbin lead the way since he had the lantern, then Jett and finally Chaz. This was Chaz's first time in the tunnels, and hopefully his last. As the three descended down the crumbling cement staircase, Chaz was trying to hide his doubtfulness. He knew the other two boys have been down in the tunnels before, and this was not their first time. He was trusting Jett and Arbin know how to be safe, and knew were to go.

"You guys know where to go, right?" Chaz called out. For a few seconds the other two didn't answer. They some-what knew their way around. "I'll take that as a *no*" Chaz answered himself out loud. They reached the bottom of the staircase when they heard very faint voices. They just stood there for a second waiting for the voices to start up again.

"Are we just going to leave him there?" Stephanie asked grabbing Jonathan's arm.

"For now, yeah. That will give us time to make it out of here. He'll wiggle free eventually." Jonathan said. Travis attempted to raise his eyebrows in agreement, but was suddenly reminded of the stabbing burse on the side of his head. He put his hand up to the side of his head as he winced in pain.

"Good idea" Travis said, realizing it was just easier to say it, then use fancy facial body language.

"Yeah but he'll be furious when he does get free." Terry added.

"At least we didn't try to kill him like he probably would have done to us." Travis pointed out.

"He'll be fine. The more important thing is that we know what we're up against. And from now on, we only come down here in numbers." Jonathan stated out loud in general.

"Why would we ever have to come down to this place again? It's nothing but one big dungeon." Stephanie argued. She was scared to death of the place she thought she was going to die in; by a monster she never helped create. Jonathan caught this vibe radiating off Stephanie and put his arm around her.

"Look, I understand how you feel. I don't expect you to ever come down here again; I say that because our only way out maybe through these tunnels. That would be the only time you would ever have to come back down here. And I'll make sure Groady is dead by then."

Terry, Travis, Jonathan and Stephanie lost all track of time. They didn't know if it was day or night. They lost track of how long they were down there. The four proceeded down the dark corridors stopping here and there trying to remember; *was it a right? Or a left?* The journey was pretty quiet for the most part. The only talking was to discuss which way to turn and landmarks that may or may not have been noted on the way in.

"I have a feeling we're going the right way." Terry shared holding her head up in a positive note. The others shouted out comments of agreement.

"Yeah I think you're right."

"I guess so."

"Yeah, I'll go with that."

"There! Did you guys hear that?" Chaz excitedly shouted in a tone that said *see, I'm not crazy.* Chaz looked at the other two for at least a visual answer.

"Where did it come from?" Arbin asked in a whisper. He was whispering because if the voices started up again, he didn't want to be talking over them. Jett and Chaz caught on to this idea and did the same.

"It sounded like from down that way" chaz said pointing in the direction he thought the voices coming from.

Jonathan stopped walking dead in his tracks and held an ear to the air. A distance of about ten feet past, before the others realized that he wasn't walking with them. They stopped, looked back and saw Jonathan in that *wait, I hear something.* Pose. They all stayed silent for a few seconds trying to listen also.

"What?" Terry asked in a quick stabbing tone. Travis just stood silent. Stephanie stood silent looking at Jonathan in the same pose.

"You heard that too right? It sounded like a kid." Stephanie asked. Jonathan turned to look at her.

"Yeah, did you hear where it was coming from?" Jonathan asked.

"It sounded like it was coming from that way." Stephanie said pointing behind Jonathan. Each one could tell what each other was thinking. *We are probably going the wrong way.*

"Let's try going that way." Travis suggested. All four turned around, and started traveling the opposite direction; passing the corridor way they just came out of. They continued walking in silence hoping to hear the voice again.

The three boys continued walking in the direction they heard the voices coming from. They stuck close together as they walked slowly down the corridor. Chaz kept looking side to side with every step. He was puzzled at everything he saw, it was like another world to him.

"I bet that was Jonathan and Stephanie we heard." Chaz stated in a normal volume to his voice.

"Yeah, but it also sounded like more than two people." Jett added.

"Chaz look for connecting tunnels on either side of us, they come up quick. It so dark down here you could pass one and not even know it." Arbin requested. "Plus it'll help us keep track of where we are." Chaz agreed to this request. A *Thudding-clank, rattle, clink* sound echoed in the tunnels. The boys stopped in mid-stride and remained silent.

"Did you hear that?" Jett asked in a whisper.

"Ye-Yeah, it sounded like,.... Like chains hitting the ground or-or something." Chaz stuttered. They both looked at Arbin for some magical explanation; in return he just looked at them as if to say, *I don't have one.* Once again the boy proceeded to slowly walk in silence.

"Di-Did you guys hear what direction the ch-chains come from?" Arbin asked.

"It almost sounded like it come from over.... That way? If we could turn left through this wall.."

Jett replied in a puzzling tone of voice. Arbin chimed in with a positive, confident energy.

"Ah! We must be near a passageway." With that, he held the lantern up and to the left shining it more on the wall. About twenty feet in front of them revealed the passageway he suspected was nearby. There they stood wondering which way to go, straight? Or take the left passageway?

This time there was no mistaking; the four heard voices talking. They stopped walking to quiet their shuffling footsteps on the gravely dirt floor and the squeaky lantern handle that was slightly swinging back and forth.

"Straight ahead! The voices sounded like they were coming from ahead of us!" Terry shared with excitement. After a second; Jonathan,

Stephanie, and Travis gave slight nods and agreeing looks that said, *Good job, we're with you; let's go!* As soon as this decision was made, they heard a bone-chilling, *thudding-clank, rattle, clink.* The sound came far off in the distance in the direction they came from. The looks on their faces that may have had of any kind of hope and excitement; immediately changed to disbelief and horror.

"Come on!" Jonathan commanded. And all four of them started walking faster, and faster.

"Should we call out to whoever may be ahead of us?" Stephanie asked.

"That sounds like a good idea." Jonathan replied; their voices now have that breathless-panting tone.

"I swore we had more time than that." Travis said in the same panting tone.

"I guess." Jonathan said. He just wanted to keep moving. "Whoever is up ahead must of just entered. If we find them we'll find a quick way out."

All three boys at the same time looked straight ahead disregarding the passageway on the left.

"That way!" Arbin said. "I just heard someone down that way!"

"I-I heard it too." Chaz agreed. "It-It almost sounds like Jonathan and Stephanie." He added. They could hear the voices, but they couldn't see anything. It was pitch black in front of them.

"Should we call out to them?" Jett suggested. "Chaz, call Jonathan's name!" Chaz just looked at Arbin and Jett in question and shrugged his shoulders. They just return the same questionable look and shrugged. With that Chaz holds up a finger in that *wait a minute* pose.

"JONATHAN?" Chaz called out, but no really in a shouting voice.

The four facial expressions change, from horror to total surprise and a little of that, *Thank god* feeling. Jonathan and the rest started walking even faster toward the sound of the voice that just called out.

"Is that Chaz? That sounded like Chaz." Stephanie said so excitedly she was almost in tears. Before anyone could get a word in, she yelled Chaz's name. "Chaz!" They also had the same problem; they could hear where the voices where coming from, but they couldn't see anything.

"Steph? Where are you?" Chaz yelled. By this time the boys had rapidly picked up their pace.

"Here!" she yelled back guessing they were following the sound of voices also.

"They're up ahead." Arbin said with excitement in his voice.

"We're coming!" Chaz yelled back. Soon enough, the two groups were getting close enough that they didn't have keep yelling for each other. They could hear bits and pieces of each other's conversations. As the boys approached closer, there was a slight glare up ahead.

"Look! Over to the right!" Jett pointed out to Chaz and Arbin. They picked up their pace even faster. Stephanie, Jonathan, Terry, and Travis could see they're coming to the end of the corridor they were in.

"Which way do we go at the end?" Terry asked out loud in general.

"Not sure." Travis replied. "I think the boys are to the rrrrright?" He said in half question half statement looking over at Jonathan and Stephanie for some kind of verification.

"I think they are to the right." Jonathan said. He was more or less pointing out there was a slight glare coming from the right corner of the passageway. Their suspicions were correct; once they reached the end of the corridor they could see a heavy glare from the boy's lantern. The two groups started running toward each other, calling out each other's names. Chaz and Jett grabbed on to Stephanie and Jonathan in a bear hug.

"We didn't think we would ever see you guys again." Chaz said in almost tears. He was so excited he forgot he was carrying a bow and arrow and almost wacked Jonathan in the head with it.

"Sorry Jonathan I forgot I was holding this." Chaz said swinging the bow off his shoulder. Jonathan and the others were impressed the thought to bring it, even being able to get in the locked room was not easy.

"You guys took the bow from the locked room I see. How did you get in there?" Jonathan asked.

"I had the key to the door." Arbin answered proudly.

"Hey guys, I hate to ruin our reunion, but I think we're forgetting about our friend Groady who is somewhere down here roaming free."

Terry reminded everyone. Everyone agreed with her and started discussing which way to go to head back.

"How did you guys get down here?" Jonathan inquired. All three boys pointed in the direction they just came from.

"We came from down that way straight all the way. We didn't even turn right or left. We came in through the basement of the abandon guest house." Jett explained. Now all seven started down the corridor back toward the staircase of the abandon guest house. They started walking at fast pace, racing back before they would meet up with Groady again. As they walked Travis pointed out a small fact everyone was overlooking.

"I don't think we have to kill ourselves hurrying back before we meet up with Groady. We are a group of seven, and he is only one."

"True, but half of us are not even teenagers don't forget." Jonathan reminded him.

"Yeah, but we have a bow and arrow as well." Travis stated. This made everyone think *oh yeah* as the pace almost slowed down.

"I don't care what we have; I want to get out of here and get cleaned up; unless we're going to kill him and end him once and for all." Stephanie protested. They all seemed to have forgotten Stephanie was held down there the longest, and probably had no food, water or bathroom. They reached the crumbling cement staircase and reentered the basement of the guest house and bolted down the trapdoor. Random sighs of relief came from the seven; they were officially out of what they considered hell.

# CHAPTER 26

## Cleaning up from the Tunnels

As they came out of the basement they saw bright sunlight flooding into the ground floor. They all got a closer look of the bruises inflicted by Groady. Jonathan and Travis had bad bruises on their faces. Stephanie had bruises on her rib cage. It was now they started to feel the pain from the bruise. Jonathan examined Stephanie's rib cage, nothing seemed to be broken.

"What time is it?" Stephanie asked to anyone in general.

"It feels like it's about seven am." Terry answered. They wanted to hurry back before anyone noticed how long they were gone. Jonathan went up stairs with the boys to return the bow and arrow. While they were up there, Arbin gave him a brief demonstration of great the bow fired.

"I see why Jimmy kept it locked up." Jonathan stated. Jonathan also noticed something is different, but he couldn't place it. Chaz known's what Jonathan is missing, but didn't say anything at first. He is waiting to see if Jonathan will catch it. Jonathan kept staring at the desk; finally Chaz lets him off the hook.

"The radio." Chaz said.

"What?" Jonathan asked.

"The radio, Isn't that what you're looking for?"

"Is that what's missing? I knew something was different. Where did it go?" Jonathan asks.

"Good question." Chaz replied.

"Do you think Jimmy took it? And if he did, why?"

"I don't know, I was thinking the same thing." Chaz said.

"Whatever." Jonathan remarked as he shrugged his shoulders. That body language kind of let Chaz know the missing radio wasn't a big deal and all that worrying over it was just a waste of time.

Jonathan and the boys returned down stairs where they met up with Stephanie, Terry, and Travis. All seven stood in the kitchen of the abandon guest house. They were discussing an alibi of where they were for the past twenty four hours. Jonathan knew people would be asking and he thought it best if they got their story straight, not that they were going to lie, but it would be easier if they were all on the same page. There was going to be a lot of explaining to do, regarding Stephanie's adventure; the others not so much they weren't gone that long.

As they stepped out house into the bright sunlight there was a slight warm breeze. The sunlight made a few of them squint for a few seconds. The air never felt so fresh and clean after being down in the tunnels. Some commented how they could almost taste the fresh air; the others joked how crazy that sounded. They all just stood at the front door for a second and just took in the sight of the open field in front of them.

It was pretty quiet on the way back to the main house The sound of shushing grass set the background noise for the small trek. They all had thoughts running in their heads of how much they needed and wanted to shower and get cleaned up. Some were imagining how many times they would have to explain their story and tell what happened, what they saw, and who Groady was. Jonathan could sense a lot of worried tension coming from the group, especially from the younger of them. Jonathan was wondering if he should speak out and give some advice, or just remain silent. He didn't want to open a can of worms, but then he didn't want to pass up the chance to give some advice that may be helpful.

"Hey guys and gals I just wanted to suggest if the others start hounding you about what happened try to keep it to one word answers. People tend to leave you alone if they start getting one word answers; get it?" Jonathan wasn't sure if Jett was testing him or was he really confused about what to say.

"What if people start asking me and stuff? I should give only one word answers? What if this only makes them ask more; trying to get more information? Or do you really believe what you just suggested will work?" Jett rattled on. Without breaking stride, Jonathan turned and looked at Jett.

"Sure" Jonathan replied and nodded in reassurance; and then looked straight ahead and continued walking; hopefully proving his point. Jett almost opened his mouth to say something ells, but seemed to have gotten the hint and decided against it. Jonathan had a feeling the others caught on. He also got the feeling with that they seemed more relaxed seeing his theory in action.

For no particular reason, the seven walk in pairs, except for the boys who were in a straight line across. In front of them were Terry and Travis, and leading was Jonathan and Stephanie. Jonathan is concerned about Stephanie's frame of mind. He knows the potential danger she just escaped from. *My god she's lucky to alive right now.* He is saying to himself, but doesn't want to tell her. Stephanie's high endurance for adventure is greater than Jonathan ever expected.

"Wha-what's going to happen when we get back to the main house?" Stephanie asked with a shaky trembling voice. The stutter in her tone grabs Jonathan by the head and turns it toward her. Her arms are crossed; her hands stroke up and down from shoulder to elbow. Her head hangs slightly down and tears running down her face, but she is not balling. Jonathan suspects her adrenalin is running out and worry, fear and reality are taking over.

"What are asking? Are you going to be in some kind of trouble? What will people say or ask? Are people going to hound you as to what happened to you down there?" Jonathan meant for those questions to be more of a blueprint. He wants to coach her on what to say o not to say.

"Yeah." She replies. *Wow! He is totally reading my mind.* She thought to herself.

"Look, As far as you being in trouble; you're not, none of these people are your mom and dad that also goes for me. You understand that right?"

"Yeah."

"As far as what people say or ask just keep your answers short. If people start hounding you tell them you're too tired or you just don't want to talk about it. You follow?" Jonathan asked.

"I guess, yeah." Stephanie said.

"If I were you, when we get back, I would just get showered, cleaned up, tend to your injuries, and try to get some rest. I would even go so far as to skip dinner. But I'm sure you must be starving."

"Surprisingly I lost my appetite." Stephanie commented.

"Well that's probably for the best; you don't have to face all those people then." Jonathan suggested.

"Ye-yeah, I guess." *There's that stutter again.* Jonathan thought himself.

"Stop worrying, you'll be fine. I promise." He said this as he wrapped his arm around her shoulder and softly gave her a hug.

Some people look up from their chores stop and stare as the seven emerge closer to the main house. Some squinted their eyes in a wincing motion once they notice the burses Stephanie, Jonathan and Travis had endured. Jonathan walked past the on-lookers holding his head up high, displaying his battle scares that are his badges of honor. It was a shame he couldn't say the same for Stephanie who must been feeling some form of shame judging from the tears and the pinched face she displayed.

Terry took a step in front of Stephanie, blocking her view from everything and everyone. Terry gently rested her hand on Stephanie's shoulder and slightly lifted her chin with the other and said; "Come on honey, let's get you cleaned up." and flashed a *stop worrying* look that actually made Stephanie's face spring back into a neutral blank stare. Stephanie looked into Terry's eyes, nodded and said

"Ok. Thanks I need it." And the two trail off down the hallway in a force field of pride and confidence, repelling any cross looks they may be receiving.

"That sounds like a great idea." Travis said while cupping the burse on the side of his head. Jonathan agreed and headed to his sleeping quarters to grab fresh clothes. The boys being boys however, decided they didn't need a shower just yet and why waist the time. They were all a buzz and couldn't wait to brag about the new adventure.

The room was dark and she couldn't see anything. The sounds of rattling chains were faint. There's not enough slack to get momentum to wiggle free. Her arms and legs were numb. The heavy footsteps were getting closer; now they were in the same room. She felt as if someone was leaning over her. The horrid stench of body odor was sign that she not along.

"Who are you? Get.....off.....me!" she shouted. Her voice isn't as loud as she wanted it to be. Her mouth wasn't tied or gagged, but she was having trouble getting the words out. A hand gripped her shoulder. Blended emotions of fear and anger made scream out and lunge forward. "Jonathan!" Flo was startled and flinches back. The pain in Stephanie's ribs stops her in her tracks.

"Easy girl, you're having a nightmare it's ok it's ok." Flo said gently placing a hand on Stephanie's hand. Stephanie cradled the side of her rib cage with one arm and saw that it was Flo sitting next to her. Stephanie slowly lied back down trying to collect her thoughts. She had that wet, sticky feeling from all the sweat. She was almost wheezing with every breath. After a few seconds, her rapid breathing slowed down to a normal pattern.

"Must have been a hell of a nightmare; care to talk about it?" Flo asked tilting her head to one side as she stroked Stephanie's forehead. After a few seconds Stephanie began to explain her nightmare.

"I dreamt I was down in the tunnels again. I heard chains rattling, than I felt him grabbing me again and holding me down." Stephanie ended her statement with a sniffle.

"Who him?" Flo inquired at the same time, she narrowing her eyebrows.

"Groady." With that Stephanie's face pinched and her nostrils flared. Her tone of voice changed from shaky to stern. Flo was thinking twice about asking her what happened down in the tunnel, but she just had to know. Stephanie knew Flo and her general demeanor. She also knew to take Flo's concern with a grain of salt. Stephanie wanted to vent about it. She didn't have time to tell Jonathan what happened when they were on their way back to the main house. They were too concerned about other people and what they would think about Stephanie's absence.

Flo positioned one knee and half her butt over the bed. She stopped in mid sitting motion, rapidly tapping Stephanie on the side of her leg. Stephanie sat up and slid over making room for Flo to sit. The two girls looked at each other with facial expressions that said; *let's talk.*

"Let's talk. I think you need it and plus you'll feel better." Flo addressed in a stern concern. "So spill it. Tell me everything that happened to you down there. Everything! I know it's tough enough for you being stranded here. I can help you and put the ice back in your veins. I feel you're like me in that way."

After a few moments of silence and collecting her thoughts, Stephanie looked up at Flo. Flo looked back at her, nodded her head and pointed her eyebrows in a sharp upward motion. *I'm listening.* Are the words Stephanie was hearing without Flo saying anything.

"Where do you want me to start?" Stephanie questioned striking a squint in one eye; like people do when they ask *what do you mean?*

"Ahh; where were you born?" Before Stephanie could answer or ever had a chance to look at her funny; Flo widens her eyes, leans in and raises her voice one octave. "How and when did you first enter the tunnels?"

"I wasn't sure if you meant after we entered the tunnel or…."

"Yes!" Flo cuts her off again. "Just before Groady captured you. What did he do to you?, to be more direct." Flo barked rolling her eyes.

"Ok, it all started when a trapdoor was discovered in the barn. One night me and Jonathan planned to go down there exploring. He couldn't go down with me so he was going to join me later. He was supposed to sit by the door and if I didn't come up at a set time, he was going to come down to look for me. We left the door sitting off-set; so if I came back and Jonathan wasn't there, I would put the door on a particular way, so he would know I was the one who set the door in place and made it out of the tunnels."

"Wait" Flo interrupted. "What's the purpose off-setting the door?" Flo asked.

"So if Jonathan wasn't there and someone come by and put the door on the correct way; he would know if it was or wasn't me that did it."

"Ok, go on" Flo insisted.

"Ok, so, I remember it was pitch black down there I somehow lit a torch. I was looking around, then I find the seats to the school bus we were riding, when we got into the accident."

"Hold on. The seats to the school bus you guys were sitting on are now down in the tunnels?"

"Yes"

"....Ok..." Flo remarked looking puzzled. "Does anybody know how or why they are down there?"

"No! That's just one of the freaky things that happened down there. Anyway, I was exploring around and after about an hour or so Groady came from behind me and put something over my head and started beating me."

"So he beat you?" Flo inquired as her eyes got bigger.

"Yes! So when I woke up I was chained down to a metal bed." Stephanie explained.

"What! To a metal bed! Did take advantage of you?"

"Thank god no! Or at least not that I know of. After what felt like forever, it was maybe later that next day, I finally heard Jonathan and that guy Travis."

"So, Travis went down there, with Jonathan?" Flo squinted in confusion.

"Yes, it was Jonathan and Travis. But they got attacked by Groady also."

"Oh my god! Did they get badly hurt?"

"I guess, you didn't see their faces?" Flo didn't know what to say. He just jolted her head back in surprise.

"No I didn't" Flo confessed putting a hand over her mouth. "Ok, continue."

"Ok, so long story short, Groady for some reason puts us all in the same room; and we're all chained down, and then he goes off somewhere. Travis actually manages to get free."

"How!" Flo intervenes.

"Not sure." Stephanie quickly replied as to tryed to speed the story up. "So, Travis gets free and he gets us free from our chains. Than me Jonathan and Travis start to plan what to do incase Groady came back. They decided if he came back, they were going to jump him and chain him down."

"So, they were going to take on Groady? But aren't they injured at this point?" Flo asked.

"Yes, they are, but wait. So Groady comes back, and Jonathan and

Travis attack him as planned. By some *act of god*, Terry comes out of nowhere!"

"What!" Flo almost screamed. "Terry too!"

"Yeah! I know right! She came at the perfect time because as the Travis and Jonathan were wrestling with Groady Terry kicked Groady right where it hurts and he went down for the count. Travis and Jonathan chained him up good, or so we thought."

"Ok, now, hang on." Flo pauses for a second. "So, now it's you, Jonathan, Travis and Terry down in the tunnels."

"Yes at least this point in the story."

"At this point in the story? Don't tell me more people found their way down there!"

"Ok, but I would be lying." Stephanie continued.

"Holy..... did the whole place find their way down there? Who ells?..." Flo reluctantly asked. Right now Stephanie is trying to hold back a smile brought on by Flo's facial expressions. Stephanie is also beginning think Flo is more upset about feeling left out and not concerned anymore than about how she is doing. *I'm actually starting to feel better* Stephanie thought to herself; Stephanie even sits up a little more and her eyes start to get brighter.

"Ok, so, um, long story short as we're trying to find our way out of the tunnels, we hear voices; we find out it's Chaz, Jett and Arbin."

"Stop!.... They made it down there too?"

"Yes. We heard them before we saw them. And they heard us before they saw us. For some time we just yelling back and forth to each other. Then we heard or we thought we heard Groady rattling free of his chains."

"So, Groady got free?" Flo asked.

"Yeah, we believe so. We didn't see him. Luckily the three boys had just come down when we met up, and they could remember the way out. We all just booked it out of there, up the stare case, and back through the trapdoor in the basement of the abandon guest house. As soon as we came up we bolted the door shut!" Stephanie said.

"Wait! One last thing; did you get a close look at Groady?" Flo asked. The memory of that hideous necklace hits Stephanie like a freight train.

"Oh my god!" Stephanie said wide eyed and holding her hand out in that *wait a minute* hand motion when people want you to wait a minute. "That reminds me! You should have seen him! What a monster! He was wearing this hideous necklace and the trinkets were human bones!"

"Human bones? Wait! How do you know they were human?" Flo was doubting.

"Groady told us. He even told us where or who he got them from….." Flo sucked in a small gasp of air as she put her hand to cover her mouth. The look of horror and shock splashed across Flo's face. Flo's face was frozen in time as Stephanie explained the necklace of discipline as Groady called it. The finger of thieves toes of trespassers, tongs of liers, and the rest. Stephanie was reading Flo's facial expressions while she was explaining the bones on the necklace and the bus driver they came from. Stephanie could read two main things. Flo is trying not to barf, and Flo is also trying to speak but she couldn't.

Flo couldn't stop imagining the horror this poor girl was rescued from. Stephanie went on to explain the empty whisky bottle that was found on the bus. And that the accident may not have been Jonathan's fault after all. Flo finally broke herself out of the the hypnotic trance she was in, and was able to speak. Stephanie knew the question Flo is going to ask.

"S-So…. Where's the bus driver's b-body?" she reluctantly asks. Stephanie closed her eyes.

"Groady claims he buried her, but he didn't say where. I don't think any of us asked. We all heard enough at that point."

"Is that everything Stephanie?" Flo inquired. Stephanie pauses for a second to reflect.

"Yeah…. That's everything." Stephanie replied. There is a tear running down Stephanie's cheek. A sign of relief and thankfulness someone took the time listen. At that moment in time; they could read each other's thoughts. They leaned forward with arms stretched out and crash into each other in a crying embrace.

# CHAPTER 27

## Leaving Soon?

"No way! That's crazy! I'm never going back down there!" Chaz commanded.

"Shhh, keep your voice down!" Jett said in a loud whisper even thought they are outside and there is good chance nobody is around to overhear them. "I can't believe Arbin didn't know his way around down there."

"Maybe that was his first time down there. He said people really don't talk about it. You heard him, Jimmy forbids anyone to go down in the tunnels. Why ells would the trap doors be bolted shut?" Chaz said. "Besides, do you know how long it would take to explore all those tunnels?"

"Incase, you didn't notice, it doesn't look like we're getting out of here anytime soon as much as I hate to say it." that comment made Chaz shoot Jett a look that would stop a charging bull. Both boys stop dead in their tracks.

"What? I mean….. We are getting out of here. I just, I just don't think it's anytime soon that's all." Jett stuttered. "I'm just saying I bet there's a way out through the tunnels." Jett stated as they continue walking.

"I guess, I was counting on Jonathan finding it by now." Chaz said.

"He will. You guys did find that radio. So it's not like we're not trying."

"I know. I-I wanna go home already. And the fact I'm almost getting used to being here….. I don't know if I should be worried about starting to feel that way." Chaz said.

"I know how you feel. We all wanna go home. And I'm sure some of the others are feeling the same as you; about almost getting used to being here." Jett says.

"Daddy!" A tiny voice shouted that seemed to be inflating two outstretched short, skinny arms. The boy's smile is turning into a look of concern and confusion. He saw the bruises on his father's face. Travis wanted to reassure his son that there is nothing wrong; despite the bruises on his face. Travis turned on his side and extended his arms to meet up with Hazelton's. Hazelton was running so fast he almost couldn't stop himself without his father's help. Travis pulled his son in making the hug magically fall in place.

"Whoo buddy, slow down." Travis said with a joyful smile. Travis was also ignoring the stabbing pain in his head, as he pretended that nothing hurt.

"Daddy?.... What happened to you face?" Hazelton asked.

"Oh, Jonathan and I were working in the barn, and the ladder came out from underneath us and the beam we were trying to put up fell on our heads; that's why Jonathan has the same bruises." Travis explained with a satisfied feeling of a good cover up.

"Wow! I-I hope you'll be ok." Hazelton wished looking at his father with that puppy-dog look only kids can do. Travis flashed another ear to ear smile.

"We'll be fine. I don't want you worry anymore then you already have; and that's an order, ok?"

"Yes sir." Hazelton replied trying to return the same joyful grin. Travis gave his son a kiss on the cheek sealing the deal that everything was truly ok and not to worry.

Hazelton heard Kasey outside the door with Star. They were about to run out into the court yard. He ran after them, and called for them to wait-up.

Terry sat by Travis's bed side. She put a soft towel on the side of his head to trying to cushion the bruise. He winced jerking his head away.

"Sorry baby." Terry said slightly stroking his forehead. "Did the shower make you feel better?"

"Yeah, I'm so tired. I think I'm going to skip dinner tonight, not really hungry." Travis Stated.

"Get some rest. You need it. Looks like Jonathans going to skip also." Terry said tilting her head in Jonathan's direction. Travis turns his head to catch a glimpse of Jonathan who is passed out. "Get some rest Hun; I'll save you some dinner." She promised, while leaning over to giving him a kiss on the forehead.

"Thanks baby" he smiled. Terry looked back before she exited the room and saw Travis fast asleep.

Jonathan heard what sounded like a small voice of a little girl off in the distance. The voice sounded like it's coming out of a tin can. He had to tilt his head sideways to here where the voice was coming from. He was pinned underneath something, but he wasn't trapped. Looking through a blurry haze; he recognized a pair of sneakers that belong to Sylvia.

"Jonathan." Sylvia called out. He started to shimmy and wiggle out from the object he's underneath. Jonathan thought he was underneath some kind of vehicle. He tried call out to answer her, but he couldn't hear himself talk.

"Sylvia." Jonathan strained to mumble. Travis almost awakens; but quickly dozed off again. Jonathan was still trying to wrestle his way out from underneath the vehicle when an upside-down head popped into view. The head was attached to two ponytails that hang down and rest on the ground.

"He knows the way out through the tunnels!" That was Sylvia! Jonathan realized. Star thought she heard Jonathan talking in his sleep.

"You kids go on ahead, I'll catch up with you." Star instructed the children.

"Is that Jonathan?" Hazelton asked.

"I think so; I'm going to check it out." Star said.

She walked into the room and saw Jonathan slightly rocking his head back and forth. He was mumbling what sounds like a girl's name. She knelt down by his bedside. A second later he mumbles the name *Sylvia.* Star is grabbed his arm and shook him lightly.

"Jonathan, Jonathan" He managed wiggle out from underneath the vehicle. He sat up in a cold sweat at the same time gasps for air. At first he didn't know where he was; and takes a second to look around the room. He was relieved to see Star sitting there. Jonathan was concerned if anyone ells heard him. He took a second look around the room and saw Travis sound asleep.

"Hey you ok?" Star asked. She remained silent for a few moments, letting Jonathan collect himself.

"Yeah." He managed gasp out. "I-I just was just having a dream." He claimed between gasps of air.

"Sounds like a little more than a dream. Care to share?"

"yeah I guess, for some reason I just can't remember what it was, but yet it was so vivid." He pauses for a few seconds. "My sister, I saw my sister, Sylvia." After a few seconds Star remembers she promised to catch up with the children. Putting a hand on his knee, she informed him she has to tend to the children and asked if they could talk later.

"Sure I'd like that. We'll meet up after dinner. I may not go, you understand." She agreed and rises to her feet. She bent over and gave him a peck on the forehead. Jonathan laid back down. He was awestruck by the dream he just had. The fading sound of Star's voice cradled to him back slight doze, but not asleep.

"Hey I thought you guys were going outside, not bothering Mr. Jimmy." Jimmy was in the kitchen. He sat on the floor under a sink. He was sounded by pieces of pipe that are bent in funny shapes. There are only two wrenches he was using, although all the pieces on the floor made it look like there should be more. The floor was wet, but not flooded. His shirt was half soaked.

Star read the look on Mr. Jimmy's face. The look resembled someone who was not working very hard, but has a lot to get done. The kids aren't being any trouble. They were just holding Mr. Jimmy up from finishing the project he had started. Mr. Jimmy was not completely annoyed because it was a nice break to talk with the children and the hard part was already done. All he has to do now was put everything back together. The children asked him a few easy questions. *What is that? What does that do? Are those the only tools you need?*

"Let's go kids, the outdoors a-waits us." Star commanded.

"Ok. Star you promised to show us how to ride bare back." Kasey reminded her.

"Yeah!" Hazelton second.

"Alright. Let's get out there and find the riding equipment. Sorry to bother you Mr. Jimmy."

"That's ok." Star and the children headed for the front door when

Jimmy gently grabs Star by the arm. "How are the runaways doing?" Jimmy asked

"They seem ok considering what they went through. Jonathan and Travis are resting. I thought I saw and heard Flo talking to Stephanie."

"Any of them seem badly hurt?" Mr. Jimmy asked.

"Yeah, Jonathan Travis and Stephanie got a little bruised up. Terry seemed ok." Jimmy took a deep breath and rolled his eyes. He grabbed a wrench and one of the pipes that looked like the letter *J*; laid on his back not minding that he was lying in a puddle of water.

"I'll have a talk with them later." He remarked clanking the wrench on the pipe "Thanks"

"Ok" She replied running off to catch up with the children who may or may not have followed through with the instructions they were given only a moment ago.

Dinner is in full swing. Jonathan, Stephanie and Travis decided to sit this one out. They just didn't feel like playing twenty questions. Jonathan decided to enter into where Stephanie was laying down.

"Hey, How ya feeling?" He asked gently as he stroked her forehead. At first the look on her face was sad. She looked up into his eyes. He had a slight smile on his face that says *everything is going to be ok*. The sight of his face made her slightly smile, and rotated her torso in his direction.

"Not as bad as I thought I would feel. Flo actually helped me out." Jonathan was taken by this and leaned back in a jerky motion.

"Oh really, how?"

"We had a like a big sister talk. I was really surprised she could have feelings like that. I thought she wouldn't care at all, but she actually talked to me like a big sister would. It was really neat. Too bad she doesn't act that way all the time." Stephanie said.

"Yeah, must be a hidden talent." Stephanie and Jonathan just laughed for a few moments. "So she made you feel better?" Jonathan questioned.

"Oh yeah, for some reason I feel strange admitting it." Jonathan gave a head-tilt and a shrug.

"Ok, as long as you feel better that all that matters." Jonathan stated.

"You guys skipped dinner too I see." Said a familiar voice. The two looked over and saw Travis was standing there. His hair is a mess, and his eyes are still half closed. He wanted to stay awake and was fighting tiredness.

"Yeah, I think it's best for us to stay away for a bit and collect our thoughts. I guess Terry didn't mind going to dinner?" Jonathan asked.

"No, she loves the attention. She'll smooth things over. There is a small chance people may not ask you guys anything at all, but don't hold me to it." Travis explained with full confidence. "Jonathan, what were you mumbling in your sleep? I thought I heard you say something." For a second Jonathan just sat there and thought. He knew what Travis was talking about, and was trying to recall the dream he just had.

"Oh man I had this vivid dream and my missing sister Sylvia was in it." Jonathan said.

"She was? What was it? What happened?" Travis asked. Stephanie sat up to attention.

"I must have been working on a car of some kind. It seemed like I was lying underneath something; anyway, her head popped into view with her ponytails hanging down resting on the ground. I thought I was flashing back to the accident, the first time I saw you." Jonathan explained looking at Stephanie.

"Then what happened! Did she say anything?" Stephanie asked

"I'm getting to that. She said, he knows the out through the tunnels." They all just sat there in a moment in silence.

"Are you sure it was her, and not me you saw?" Stephanie questioned.

"No, it was Sylvia. There's no mistaken it. It was just dream I guess." Jonathan said snapping out of it.

"Yeah but it must have meant something. Why ells would she mention the tunnels?" Stephanie pondered.

"Yeah, that is odd." Travis remarked.

"Like I said, it was just a dream." Jonathan said.

Travis, Jonathan and Stephanie hesitated for a while before making a *guest appearance*. They wanted to wait for the right time to *reintroduce* themselves to everybody. They wanted just *blend-in* rather than being the center of attention. They figure the campfire would be a good time to join the rest. It would be dark, other people would be talking about their day, and they wouldn't be center of attention. They were hoping they could tell their story to everyone at the same time; and not explaining it over and over again.

The three walked into the main hall that led to the kitchen and the dining room. People were still in the kitchen doing last minute clean up. There were three plates of food left aside on the dinner table. Kasey was the first person they saw. Her eyes widened with joy.

"We saved you some dinner." She said with a joyful nod.

"Aww. Thanks Hun." Jonathan said patting Kasey on the head.

"Are you guys joining us at the campfire?"

"Yes Kasey, as soon as we're done eating and help finish cleaning up." Jonathan said.

*Crackle, pop,* echoed from the wood in the fire. Travis sat next to Terry, Stephanie sat next to Flo. They both gave each other a look that finalized their sister-hood they shared earlier that day. Jonathan went to sit down, but was asked to get a bottle of spirits before he could do so.

"Sure Jimmy, be right back." Jonathan was actually happy to do so. Jonathan returned, handed the bottle to Jimmy and took a seat between Star and Stephanie.

"Thanks Jonathan. You're always so helpful." Jimmy said.

"I try Jimmy." Jonathan said with pride in his voice.

"We sure are going to miss you all." Jimmy said with a smile in his eyes.

"Congratulations! You guys found a way to make it home?" Star asked. Jonathan looked at Stephanie; her eyes widened, accompanied with a mouth open smile. Kasey's face lit up and begins to chant.

"I'm going home, I'm going home" said a tiny voice a few seats away. Jonathan was in shock. He didn't know what to think. And he certainly had no idea what Jimmy was talking about. All he could do was remain speechless. Jonathan looked at Stephanie again as if to say *I have no idea what Jimmy is talking about.*

"What are you talking about Jimmy? You know something I don't?" Jonathan said trying to hold a smile.

"You can't stay here forever, right?" Again; a short pause from Jonathan.

"True." This time Jonathan had a straight face, except for some a hint of confusion.

"Well then you all will be leaving soon." Jimmy said. Jonathan once again took a glance at Stephanie. She now had the look of confusion. Jonathan almost couldn't believe what he was hearing. He took a quick look around, at the other commune people. They all have straight faces. Jonathan had strong hunch this had something to do with the tunnels, and the fact Jonathan confronted Groady may have woken a sleeping beast. Jonathan returned his gaze on Jimmy.

"I guess, do you have a radio I can use to call for help?" Jonathan locked eyes with Jimmy. They both knew there's a radio. Jonathan and Chaz saw it and almost got it to work.

"I have a radio, but it doesn't work." Jimmy fired back.

"Mind if I take a look at it and try to get it to work?" Jonathan inquired; their eyes still locked on each other.

"There are parts that have to be replaced and there is no way to get them, not way out here." Jimmy said, again with the smiling eyes this time with a raised eyebrow. A brief silence took over the conversation. A few *crackles* and a loud *pop* shattered the silence. Jonathan's eyes squinted, powered by his charming smile. He didn't ask how soon was soon. Jonathan didn't want to talk about it. Not now, not there. That was more of a private conversation, if that was possible. *It's time to end this conversation for now, before one of us looses our cool.* Jonathan thought.

"Ok, I'll work on that. Thanks for the heads-up." Jonathan stated holding his composure.

Jonathan felt the warm touch of her soft hand, not realizing who it is. A second later Stephanie came into view. Still half asleep, he managed to take part in a conversation he knew was coming, considering all the wine the consumed.

"Hey" he mumbled, trying to hold a gazing at Stephanie.

"I can't sleep. Are we getting kicked out of here? How are we supposed leave?" Stephanie whispered. All this rambling woke Jonathan even more. He leaned up one elbow. "Doesn't he think we're trying? I don't get it." Worry and doubt took over her mind and body. Jonathan grabbed her hand gently, opened his eyes wide enough to look into hers.

"Relax, I have a plan. I was thinking of it when we were in the tunnels. You remember that dream I had? The one with my sister?"

"Yeah" she whispers.

"In the dream, it seemed like my sister was trying to tell me something. She said, *He knows the way out through the tunnels.* I think that's a sign of something" Jonathan said.

"Do you think she was talking about Groady?"

"I don't know. It sure sounded like it. Look I know you're worried. I just don't have the answers right now. Jimmy sprang that up on me just tonight. I had no idea that was coming. We'll talk in the morning, ok?" The conversation didn't settle Stephanie's worry any, but she knew Jonathan was tired.

"Ya, sure, night." Stephanie replied.

Jett couldn't help but to overhear Jonathan and Stephanie's conversation. This was great chance to tell Jonathan how he felt about going back into the tunnels. Jett waited for Stephanie to leave.

"Jonathan, Jonathan" Jett said and gave his shoulder a slight nudge. There was no response; just a soft snoring buzz. Jett tip-toed back bed and figures he'll try again tomorrow morning.

# CHAPTER 28

## Making Plans to Leave

Jett couldn't wait to talk to Jonathan. As soon as people started waking up He sprang out of bed and ran over to Jonathan, not realizing he may be hung over. Jonathan is still in his clothes from the night before.

"Jonathan! You awake?" Jett asked while shaking Jonathan's arm vigorously. Jonathan slowly rocked his head to one side and moaned softly at first. After a short time he woke up to Jett's face full of life.

"Jett?" a half sleeping, groggy Jonathan squinted.

"Jonathan, you awake?" Jonathan put a hand on his head, like that's going to suppress any pounding.

"Uuuh, somewhat. What is it?" Jonathan asked in a quiet tone; still holding his head.

"I heard you and Stephanie talking last night; about us having to leave? And the dream you had about your sister and how she said *he knows the out through the tunnels.* "Jett raddled off.

"And? What about it?" Jonathan mumbled.

"W-Well I was almost thinking the same thing. I mean, I think there's a way out through the tunnels also." Jonathan's eyes widened enough to be able to look at Jett without squinting. Jett reads this and moves back a little thinking Jonathan was going to spring up.

"I need coffee. I understand what you're saying. I just need some coffee and about two hours to wake up." Jonathan pleaded

"Two hours? Why so long?"

"Jett, Please!" Jonathan pleaded once again. Jonathan made his way to the main dining hall. A dark, strong cup of coffee was playing in head, cheering him on to that first sip. Finally, coffee! He managed to have two uninterrupted cups. Now he was almost ready to take on the day. After last night's *pot stirring,* he had a lot of explaining and planning to do.

"Jonathan, Jonathan!" Kasey called out running up to him. "When are we leaving? I'm all packed. I can't wait!" She bellowed. *I hate Jimmy for this; he's going to get his.* Jonathan thought to himself. He reached out and put a gentle hand on her shoulder; mainly to stop her from bouncing around.

"Kasey, calm down we're not leaving today. Jimmy shouldn't have said anything." Kasey's facial expression went from extremely happy, to now coming to a halt; somewhere between, *sad and wanting to cry.*

"So when are we going hommme?" Kasey wined. Jonathan knew the stretched out *m- sound,* was the possible start of a melt- down. It's time for some reassuring eye to eye contact; even at the risk of head-splitting head rush on the way up. Jonathan restored hope in Kasey that they will be going home, just not now.

A moment later, he caught up with Jett. Jonathan tried to explain to Jett what Jimmy had said at the campfire last night. Jonathan also explained about radio he and Chaz found, and how it was gone now. He also explained how Jimmy didn't give him any expected timeframe that they should be *rescued* by.

Jett told Jonathan about how Arbin had the key to the room where the radios was; that's how they got the bow and arrow. They also discuss the dream Jonathan had and the message his sister could have been telling him. Jett mentioned the fact that Chaz was totally against the idea of going back in the tunnels.

"I think once Chaz hears the whole story he'll understand better." Jonathan said. "Did you tell Arbin this?"

"No, he wasn't around when me and Chaz were talking about it."

"Ok, do me a favor; don't talk about this to anyone. I don't want rumors to spread more so then they may have already. I have to talk to Jimmy and find out why he's saying all this." Jonathan said. Jett nods in agreement.

On the way back to his sleeping quarters to change his clothes; Jonathan looked in the girl's room. He caught a glimpse of Stephanie's face as he approached the doorway. She looked very unhappy, even heartbroken. He kept walking past, now he got a full view of inside the room. Flo was at the other end of the conversation. *That explains the sad look.* Jonathan thought to himself. He continued on his way to get some-what cleaned up. Although, he felt bad for Stephanie he didn't have time for girl drama.

"Jonathan agrees with me that we should go back down in the tunnels and find a way out of here." Jett said.

"He didn't say that! You're-you're lying!" Chaz managed to stutter.

"Am not! Come on let's go ask him now!" Jett protested. Chaz really felt it was a great idea, but for some reason he was in denial. When they went down in the tunnels he was scared, scared to death. After they all resurfaced on to the basement floor; it was then he started to feel different. This is the second time Jett was toying with the thought of returning to the tunnels. Now there's an added energy powering this runaway brainstorm, Jonathan. Knowing this, made Chaz seal the deal.

"We'll need Arbin to get the key for us. I think it would be good idea to take the bow and arrow with us." Chaz said.

"Bout time you put your other foot in the railcar and got on board." Jett said thinking he was funny. Chaz turned and gave him a funny look.

"Shut up. That doesn't even make sense." Chaz laughed.

"Does so."

"OK, we'll ask Jonathan." Chaz suggested still looking at Jett and shaking his head. The two boys promised not to mention the idea to anyone ells. Although they may have to tell Arbin, they do have to get the key after all. Jett and Chaz started heading over to the barn to find Arbn.

"Look, Stephanie I don't know what to tell you. I don't know why Jimmy would say that." Flo said.

"Is he really just going to through us out like that? What's he going to do, banish us all to the tunnels like he did Groady?" Flo just looked up at the sky and then back into Stephanie's eyes.

"Steph, calm down I'm sure he's not going to banish you all to the tunnels. Well, maybe just Jonathan." Flo joked.

"What!"

"I'm kidding. Chill out girl. Listen, Jimmy knows you kids need to get back home soon. He's just scaring Jonathan into hurrying up." Flo said.

"I don't get it. What happened to the radio that was working, but now is mysteriously missing? I mean, what ells are we supposed to do?" Stephanie started to tear up.

"I don't know. How did you guys find your way here?" Flo asks. Stephanie sniffled.

"I climbed the tallest tree closed to us and that's how I spotted this place." Flo tossed her hands waist high with her palms facing up.

"Can't you just do the same and look for a different place?" Flo suggested.

"This is the middle of nowhere. I tried that, and almost killed myself. Didn't you hear about that?" Stephanie said.

Flo rested her hand on Stephanie's shoulder, tilted her head slightly and raises here eye brows

"Look, I'll talk to Jimmy and See what the deal is, but I can't promise anything, ok?" Stephanie doubted Flo could do anything to help. The one thing Stephanie wanted to know was; was Flo really sincere when they were having their *girl-talk.*

"Flo, did you mean all that stuff you said before? Ya know, when I was having that nightmare and you calm me down." Stephanie asked.

"No, you'll be gone soon and this is just my nightmare." Flo seemed all too happy to say grinning. She topped off her comment with a set of blinking eyes. That was probably the meanest, cruelest thing anyone could say to a person in their time of need. This made Stephanie burst out in laughter; and then she embraced Flo in *big sister* hug. Flo's eyes open wide in disgust; as if she was being hugged by a sweaty fat guy or a stinky grandma. Stephanie knew Flo hated mushy times like this, and she laughed even more.

"Last minute good buys?" The perfect ice-breaker he though. The two girls looked up and saw Jimmy standing there. He had a half faded smile and a commanding look in his eyes. Stephanie didn't want to stick around to hear what Jimmy had to say, or answer any questions he may have. Before he has a chance to say anything ells, she slinked between him and the half of the doorway he was blocking.

"Gotta run, thanks Flo." She chimed, throwing back a quick glance and waggling her fingers as she used her hand to brace herself making a sharp turn around the doorway. Flo didn't bother to answer back, nor did Stephanie wait to hear for one.

"What was all that?" Jimmy asked raising one eyebrow.

"Nothing, just some girl-talk. So why all of a sudden ya know, wanting them to leave? I know there're not welcome to stay forever. I was just wondering the sudden hurry for them to leave." Jimmy stepped all the way into the room, and closed the door. Flo mentally got herself ready for a stern explanation; but hopefully not a long one.

"I'm afraid they're causing a lot of trouble. That little stunt they pulled woke a sleeping beast; a beast I prayed would never haunt us again. And now I have to clean up the mess... again!" Flo took a deep breath and exhaled in concern. She was remembering the trouble Groady caused. It had been so peaceful with Groady locked in tunnels and forgotten about. He was now awake, and there was new flesh and blood prowling about. This new flesh and blood he had a taste of, and is going to want more. Flo was now beginning to understand this.

"Did you give Jonathan and his people permission to go in the tunnels?" Flo asked. *His people* she reflected. Stephanie is part of *his people;* the girl that was just here a moment ago. The girl that looked up to Flo as a big sister is now one of *his people*, a stranger once again.

"I had no choice in the matter. They went in there without me saying anything. By the time I found out what they did, it was too late. That girl Stephanie was missing. I knew Jonathan wasn't going to just leave her there. Not only that, Travis got caught up in their mess. Have you seen what Groady did to his face?"

"Yeah I saw." Flo winced holding the facial expression trying to imagine Groady himself and the rage he possessed. Jimmy read this expression and finalized his point of view.

"Now you see why it's best that they just leave? Don't get me wrong Flo, I feel bad for the kids, but I have you all to worry about."

"So what do we do about this?" Flo asked.

"I don't know yet. I need your help; can you go around to all the trapdoors and make sure they are bolted down? I don't need any surprises. Once I figure out what to do I'll let you know." Jimmy knew all the trapdoors were bolted down. He just wanted to keep Flo busy for a while; and keep her mind occupied. She can be a handful if she had nothing to do. "Oh, and let me know when you're done, no hurry." He said disappearing through the door into the hallway.

The coffee was harsh and bitter tasting; at the same time that cup of coffee was Jonathan's best friend. Every sip stretched his imaginary green energy level bar. Unlike in video games; this bar has no max limit. At that moment, all he wanted was more coffee.

"Hey sleepyhead." Jonathan looked up and wasn't surprised to see Jimmy standing there. He just wasn't ready for the unpleasant conversation he about to have. *Let's get this over with.* Jonathan thought.

"Morning sunshine." Jonathan replied trying to form some kind of smile, but failing at it. Jimmy just glared at Jonathan blankly; as if invisible laser beams were shooting from his eyes and burning a hole right through Jonathan. "Look, I know you want us out of here. Just tell how long we have; today, tomorrow, in a week?" Jimmy continued to hold his gaze on Jonathan for a few seconds. This was getting Jonathan really angry.

"I'll give you two weeks. I think we've been generous enough. And I'm sure the children want to get back home to their moms, dads, siblings, maybe pets they miss. I won't even mention the problems you stirred up by finding your way down in the tunnels and the danger you put my people in. Any ideas how I'm going to fix that?" Jimmy said holding back anger.

"Well, now that you mentioned it." Jonathan sarcastically emphasized the word *mention.* "If he's that much trouble, why don't you just kill him and be done with it?" Jonathan asked that out of tongue and cheek.

"You know that's not how I do things." Jimmy said looking at Jonathan sternly. Jonathan was getting tired of this conversation. Besides, he had to get started on finding a way to get himself and fifteen children back home from the middle of nowhere.

"I get it. Look going to do my best to make sure we're gone in two weeks." By now Jonathan was already exhausted and it was only morning. For a few seconds they both stare at each other in silence.

"Hey Jonathan, I….." Star stops dead in her tracks with her mouth hanging open. She didn't realize Jimmy was in there. She put her hand over her mouth. "Oh!" They both look at Star, but in different mindsets. Star could read Jimmy's thoughts, and gave him a *puppy dog* look that said *I'm sorry to bother you.* Jonathan looked at her with relief in his eyes. Jimmy explained to Star she wasn't interrupting anything, gave her a friendly grin and exited the room. Jonathan was staring at the cup in her hand hoping it's a cup of coffee for him. Star relaxed her tense gaze.

"I figured you could use some coffee." An opened mouth smile take over his face. A slight tremble escapes both hands while reaching for it. The steam looked so good. He felt the warmth of the coffee a split second before he can wrap his hands around cup. That imaginary green energy bar stretched longer again, even more so when he takes a sip. Jonathan let out a sigh of relief and looked up at her thankfully. "You're welcome." She replied smiling. She could tell he was thinking, *thank you.*

"How much of the conversation did hear?" Jonathan asked.

"Almost all of it. So, what's going on? He seemed pretty peeved." Star said.

"Well, Jimmy claims I caused a lot of trouble. The main thing he was complaining about was us going down in the tunnel and waking Groady up. And I guess me and the other children just being here in general. He said I have two weeks for me and the rest of the children to find a way out." Jonathan said slightly shaking his head. Star gasps a little. She sat on the bed next to him and put one arm around his shoulders and the other hand on his knee.

"Jonathan, I'm sorry to hear that. Is there anything I can do to help?" She said rubbing his shoulders.

"Thanks, I'm sure there's something you can do; but I can't think of anything right now. I think now I need to find Stephanie." He paused for a few seconds. "After I finish my coffee." She nodded in agreement.

Terry walked out of the main house toward the farm. She has volunteered to help gather food for the afternoon lunch. Up ahead of her, she saw her son Hazelton and Kasey. The two children were walking side by side, with an oval wicker basket between them. The basket is bopping up and down, resembling a row boat on a rippling lake. At times the basket stretches out and stops bopping for a few footsteps. Hazelton and Kasey spring back together and the basket continued bopping up and down once again. This walking pattern goes repeats over and over until they reach what looks like a long straight row of weeds.

"Hey kids, you helping out?" Terry asked as she gently rubbed her son on the head. The kids squint against the sunlight as they looked up at Terry. Terry squatted down to meet the kids eye to eye. She wanted to spare them from looking into the sun. Hazelton looked at his mom with humble eyes and claimed he knew what veggies were ready to pick and he would show Kasey.

"I know which ones to pick mommy." The little boy bent down and popped up holding a carrot that was just right. He dropped it into the basket. "I'm going to show Kasey." Kasey didn't say anything. She just looked down at the ground. The expression on her face was completely blank and emotionless.

"Kasey, what's wrong dear?" At first Kasey didn't say anything. Terry rested a hand on Kasey's shoulder. Kasey looked at her with sad puppy dog eyes. Terry tilted her head to the side and gave Kasey a slight smile. Kasey looked down at the ground again.

"Why is Kasey so sad mommy?" Hazelton asked. "Kasey? What's wrong?" Hazelton continued. Terry has an idea, but she's not totally sure. Maybe Kasey will feel like talking once they get boarded from picking veggies. Terry thought to herself.

"Come on kids, we better get picking. We have a lot to get. You kids start here; Hazelton will you show Kasey what to look for so she can pick ones that are ready." Hazelton staggered off on the unlevel ground to the start of the row, almost dragging Kasey with him. Terry thought for a second and figured she'll talk to Kasey later. She knelt down and began to pluck oval shaped red peppers.

"Jonathan was supposed to find our way back home." Kasey said. Without turning to look at her, Hazelton questioned what she just said. "Jonathan was supposed to find our way back home through the tunnels." Not knowing what Kasey is talking about, Hazelton spouts off any comment hoping to guess it right.

"Maybe he just got lost." Hazelton said. Terry overheard the word *tunnel* and looked back at the children. She didn't want Hazelton knowing anything about the forbidden tunnels. She got to her feet and made her way over to the children.

"Kids?" Terry called out. "How ya making out?" Before Hazelton or Kasey has time to answer, she asked another question. "Hazelton, are you showing Kasey what to look for?"

"See mom? Look what we picked. I Showed Kasey what to look for; to know if they are ready to be picked."

"Good job dear. Kasey, are you getting the hang of it?" Terry asked.

"Yeah, I think so." Kasey let her voice trail off in a soft tone.

"Kasey come over here, I just wanna show you one thing real quick. Only take a sec. ok?" Terry said nervously. Kasey followed Terry about fifty feet away from Hazelton; she doesn't want him to hear what they were talking about. "Kasey dear, what did you say about Jonathan and the tunnels?" She asked trying to hold a soft grin.

"Jonathan was supposed to find our way back home through the tunnels.... At least that's what Mr. Jimmy said." Terry tilted her head and looked off into space for a second as if in thought and then looked in Kasey's eyes.

"What do you mean?" Terry asked in surprise.

"Mr. Jimmy, he told Jonathan a man named Groady knew a way out of here through the tunnels. Why didn't Jonathan just do what Mr. Jimmy said?" Kasey asked looking at Terry with sad eyes. Terry softly took Kasey by the hand.

"Kasey, I have a secret to tell you, but you can't tell anyone ok?" Kasey's eyes brighten a little and she nodded. "I was down in the tunnels with Jonathan at the time. In fact, it wasn't just me and Jonathan; Mr. Travis, Jett, Chaz, and Stephanie were there as well." Now Kasey had the same head-tilting motion.

"Then, what happened? Why are we still here?" Kasey asked.

"There was a little problem down there. You see, Groady is a bad man who stopped Jonathan and Stephanie from trying to find the way out." Terry leaned in close to Kasey softened her tone. "That's why Jonathan and Mr. Travis have burses on their faces." Kasey's face pinches up in confusion.

"They got beat up?" Kasey asked. Terry nodded with a sad expression.

"I'm afraid so dear." Kasey slowly looked down at the ground. "Hey, don't worry; they're big boys they'll be ok. Jonathan is going to try again real soon. He's planning everything now." Terry said.

"I wish there was something I could do something to help." Kasey said still looking down. Terry gently placed a hand under Kasey's chin and lifts her head.

"I think there is." Kasey's eyes widen. "I know it would be a great help to Jonathan if we didn't ask him when he was going back down in the tunnels. He needs time to think. He understands you're in a hurry to get home, he is also." Kasey took a deep breath.

"Ok, I guess so." Her tiny voice agreed. Terry thanked Kasey for understanding and leaned in and gave her a hug.

"Hey!" Shouted Hazelton. Terry and Kasey looked at each other and then quickly turned around and see Hazelton dragging the basket that was now almost full of carrots, peppers, cucumbers, and a few potatoes. Terry sprang to her feet.

"Sorry dear, I was just showing Kasey different veggies and how they look when they're ready to be picked. Wow, look at all the stuff you gathered." Terry said squatting down to meet Hazelton eye to eye.

"Yeah! Look Kasey, see what I gathered?" Before Kasey could answer, Hazelton shout out another question. "Do you think we have enough?"

"Me and Kasey saw some peppers and stuff that's ready to be picked; and then we should have enough. Can you kids carry the basket over here?" Terry said.

"Ok mom. Kasey, help me with this, here I'll get take the heavy end."

"Ok Hazelton" Kasey's tiny voice squeaked. When the basket was full, the kids picked up the basket and walked back to the main house. Once again the basket looked like a row boat bopping up and down on a wavy lake.

# CHAPTER 29

## Missing Again?

"I don't think that's such a good idea. I get the feeling we're in enough trouble. Jimmy doesn't seem happy." Arbin said; his voice just a little louder than the milk that is squirting into the bucket. Still looking down, Arbin adds "Besides, I'm not risking being shunned for you two." Jett and Chaz look at each other. Chaz's face brightened. Jett's eyes slightly squinted in question.

"Look Arbin, You can hold the key the whole time. All you have to is get us in room, I'll get the bow and arrow. You lock the door, and your job is done. I'll hide it in the basement and it'll be there if / when I need it." Jett explains. Arbin let out a stressful sigh. Jett and Chaz look at each other in pop-fly suspense.

"I guess." Chaz and Jett's shoulders settle down in catching relief. "But! We do it when I think it's safe! Not now!" Arbin commanded.

"OK deal!" Chaz agreed. Assuming Jett wouldn't mind, Chaz volunteered them to help Arbin in the barn, as a *thank you*. "Hey what do need us to do in here?" Arbin has Just the chore for them.

"You guys can clean the manure out of the stalls." Arbin suggested turning around looking back at them.

Walking across the field away from the all the houses, is leaving behind an invisible trail of worry. The beam of heated ray rinsed down any leftover doubt. The negative energies soaked into the ground, disappearing hopefully for a very long time. It felt peaceful to get away from everyone and all the busy stuff going on. The bright sunlight made it difficult to scan the tree line. She remembered her last attempted at this, and how she almost killed herself. That really wasn't going to stop her, just make her more careful.

It's the same issue that came up over and over; the first branch is unreachable. This problem limited her choices. *If I can reach way up there, the rest is easy* she pondered. *That's it!* she suddenly had an idea. She flashed back to when the tree guys her dad hired one time used a thick strap and spikes on their shoes. They clawed their up the tree and used the strap that was wrapped around them and the tree itself. It was a long shot, but it may be worth a try. She would have to scrounge around for the stuff that would be needed. She was hoping Jonathan will help her with that.

She began brainstorming where she might have seen such items around. After a few seconds the barn came to mind; all the horse riding gear; the straps and buckles. The sun was beating down on her and she decided to find a shady place to sit a while. She was enjoying the calm quietness. It's so calm and peaceful; her eyes started to get heavy. *Just a fifteen minute nap* She thought to herself.

The old wooden door creaked open with ease. *I caught ya!* Jonathan thought to himself as all three boys looked up through the mist of guilt they didn't realize they are giving off. Jonathan couldn't help an, *ah-ha* moment he was having. Without any pleasantry greeting, Jonathan jumped right into it.

"Alright, spill it." Once the boys stopped looking at each other, their expressions collectively tried to land on *what are you talking about?* Jonathan wasn't falling for it. "What are you doing, have done, or are about to do?" he demanded. A brief silence took over the inside of the barn. Jett took the bull by the horns and explained to Jonathan what the plan is.

"We were going to get the bow and arrow so we can take it with us back down in the tunnels." Jett explained in a telling voice vs an asking voice; hoping Jonathan will just blend right in.

"Wait! Who is doing what?" Jonathan asked. Jett and Chaz knew Jonathan wasn't as strict as Jimmy or someone from the commune would be. Jett threw his hands up in a *let me explain* sign.

"Arbin was going to see if he could get the key to the room in the guest house. Me and Chaz were going to get the bow and arrow and hide it in the basement. Arbin is going to lock the room and return the key before anyone could find out anything is missing." Jonathan thought for a second.

"When was this going to happen?"

"Whenever Arbin felt it was the right time." Jonathan looked at each of the boys; who half nodded probably afraid to give a full nod.

"Ok, great. Let me know when that's done." The three boys looked at each other in surprising happiness.

"Ok! Sure!" Jett promised.

"By the way has anyone seen Stephanie? I've been looking for her." Jonathan asked. The boys shook their heads claiming not to have seen her. Jonathan left the barn leaving the boys in their emotional victory.

"Your little friend seemed to have gone astray again." Flo said as only Flo can. The tight lipped smile is an invite for her and Jonathan to have a sarcastic battle of the wits. But he honestly had no time to goof around as much as he'd love to put her in her place.

"I know, have you seen her at all today?" Jonathan asked with no sarcastic tone. Flo was taken back by his reaction. She didn't know what to say. Her face almost went blank.

"Yeah, I saw her this morning and then Jimmy came by and then she left." She replied still puzzled by the fact he was serious.

"Did you talk to her? What did she say?"

"It was just some girl talk. I told her not to worry about what Jimmy had said about wanting you guys to leave. I was trying to calm her down." Flo explained.

"Was she that upset? What she crying?" Jonathan asked.

"What do you mean was she that upset?" Flo said squinting at Jonathan. "I'm not comforting to talk to?" This remark left Jonathan speechless. There's so much to say he didn't know what to say.

"Sure you are Flo. I'm just trying to find Stephanie, that's all." Flo didn't say anything and turns to walk away, then stopped and spun back around; catching Jonathan by surprise.

"Oh there is one thing we did discus, she told me how she found this place, about how she climbed a tree. I suggested maybe she should do the same thing again." Jonathan's face brightened a little. Now he may have some idea where she may be.

"That actually makes sense, thanks." Jonathan said sincerely, and turned around to finish washing the pile of dishes that was growing bigger. Jonathan was brainstorming on how to begin to look for Stephanie as he was washing dishes. He had an idea that will require the help of Jett and Chaz. *Man, didn't this kid learn the first time about running off by herself?* He thought.

Jonathan spotted Jett gathering wood for the evening's campfire. Jett had a nervous look on his face, which gave Jonathan a concerning feeling. They must be up to something Jonathan suspected.

"Hey, what's up?" Jett spun around so fast, the toe of one foot caught the heel of the other. He did some weird two-step trot and regained his footing. Jonathan was impressed Jett didn't drop any of the wood he was carrying "You ok? What's wrong?" Jonathan asked trying not to laugh at him.

"I'm fine." Jett blurted out. Jonathan didn't say anything, but just looked at him visually prying him for more info. "We're going to get the bow and arrow later tonight when everyone is at the campfire." Now Jonathan understood why Jett is acting so funny.

"Do you know what time? I need you and Chaz to help me." Jonathan asked.

"Not sure, I'll tell them I can't do it tonight? What do we have to do?" Jett almost had relief in his voice. Jonathan could tell something ells was going on, but he has no time for playing guessing games.

"What's going on Jett? Are they bulling you into doing something you don't want to do? Just tell me." Jonathan said.

"No, no. I'm just, not sure how we're going to do this." Jett admitted as he uncurled his arms and let the wood fall to the ground with wind chime clunks. Jett looked up and found Jonathan still holding his gaze.

"Are you bullying Arbin into doing something he doesn't want to do?" Jett's face pinched in disbelief.

"No." Again Jett did that *let me explain* hand motion; which was starting to become his signature expression. "I'm just not sure we're doing it right. None of us really planned it out. Arbin just said we'll do it tonight." Jonathan just rolled his eyes.

"Do you want me to go with you?" Jonathan finally asked. "It's really not that big of a deal. It shouldn't take more than five minutes. I need you and Chaz to help me find Stephanie, she missing … again." Jonathan stated shaking his head. Hearing about Stephanie missing again made Jett snap back into reality.

"What happened?"

"I don't know. Are you done here or do you need more wood?"

"Just two or three more handfuls." Jett said excitedly. Jonathan gave him a hand to hurry him up.

Jonathan and Jett made their way over to meet up with Arbin and Chaz. Jonathan found out those two are just as a nervous wreck as Jett is. *Another babysitting stunt* Jonathan thought. The boys seemed to become more relaxed now that Jonathan was there. They know he'll make sure they don't mess this up. All four of them discussed how they're going to pull this one off. The discussion was Jonathan telling them how they would go about getting the bow and arrow.

"Do you have the key Arbin?" Jonathan asked.

"Yeah." Arbin pulled they key out of his front pocket and opened his hand in a small cup. He gave them a quick glance of the key, then immediately closed his hand and shoved the key back in his pocket.

"Great! Let's do a walk-through so when the time comes we know exactly where to go and what to do. Come on, let's get to the room and make sure we have the right key. We don't want anything going wrong" Jonathan suggests. Without questioning him they all made their way to the guest house. Jonathan had a casual strut. The boys however were leaving behind a trail of guilt and suspicion, with their heads turning and bobbling around. Jonathan noticed their body language and shouted back a sarcastic comment.

"You guys are going to give yourselves whiplash." Jonathan wasn't sure if Arbin knew what whiplash was, since he has been home schooled his whole life. He may not have been taught what that was. The boys stop bopping around and asked Jonathan what he was talking about. "Never mind" Jonathan sighed shaking his head. They finally reached the locked door in the abandon guest house.

"Now what?" Chaz asked

"Arbin make sure you got the right key and see if it actually works." Jonathan said. Arbin did what Jonathan instructed. As soon as the door unlocked, Jonathan entered the room. He grabbed the bow off the wall and found the arrows. He left the room. The boys followed him. "Arbin lock the door." Again Arbin did as instructed. Jonathan lit the candle and headed down the stairs and to the basement. He placed the bow and arrow behind a pile of junk in the corner of the basement. There's no need to hide the bow and arrows, because all that darkness does most of the hiding. All four of them exit the basement through the basement doors, and into the twilight.

Jonathan closed the doors and looks at the three and said,

"Is that what you guys needed to do?" The boys just stood there in silence and bewilderment; not really knowing what just happened. Jett opened his mouth but nothing came out. Chaz managed to say something as he suddenly realizes what they were just tricked into doing.

"Wait! What? I thought *we* were supposed to do that." Chaz said extending his arm toward Jett and Arbin. Jonathan shrugs.

"Yeah, but you guys were taking too long, making a big deal out of nothing. Now it's done. It's getting dark and I'm running out of time. I need all of your help to find Stephanie. Arbin return the key before anyone notices it's missing." Jonathan said.

# CHAPTER 30

## A Road to Where?

Off in the distance, Star could see Jonathan and the three boys across the field. They appear to be evenly spaced apart about fifty feet between them. They resemble a small search party. Star wondered if they are looking for Stephanie. She decided to walk across the open field toward them. The trees look like black silhouettes against the dark blue sky. It's not quite a full moon and stars are faint in the early night sky. Jonathan noticed Star walking in his direction; she walked faster as she got closer.

"Any luck?" Star asked.

"Na, not yet." Jonathan replied.

"She'll come back soon" Star said trying to reassure. Jonathan couldn't help starting to get angry.

"I really hope she didn't go back in the tunnels again." Jonathan pleaded.

"Do you think she would have?"

"I doubt it, but with her you never know" he said. Star didn't blame Jonathan for getting angry.

She felt a chill on her skin and finally opened her eyes in total darkness. This feeling made her spring to her feet. A second later she felt dizzy and fell back down, but remains awake. She must have given herself a head rush. After a minute or two she finally remembers how she got there. She was supposed take only a fifteen minute nap. She managed to stand up. Turning around in circles, trying to figure out where she is. Something far away caught her eye; it was faint blinking light. *Is that the campfire?* She thought. After a few more minutes she now knew she is deep in the woods. She started to walk in the direction of the light, taking giant steps trying to step over heavy branches. Leaves and twigs crinkle and snap with every step.

Jonathan and Star found themselves ahead of the boys. The brush was getting heavier, the deeper in they go. Jonathan stopped and put his hand out motioning Star to do the same. He thought he heard the crunching of leaves. The sound came from ahead of them. They could only see about thirty feet ahead of them; and that visual gap is rapidly getting smaller.

The two stood frozen, trying to listen for crunching leaves. Jonathan continued walking forward. He was being careful to step on clear ground and not make additional noise. Star tried to do the same, but she was a little noisy at it. This caused Jonathan to stop every few feet to listen for more crunching leaves and crackling twigs.

Her eyes didn't adjust the darkness as much as she thought they would. She stayed focus on the light up ahead; she was hoping it was the campfire. *What ells could it be?* She asked herself. The forest was causing her to trip and stagger with almost every footstep. A few times, she even had to catch herself from completely falling on the ground. Being more annoyed then anything made it difficult to maintain focus on balance and body coordination. The snap of a heavy branch almost echoed as she stumbled, breaking the rest of the fall with her palms. She managed to keep the upper half of her body from hitting the ground.

Jonathan stopped again, this time Star did the same time.

"Did you hear that?" He asked. She did hear it, but she thought it was just her mind playing tricks on her.

"Yeah! It sounded like it was coming from over there." She was pointing to the right from where they were standing. Before they could say or do anything ells, they heard the faint sound of rustling leaves. They both continued on in the direction of the rustling leaves. Taking leaping steps seemed easier than trying to walk. Jonathan was having a hard time seeing what's in front of him and watching his footing as not to get tripped up. He stopped every few feet to take a second to regain his vision. He thought he saw someone a little ways in the distance. He remained still. Star grabbed him by the shoulder. Unable to get the words out, she just pointed franticly. They saw a silhouette of what looked to be a person.

Once she is on her feet she stood still, perfectly quiet. *Did someone just call me name?* She franticly looked in the dense forest hoping to hear something. After a few seconds she slowly moved forward, watching her footing. At first she walked softly, but if someone was searching for her the sounds she was making may be the only link to them. She picked up her pace once again, a split-second flash accursed. The feeling of hair against her cheek knocked her to the ground. Losing all of her senses, she just sat there in bewilderment.

"Stephanie! Are you ok?"

"Jett?" She looked closer. It was Jett. Now she was starting to feel the pain of the collision they just had. She was so happy to see a familiar face she ignored the pain. "Jett! What are you doing out here?" Stephanie asked.

"We've been looking for you. What happened?" She explaind how she went a walk and it was so peaceful she sat down just for a minute. Apparently she fell asleep and waking up a few moments ago. Jett got so caught up in finding her; he almost forgot to call out to the others. He had to let them know she was found.

"Who ells is out here?" Stephanie asked.

"Me, Jonathan, Chaz, Arbin, and that Star lady." The two finally got up and heard Star and Jonathan's rustling footsteps. Jett and Stephanie called out to them and they were reunited once again. For the first time in Jonathan's life, he found out what it felt like wanting to hug and yell at someone he cared about. Jonathan gave Stephanie a hug and yelled at her for running off like that.

On the way back; Stephanie apologized to everyone but mainly to Jonathan. The dancing light of the campfire was the only indication guiding them in the right direction. By now it was full darkness and that was the only thing they can see. Stephanie wanted to explain to Jonathan her idea of climbing the tallest tree to find some way out of there, but she felt uncomfortable talking in front of Arbin and Star.

Kasey spots what she thinks is Jonathan and the others. She jumps out of her seat. A hopeful smile replaces the frown. "Look!" she shouts pointing between Flo and Terry who just look at Kasey with concern before turning around. Six shadowy figures emerge from the forest, a small army marching across the field. Stephanie and the rest of the approaching silhouettes recognize the tiny high-pitch voice even in a crowd.

Kasey stirred up a small breeze as ran between Terry and Flo, who leaned aside clearing a path. Kasey wrapped a set of tiny arms around Stephanie's waist almost making Steph stumble back.

"Well, looks like someone missed you." Jonathan joked. Normally Stephanie wouldn't be as emotional, but she was actually felt guilty about going missing again. She squatted down and takes Kasey in an embracing hug. Stephanie stood up still holding on to Kasey; and sat Kasey's little bottom on her hip. The boys really didn't pay mind to Kasey's joy. They found a seat by the fire. They just wanted to rest.

"Jonathan did he tell you the way out thought the tunnels?" Kasey asked. Stephanie and Jonathan just look at each other in total confusion.

"What do you mean? Did who tell me?" Jonathan asked.

"You know, the bad man in the tunnels. I told you he knows the way out. You were still half asleep at the time, but I figured you heard me anyway."

"Oh." Jonathan said as he reflected back to the dream he had about his sister. Stephanie gave Jonathan a blank look. *Maybe it was Kasey and not his sister in that dream.* She thought. She never brought the thought to Jonathan's attention.

"Looks like the Sheppard found his lost sheep." Jimmy commented. "Please, sit. We saved you a seat." Kasey took the seat she sprang out of. Jonathan and Stephanie found a seat a few seats apart from one another. Still a little groggy, Stephanie fell into her seat. Being in a some-what safer place, she was able to plan her idea more clearly. Jimmy offered the something to drink for the returning *herd.* Jimmy continued the conversation they were having before the silhouettes reappeared. "So Hazelton, how did it feel milking a cow? Think you can do it on your own?"

"I, I'm not sure. I'm afraid the cow will get mad at me." Travis rubbed Hazelton's head laughing. Some other people chuckled as well.

"The cow won't get mad at you son. Be *one* with the cow." Travis said.

"Does that mean you have to wear brown clothes while you do that?" Hazelton asked. The chuckles turned into full laughter. Terry spit out her wine as she is in mid-sip. This made people laugh even harder.

Stephanie finally caught Jonathan alone and told him her idea about using some of the horse riding equipment to help reach the first branch of the taller trees.

"We just have to find a way to strap some kind of climbing spikes to my feet." Stephanie said. Jonathan is impressed with her idea, and is wondering why it wasn't thought of before.

"Why didn't we think of this before?" Jonathan inquires.

"I don't know, I guess it just didn't come to mind. Do think we could find that stuff in the barn?" She asked

"I would think so. The *spiked shoes* are going to be a little tricky. I'm sure I've seen some kind of straps and buckles in there before." Jonathan said. "We'll figure it out in morning. I'm going to get some sleep."

Stephanie was thinking of going back outside to rejoin the others at the campfire, than decided against it. She didn't want to be the center of attention being bombarded with questions of her whereabouts.

The mattress felt so cozy compared to the ground she awoke on a few hours ago. She was trying to think of what she could us as some sort of grappling hook for her feet. Straps were easy, if need be, she could use a belt even. Her eyelids were getting heavy. Then everything went black.

For a change the tables are turned. At first a blurred vision of somebody, then Jonathan came into her focus. He has a handsome smile she thought, but would never admit it.

"Hey sleepyhead." He sat there for a few seconds and lets her wake up a little. "You coming for breakfast?" He had an unusual glow to him this morning. Seeing this she perked up a little and almost sat up.

"What time is it?" she asked. Jonathan shrugged.

"About 6:30am." Now she sat up all the way.

"You seem to glowing this morning." Stephanie was actually about to smile. "What's up?"

"What? I can't be in a good mood?" Jonathan said.

"Sure you can, I'm just wondering why?" She asked as she got out of bed.

"I think I have an answer to our puzzle. Come on, let's have some breakfast. I was up extra early helping make it." Jonathan said.

After breakfast Jonathan led her to the barn. He showed her the straps she can use for her stunt. He explained what they can do for the spikes she needs. He showed her a three prong claw like tool with a wooden handle used for gardening.

"We can strap these to the inside of your legs like this." He placed the tool with the handle pointing down his leg, just below his knee; the prongs were pointing on the inside of his leg. "One on each leg and you'll close your legs on the tree digging tools prongs into the tree." She didn't seem all that convinced. He read this and knew she'll understand when she sees it in action. "Come on, I'll show you."

A gray sky is blew a steady warm breeze across the earth. The leave's heavy rustling were cheering down to her. They stood at the base of the tree and admired its mighty. They were going to roll-play how to work the straps. Stephanie had a specific way she wanted to do this. She remembered the tree guys her daddy hired that one time, and was going to do *almost* what they did. They have a leather strap about one inch wide and about six feet long.

Her arms aren't long enough to wrap around the tree; so she put the strap on the ground and walked one end of the strap around the tree. Now her arms complete the circle. She took the strap and pulls herself toward the tree at the same time took her feet and pushed herself away from the tree. These two forces able her to get her feet off the ground; but it was hard for her to climb up.

"What if you try wrapping the strap around your whole body? That would leave your hands free to help climb." Jonathan suggested. With a doubtful expression she gave this a try. She is able to climb up, but she was having trouble resetting the strap; as soon as she takes pressure off the strap to move it, her feet slide down.

"What?" She said looking at Jonathan who is just shaking head. "Fine! I'll try those ridicules hooks."

Jonathan helped her fasten the three prong hooks to her legs as planned in the first place. Once again she managed to support herself off the ground. The prongs made her feel award. She now has to grasp the tree with the inside of her legs for the prongs to be affective. She felt the prongs digging into the bark. The strap was around her body braced under her armpits. The hooks allow her to support her body weight without her legs sliding down. With her legs hooked into the tree, she threw her arms up looping the strap another foot and half higher. She pushed her body away from the tree, putting tension on the strap. She is suspended in with the strap and the hooks on her legs. She now threw her legs up and dug the hooks in the tree, lifting her body up. *I think this may work.* She thought.

"Looks like it's working. Are you ok?" Jonathan asked. He is surprised and happy to see her plan in action.

"Yeah, I just have fifteen more feet to go." She replied. She was so shocked she can't stop laughing. Jonathan was concerned about this for some reason.

"What's so funny?" He asked fearful her may fall.

"Nothing, this isn't so bad, it's almost fun." She said climbing her way up another foot.

"Ok, just be careful and make it to the first branch." She didn't reply until she reached the first branch. Looking down at him she jokingly shouted,

"What's the problem?"

"Ha ha. See anything yet?" She just shakes head and released the strap from her waist.

About fifteen minutes went by and she was almost out of sight. He could barely see her rustling the leaves as she climbed. He took a few steps back to try to get a clearer view, but she was out of sight. He gave one last yell up and got a muffled response. He thought she said, *the air is cooler up here,* but he was not sure and he'll just wait for her to come down.

She felt a stray, cool raindrop splash on her hand. The sky turned from light gray to dark gray. *Five minutes, I'll see how much higher I can get in five minutes.* She thought. She looked down and realized this was the highest she has climbed. She still hasn't reached the top of the tree. Looking down, she saw past the commune. There was a clear patch a little ways up the tree where she would be able to see all around her. It was about twenty up, but she reached it in no time. She actually saw an air plane. Her first instinct is to wave at it, but for obvious reasons she couldn't. Besides she was so buried in the thick of the tree, they probably would never see her.

She spotted something so mesmerizing she had to get a secure grasp on the branches she is on. She may be there for a while. She took a mental note of the layout of the commune and the newly found land marks. She guessed it's about a mile from the commune. *That has to be the end of the tunnels, how ells would he get out.* She couldn't wait to tell Jonathan what she found. About a half mile further in the distance was a road. She waited there for a while to see if any cars pass. Her trance is broken by a splashing raindrop that bounced in her eye. She shook it off and before she knew it the sky is now turning black.

Stephanie decided she has seen enough for now, and she better hurry down before she gets drenched, not to mention any lightning. Her decision proved to be too late as it started to pour, but the tree shaded the rain for now. She was almost running down the tree. After about fifteen minutes, Jonathan finally came into sight. He was franticly looking up shielding his eyes from falling rain.

"I'm coming!" she yelled.

"Great!" he yelled back. She stopped for a few moments as she stood on the first branch trying to figure out how to climb down. It seemed like Stephanie was tired of thinking about it. Before Jonathan or even she knew it, Stephanie climbed down the trunk with the leather strap wrapped around her waist. She almost slid down the tree. Jonathan was at the bottom, arms spread out waiting to catch her. She landed hitting the ground with a hard *thud*. "You ok?"

"Y-Yeah! I-I'm fine!" she said. Jonathan took a second to looked her over for any scratches or cuts she may not have noticed. She was clean of any such marks. Their clothes were sticking to them. The wetness covered their bodies in a chill. The dark sky and pounding rain made it seem like it was late in the afternoon, maybe evening. They managed to keep up with each other's fast paced walk.

"I saw s-something, a shack or something. It-it looked like it was about a mile away. I-I also saw him!" Stephanie panted out. Jonathan turned and looked at her.

"Who?"

"Graody! He came out of the shack! It looked like that there was a spot for a campsite or something on the side of the shack. Is that where the tunnels lead?"

"It's possible, If he's been locked down there and you saw him outside. What was he doing?" Jonathan asked. Her face squinted-up as she turned to stare at the ground.

"He-he was dragging a-an animal of some kind."

"Did you see any kind of campfire lit?"

"No, It looked like a circle made out of rocks."

"What ells did you see?"

"Oh! I saw a road! It was about maybe a mile or less from that shack. And I saw a plane! I know it didn't see me, I was buried in the leaves of the tree." This made Jonathan perk up.

"Did you see where the road or the plane went?"

"The road curved out of sight and like I said, I was buried under the think leaves of the tree. I doubt the plane saw me." Dripping wet they enter the main house. The air wasn't any warmer, but they weren't getting rained on anymore.

Jonathan already has some ideas of how to get the children and himself home again. One idea may involve Stephanie going back up in the tree again if she is willing to do so. His idea is to have her go back up in the tree and watch the road and the shack. It would help to know if there is a time of day when cars would most likely be traveling on the road. Jonathan wasn't so worried about Groady, he planned on taking care of him.

It felt good to be in dry clothes again. Jonathan knew it was later then he thought because he heard noises coming from the kitchen. The sound of people chatting, random pots clanking; knives tapping on cutting boards echoed down the hall. It was close to dinner time. On his way to the kitchen he saw Stephanie asleep in the room. Her wet clothes were hung over a chair. Jonathan will also have to talk with Jett and Chaz. Some of Jonathan's plan involves a *dry-run* though the tunnels. If he was going to be leading fifteen kids though the tunnels; he wanted a clear path. That meant taking care of Groady before they left. He was starting to get himself overwhelmed. Maybe helping out in the kitchen will give him a mental break and clear his head.

He saw Kasey climbing on a chair to reach the counter top like an adult. She had been given an easy job rising off the veggies that came in from the garden. He hurried over and she stopped in mid climb looking at him hoping he helps her on the chair. He grabbed underneath her arms and lifts her high enough so she is standing on the chair.

"Thanks Jonathan." She said in a shy squeaky tone.

"You're welcome honey." Jonathan said. He wanted to ask her about what she said to him when he was half asleep the other morning. "Hey Kasey, what ells were you trying to tell me that morning about Groady and knowing the way out of the tunnels?"

"I overheard Mr. Jimmy telling someone that he told you Groady would tell you the way out through the tunnels. I thought you heard me. Didn't you hear me?" The question painted a sad look of concern on her face. He had to explain he did hear her, but he was having a dream about his missing sister and her voice was part of the dream.

"I did hear you Kasey. At the time; I was having a dream about my missing sister and I thought it was her talking to me and I didn't realize it was you. Thank you for telling me. I'm working on it. Please don't lose hope. We all need to go home." He said this using his *inside voice* and gently squeezed her shoulder with a hopeful smile. She sadly looked down at the ground and just replied

"I guess." Instead of lifting her chin up, making their eyes meet, he gently places his other hand on her other shoulder.

"Hey, we'll be home real soon, I promise, ok?" Jonathan said. She replied a confirm out of *tongue and cheek* still looking down. He gave a soft hug and grabbed a half red and green pepper.

He started to rinse it off to give her a subtle hint she should get started rising. Kasey grabbed the next pepper to rinse and her eyes start to sarcastically roll. Jonathan turned around and saw Flo standing behind him. Now he understood what Kasey was expressing. It's actually a good thing Flo was there to break the tension.

Jonathan used Flo's sudden appearance to his advantage to make

Kasey laugh and put her in a good mood. He spun around, looked at Flo said something that made Kasey chuckle.

"Flo." Jonathan started out. "You're looking different, I like it." Kasey covered her mouth to try to hide the fact that she was laughing. Jonathan looked at Kasey to make sure she didn't lose her balance off the chair, and flashed a wink. Flo stared at him blankly.

"Are you finished?" Flo asked holding her gaze.

"I am; apparently you are not." He said and wanted to end this conversation. "What do you need Flo?" Flo remained in her *fixed stare.* Jonathan had no patients for her attitude and turned around and started to cut up the veggies Kasey just rinsed.

"There's some riding equipment and some gardening tools missing from the barn; any idea where they might be?" Jonathan knew exactly what she was talking about. He also just now figured out Stephanie never returned the stuff when they were done with them. He shook his head slightly and dropped his head down for a split second.

"I'll get them for you. Stephanie must not have returned it like I thought she would. She had them because apparently someone put the buzz in her ear and doing her famous tree climbing stunt, any idea who might have done that?" Jonathan didn't turn to look at her as he spoke. They both knew it was Flo who gave Stephanie that idea. Flo just turned and walked away.

Jonathan was finished cutting up the veggies Kasey rinsed and decided to check on Stephanie. He entered the room and sat next to her as she slept. She slowly started to wake up; but made no effort to get out of bed.

"Hey, how ya feeling?" Jonathan asked.

"Fine." She replied looking at him; wondering why he's even asking.

"You did great climbing. I am surprised you made it up and down so fast."

"Yeah, no big deal. Having the straps and the hooks helped out a little also." She shrugged.

"Oh! Where did you put that stuff? Flo was nagging about that a few minutes ago; like all of a sudden she needs it and she didn't see it in the barn." Jonathan said.

"Oh I have it over there on the side of the chair where my clothes are hanging. I was going to put them back after dinner. I didn't think anyone was going to be looking for them."

"I'll put them back. Get some rest. Do you want me to wake you for dinner? Or do you want to skip dinner tonight?" Jonathan asked.

"I don't know." she said with a yawn. He's guessing she may sleep though dinner.

"I'll check on you just before dinner to see how you feel. I'll return the stuff to the barn in the mean time." Jonathan said.

"Thanks Jonathan." She said softly as she half dosed back to sleep. He gave her a slight smile and a wink as he left the room.

Jonathan met up with Chaz in the hallway. Jonathan asked where Jett was. He wanted to talk to them both at the same time. He didn't want to repeat himself over again. It would be easier to talk to them at the same time; they could share ideas.

"I saw Jett with Arbin around the guest house when it started raining. Why what's up?" Chaz asked

"I wanted to talk to you both at the same time, but I at least want to tell one of you for now." Jonathan said.

"What is it?" Chaz asked. Jonathan was hesitating telling Chaz since he was just a kid and all. Jonathan didn't want him to tell Jett any wrong info. On the way over to the barn, Jonathan explained to Chaz what Stephanie saw while she was up in the tree. He also explained how he wanted to try to find a way out through the tunnels. That will lead into how Groady had to be taken care of. Before he can explain all that, Jonathan wanted to make sure Chaz understood why all this planning was being done.

"You do understand what's going on, about what Jimmy said, don't you?" Chaz had an idea, but didn't want to say it and be wrong.

"I'm not sure what you mean." Chaz said. Jonathan was going to make this short and sweet.

"Ok, Jimmy made the comment the other night that it's time we need to leave." Jonathan paused for Chaz's reaction not knowing what to expect. Jonathan now knew Chaz really had no idea about what Jimmy had said judging by his response.

"W-what! why? W- What happened?" At this point Chaz turned into a babbling mess and needed to calm down.

"Calm down. I have it all planned out; or at least half planned out. This is where I need you and Jett to help me and Stephanie." Jonathan explained the idea he had for going through the tunnels. He also made it clear they need to find out what's at the end of the tunnels. Jonathan didn't want to lead these kids down another dead end path. Chaz leaned up against the wooden boards of the stall for a second staring at the ground, then looked at Jonathan and suggested that they travel outside the tunnels on the dry-run. That way they have less chance of running into Groady, and if it was going be a nice day; who cares about the mile or two hike. They could be there and back in a day. Jonathan thought about the idea for a minute.

"I get it, but who'll go with me?" Jonathan asked.

"I'll go with you." Chaz volunteered. Jonathan wasn't so sure about that idea. Between Jett, Chaz, and Stephanie; each has a great quality. Jonathan wishes he could put them all together in one person. Chaz was more of a thinker, Jett has the bravery, and Stephanie kind of has both and possibly additional common scene. Although he almost feared Stephanie would want to go inside the tunnels and run into Groady and it would only be the two of them. His other concern about taking Stephanie was some unnecessary drama like getting them totally lost. Jonathan likes Stephanie's bravery, but there are times when she gets overly enthusiastic.

"Are you sure you're up to it? Who knows what we'll encounter out there." Chaz stood up straight, threw his shoulders back. With his eyes widened and his neck extended he replied.

"I'll be fine. We should be in and out. Stephanie guessed two miles? You figure about two hours to that shack and another thirty minutes to the road. We take one hour exploring time, then about two and a half hours back. No side adventures." That's just what Jonathan wanted to hear. He nodded in agreement.

"Alright that sounds like a plan. If Jett finds out he can come with us too. Stephanie is a good kid and means well, but I think she'll hold us up. We want to be in and out." Jonathan said. This time Chaz nods in agreement. "Let's start heading back and help out with dinner. I asked

Stephanie to draw out some kind of map of the land; we can use that to guide us." Jonathan said.

They entered the main house just in time when the food is being brought to the table. Chaz grabbed a bowl of potatoes from Terry' hand; in her other hand she had a plate of chicken. Chaz didn't realize how hungry he was until he saw it.

"I'm going to see if Stephanie wants to come to dinner." Jonathan said as a general statement, not really addressing any one person. Chaz looked at him for a second not sure if that was a signal to go with him. Jonathan didn't even look back so Chaz remained helping set the table.

The sound of a sniffle was a soft whisper in Jonathan's ears. Before he entered the doorway he saw Stephanie lying in bed motionless. As he approached in front of her; there's a tear running down her cheek and her eyes are red. He walked over and squatted down.

"Hey, what's wrong?" She remained motionless not answering. "Hey, what is it?" he asked in a calming voice. Now he had a hand on her shoulder and the total look of confusion on his face. She finally looked up at him after a second.

"I just got my hopes up. We're never going home. What's Jimmy planning for us? Is going to banish us to the tunnel like he did Groady?" she whimpers.

"We found Groady, someone will find us." Jonathan said. She didn't say anything and broke her graze at him and looked straight ahead. He felt her frustration and felt it was time to let her in on the plans he and Chaz came up with.

"Relax." He said rolling his eyes, hoping she'll think she's over reacting. In his heart he felt she was right. He really had no idea how they're going home... If they make it home. He had no intentions of letting her and anyone ells know he had that doubt in his mind. "Me and Chaz thought of a plan." He paused to see if she perked up. She did not. But she did question what it was.

"What's that?" she asked.

"We plan on starting out early tomorrow morning. We're going to hike the two miles and check out the shack you found, and then we're going to hike the rest of the way to the road to see if we can find someone driving by. We're not going in the tunnels for a lot of reasons, Graody being one of them. We plan on returning back late afternoon."

Jonathan noticed a look that came across her face that indicated she didn't want to be left out of his plans. He knew she was going to be thinking that and has a reply ready for her.

"Ok, what time do we leave?" Stephanie inquired.

"I think it's best if you stay here, because I need someone to answer any questions if people ask where I am. Plus it's best if you stick around and don't do anymore disappearing acts. That'll hopefully put Jimmy at ease and not be in a rush to kick us out. You've actually did a lot for us by seeking out the landscape." Jonathan explained. She considered the idea for a second or two and finally visually agreed, without her saying a word.

"Let's have some dinner and relax by the campfire, we can use it. We made a big step forward today and it's time to chill. We'll start fresh tomorrow morning." Stephanie agreed, and they join the others for dinner. Their time at campfire managed to be relaxing; and Jonathan was surprised it was. He noticed Chaz a little punchy and nervous. Jonathan was trying to give him eye contact asking *what's wrong.* But Chaz didn't seem to be getting the hint. Jonathan is guessing Chaz was getting cold feet. Jonathan was not worried about it; if worse came to worse Jonathan would just go alone. Later that night Jonathan finally had a chance to question Chaz why he appeared so nervous.

"You getting cold feet about tomorrow? It's ok if you are; you don't have to go if you don't want to." Chaz didn't answer for a few seconds; and Jonathan didn't want to force an answer out of him. "Think about it, let me know in the morning." Jonathan said.

"I should be alright. I'm just doing last minute planning." But there was one thing would keep Chaz from going. "Jonathan, what if it's raining tomorrow? Do you still want to go?" *Ah-ha,* Jonathan knew there was something bugging Chaz.

"I don't know. If it's raining in the morning we'll just wait. This shouldn't take all day if all goes well. Let's get some rest we'll worry about it in the morning." Jonathan was so tired he didn't even hear if Chaz replied back.

# CHAPTER 31

## Looking for Help

"How long do you think the rain will hold off?"

"Not sure. I wouldn't be surprised if it didn't rain at all." Jonathan didn't want to admit the fact that he's feeling overwhelmed. The forest is a lot denser then he imagined. At times they didn't engage in conversation. There are mentally preparing for whatever the unexpected may bring. A *crunch, snapping* sound was the only thing they head at times of the hike. The leaves and twigs are screaming many tones of that *crunch-snapping* sound when they walk. Sometimes both sounds are muffled. But many times the sounds echoes, slicing through the dense eeriness.

By this time the forest was looking the same no matter which direction they looked. He was guessing they may have hiked about a mile by now. Jonathan couldn't fight the paranoid feeling that was taking over him. He was always the calm cool one. Maybe it was the fact that they couldn't see what the direction they came from. They stopped for a second to rest.

"Hey Jonathan, you ok? You don't seem yourself."

"Yeah." He took a short pause. He almost had that dizzy feeling like he did back at the sight of the accident. He finally shook his head to free himself from his hypnotic daydream. "I'm ok, I'm just trying to get my sense of direction back." Jonathan's facial expression seemed to return back its normal confident self again.

"Oh, that's good to hear. For a second, I thought I lost you. We should probably keep moving. I bet we're not far." Jonathan nodded in agreement and they continued hiking on. They were hiking along and then Jonathan noticed something missing; the sound of crunching leaves and snapping twigs. He looked down and noticed the ground is once again clear; like a path they never expected to be on. Jonathan didn't mention this fact and just kept hiking.

"What's that?" Jonathan looked up and saw a dark shadow tied between two trees. When they approached closer, the shadow resembles two arms. As they got closer, they realized they weren't arms, but are hooves. It's a deer. The body cavity is cleaned out. Below, underneath the deer's lower hooves is a freshly dug pit.

"Looks like someone gutted this deer and buried its guts and took the meat." They both have the look of horror and caution on their faces. "We must be close to Groady's shack." Jonathan said. "This must be fresh. I'm sure Stephanie would have seen this yesterday." They proceeded forward along the clearing. The cool breeze was both, refreshing and a warning that rain maybe coming soon.

"Look! That must be it!" up ahead in the distance, though the misty air Jonathan saw a lop-sided shack. They both stopped walking to steady their vision and focus on the structure. Without any words being said they both made their way toward it. They approached what looked to be the back side of the shack. Jonathan put his hand out and they stopped walking. They are about fifty feet from the shack. Jonathan started to walk slowly, watching his footsteps as not to step on any noisy on the ground. He motioned to stay in place and wait as he proceeded forward. He disappeared in front of the shack. A few moments later reappeared and motioned to come forward.

The shack seemed to be twelve feet long and nine feet wide. There was an oval shaped hump in the middle of the floor. The hump is about six feet long. Jonathan took a step on it. The oval shape felt softer than the rest of the ground around it. In the corner of the shack was a trapdoor. The trapdoor wasn't bolted down.

"This must lead to the tunnels back to the main house." She said squatting down to look for a handle.

"I would imagine so. Hey Thanks again for coming with me. I wasn't surprised Chaz got cold feet. I almost expected that to happen." Jonathan said.

"Yeah; sure thing. I needed to get away anyway. You wanna pry this thing up?"

"Yeah, I wanna take a quick look in there; and I also want to make time to look for this road Stephanie spotted." Jonathan said.

"I wonder how he lifted it up if it has no handle." She asked.

"He probably leaves the lid up when he's here. I'm guessing he maybe in the tunnels since the lid is on flat." They managed to pry the trapdoor open. It is dark. There were no steps like the other trapdoors; it's just a hole descending straight down. They could only see a few feet. They noticed a structure made out of branches that are tied together by vines or something. The structure resembled a latter of some kind. Jonathan placed one foot on the first step of the latter to test its strength. It whimpers out a *creek* but managed to hold his weight.

"Do have any matches on you?" She asked. Jonathan patted his pockets down and found book matches. He just looked up at her in surprise, not knowing he had them. He lit two at the same time and they saw the latter went about ten feet down and ended on a dirt floor. The matches went out and Jonathan climbed out of the hole.

"Thanks for reminding me, I didn't think I had those. We'll have to explore this later." He said. "I have to find this road first."

"Ok, sure." She really didn't want to go back down in the tunnels anyway. The two walked out of the shack cautiously, looking all around them. They didn't want any surprises like groady finding them.

"Stephanie said the road is straight ahead from here. She guessed it was about a half mile away." Jonathan said.

"Are we ready then?" she asked.

"Let's go." He replies and the two set off to find a mysterious road to nowhere. After what seems like forever they are starting guess Stephanie miscalculated the distance.

"Jonathan, how long do you think we've been hiking?"

"Not sure, about an hour, if that. Stephanie must have been a little off. She was spot on about the shack though." She gave a small sighing pant and kept hiking. The terrain was getting rough; not to mention they're getting tired of hiking up hill. They finally stopped to rest. They looked back down at the hill they were hiking up. The shack almost looks like a dot.

Jonathan grabs her by wrist and gently pulls her over behind a tree.

"Whata-ya doing?" She asked in surprise. Jonathan remained silent for a second and pointed down the gully toward the shack.

"Did you see that? Groady. I just saw him." He said.

"Where?"

"He just walked in the shack!"

"What was he doing?" she asked.

"I don't know." The two sat there for a minute waiting to see what Groady will do next, if anything. For all they knew, he could be going back in the tunnels. Groady reappeared from the shack. He went over to the fire pit, the one that Jonathan and Star didn't notice before. They sat on the ground as if they are watching a movie. After a minute or two, smoke bellowed from the pit. Soon they saw flames. After another minute, Groady placed something over the fire. They couldn't really make out what it was. After about ten minutes Groady flipped over whatever it was on the fire. Star finally put two and two together.

"I bet he's cooking that deer we saw ya-know; the one that was gutted." Star suggested.

"I guess so." Jonathan said. He gazed up at the sky. The clouds were turning from light to dark gray. It was nice just to sit there and watch what Groady was doing, but Jonathan knew they should get moving soon. He didn't want to get caught in the rain. He planned on them being back at the commune when the rain started.

"We better get going it looks like it doing to rain soon and we still have at least a two hour hike back." She agreed and they continued hiking up the hill. The hill they started is now a steep incline. At times they are on all *fours* grabbing at visible roots and rocks as footholds. Jonathan is guessing you can see the steepness of landscape from high up. It would have been nice if Stephanie warned him about this beforehand. Jonathan is guessing she thought it wouldn't be an issue.

"If we don't find anything soon I think we should head back." Jonathan said.

"That sounds like a great idea. It feels like we hiked over what she claimed we would be."

"Yeah I know, as much as hate to turn back, I hate being wet even more." Jonathan said. There was a *shushing* sound over their heads. They both looked at each other in question.

"What was that?" Star asked.

"I don't know! Sounded like it came from up there." Jonathan said motioning by pointing with his chin. Jonathan saw a spot on the hill that was not so steep to climb up.

"Hey, let's go over that way. It's not so steep." Jonathan said. The two made their way over to left. Jonathan was correct, once they made it over to the direction he suggested, the climb was much easier. They heard another *shushing* noise.

"That sounds like a car going by!" Jonathan said with excitement. Star just gave him a funny look.

"Are you sure? I don't see a road." Jonathan was so sure; he quickly hurried up the incline. He was almost running, not waiting to see if Star is keeping up.

"Slow down!" she called out trying to keep up. Jonathan stopped and took in a deep breath. Star noticed his eyes were fixed on something and was wondering what it is that made him stop dead in his tracks. Once she caught up with him, she saw it also. Jonathan was wondering the last time Star saw a paved road, one with painted lines. He ran up and stood on it as if were paved out of gold. Star just looked in amazement. They looked right, and then left; like they were two kids about across the street for the first time by themselves.

"I almost forgot what the highway looked like." Jonathan said with a hopeful smile. The commune seemed a world away. If a car came by right now Jonathan would have to hold back from jumping in front of it. He was actually thinking of doing it. He wouldn't do it to be suicidal; he just to tell someone what happened and where they were.

"What is this? I mean what road is this?" Star asked. For a second Jonathan thought she just landed here from outer space. He was so jazzed he can't stop smiling. At first Star thought he was laughing at her; and was starting to get annoyed.

"What!" she finally snapped.

"Nothing, relax. I think this is the road the accident happened on." The two just stood there on the road. Jonathan didn't want to leave, he didn't want to hike the two or three miles back to the commune. He almost wanted to hitch a ride to somewhere, anywhere and take Star with him. *Take Star with me.* He thought. He just figured out how much he liked her. He could just ask her to go with them if they got rescued, but she would probably say no.

"What do we do now?" she asked. Jonathan wasn't sure what to do.

"We'll wait here for a little bit for a car to come, I'll flag it down and tell them where we are and we need help." Star wasn't so sure that was a good idea. She knew Jimmy would be furious about people knowing about them. He worked so hard finding solitude. Jonathan could see Star's face go blank. She wasn't smiling; her eyes were dull as she just looked around.

"I guess." She sulked. A drop of rain breaks their hypnotic day dream; and another, and another. They looked up and saw the whole sky covered in a dark gray. The sound of angels bowling was soft and drawn-out. They both glanced at each other, and decided it's time to head back. No doubt they're going to get caught in the rain.

The sound of a faint, empty wind noise came from behind the bend in the road. Jonathan grabbed Star by the arm just as she takes her first step down the embankment. She just looked at him in question. Jonathan couldn't make out if that's a car approaching or another roll of thunder. *Thank god!* he almost said out loud. Jonathan waved his hands in the air crossing them over his head in that *distress* motion.

The blond haired girl was lost in her thoughts; thinking of meeting her boyfriend and her care free life style. Her hair is pulled back in a ponytail. She was wearing a black skintight jogging outfit, pink sneakers and a pink headband. Her eyebrows were a little wider then pencil thin, as if to be painted on. She has her left foot on her seat next to her butt; with her knee pointing up, her leg was resting against the Jeep door. She was nodding and bopping her head to the beat of a Lady Ga-Ga song that was so loud; Jonathan and Star will soon be hearing it over the wind noise the Jeep is making.

Her phone lights up. A picture of a crew-cut, flat-topped blond haired boy comes to life on the screen. In the picture; the blond haired kid has his arms wrapped around a blond girl kissing her on the cheek. The girl in the picture is smiling so wide, it starts to blend into laughter. In white letters, the name Justin arrears on top of the screen. She taps the icon of the message bubble. "Here now baby" it reads; this make her more giddy and lost in thought. Her first instinct is to reply to the message, but something shouts in her head, *Look up!*

For a second, she didn't notice the bend in the road, but what she did notice was that there wasn't a guardrail. She dropped the phone on the passenger seat and firmly tapped the breaks and sharply cut the wheel. She soon regained control of the Jeep. As she turned the corner, she saw a young couple.

The woman was standing off to the side of the road. The man was almost in the middle of the road waving his arms overhead. She pulled the steering wheel once again and swerved around him, almost hitting him. She brought the Jeep to sudden stop that almost made the tire screech on the blacktop. For a second she was in shock. *Who and why would someone jump in front of a speeding vehicle?* She thought.

Her heart was pounding. She considered just putting her foot on the gas and taking off, but her big heartedness won't let her do that. She tried to relax a little remembering the taser Justin gave her for safety.

She turned it on and pulled the trigger for a second just to test it. A blue lightning bolt bounced between two metal prongs. A *buzzing-zap* sound shouted from the lightning bolt. She was ready if she needed it. She pushed a button and the passenger side window went down. Jonathan remained a foot or so from the Jeep. He didn't want to frighten the girl and risk having her just drive away. The Jeep was high enough that he didn't have to duck down to look at her. The scent of her perfume was sweet and candy scented. It floated out of the open window and hits him before he reached the Jeep. The smell took him back to what that outside world is like as he remembered it.

"Hey! Thanks for stopping. Listen I know you can't help me by yourself; tell the police I am stranded with fifteen kids in a commune four miles in the woods. Their bus hit my truck and we found our way to this commune and we've been stranded there for months. Contact the Wilkinson's camp for the gifted. They may have been looking for us." The girl didn't know to do but just stare at Jonathan. He said one last word. "Please!" Just then the girl noticed Star slowly coming over.

"Who's your friend?" The girl snapped making the taser visible for Jonathan to see. Jonathan turned around and franticly put his hand up and motioned for Star to stop where she was. He turned back to the girl and now saw the taser.

"Wait! She's one of the people from the commune. Just, please, do what I ask. Just contact the camp I told you about or the authorities. Remember this bent in the road; we're four miles in the woods straight that way. Tell someone we are here and need help."

"Mister!" Jonathan really doesn't like being called that. "There's a hundred bends in this road. This is probably one of the longest stretches of highway in the U.S. It's at least sixty miles through the mountain. You're the only sole I saw in two hours." Jonathan started look around for a distant land mark for someone to look for, but there was none; everything looked the same.

"Look! Just call the authorities, or the camp. I'm almost sure they'll handle it from there. Please!" After a second she reached in the glove box and wrote down the name of the camp.

"Ok, I won't be around any people for another hour or so. I'll tell someone about you and the children." She sped off without hearing any kind of reply from Jonathan.

That was the first time Star saw a vehicle in real life. Star is about Twenty two-twenty four years old. The commune and its people are all she knows. Jimmy made it that way. He must not have figured any of his people would be able hike that far.

The two start the journey back toward the snack. The rain was steady, but seemed to have lightened up a little. At first they didn't relies how wet they were. They barely speak to each other. They aren't mad at each other; they are just in deep thought. Star was in aww at what she just saw. Jonathan finally feels some sense of accomplishment.

"Hey! Should we rest in the shack for a second, and see if the rain stops. I'll make sure Groady's not in there first."

"I guess," she replied. They entered the shack, but there's really no place to sit. They were too wet to sit on the floor, so they leaned against the walls of the shack. "Jonathan?" Star address softly.

"Yeah? What's up?" He almost knew what she is going to ask.

"What was all that back on the road? The vehicle? The girl? Is that what the outside world looks like? Do people dress like that? Was that music we heard coming from the vehicle?" Star asked. That was just what he thought she would ask about. He looked at her with a grin.

# CHAPTER 32

## Explaining the Real World; Heading Back to the Commune.

"Yes Star, That is the outside world. The vehicle was a new Jeep, nothing special, one of many types of cars. That was music we heard coming from the radio. A song by a singer called Lady Ga-Ga. The girl was dressed in a skin tight gym outfit. He felt bad for Star not knowing to world as he knew it.

"I-I just never knew. I mean, I always knew there was an outside world. I just didn't know what it looked like. Did you find the girl attractive?" Star asked.

"Yes! very attractive. Why?" Jonathan answered holding a grin; remembering the outside world himself.

"I don't know; I was just wondering that's all." Jonathan knows he should tell Star how he feels about her.

"Star," He paused for a minute as she looked at him. "If we get recued, do you want to go with us? With me? Hey, I just want to say; I'm attracted to you. But if feel you want to stay you can. I'm not going to force you to come with me. You don't have to give me an answer this second." She just looked at him blankly.

"I don't know what to think." She said. Jonathan didn't want them to lose focus on getting back. They were out longer than planned. It'll be dinner time soon and he was getting hungry. He's guessing she's hungry too. He checks outside to see that it's still raining.

"Do you want to wait for the rain to stop, or should we chance going through the tunnels?" he asked. Her head was leaning the side, almost resting on her shoulder. Her saddened eyes were staring at the ground. All she needed was a tear to be running down her cheek, thankfully that wasn't happening. Jonathan suspected she didn't want to go back. He couldn't stand to see Star like this; it was starting to bring him down. He had to snap her out of it. Finally, without saying anything she just shrugged.

There was something different about the air around them, it seemed quiet and still. His eyes brightened a little. He looked outside and was glad to see it stopped raining. He didn't know for how long, but it stopped for now. Jonathan broke free of the depressing spell Star casted on them. He grabbed Star by the wrist.

"It stopped raining! We should get a move on it, who knows when it will start up again." Star was not feeling his happiness, and was feeling left out. She made no effort to move. Seeing Star sad like that, made Jonathan feel he had a problem on his hands. How was he going to make Star snap out of it? He did the only thing he felt may work.

Jonathan turned around and took a step closer to her. Their bodies were almost touching. Jonathan is so close; Star can smell the lingering scent of the perfume from the girl in the Jeep. The sweet candy like scent slightly enters her nose. She can almost taste it. He cradled her chin and cheeks, and gently tilts her head up so they are now looking eye to eye. He places his lips on her lower lip. Jonathan held that pose for a second, waiting for her to pull away, but she didn't. When he didn't feel her resistance, he pulled them closer, now their bodies were touching. He repositioned his lips so he could gently clamp both of her lips together. He made their lips do that soft clicking sound as he pulled away from her.

*That did it!* He thought to himself. He looked into her eyes and they were wide and life like again. The spell seemed to be broken. He was not sure if he should have done that; judging by the look on her face, she was not sure ether. Jonathan said something to break the tension.

"Welcome back; you ok?"

"Yeah, I think so. What just happened?" Why'd you do that? Star asked, feeling glad he did so.

"We kissed; and now you seem back to normal. I thought that would help you get your head on straight. You weren't looking so good for a second. Are you mad at me?" He asked placing a hand on her shoulder.

"So, did you kiss me because you actually like me or did you kiss me to snap me out of some kind a trance you thought I was in?" Jonathan really didn't want to have this conversation now; he really wanted to start heading back. Once they are on their way back then he'll talk about it.

"Both! Look, I did kiss you to snap you out of your trance; but I admit I have grown attracted to you in our time together. I'd like to talk about it more on the way back." Jonathan said.

"I guess so. We should make it back just before dinner if we hurry." Star said. Jonathan agreed and they start heading back hoping they beat the next rainfall. On their back their minds were racing about what just happened; what they saw and the girl they met. Star saw a world she never knew existed. She wanted to know more about it. She was mesmerized about the girl, her vehicle, the music she was listening to and the clothes she was warring. Star wanted that life style and was starting to resent being in the commune life.

"We're making good time; we'll make it back in plenty of time for dinner." Jonathan said.

"Jonathan I have to tell you something." At this time Jonathan was so jazzed, he could handle anything she had to say.

"What's up?"

"I want to go with you." Jonathan just turned his head and looked at her in shock. "If or when you get rescued, I want to go with you. I don't want to be here anymore." Star said.

"Wait! Do you want to go with us to get away? Or do you like me and want to be with me? I understand if you just want to get away from here. So please be honest. I'll take you with me either way." Jonathan stated.

"I don't know. I like you a lot. I've grown attached to you too. But once I saw that girl in that Jeep; she seemed so free. It seemed like she did what she wanted, when she wanted. I want that. It seems like I'm living under the command of someone and I don't want that life anymore." Jonathan figured that's what she was thinking.

"Ok. When I figure out a plan I'll include you and you'll come with us. Sound good? You don't have to decide now, you have time." He said. Jonathan had a thought about Groady he kept to himself; a thought he wanted to share with someone ells. Now was a good time as any. "Hey Star?"

"Yeah?"

"It's going to sound strange, but I keep having this thought about Groady." Star looked at him with confusion.

"What about Groady?" she asked.

"Well, I don't think he was really *banished* to the tunnels. I'm starting to think he was sent there to keep a watch on the people in the commune to make sure they didn't try to leave." Star was confused she almost stopped walking to question Jonathan.

"What do you mean?" she asked.

"When we were all held captive down in the tunnels, he could have killed us all and no one would ever know. Instead he beat the crap out of us. I mean, thankfully he didn't even take advantage of Stephanie. From what I've heard about Groady, I was sure he was going to kill us. And think about the shack, how close it is to the road. Sure it's well over a mile hike up hill to get there, but still. Ya know what I'm saying?" Star thought about it for a minute.

"I guess," She replied. Jonathan explained to Star everything that happened to them when they were held captive in the tunnels, now that had the time and privacy. They talked about a lot of things. Jonathan felt good about the kiss he gave Star; he was hoping she felt the same way.

The sky was turning that gray color, and there was a cool breeze blowing. Jonathan would have normally been worried about the rain, but was too excited and couldn't wait to get back to Stephanie and tell her the great news. They were about half way back, when Star felt a cool wetness on her hand, and then one on her cheek. Jonathan stopped for a second to take a deep gaze at the sky.

"What is it?" she asked.

"We better pick up the pace, the heavens are about to open up again. Did you see flash of lightning?" She acknowledged that there was a flash of lightning; and they continued walking at a faster pace. The Sky was turning from gray to dark gray. The breeze was getting stronger, but not cooler.

"Look!" she shouted. Jonathan could tell by the tone in her voice they must be getting close. When Jonathan looked up he saw a person coming toward them. He squinted to try to make out who it is.

"Can you see who it is?" he asked. There was a pause for a minute and then she stuttererd a name in question.

"Ch-Chaz?" Jonathan stopped for a second so he could get a better look at how the person was walking. Since the accident, Chaz gained a slight limp because of his leg injury. Besides, Jonathan didn't think Chaz would be brave enough to hike all that way by himself. Whoever it is has a straight walk.

"I don't think it's Chaz." Jonathan stated. "Chaz has a slight limp" The two continued forward.

"Who could it be then?"

"I'm not sure. It may be Stephanie looking for us. We're coming back later then we planned on." Far off in the distance; the sight of the buildings of the commune were just coming into vision. "That is Stephanie" Jonathan said.

"Why is she coming out in this rain? I hope everything is ok." Jonathan rolled his eyes.

"I'm sure everything is fine. She just feels left out." Star suddenly remembered what she planned on asking Jonathan; but forgot about till just know.

"Hey! That's what I wanted to ask you. Why did you ask me to go with you on this hike, instead of Stephanie?"

"I wanted to ask Stephanie. I also wanted to go and come back and not get side tracked. Stephanie would have been great to go with; but she would have had us off the beaten path. I was afraid nothing would have gotten done." Jonathan explained.

"Does she know that?"

"No! And she not going find out either." Jonathan commanded. Stephanie reached them in record time. She is in such wonder, she seemed not notice the rain.

"Hey! You guys ok? I thought you would be back sooner. It's almost dinner time. What happened?" Stephanie asked over excitedly. She knew a lot happened to them. She could read Jonathan's eyes.

"Relax, your estimate of distance Is a little off. The shack was about four miles away not two; and from the shack to the road was two miles not a half mile. That held us up." Stephanie's face wilted a little and her eyes sank in their sockets.

"Oh, sorry." Stephanie said. In her mind she was took the blame for their, what seemed now to be a pointless hike. Star was looking at

Jonathan with high anticipation. Jonathan winked at Star with a slight grin. He places a hand on Stephanie's shoulder. Stephanie didn't even bother to look up at him.

"Yeah, that and the girl in the Jeep we met driving along the road." All at the same time, Stephanie's head sprang up, eyes almost popped out their sockets and her lower jaw dropped. She remained in a fixed stare for a few seconds. Jonathan turned to look at Star and then turned back at Stephanie.

"Your face is going to freeze that way ya-know." After a few seconds she was finally able to stutter out one word questions.

"Who? What? Where? What'd she say?" Stephanie rambled on. Jonathan was going to tell Stephanie everything, just not at that second. They were getting close to the main house now, and he didn't want anyone to over hear them.

"Listen I'll tell you everything after dinner. I promise. I just don't want you to say anything to anyone!" He said grabbing her shoulder. Her eyebrows narrowed and her eyes squinted. Once Jonathan felt her start to pull away; he let go of his grip.

"Sorry Stephanie, I didn't mean to grab you that hard. Listen, the last thing I need are rumors to start flying. I don't want the kids to get the wrong information and get their hopes up and being let down. Like I said I'll tell you everything after dinner, I'm not sure I can even trust Jett and Chaz." Jonathan explained. Stephanie was finally understanding the point Jonathan was trying to make; and agreed not to say anything.

It felt great to get out of wet clothes and a shower; dry clothes feel like wearing a hug. At dinner, Stephanie kept bouncing around in her seat. She took small portions and fast, choppy bites. Her busy hands caused her to spill her glass of juice, that hit her plate with a loud *clank*, and startling some people out of their daydream.

"Oh! Sorry!" Stephanie said trying to wipe up the spill. Luckily the glass was almost empty. She glanced up at Jonathan. He had a fixed gaze on her with a look that said, *chill out!* Stephanie read this and continued through dinner in slow careful movements.

"That's ok Steph, it's just spilled juice. It wiped up like nothing ever happened." Flo said as she rolled her eyes ending the roll peering at Jonathan. If her stare were a fist, it would have given Jonathan a black eye. Stephanie caught this eye contact and almost laughed. Jonathan just shook his head and looked down at his plate and continued eating.

In the kitchen Jonathan was at the sink washing pots and hanging them to air dry. Flo came up to him and looked at him crossly.

"What's your problem?" She asked with a sneer. This made him slightly jump and he turned his head like a kid caught in the cookie jar. Flo looked different to Jonathan. She was leaning sideways against the counter. Her hips were extended out supporting her body. She had her arms crossed below her chest. It was as if Jonathan was looking at her for the first time. It was at that moment that he absorbed the curves of her body, her wavy hair, and crystal eyes. The sight of her was hypnotic. *God, I'm going to miss you Flo.* He thought to himself. Jonathan didn't realize the spell he was in.

"Hellooo!" She finally snapped. Jonathan did a double-take.

"Wait, what, what is it?" he asked. Keeping a *death stare* on him she asked in a louder voice,

"What's your problem? Why the nasty looks at Stephanie?" Jonathan was wondering what she was talking about. It's not her busyness what's going on between Stephanie and him.

"Nothing, she's being all clumsy stilling drinks and stuff. Why? What's it to you?" Jonathan remarked giving Flo that look that scans a person from head to toe. Flo's eye language changed. It went from death stare to a concerned / sadness. Jonathan had no idea what was going on. He was wondering if Stephanie told her something. Without saying a word Flo stormed off. Jonathan followed her with his eyes; as he remained standing in place.

Jonathan explained to Chaz and Jett about what happened earlier that day. He didn't tell them the full story. He certainly didn't tell them about flagging that girl down as she was driving by. He knew they wouldn't be able to keep a secret. Jonathan was on his way to finding Stephanie and was trying to think of a private place for them to talk. He was thinking maybe just taking a walk out into the field is a good place. He finally found Stephanie in her room about to leave.

"Oh, Jonathan I was just about to find you." Stephanie said.

"Really? I was doing the same for you. We'll have a good talk; but first, did talk with Flo after we came back?"

"No why?" she asked.

"Because she was on my case about the way I was looking at you when you spilled your drink." He said.

"I didn't say anything; I didn't even talk to her today." Stephanie narrowed her eye brows and just looked down at the ground.

"Whatever, let's take a walk we have a few things to discus." Jonathan didn't start the conversation until they are entering the field and far away from everyone.

"So, what happened?" She asked in great excitement.

"Ok, aside from your judgment of distance being off, I think the shack is where Groady buried the bus driver. There was an oval shaped patch of dirt in the middle of the shack. There was also a trapdoor in the corner of the shack."

"OK, that's kinda creepy. So about the girl…" Stephanie said impatiently.

"Ok, we made it to the road. That's when we met her. We heard her Jeep from around the bend. We actually heard the music she was blasting before we saw her. When she came around the bend, I kinda jumped in front of her Jeep." Jonathan said.

"You did what!" She asked in disbelief.

"Otherwise she would have just kept driving and not have stopped."

"You're-you're lucky she did hit you!" Stephanie stuttered. "Was she young or old?"

"She was real young, maybe about nineteen. Anyway, when I approached her car I noticed she had a taser ready."

"A what?"

"A taser. It's a self defense weapon used to blast someone with an electric shock if they try to mug or rob you. I explained to her what happened to us and where we were. I tried to explain to her to remember this bend in the road where we were, but I don't think she was getting it. I also told her about the summer camp you kids were on your way to. I told her to contact them and tell them about us." Stephanie just remained silent for a minute as a look of doubt washed over her face.

"Do you think she'll tell anyone about us? I mean if so, did she give a time when help will arrive?"

"No mention of when help may be coming, but, a strange guy jumping in front of your car. That's a story worth telling anyone. I hope she tells the cops, that's just what we want." Jonathan pointed out. Again, Stephanie remained silent for a moment. She was trying to think of more questions, but none come to mind. Stephanie asked one *last chance* question.

"Did she say anything ells?" Just then she thought of the question that was burning to get out. "Oh wait! what was her name?" Jonathan almost did a double take. *Her name?* he didn't get her name. He was also trying to think of anything ells he and the girl talked about.

"I didn't get her name. Oh, she did say one last thing. It really isn't important, but I figured you'd want to know. When I tried to get her to remember the area we were at, she commented that the road was about sixty miles long and she would easily to forget." Stephanie really didn't know why she needed to know this.

"Oh." She said shrugging it off. Jonathan decided to explain what was on his mind.

"The road you found may be the road we met by the accident. The girl said it was one of those roads that went on forever. She claimed she was driving for two hours and we were the only people she saw; just saying."

Stephanie pretty much heard all she needed to know. Jonathan could see her thinking. He didn't even get to the part about Star wanting to go with them. He didn't want to overwhelm her. The truth is that, he was not sure himself what to make of it. For now he was not going to say anything about Star, they have enough to worry about. Jonathan's eyebrows narrowed together and his face pinched from the question she asked next.

"What was playing on the radio?" Stephanie asked.

"What!"

"What was playing on the radio?"

"I don't remember; what does it matter?" Jonathan was really trying to remember but wasn't telling her.

"I'm just judging that's all." She admitted.

"I think it was some song by Lady Ga-Ga; if it's so important."

"It really isn't. Have you told Jett or Chaz?" She asked

"I didn't say anything to them. I'm probably not going to until I know for sure what's going on. Unfortunately for now it's going to be a waiting game, but I don't plan on waiting too long." He said.

"How long do you figure and what do we do in the mean time?" She asked. Without hesitation he answered.

"Get everyone ready to leave; but! Do it in such a way as not to let the cat out of the bag. Meaning...."

"I know what you mean." She said sharply.

"I figure wait one to three days; maybe in that time take one more hike to the road. I really don't want to make these kids hike unless there is a sure way of being rescued." Stephanie slightly tilted her head and half rolled her eyes as she looked him.

"So what you're saying is that we have to wait for help to find us." Stephanie said. Jonathan looked up as if to be looking at something invisible in the air above his head, and then at her.

"Almost." Stephanie held her sarcastic gaze on him. "Look, do you really think someone is going to pick up fifteen kids on the side of the road? And that's *if* someone drives by. Besides if someone does come by, do you think there're going to able to have a vehicle that will be able to hold seventeen people?" Stephanie didn't admit to herself that Jonathan was right.

"I guess so..." Jonathan read the sadness in her eye language; and placed a gentle hand on her shoulder.

"Stephanie, I know it's dragging on, but we're at the homestretch, sorry about the pun. Hey! If I have to hike to the highway and get a hold of a bus somehow I will. Well, the one big problem to that plan is that once you reach the highway you're still at least 20 miles from the nearest person." Hearing that really didn't make her feel any better.

The two just sat and pondered on what the day brought. The bouncing flames from the campfire look like a match head. Jonathan felt invisible. He knew the darkness had shielded them from everybody. He was hoping Stephanie felt the same way. She was staring across the field hypnotized by the bouncing flames. The look on her face was not a blank stare; but a mindful wonder. That warm hug feeling embraced them as they imagine what each other is thinking.

Jonathan took a look around and knew they have been gone for a while. The surrounding trees were now under a blanket of night. He looked up and the stars were reminding him that it was getting late. He looked over at Stephanie and she was almost just a shadowy figure; he couldn't see what expression she has on her face.

"Hey! You up?" Jonathan asked.

"What! Yeah, I was just….." Stephanie trailed off.

"I know; in deep thought." Jonathan said. The two shook off their daydreams and verbally regrouped. "Do you wanna start heading back or just sit here for a bit longer?" Jonathan asked.

"I guess we should start heading back. When do you think we should tell Chaz and Jett?" she asked

"I don't know. Like I said, not till I know more about what's going on. But there is one thing I thought of while I was out earlier today."

"What's that?" Stephanie asked.

"It's about Groady." Just then he felt her hand grabbing his arm. He could feel the chill that ran up her spine.

"You ok?"

He asked her and suddenly stopped walking. He felt bad now bringing it to her attention.; he didn't think she would react that way. After a second she let go of his arm and they resume walking.

"Yeah, what about him?" she finally responded.

"I'm Sorry, I didn't know you were still on edge about it. Anyway, for some reason I don't think he was *banished* to the tunnels."

"What!" He felt her questionable glair.

"Yeah, I don't think he was banished to the tunnels. I think he was sent there to make sure no one in the commune escapes."

"Wait! That doesn't make sense. You think Groady was sent in the tunnels and not banished down there?" she asked breaking the sentence up, pausing between some of her words.

"Ok, we saw Groady today. He was outside milling around the shack. I'm sure if he really wanted to he could have wondered to civilization. And also, he could have killed us when we were in the tunnels. No one would ever know, but he didn't. Do ya see what I'm saying?" The two ideas bounced around in her head, were trying to puzzle together.

"I guess. So, you think Jimmy sent him to the tunnels to play watchdog?"

"Exactly!" Jonathan said, as if to finalize his point.

"That's weird, why would Jimmy wanna keep people hostage? Besides, I don't think anyone is going to travel all that way to an outside world they know nothing about."

"I don't think Jimmy is trying to keep people hostage. More like trying to keep them hidden." Jonathan said.

"Well he sure picked the right area." She said as they were getting closer to the group sitting in a circle around the campfire.

"What do ya feel like doing? Wanna join them, or just go off somewhere ells?" Jonathan inquired. Stephanie wasn't sure what she wanted to do. It really depends who was around the campfire. For some reason she had this strange urge to be with Flo. Stephanie couldn't explain to herself or even Jonathan why Flo makes her feel good; maybe its Flo's tough attitude.

"I don't know, I think I just wanna be alone. I could use some peace and quiet to think. What do you feel like doing?" She asked.

"I think I'm going to see if I can talk to Chaz and Jett alone. I'm going to tell them what we saw on the hike, but I'm not going to tell them about the girl in the Jeep. I think that would just set their minds racing and they would start talking and that would be opening a can of worms. I do feel I have to tell them something." He said.

"I guess." She shrugged and went off to her sleeping quarters to lay down and think. After a moment Jonathan decided that good idea and does the same.

# CHAPTER 33

## The Girl and the Plane

The next thing Jonathan knew, he was hearing footsteps and hustle and bustle all around him. He could also hear the faint sounds of water running and pots, pans, and dishes echoing from the kitchen. He sat up pretty quickly; he felt like he was asleep forever. He looked around the room and noticed Travis buttoning his shirt. He looked half asleep; almost like he was forcing himself to be awake.

"Rough night? You look half asleep." Jonathan said.

"Oh, the women talking and chattering on kept me up half the night. I was starting to think they would be up all night."

"Who was?" Jonathan asked.

"Flo and I think Stephanie? I know one of them was Flo, I could recognize that laugh anywhere." Jonathan pinched his eyebrows together and slightly jerked his head back.

"Laughter? Flo?"

"Yeah! I couldn't believe it myself. It's rare, but it does happen." Travis said.

"Did you hear what they were laughing about?"

"I couldn't make it out what they were saying it was muffled; but that laugh is unmistakable." Travis shook his head. "Well, we better grab some breakfast before it's all gone. Hey, you going to be around later? I could use your help in the barn. The roof is leaking." Travis asked.

"Sure, what time do you think?"

"I'm not sure, I have a few other things to get done first, but I'll come find you."

"Ok, whenever." Travis thanked him and headed for out to grab some breakfast. Before Jonathan could stand up, Stephanie floated in the doorway.

"Morning!" She chimed. Jonathan turned around and was surprised to see Stephanie so bright eyed. Seeing her like that, made him brighten up himself.

"Morning sunshine!" He cheered back." You're chipper this morning."

"And why wouldn't I be?" Her cheerfulness almost made him forget to ask about if she was talking to Flo last night.

"Hey! Heard you and Flo were chatting it up last night." Jonathan was glad she and Flo were getting along, but he was concerned what Stephanie might have told her.

"Yeah, we got caught up in conversation ya-know; girl stuff. Why?"

"No reason." Jonathan chuckled. Stephanie looked at him puzzled. "Travis told me this morning he heard you guys talking but it was muffled. Flo's laugh gave her away. We both had to stop for a second and think to ourselves, Flo and laughter. Did you mention anything about what happened yesterday?" Jonathan asked changing his tone of voice.

"I told her, but she seemed not to care. Why?"

"I just thought we agreed not to say anything to anyone." He said.

"Oh, I thought we agreed not to say anything to Jett or Chaz. I really don't think it's a big deal." She said snidely. Jonathan could see she was getting annoyed for some reason. He doesn't want to ruin the good vibe she seemed to be floating in, and decided to shrug it off.

"I gotta help Travis sometime today to fix the roof on the barn. He didn't say why. Sorry if I annoyed you; I didn't mean to ruin your vibe." After a moment of awkward silence he suggested they grab some breakfast.

"Common, let's grab something to eat. I'm starving." He said.

"No thanks; gotta run." And she swept out of the room almost as gratefully as she floated in.

Travis and Jonathan are studying the roof of the barn, and then bring their gaze down to look straight ahead as the barn door creaked its way open. Jett, Chaz and Arbin are silhouetted against the bright sunlight. Travis and Jonathan look at each other and then back at the boys. The three notice this and realized they just walked into some kinda labor trap.

"What timing; just the young fellows we're looking for" Travis said with triumph. The curious, bright eyed trio suddenly had long faces and sagging eyes.

"Relax, It's going to be easy work. We just need you guys to hand us stuff so we don't have to climb up and down the latter. But I need at least one of you to come on the roof with me. The roof has a leak and we just have to replace a few boards." Jonathan explained.

Jett volunteered to go on the roof. In a short moment Jonathan and Jett were on the roof. They started to pry off the boards Jonathan and Travis just inspected from the inside. Travis, Chaz and Arbin remain on the ground.

"Heads up!" Jonathan yelled down as he looked for a clear spot to drop the last board. Travis climbs half way up the ladder and saw what Jonathan had pried off. Travis gives a nod of approval headed back down the ladder to start handing up new pieces of board for Jonathan to nail down.

Travis handed Jonathan the first piece of board. He seemed to be looking past Jonathan into the distant sky. Jonathan didn't notice it at first, but after watching Travis for a few seconds; he turns around to see what Travis is being hypnotized by. Soon, all five of them were staring at what appeared to be some kinda crop plane. It glided out of sight without making a sound. Jonathan was guessing by the look on Travis's face; it has been a while the last time he saw a plane. After a minute or two, they resumed working on the roof.

A little less than ten minutes pasted when two faint sounds flew overhead. The sound of a slight rumble and the sound of buzzing seemed to sputter across the sky. This time all five heard it and looked in wonder. The plane was closer than it was a few minutes ago. Jonathan couldn't help but think *they finally found us.* But he didn't want to get his hopes up. The plane flew over slow; than once it passed them it gained elevation and faded out of site.

"Victor 1 to base."

"This is base go ahead victor 1"

"I just flew over site as described. All I saw was a few people repairing the roof of an old barn, didin't look like much from hear. Is there any more info on that missing party of children?"

"No, just that they're supposed to be in a commune of some kind. Did you see any one ells or other houses around?"

"I did see a few other buildings and what looked to be a small farm land of some kind. You want me to take one more pass?"

"Naw, bring it in looks like there is a storm coming."

"Roger that."

Chaz charged up the ladder. Before he could get a word out, Jonathan answered his question.

"Yes! We saw the plane." Jonathan said.

"maybe that was for us" Chaz said franticly. He started to ramble on once again. Jonathan raised a hand in the *stop* motion and held eye contact with only Chaz and Jett.

"Hold on, I don't want you guys saying anything to anyone yet. I know you're excited, I don't want you spreading rumors. That plane could've just been lost for all we know." Jonathan said.

"Yeah but that's the only other sign of life form other than us we saw in two months." Chaz cheered.

"Yeah I know, but still let's not get our hopes up; like I said that plane could've been lost. For now let's get this roof finished; there are a few things I may need your help with." Jonathan said. As soon as they were done with the roof, Jonathan was on a mission to find Stephanie. He finally found her inside gathering up her belongings as if to be packing her clothes. *How ironic* Jonathan thought.

"Hey!" Jonathan said, almost keeping his voice down. Stephanie looked up and saw the excitement in his eyes. "Any one ells in her?" Jonathan asked.

"No, What's up?" She suddenly perked up. Jonathan turned and closes the door gently. Now she was really confused. "What's going on?" she asked with a soft tone in her voice. Before he told her about the plane Jett, Chaz, and he saw; he told her not to get overly excited. She agreed.

"Me, Chaz and Jett were helping Travis repair the roof on the barn and I think we saw a search plane!"

"What!" She almost shouted. Jonathan placed a finger in front of his lips making that *shh* sign. She continued using her inside voice. "Wait! when, what did it do? Did they see you?" She fired off.

"We were on the roof and Travis noticed the plane first because he was already looking up, handing me a piece of wood. It wasn't making any noise."

"What kinda plane?" she asks cutting him off.

"Listen to me! I think it some kinda crop plane, it was small. Travis was looking at it as if he didn't know what it was; it was like he didn't know what a plane was. The plane flew out of sight. We all shrugged it off and went back to work fixing the barn. About ten minutes later we all heard this buzzing / rumbling sound. And the plane was flying over us again, this time even lower. Then the plane just flew out of sight. We didn't see it again that was about two hours ago."

"Do you think they saw you?" She asked.

"They had to have, they were flying low enough. My only question is; did they know who or what they were looking at?" The two just stood there in wonder. Their energy field was shattered by a tiny voice that made them jump out of their skin. Now they heard a chuckle. Jonathan and Stephanie spun around. Kasey was standing there holding her hand covering her mouth. Her eyes were smiling from ear to ear. Jonathan and Stephanie turned and looked at each other for a second. Jonathan walked over to Kasey with a friendly grin and squatted down to eye level.

"What's up sweetie?" After a second she uncovered her mouth and almost broke into laughter.

"I scared you." Kasey giggled.

"I guess you did. What's going on?"

"Did you see that plane?" Kasey asked. Jonathan's head got warm, and he felt sick to his stomach. He didn't want to be the one to have to tell little Kasey that the plane she saw, may not be looking for them.

"I did see it, but I don't think that was a rescue plane sweetie. I'm not sure what it was."

"It wasn't." Kasey replied. Jonathan turned and looked at Stephanie for a second and back at Kasey.

"Oh? What makes you say that?" He asked.

"Mr. Jimmy. He said that the plane flies by every few months and they may or may not tell someone about us." To Jonathan's surprise

Kasey didn't seem overly excited about seeing the plane. At the same time he was thankful knowing she was so calm about it.

"What ells did Mr. Jimmy tell you about the plane?" Jonathan inquired.

"Nothing, that was it. Are you coming for lunch? It'll be ready soon." Kasey said.

"Sure Kasey, we'll be there in a minute. Ok?" Jonathan said rubbing the top of her head.

"Wait! There was a plane coming the whole time?" Stephanie protested. Jonathan's mouth opened, but nothing came out. He started to say something, but only stuttered. He could only shake his head, at the same time through his hands in the air waist high, palms up. Jonathan tried to offer some lame comment.

"I don't know! I don't live here!" She really didn't find that funny. Jonathan wasn't trying to be funny. He was just as confused as she was. "And if I knew there was a plane coming, don't you think I would have told you. Do you honestly believe I would have gone on that five mile hike in the rain if I knew there was going to be a plane flying overhead the next day?" Jonathan protested, without raising his voice. Jonathan convinced Stephanie to calm down and grab some lunch.

After lunch, Stephanie and Jett were heading out toward the barn. They were hoping to find Jonathan there. They wanted to tell him Stephanie's idea about somehow signaling the plane if it came by again. The only person they saw was Travis. He was admiring the work he and Jonathan had done earlier.

"Hey, have you seen Jonathan?" Jett asked, looking up at the recently repaired roof. Travis was answering Jett, all the while examining the roof.

"I haven't seen him, only this morning and at lunch. But if you do see him, ask him…." Travis stopped talking as he noticed Jonathan walking in their direction. "Oh, speak of the devil. Sorry, no pun intended." Jonathan walked over being hypnotized by the roof along with everyone ells.

"Looks good." Jonathan commented.

"Yeah, we'll know better the next time it rains to see if it still leaks.

I think we got it though. Do you think you can give me a hand later? One of the stall doors is falling off and it's a lot easier with two people." Travis explained.

"Sure, just find me." Jonathan said. Jonathan was reading the facial expressions on Jett and Stephanie's faces. He had a strong feeling they wanted to talk to him. "I have a few things right now, when did you want to fix the door?"

"Oh, later, maybe after dinner; no hurry." Travis said casually.

"Where did you go I was looking for you?" Stephanie asked.

"I went to look for Jimmy and ask about that plane we saw. I was wondering why he didn't tell us about it" Jonathan said.

"Yeah, I agree. I have an idea if we see that plane again. We have to find some way to signal to it." Stephanie said.

"What did you have in mind?" Jonathan asked

"I'm not sure. One thing I thought of; if the plane flies by again we all position ourselves somehow so we spell out *SOS*, like a human message board." Jonathan thought for a moment.

"That's an excellent plan, but... you would always have to have everybody ready at all times. Too bad we couldn't go back in time, or at least know if and when that plan is going to come by." Jonathan said.

"I thought of that, that's why I thought of forming in block lettering." Jonathan had a doubtful look on his face; she explained what she was talking about. "Like the *O* can be done with four of us." Jonathan was slowly catching on.

"So, the *S* could be done with six people." He guessed. Stephanie nodded her head.

"Yes. It does take a lot of planning. The other thing thought of was just waving my arms franticly." Stephanie said. Jonathan raised his eyebrows and tilts his head slightly, as if to agree that's a better idea. After a second in deep thought Stephanie made a decision. "Ya know, the whole *SOS* thing was dumb idea anyway. There's no time for that, looks like we're back to waiting again."

"I have a feeling that the plane will be back soon." Jonathan said.

"What makes you say that?" she asked.

"Because when the plane flew by; the pilot did a double take. It was like he saw something that stunned him. That makes me think he'll be back soon." The tone of Jonathan's voice and the look in his eyes made Stephanie do a double take herself.

"You're serious; I can see it in your eyes. How long do you think before he comes back again?" Stephanie asked.

"I guessing by tomorrow sometime; I could be wrong though." Stephanie had the same feeling; at the same time she didn't want to get her hopes up. She was tired of getting let down. This whole ordeal was taking a toll on her mentally. Broken promise, after broken promise; a positive attitude was becoming not so easy to hold on to. Jonathan could read this in her eyes and didn't know how to reassure her not to give up hope.

Stephanie, Jonathan and Jett stroll toward the garden. Kasey and Hazelton were gathering veggies for the nights feast. Star was with them. She saw the three and called out to Jonathan with eye contact. He went over to see what Star had to say, while Jett and Stephanie tended to the two children.

"Hey, I heard though grapevine your rescue plane finally came through. So when are we leaving?" she asked. Stephanie glanced over. Jonathan wasn't sure if she heard what Star just asked. He was hoping not; he didn't want to get into a heavy conversation now. Then he suddenly remembered what Jimmy told Kasey.

"That plane wasn't for me. Jimmy said that was just a crop plane that flies by every few months. I wish it were a rescue plane." He said hoping that would end her crazy idea of going with them.

Jonathan was almost regretting kissing her that time when they went to search for the road. *The things people say and do huddled together in the pouring rain, in hopes to stay dry.* Jonathan thought. Stephanie's trance was broken by Kasey tugging on her hand.

"Do ya think this one's ready Stephanie?" A tiny voice floated up to Stephanie's ears; forcing her head to look down.

"What? Yeah, sure that looks fine Kasey." Stephanie said examining the rest of Kasey's gatherings. "Oh Kasey dear, this one needed a little more time." Stephanie pointed out, holding up a cucumber. "But that's ok, we'll still eat it. Just try to remember for next time, ok?" Kasey just nodded her head in agreement.

"Look Star, I'll let you know if something comes up. I don't want you to get your hopes up." Jonathan tried to explain. Star's eyes went dim and her lips fall strait.

"Yeah, I guess so." She sulked. Jonathan felt no need to explain further.

Stephanie's mind was racing with what she thought she overheard between Star and Jonathan. She wanted to have a talk with Jonathan, now!

"Kasey dear, why don't you let me and Jonathan carry that inside for you?" Stephanie said loud enough for Jonathan to hear; all the while raising an eyebrow. Jonathan read this and walked over, looked down and gave Kasey a friendly smile. Jonathan and Stephanie each grabbed one end of the basket full of fruits and veggies and made their way to the main house. Jonathan could feel the energy radiating off of Stephanie, and he was waiting for her to explode in protest.

"What was that! You're taking Star with us?"

"Listen, I'm not taking her with us. If she wants to tag along to get out if here that's up to her. You guys are the ones I'm worried about." Jonathan reassured her.

"What's her problem? Why does she want to leave?" She asked.

"I don't know. Maybe seeing the girl in the Jeep triggered something. That was probably the only link to the outside world she has ever seen." Jonathan said.

"And what if she does want to go with us? I don't think Jimmy is just going to let her go." Stephanie said.

"Like I said that's not my problem. I just have to worry about us." Hearing that seemed to calm Stephanie down. They put the basket on the counter by the sink and Jonathan began to wash the fruits and veggies. Stephanie went back outside to bring the children the empty basket. Jonathan was hoping she didn't say anything to Star.

Stephanie returned to the garden just in time to see Kasey and Hazelton struggling to hold the food they picked. They unwrapped their little arms and drop their collecting in the basket.

"Wow, I came just in time, Huh?" Stephanie said. The two nodded and ran down the edge of the garden leaving behind the basket. Stephanie went to open her mouth, to tell them they left the basket. She decided against it, when she thought of how funny it would be when they figured it out themselves. Stephanie asked Star about the whole idea of Star going with them if they got rescued.

"Hey, I need to ask you something." Stephanie said.

"Sure what's up?" Star replied.

"Ah, Jonathan mentioned you maybe planning on going with us when help comes. Is this true? I mean, why? I don't think Jimmy's going to be happy about that, do you?" Star thought for a moment. She didn't know how to respond. She thought that was just between her and Jonathan.

"It was just an idea. Jonathan kinda hinted that he wanted me to go with him. I don't know how Jimmy would take it. Honestly, I'm not sure I could leave everyone here. It was just a thought." Star explained.

"Wait! Jonathan said he wanted you go with us?" Stephanie asked. Star thought for a second.

"He really didn't say it. He more or less hinted it." Stephanie's eye brows narrowed in confusion.

"What do you mean he *hinted*?" Stephanie asked.

"When we were on that hike, we got to talking and we kissed." Stephanie didn't see that one coming.

"Oh! Ok. I guess. I was just worried about what Jimmy would have to say about the whole thing. I didn't want him coming after Jonathan, that's all." Stephanie said.

"Like I said, it was just an idea." Star reminded her. Before anything ells could be said, the sound of squeaking wicker was being mixed with the soft thudding of fruit and veggies. This broke what could have been a very awkward silence.

"Ok, we're done." a tiny voice said. Without hesitation, Stephanie picked up the basket. She thanked the children and made her way to the kitchen to meet up with Jonathan. On her way over, she had a new thought to dwell on. She kept imagining Jonathan and Star kissing. *Stop it Stephanie! Focus on getting recued; and figuring out a way to signal the plane if it comes by again.* She told herself. For some reason the barn roof caught her eye. There was the new plywood on the one side. Seeing that gave her a great idea. She suddenly perked up and hurried to the kitchen.

"Hey! I got some more for dinner" Stephanie said. Jonathan saw her wide eyes and half smile.

"Thanks." He said absorbing in her new found great mood. "Must be a magic garden." Jonathan joked.

"What?" she asked

"Never mind. You seem be in a better mood." He could tell Stephanie had something to say. "Are you going to tell me or just stand there?" He commented.

"I just thought of a great idea to signal that plane and nobody has to sit around and wait for it to fly by, but I need some paint." She blurted out.

"Paint?" why?"

"Just, where would paint be?" She asked

"I'm not sure, maybe the barn or in the basement down here. What are you up to?" He asked. Just then Flo entered the kitchen.

"I'll explain later." She shouted back leaving the kitchen, toward the front door and outside.

"Explain what?" Flo asked. Jonathan thought it best not to tell Flo and get into a deep discussion. He really didn't know why Stephanie needed paint for anyway.

"Nothing, just a childish idea he has in her head." He said rolling his eyes. Judging by the stare she has on him; he knew she didn't believe him.

"Or you just don't want to tell me." She claimed tightening her gaze. Jonathan looked up in space for a second in that *oh god* pose.

"Do you need help with something Flo?" Jonathan asked. Flo raised her eyebrows and shrugged as she grabbed a red pepper and started cutting it.

"I just came to help out. That's what we do. Is there a problem with that?" she asked *as lasers shot from her eye sockets.* After dealing with Star and Stephanie, Jonathan was warmed up, and ready to give Flo a run for her money. *Insert slam here.* He thought.

"No, love having you." He winked at her. "Stand here, next to me. I feel we don't see enough of each other. How are things going?" He said holding a smile so hard it made dimples in his cheeks. She didn't know how to respond. She was thinking of a good come-back. He could tell by the way she had to look back down at her hand so she didn't cut off a finger. This made him smile even wider. She said the only thing that comes to mind, even if it is a cheap shot.

"So, when ya leaving? I thought you'd be gone by now." Without any hesitation Jonathan fired back.

"We're not leaving; we're going to stay, here, with you. You really have grown on the children and me as well." Jonathan put the knife down, took a step closer to Flo and wrapped both arms around her and nuzzled their heads together. She said nothing, just made a loud chopping sound with her knife. It knocked the cutting board so hard it echoed though the kitchen.

"Hey you too, get a room." said a voice from behind them. They turned and saw Jimmy standing there. Just the guy Jonathan was looking for. He released his grip on flow and continued cutting vegetables. He really didn't know what to say to Jimmy to break the ice. Then he thought of something.

"Jimmy, have you seen Stephanie?"

"I haven't seen her. Why?" Jimmy asked.

"She was looking for paint for some reason."

"What did she need it for?" Jimmy inquired.

"don't know" Jonathan said shaking his head. "And I honestly almost don't care."

Jonathan was debating whether or not he should ask Jimmy about the plane they saw, and why he didn't mention that a plane comes by every so often. Jonathan decided against asking Jimmy about the plane, as he could hear Travis and Terry instructing the children on the easy kitchen work to be done. Jonathan was guessing two other people that had joined him and Flo were also cutting up of vegetables. The kitchen was in full buzz.

# CHAPTER 34

## Going Home

Terry looked over at Hazelton's dinner plate and could tell He needed help cutting his meat. He was only eating the veggies, not his favorite but easy to cut.

"Need help buddy?" She asked. Without saying a word he leaned back and moved his hands away from his plate, a sign that said *yes*. She cut his steak and he continued to eat. Jonathan looked over at Stephanie and noticed she has faded blotches of red paint on her hands. He looked up at her face and her eyes were brilliant with energy. She had a slight smile. Jonathan was concerned she did something Jimmy may not like; but he knew he'll find out what she did soon enough. Before campfire, Jonathan finally caught up with Stephanie.

"Hey! What did you need red paint for?" Jonathan asked. She told Jonathan all about the red paint and what she did. He was impressed. He warned her to try to scrub the rest of the paint off her hands before people start asking questions.

A few days of labor and washing proved to be the best way to remove paint from hands without any real paint remover. Jonathan was making plans to hike to the highway again. This time he was not coming back without help on the way. He had this nagging feeling to take Stephanie with him this time. He only hesitated because he knew how she can get side tracked and prolongs things. He really didn't want to go through the added trouble of one more person to worry about. Judging by Stephanie's reaction the last time, Star may not feel so welcome, but Jonathan did enjoy Star's company. It was nice to be with someone he was eye to eye with.

A clear blue sky was always nice to be piloting a small plane in. The pilot knew the clear wasn't going to last long, as evening was setting in. This flight proved to be very different from the others he had taken. The first thing he does before radioing the tower was look for a place to land if he had to do so. There's a field below that looked big enough to land and take off, assuming the ground is smooth. If that wasn't going to work he was looking for a second choice. The nearest road of any kind is a highway about five miles away. The pilot figured a chopper could be used if worse come to worse.

"Victor 1 to tower" A static filled voice called out.

"This is tower."

"Tower, I have strong reason to believe that the party of children that went missing over two months ago is in that commune." Said the pilot.

"Oh, what makes you say that?" asked the tower.

"Someone painted the letters *SOS* on roof of one of the houses, and I know it wasn't there before when I flew by a few days ago."

"Ok, is there any place to land that you can see?" asks the tower.

"Not really, maybe a chopper would be best. The nearest road looks to be about five miles away." The pilot replied.

"Ok, if you can't land bringer in. We'll have to figure out something."

"Roger." answered the pilot. He had a strong feeling to try and signal the kids below and let them know help was on the way. The pilot circled back and passed by the guest house and took one last look at the roof with the letter *SOS* painted on it; and also the landscape. He wanted to know what kind of aircraft could land the small field.

Chaz and Jett both look at each other in confusion. They heard a sound that they heard once before, but couldn't place it. The sound was a cross between a hum and a rumble. At the same time they remembered where they heard that sound from and they both looked up.

"Come on!" Jett said tapping Chaz on the shoulder. They made their way into the guest house and reached the roof top just in time to see the plane fading smaller and soon fade out of sight. They both exhale in half disappointment.

"Do you think they saw it?" Chaz asked

"Yeah! It's big red lettering." Jett reassured. "I saw, they slowed down as they flew overhead. Let's tell Jonathan." The two found Stephanie and told her about the plane they just saw.

"Did you tell Jonathan?" She asked

"No, we haven't seen him. Know where he is?" Jett asked.

"Yeah, he was just here; I think he went in the basement with Travis." The three went outside where the little daylight was fading and soon will be gone. They gazed at the sky like their waiting for the mother ship.

"Stars look great tonight." They turned around and saw Jonathan at one end of the ladder and Travis at the other end.

"Oh, we were just looking for you." Jett said.

"What's up?" Jonathan asked.

"If you're busy, it can wait." Jett said.

"We're just brining this to the barn. I'll catch you in a few." Said Jonathan.

Later at campfire, Chaz and Jett Managed to meet up with Stephanie and Jonathan. The boys could tell by the look on Jonathan's face, Stephanie had told him the news about the plane. It was then Jonathan told them he was planning on hiking to the highway again and not returning without help on the way. Jonathan said this looking at Stephanie with a stern gaze. She just looked back at him with a sarcastic smile.

The next morning started out cloudy with heavy rain. The weather finally broke later that afternoon. The sky became bright blue. The last of the clouds could be seen trailing off in the distance. The sun became strong and was beating down. The sounds of chirping birds were carried by a steady cool breeze. Quietness echoed though the compound, as everyone was still hibernating from this morning's rain.

The silence was broken by a far off rumble; this wasn't the same rumble from the plane that was heard a few days before. This was heavier, and seemed to have a stutter to it; like a strobe light effect. The sound got a little louder and just maxed out. After a few seconds, there was no mistaking it was a helicopter. Jonathan and some of the kids ran outside to see what it was. They saw it getting lower in the center of the field far from the main house. Jonathan, Stephanie, Jett, Chaz, and Kasey just stared at the helicopter. By this time the helicopter landed; the whipping blades moved slower and slower. The *swishing* air that was being stirred from the blade also slowed down.

The pilot got and stood in place for a second as he looked up and saw about thirty or forty people looking at him. He also saw a young man, two boys about ten years old, a girl who looked to be about fifteen years old, and a little girl about five or six years old. They were running in his direction; all with a look on their faces that said *help us!* Behind them, there was a stream of children ages from five to twelve or thirteen he was guessing. *This must be the missing party.* He thought to himself.

"God, am I glad to see you!" Jonathan said shaking the man's hand and pulling him in for a bro hug. The pilot returned condolences

"The names Vic. Are you with that missing party?" the pilot asked.

"Yes, there's sixteen of us. I hope you have the room."

"I should, I'll squeeze you all in somehow. Do you need to pack anything?" Asked Vic. Jonathan told the children to get there things, there're going home. He almost started to cry after he said it; he waited over three months to so that.

By this time everyone from the commune was outside. Brief, very brief good-byes were exchanged. Hazelton gave Kasey a hug. They couldn't help but to start crying. Terry and Travis went over to comfort them. Star went over to Jonathan.

"I guess I'm staying after all, huh?" She said looking at the ground. "It was a stupid idea." Jonathan lifts her head up gently with his fingers.

"You never know, I may be back. I know where you live." There is a short, silent pause. "That's a joke in the outside world." Jonathan explained. Star just shrugged. He gave her a soft kiss and hugged her good-bye.

Stephanie slows her pace down and makes eye contact with Flo. Stephanie didn't know what to say to her. They just lock eyes for a second, finally Stephanie breaks the silence.

"Bye." Stephanie said with a blank stare, Flo returns the comment.

"Good bye Stephanie." Flo said. This made Stephanie's eyes widen and she took a deep breath. She opened her mouth to say something but couldn't find the words. Stephanie remembers the *girl talk* they had that one time, and how glad she felt after words.

"Thanks for all your help." Stephanie finally said.

"Sure, no big deal." Flo said.

"When's the wedding?" Jonathan said to break the awkwardness. Flo looked at Jonathan and squinted her eyes in what looked to be mix of anger and sarcasm. Jonathan put his arms out to embrace Flo in a hug; also out of sarcasm. "I'm going to miss you most of all scarecrow." Jonathan said. She put her hand up thumping him on the chest and stopped him in his tracks.

"Go….. Away." She said in a slow drawn out emphasis. He was more than happy to do so.

"I don't totally hate you in fact I'm going to miss you actually." Flo just held her gaze, that did soften a little; closed her eyes and gave a nod of approval. A nod that said *whatever.* The sound of the chopper blades reached Jonathan's ears. He noticed the blades were in full swing. Jonathan was wondering why he didn't hear them start up. Without warning, Jonathan felt a hand on his shoulder.

"We're waiting for son." Jonathan turned and saw the chopper pilot and then noticed he was to only one not on the helicopter. The pilot turned to look at Jimmy and they gave each other a nod.

"We should be at the base in about Thirty minutes." Vic shouted over the chopper noise. The kids were ending their wild adventure with a helicopter ride. Jonathan was wondering what they were thinking; happy that there're finally going home and jazzed about being in a helicopter. He could see the children staring out of the windows in aww.

"Sounds good to me." Jonathan said. "How did you finally find us? Did a girl in a jeep happen to tell you?" Jonathan asked.

"I think so, my boss said his daughter mentioned the area. It's a good thing I saw your smoke signal; that's how I spotted the commune." Jonathan looked at him with total confusion and looked back at Stephanie. She is too fixed on the sights from the window.

"Smoke signal? We didn't send any smoke signal." Vic looked at Jonathan with the same confusion.

"You didn't? That's how I found you. I saw a burly guy sending smoke signals. It looked like he lived in a snack in the middle of the woods a few miles from the commune. If that wasn't you, who was it?" Vic asked

"I don't know." Jonathan said. Vic just shrugged and radioed the tower.

"Vic1 to tower." A static filled voice blurted out of the tiny speaker.

"Tower here."

"Tower my E.T.A. is about 25 minutes and I have that missing party, sixteen people in total."

"You have them with you now?"

"Affirmative." There's a brief silence as the tower operator leaned back in his chair and sighed a sigh of relief. "Tower?" Vic repeated.

"Yeah! Sorry, you're clear to come in for a landing. I'll contact the Wilkinson's camp and let them know the children are finally going to arrive. We'll have a bus waiting for them when they get here."

"Roger that." Vic said.

"......ok, I'm contacting parents now!" Linda Schmerginhertz hung up the phone in a mental tornado. The air traffic controller just alerted her about the arriving children that were supposed to be there a little over three months ago.

She got on the radio and called out for Tom the park ranger to immediately report to her office, urgent. Five minutes later Tom came strolling and found Linda opening and slamming file drawers, digging and shuffling files around on her desk. She set aside the ones she wanted. This was the fastest Tom has seen her move in a long time. He knew something was up and is almost concerned.

"What's up?" he asked.

"Remember that missing bus load of children a few months back, well they were found and are finally going to be arriving in about three hours. I need your help to contact parents and let them know to come here as soon as they can." Tom's face went blank, and the color drained out of him. He remembered the whole ordeal. For a few seconds he didn't respond. Linda had to snap him out of his trance.

"Tom! Did you hear me?" Linda shouted.

"Yeah! I got it, sure, ah, just give the numbers and I'll get on it now."

The passenger compartment of the chopper was shouting with silence, only the thunder thudding of chopper blades could be heard. Sixteen pairs of eyes stared down at the commune, the people watching, and the houses gathering closer together, and the painted *SOS* that is painted on the roof of one of the houses, as the chopper gains elevation. Although nobody was saying anything; they all had the same thoughts. How they got there, the people they met and were now are leaving behind, what they learned about living off the land, and the way of life they missed.

Parents started arriving at the Wilkinson's camp by the dozens; even the parents that have been divorced manage to pair up. Mass confusion and lots of questions from overwhelmed parents filled the campgrounds. Linda and Tom were doing their best to instruct parents of the children's arrival. One parent asked *how are we going to know which bus it is?* Tom remarked that it probably would be the bus with the children calling out for mommy and daddy. He also mentioned they would have a police escort.

Camp counselors were running around trying to answer questions and calm parents. Some parents had been there for two hours and still parents were arriving. The entrance to the campgrounds started out with a half mile dirt road that was private, before you see any buildings. The children all crowded to one side of the bus as they saw the first building, a sight they should have seem over three months ago.

The sound of police sirens were heard by the waiting parents. They all stopped to look. Children in the bus were seeing their parents for the first time in three months; as waving arms and cries for mommy and daddy blast from the windows of the bus. Parents started to franticly wave at the bus calling their child's name.

The first police car pulled ahead with sirens wailing to slow down the rush of parents. The bus finally came to a stop and sat there for idol for a minute. Camp counselors approached the bus and wait outside until the bus doors opened. There was no holding back emotion. Crying children rushed out and into the arms of crying parents. After the bus emptied out Jonathan finally stepped out and took in the sight of parents and children reconnecting.

The bus driver looked at Jonathan and asked him if he wanted a cigarette; he took it. Jonathan didn't realize how much he missed it. The cigarette suddenly triggered a memory Jonathan had lost. Stephanie looked behind her parent's shoulders and saw Jonathan having cigarette and just then found out that he smoked. She also thinks she saw him holding back tears. She slowly let go of her parents and ran over to Jonathan.

"Hey what's up?" Stephanie asked. "I didn't know you smoked." He took a deep breath.

"Having this cigarette suddenly made me remember what happened just before the accident. I was reaching for a pack of cigarettes that slid off the front seat on to the floor." She just looked at him blankly, and wondered, *your smoking habit caused this?"*

"I'm so sorry Stephanie." She wasn't mad at all. She just grabbed him and gave him a hug.

"It's ok Jonathan. We're home now that's all that matters." He loved her for understanding. "What are you going to do now?" Stephanie asked.

"I'm going to find a way home." He replied.

"Come on, We'll give you a ride." She said and walked over to her waiting parents. "Mom and dad, this is Jonathan. Please, we have to get him home. He saved us. I'll explain on the way." She said with tear filled eyes.

Jonathan, Stephanie, and her parents were fallowing the line of cars exiting the camp sight. Although Stephanie had never been there before, she felt like she was at the camp the whole time and not at some far off commune. To her the whole ordeal felt like a bad dream she finally woke up from. They drove down the dirt road passing the sign that read, *Thank You for visiting the Wilkinson's camp for the gifted, your journey begins now.*

**The End.**

# Destiny's Path

Funny how words can change where a life goes
Like advice from people who could never know
Or guess where it is that we think we are bound
We just keep moving forward to a distant sound

Deep down in the recesses of our troubled mind
This journey is taking us to a place hard to find
Often in dreams we get glimpses of this place
Is it truly real or just based on timeless space

Most of us think we know what we really need
Searching through life moving at warp speed
When what need to do is slow down the pace
And finally, we realize it's a journey not a race

So, when searching for your unknown destiny
Try to remember it's not just about you or me
But about looking beyond our narcissistic self
It's by helping others we find peace and wealth

# Don't Let Go

When you're down with a darkness all around
Hold to your dream don't let go
Stop, listen to the music and enjoy the sounds
Sing along when you're feeling low

Living is the game of life and all of us have to play
No matter the cards don't let go
Listen to the man who's singing your blues away
Sing along and enjoy the show

To win the game of life you must follow your dream
Be determined and don't let go
Don't just be ordinary, be original and be extreme
Stay with the plan you made to grow

Win—Loose—Draw: Success is never letting go

# Eagle Eyes

Had dinner with a beautiful friend last night
The lady sees life with a laser sharp insight
Never judging without getting all the facts
Thinking through wisdom before she acts

She's seen the waste of relationships past
And learned with joy how to make them last
Living in harmony with the man she chose
She has some thorns but still his Wild Rose

They are the guardians of our ancient earth
Waiting for nature to produce its new birth
Sharing a land giving voice to quiet splendor
Saving our vast resources never a spender

# Forgotten Dreams

I woke up from a dream late one night all alone
Nothing left to remember the thoughts were gone
How nice that would be, forgetting a painful past
Seems like some memories want to linger and last

When you are down, listen to the sounds of silence
Remembering the past pleasures vivid and intense
As you move through life give yourself the right
To enjoy new experiences every day and night

Don't let others determine your right and wrong
The paths you choose are made by you alone
A heart's journey takes you where you need to be
Like a butterfly moved by the wind and floating free

# Forward

Onward in search of your life's destination
Moving forward in life with glad anticipation
Don't allow anyone tell you that you can't
Efforts fail so don't quit, move on with intent

Life is an exciting journey starting every day
Don't ever worry what others have to say
You are the one who has to make the choice
Don't let others deceive that quiet inner voice

Search for happiness always day and night
Always keeping your goals clearly in sight
Find in your life what it is, you really need
When you achieve success, you'll be free

In short:
"Be Everything You Can Be"

# Free Thinking

Free your mind to seeing the things beyond today
We see in the past many ways not to go astray
Yet all of us continue to repeat the same mistakes
And we say how does this happen for heaven sake

We are all victims of societies clichés and doctrines
Ignorance shouldn't be the guide to life and actions
Open up to the possibility words aren't always true
So think before saying yes to ideas without a clue

While they speak with emotion, fire and conviction
Some have the one goal and that's to create friction
Learn to study and think before joining the masses
Always be careful when using rose colored glasses

When you decide by emotion it easy to be misled
Be very cautious about the areas not safe to tread
Opinions are easy to have while truth is hard to find
Avoid useless controversy, keep your peace of mind

# Friends and Family Lost

When I think of you on those lonely nights
It's a strange sadness that I feel
Remembering good times fading from sight
Makes me think It can't be real

You were a constant joy in my happy life.
Now the joy has gone away
And the pain of loss cuts me like a dull knife
So much more I wanted to say

You can't know or hear what's in my heart
The loss I feel way down deep
Saddened, for our life was so quickly torn apart
A memory is all I have to keep

Yes, it's hard to sleep on those lonely nights
The pain of loss can be so hard
Trying to forget with no way to make it right
My heart locked behind cold bars

Even with the memories I hold so very sweet
I'm hurt you left me so alone
I know that death is something we can't beat
It's so sad that you are gone

# Friendship

I think of beauty and it's somehow you I see
A lady who now has become a friend to me
You put a wonderous smile upon my face
And always greet me with a warm embrace

Sometimes it's nice to simply sit and talk
Or enjoy the mountain views as we walk
The aurora around you draws your friends
What a joy to see the love you have within

When I chance a look into your eyes, I see
A sweet tender heart living a life kind and free
Your journey has purpose as you move along
As a special friend, to you my heart belongs

When I think back on the times, we shared
It's amazing how much trust we dared
Telling each other about hard times past
A friendship developed that will always last

Stephen, A Brother Gone too Soon!

# Gone Gone Gone

Some days it's hard to remember your face
Then on others I see you in every place
I miss that I can't talk to you at any time
I catch myself searching but just can't find

When most people talk with me about you
I am filled with memories I want to pursue
Always a smile which warms my heart
You knew how to make us all feel a part

You left me, and the world became darker
Now all that's left is a cold stone marker
Where I have to go when I want to talk
For me to visit there it's a long hard walk

Wish we could again walk, talk, and play
It's sad that you are gone, gone, gone away
But as I watch the beautiful sunrise sky
I'll see you again, in that great by and by

# Greg Ryder

## *A Friend Gone*

A singer, a writer of songs and lover of life
I know for many your death cuts like a knife
Your music and life touched many a friend
To pay you tribute I don't know where to begin

My mind is flying as I remember our past
A friend who is gone and now at rest
To know you are gone makes my heart break
I must ask why it was you, death had to take

The last we talked you had learned to forgive
You said I have to let things go if I want to live
To see you make peace with your past
Made me believe your peace would last

Having known you made many lives better
Listening to you sing will always be a treasure
You would always work in a Marty Robins' song
While I drank a gin and tonic and sang along

Greg it's sad to know you're gone!

# Journeys

Someone will always say I'm crazy
And that's really alright with me
It's ok, because I'm happy just to be

I'm looking and living for the upside
Not looking back, living without regret
I'm on a roll and I'll be taking every bet

You might try and say I can't have it all
But I'm of the belief why not take a shot
At least by doing so I'll have lived a lot

I've seen and climbed majestic mountains
And fly-fished cold clear streams and rivers
And I have enjoyed what life has delivered

Now I'm thinking if there is a master plan
Take the time to make your choice and begin
Might just be a way to be happy until the end

# Just Friends

Lady has eyes that will light up the day
One look deep inside and you'll have to say
She's seen the joy of life and pain of death
But chooses to live happy till her dying breath

If you're lucky enough for her to call you friend
Better hang on tight for this ride will not end
Her look or touch can heal a broken heart
So, in her circle allow yourself to be a part

Share back the love she freely gives
You'll have a friend who always cares
She loves on levels that most cannot see
But if you try and win then happy you will be

# Listen to the Music

Music is the tool to give your heart wings
And allows the tired mind to simply sing
As you hear a song that makes you grow
Enjoy the lyrics and rhythm fast or slow

When the artist pens a new classic song
Whether it's about love, right or wrong
It's good to feel the music and let it roll
Moving our troubled heart, mind and soul

Sometimes the best music is a simple verse
That keeps the ugly world from getting worse
Music adds peace and value to everyday life
Often clearing our minds of the daily strife

So, when you listen to your old favorites
Songs that pull the heart like a magnet
Share your joy with all those around you
Allow your joy to light up your soul anew

# Live Large---Live Long

You know if you're living life that worn and torn
Don't let life's troubles and woes take you down
Remember I was there before you were born
Never allow hopes and dreams to perish or drown

Just do it. Live long live large,
Or don't live at all. Just do it.

If you're leader of the pack or standing in the back
No matter which, live your life and stay on track
Don't make it about money and material things
Live from the heart and let your life take wings

Just do it. Live long live large,
Or don't live at all. Just do it.

Live the life you want to live and chase your dreams
Remember I've been doing this forever it seems
Listen to a traveler who's been down the road before
Never settle for a little life surely owes you more

Just do it. Live long live large,
Or don't live at all. Just do it.

Tidwell Brothers

124

# Message for Dad

As a father I know I should have done more
I know I didn't match the qualities of my dad
But then again, it's not about keeping score
I still try to achieve the wisdom that he had

I would like to once again just sit and talk
And this time take his messages to heart
Learn to talk his talk and walk his walk
It's sad to realize to late he was so smart

He set a very high standard for me to see
Trying, I knew, his level I wouldn't achieve
Maybe coming close, I became a better me
Yes, he taught me how to trust and believe

As I write these thoughts my eyes have tears
You were my hero, that I want you to know
And I am thankful when I remember our years
Your wisdom shared is why I continue to grow

# Miss You

Honey, I thought of you again today
About that I'm not ashamed to say
You helped me learn to trust again
By being first a loyal honest friend

Although death has pulled us apart
I will always have you in my heart
You didn't willingly leave my side
For you dearly loved me till you died

As I begin to travel back to the light
I know you want me to be alright
So, as I now seek my life made new
I hope to find another as kind as you

# Moms

Moms love us from their heart and soul
Making our life happy was their total goal

Moms are always planting positive seeds
Looking always to meet our simple needs

Moms are the compass through our youth
Guiding and encouraging us to seek the truth

The happy life we have finally learned to live
Comes truly from of the love she had to give

# No! To Sorrow

I won't ever stop believing in my tomorrows
Trying to forget all my tears and sorrows
Even while making rhymes of yesterday's
Remembering what the wise ones had to say

When love is gone, all that's left is a tear
No, is the saddest sound you'll ever hear
It's now time to start moving on to tomorrow
So, don't look back at choices filled with sorrow

Listen to some music and dance with the ladies
Taking trips and dreaming of new exciting places
Planning how to build new memories that will last
Sharing good times beyond the sorrows passed

# Puppet on a String

I see people living a life of wealth beyond belief
While there are others living with financial grief
Can I get richer based on who or what I know
Leaving the poor far behind with nothing to show

Is someone poor in wealth due to fate or chance
Or is it maybe their socio-economic circumstance
Are we rich as a result of parents having money
Could it be we simply had a greater opportunity

It's wrong to grow up thinking you can't succeed
Being locked forever in the box of constant need
With desire we can shake the bonds of ignorance
Gaining knowledge will help you make a difference

Don't let society, friends and family ever tell you no
You are responsible for your choice to stay or go
Go forward and reach for the elusive golden ring
Choosing never again to be the puppet on a string

# Retrospection

Why would today I think of you again
When that disappointment is at an end
Your cruel words left us with nothing
While old love was your new something

Why stay when her heart is with another
Yes, I should have listened to the others
Sad when divorce turns out to be the key
The one awful option to finally set you free

How does love die with such a happy start
All the dreams in an instant are torn apart
A love that's not returned has a painful end
Admit your mistake and learn to love again

# Searching For Meaning

Are you a leaf just blowing on the breeze
Or that leaf that is the beauty of the tree
It's easy to accept the worlds status quo
But then you cease to develop or grow

Don't let your life take you where it will
Decide it's time to live your life for real
There's so much beauty don't let it pass
Don't continue to live your life in the past

Charge on into the dark unknown places
That you were at one time afraid to face
Choose courage, you'll find it reassuring
As you search for your life's true meaning

A little added effort gives so much more
Life is not just a battle but the larger war
So, plan to focus on that coming final goal
Your victory offers more than silver or gold

# Searching for Success

Life can be tough while trying to find our way
Looking this way and that day after day
Searching for meaning in the hand you're dealt
Living the difference of poverty and wealth

When you don't know what you're looking for
You feel like life is just an endless loosing war
Many in life are born rich with a silver spoon
Maybe I was just born to late or maybe to soon

But there is a way to get from here to there
It must be done by me cause no one else cares
Life comes down to the choices we will make
So, stumble forward through all your mistakes

You must know it's possible to make it to the top
Keep trying never give up and never ever stop
Others can succeed with seemingly little strife
Success is your destiny, move on to a happy life

# Silence

When you really listen, silence can talk to you
And what you learn is usually honest and true
Winds of chaos with its noise will always blow
Let the muted sounds of silence to gently flow

Silence can be a best answer to an angry voice
Now it's your attacker that has to make a choice
Never think that your silence says you're weak
Just be careful with answers before you speak

They say silence is golden, a gift of quite peace
Listen and allow your stress to slowly decrease
Sometime silence says what needs to be said
Use not words but the wisdom of silence instead

# Stop Look Listen

When l stop to look up and see the starry sky
Life makes me think of the sweet by and by
And all the things my parents shared with me
Yes, they made me the man I turned out to be

Sadly, I made some awful turns along the way
Yet I'm determined to be a better man every day
With the lessons learned some left ugly scars
But they also taught me how to love and care

I see so many folks are struggling every day
Maybe I can help them move on and be unafraid
I want to be one who brings hope and laughter
And maybe claim a place in the great here after

# Stormy Weather

Some of you will think this poem is about you, listen up
Just maybe there is something here to help you develop
What's holding you back, "it's who you think you're not"
Often our failure comes from what we've been taught

Don't be afraid to be different, dare to get out of the box
When you're seeing success don't let yourself be shocked
Look to the front and move ahead, let go of what's behind
Because this is where success and happiness, you'll find

When stormy weather comes don't let yourself be afraid
It's through these cloudy days successful plans are made
Learn everything you can about the place you want to go
It's not easy, but, if earned, you'll get what you are owed

We are given opportunities and choices we have to make
So now it's time to think about the path you want to take
Often times you wonder how some people ever achieved
Don't get caught up in who you're not, just believe

# Surprises

Life has surprises that are both bad and good
Don't waste time wondering what they'll be
Realize at times they may not be understood
Travel onward to the wonders your yet to see

When life has delivered an unwanted surprise
Don't be disappointed look to the joys ahead
It could be as simple as the evening fireflies
Or just throwing off a burden you want to shed

Don't carry the guilt of mistakes like a yoke
They are simply lessons that you had to learn
Ugly things of life usually disappear like smoke
Move forward so joy and peace can be earned

There aren't many secrets in finding our way
Trust your choice of the path you need to take
If it's work or play stay the course never stray
Don't doubt the difference your life can make

# Thanksgiving Day

So many things we can give thanks for every day
A day we justify the good things we want to say
This is when we should realize everyday matters
And being thankful becomes part of our character

Thankful for friends and thankful some went away
Now maybe that's something I shouldn't even say
But if they are not adding joy to life, say goodbye
It's hard to understand, but time to stop asking why

Life tells us you can't quit or give up on someone
But while compromising self, what do you become
There's no wrong in removing negatives in your life
Time to improve your life by ending useless strife

So today be thankful for your life's lessons learned
And may blessings shared be returned

# The Road

Moving along a wonderous and unmarked highway
Beauty sometimes leaves us without words to say
Look around and enjoy the sights there are to behold
Watch the sunsets turn the heavens into solid gold

The road is your journey to somewhere yet unknown
Look for pleasures no matter the curves you're thrown
Life's road is full of twists, turns and ups and downs
Always look for wonder passing through every town

Happiness can be choosing the road far less used
Where you chance to see sights and be amused
Take to the open road and experience the mystery
Of making memories and learning Americas history

When it gets tough take to the road, where life's richer
It can give you a much better view of a hopeful future
Don't be discouraged when a journey comes to an end
"Hit the road again" for this is how our memories begin

# Things I Can Do

You and I know I can't ever walk on the waters
Just be willing to learn to see what I can see
You don't expect of me the miracle of Galilee
I will learn to be the man you need from me

I can't forgive you of your sins and transgressions
But I can accept your apology to let us start again
To say you're sorry means you change your actions
And start a new way of dealing with our infractions

No, I can't turn the water into wine like Jesus did
But I can provide what I need for you and the kids
To live a life of happiness and peace along the way
Allowing for the necessities and the things of play

I won't be able to raise a loved one from the dead
My job is to help us go through this time of dread
And go on and live a life filled with peace and calm
To surround our injured hearts with a healing balm

# Tomorrows

When I look back at my life, I have to say
Life was really good from time to time
Yes, there was some happiness every day
Rivers to cross and mountains to climb

Always an endless hope for my tomorrow
Just knowing that time was on my side
A journey forever dodging any sorrow
Enjoying little pleasures life did provide

Many things happened I can't understand
With the many friends I had along the way
While some of us traveled hand and hand
Some left me for reasons they couldn't say

Not knowing why would make me wonder
Was there something wrong in what I chose
Or were our days together simply numbered
In looking back, I will never know I suppose

Journeys are about tomorrow not the past
Some love and friendships will never fail
And it's those relationships that always last
A search for peace and love can now prevail

# Trying Is Not Failing

When our eyes finally met from way across the room
I knew that words would be slow to come
Others conversations are pretty as flowers in bloom
Beautiful words are natural for some

So many words flooded in, my mind was just a blur
When all I wanted, was to say hello
All I knew was, I wanted to walk up and talk to her
Before she decided she had to go

Don't be afraid, go forward and take a chance today
It's ok for you to try and fail
Let your heart to tell your mouth what it wants to say
Maybe just maybe you will prevail

If you fail remember you will live to try another day
And your chances might improve
Not trying you will feel the loss as she walks away
Never fear it's the only way

# What's Coming

Someday we will see heavens streets of gold
And live a life where we will never grow old
A life without pain, loss and no more death
A beautiful thought that takes my breath

Seeing loved ones who have gone to sleep
Thanks to the sacrifice that wasn't cheap
We will be dressed in robes white as snow
That should be a message all want to know

When life is tough and so hard to understand
It might not be a part of what you have planned
Perhaps it's about a plan set in place long ago
If you believe and trust, it's all you need to know